THE TROUBLE WITH JENNY

Wind River Chronicles, Book 1

KATHY GEARY ANDERSON

For Kurt, the hero of my personal love story. Ours is my favorite friends-to-more story. You are my home.

Chapter One

E ver since her parents were killed in that awful train wreck fourteen years ago, Jenny Westraven had never felt like she belonged anywhere. Until now. Never mind the stuffy room smelled faintly of linseed oil or that her chair was rigid and unyielding. Never mind her fingers were cramped, and her neck and shoulders ached from the day's work. The fact was—she loved working in this small lawyer's office in Newark. Could it be she'd finally found her destiny?

She pulled a clean sheet of crisp white stationery from the pile beside her and threaded it into the rollers of her Remington Standard typewriter. Glancing at her notepad, she began to type.

April 27, 1900.

George S. Barnwell, Esq., Passaic, N. J.

Dear Sir: We beg to acknowledge . . .

Her fingers flew across the typewriter's keys, navigating all the "whereases" and "hereafters" with ease. One month on the job and she already spoke the legal language with a fair amount of fluency. Who knew? Maybe she was cut out to be far more than a mere typewriter girl. After all, hadn't she mastered the intricacies of stenography and typewriting in ten short weeks, graduating top of her class at the Newark Business College?

. . . Very respectfully yours, Goddard and Bennett, attorneys-at-law

With a flourish, she pulled the letter from the typewriter machine and scanned its contents. Not a single error or misspelling. Yes, she very well could be selling herself short.

While Jenny Westraven, typewriter girl, sounded grand, Jenny Westraven, attorney-at-law, sounded even better. She could picture her name in gold letters, forming a base beneath the names arched on the window of the door in front of her: Goddard, Bennett, and Westraven. She loved the sound of that.

Uncle Clarence and Aunt Matilda would—

Well. She knew what Uncle Clarence and Aunt Matilda would do if her name were to appear in gold letters anywhere other than on a society invitation. Uncle Clarence would suffer apoplexy, and Aunt Matilda would succumb to the vapors. No matter. She'd stopped trying to please Aunt Matilda years ago.

Jenny had just positioned another page of stationery between the machine's rubber rollers when the door to the firm's outer office flew open, and Ben stepped in. She steadied her paper as it fluttered in the cross breeze. If only she could steady the fluttering in her heart.

Honestly. Why was she reacting to him this way? It was only Ben. A grown-up, broad-shouldered, extremely handsome Ben, but nevertheless . . . just Ben. Or *Mr. Bennett* now.

He'd been Ben to her for so many years, she kept forgetting to call him by his proper name. Thankfully, neither Johnny nor Mr. Goddard seemed to notice. *Ben* had, of course. He'd catch her eye each time she stumbled, one eyebrow raised. The laughter in his eyes reminded her of their childhood summers when the two of them and Ted ran free and wild.

But that was then.

Now he was her boss, and she'd do well to remember it. *Mr.* Bennett he was, and *Mr.* Bennett he would remain. She rolled the paper into position, determined to look as busy and professional as possible. Yet, from the corner of her eye, she watched him toss his hat to Johnny and shrug out of his topcoat.

"Did you win or lose today, Mr. Bennett?" Johnny caught the hat midair and set it on a ledge beside the coatrack.

"I'm afraid the jury is still out. Judge Williams will render a decision in the morning. Is Mr. Goddard in?"

"No, sir. He said not to expect him. Said he had plans to go to the opera with his daughter."

"Oh. That's right. I'm supposed to join them." Ben pulled his pocket watch out of his waistcoat and strode by Jenny's desk without so much as a nod in her direction.

"I've got some paperwork I need to finish before I go. See that I'm not disturbed, will you, Johnny?" He ducked into his office and shut the door.

Not that she minded, of course. If he wanted to ignore his typewriter girl as if she were no more than another stick of furniture in his overcrowded outer office, who was she to care? Their relationship was professional. Strictly professional. She turned to her notes and began punching the typewriter keys.

She could go to the opera herself, had she a mind to. Which she hadn't. She didn't come to Newark to become part of yet another round of social events. Though the opera and theater were by far her favorites. And on the arm of the charming Mr. Bennett, she'd be sure to enjoy herself.

Only . . . Nell Goddard would be the one enjoying his company tonight. She'd met Miss Goddard a few days ago when she'd visited the office. She was pretty enough—in a cold sort of way. Far too high in the instep to pay the typewriter girl any mind. And far too proprietary with Ben. But, of course, she was. They were courting, after all.

Jenny's fingers slowed on the keys. She understood Ben's attraction for the girl. After all, he was hoping for full partnership, and what better way to achieve that than to marry his boss's daughter? She gave the carriage return a swift push. She was happy for Ben. Really, she was. Still. One would think he didn't have to talk quite so much about the wonderful Miss Goddard during their Tuesday night meals at Aunt Bethany's.

Another cool draft, laden this time with the sweet scent of gardenias, cut into Jenny's thoughts. A plump, middle-aged woman pushed through the office door. Clad in a sensible gray suit with a frilled white shirtwaist, she reminded Jenny of a pigeon, except for her hat. Jenny had seen many a fancy hat in her day, but none to rival the feathers and furbelows on this one. And the colors! A riot of red, purple, yellow, and green clashed atop the woman's head. How did the woman's neck support such a monstrosity? Jenny stifled a giggle. If only Ben could see this.

Johnny slid off his stool. "May I help you, ma'am?"

"Yes. I'd like to speak with Mr. Goddard."

"Do you have an appointment?"

"No. I do not."

"Well, he's not in right now. If you want to see him, you'll have to make an appointment and come back next week."

"Next week!" The feathers bobbed and dipped. "I can't possibly wait until next week. I need to speak to him today."

"Well, you can't speak to him if he's not here."

Jenny cleared her throat. "Excuse me, ma'am."

The hat turned her direction, the woman's eyes peeping out from beneath a fringe of feathers. Was it her imagination, or did those eyes narrow a bit when they landed on her? She plunged ahead regardless.

"If you need a lawyer today, perhaps you'd like to speak with Mr. Goddard's associate?"

From behind the mountain of feathers and lace, Johnny made a cutting motion across his throat, shaking his head vigorously.

She ignored him.

Ben would forgive her once he saw that hat.

"Shall I tell him you're here?"

"Oh, I don't know. Mrs. Green said I ought to have Mr. Goddard."

"I'm sure you'll find Mr. Bennett every bit as good." She jumped up before Johnny could stop her and rapped on Ben's door.

Pushing it open, she stuck her head inside. Ben sat in his shirtsleeves and waistcoat, his jacket draped over the back of his chair. His thick, dark hair was disheveled as if he'd plowed his fingers through it while he worked. He raised his head and crooked an eyebrow.

"Yes, Miss Westraven?"

"Your four o'clock appointment is here."

"My four—"

She stepped aside to allow the woman entrance, struggling to hide her grin when Ben's eyes snagged on the hat. He rose to his feet.

"Come in, Mrs. . . . ?"

"Dalrymple. Clara Dalrymple."

"Of course, Mrs. Dalrymple. Please, have a seat."

Jenny didn't want to miss a minute of this. "Would you like me to take notes, sir?"

Ben turned to her, the glint in his dark gaze promising retribution in full once Mrs. Dalrymple left. "By all means, Miss Westraven. Join us."

By the time she returned with her stenographer's notebook, Ben had recovered his jacket and seated Mrs. Dalrymple in a comfortable chair. Jenny took the high-backed chair at the small table to the right of Ben's desk.

She loved his office. Though small, the high ceilings and tall windows gave it a feeling of airiness. Late afternoon sun spilled in over the warm mahogany floor, painting a pattern of light across the rich burgundy of the wool rug. Pen poised above her notepad, she waited for Ben.

He rocked back in his seat and steepled his fingers across his chest. "So, Mrs. Dalrymple, what can I do for you?"

"I need you to tell me if my divorce is legal."

Jenny gaped at the woman. Mrs. Dalrymple looked nothing like she imagined a divorcée would look. Apart from the outrageous hat, she looked like any other sensible, middle-aged matron. Yet there she sat, baldly proclaiming she was divorced.

"When did you obtain it?" Ben sounded as if he dealt with divorced women every day. Well, maybe he did. She hadn't considered this part of lawyering before.

"*I* didn't. My husband did. Or says he did, anyway. He got one of those Western divorces about a year ago. My previous lawyer said it was worthless in New Jersey, but Walter doesn't think so. Thinks he's married to *her* now. Brought her back to Bloomfield to live just last week. I told him I won't stand for it. Him, bold as brass, living in the same town as the children and me. It's wrong. That's what it is. Dead wrong."

"Forgive me, Mrs. Dalrymple," Ben held up a hand as if to slow her stream of words. "You mentioned a previous lawyer? Can you tell me why you're no longer utilizing his services?"

"Because he's dead. Up and died last December and left me in the middle of this mess. Now, here's Walter and that . . . that . . . *jade,* living no more than three blocks from me, with people talking and whispering and laughing behind my back. Well, I won't stand for it." Mrs. Dalrymple pulled a large handkerchief from her pocket and dabbed her eyes.

"I can see how the situation would be intolerable." Ben's voice gentled. "Perhaps you should start at the beginning. When did your husband first mention a divorce?"

"Well." The feathers on Mrs. Dalrymple's hat listed dangerously to one side as she tipped her head to consider Ben's question. "It must've been a little over two years ago. I remember it was right after our youngest, Sammy, was born, and he turned two last January. We'd been arguing over my husband's newest clerk, Miss Jeffries. Miss *Jezebel,* more like. I said it wasn't seemly, having a woman like that working for him. Women and men working in the same office are nothing but trouble." Mrs. Dalrymple sniffed and threw a glare in Jenny's direction.

Jenny lowered her gaze to her steno pad. Oh dear.

"And your husband mentioned a divorce at that time?"

"Yes. He said he wouldn't tolerate a wife who wanted to

dictate his business affairs. Told me he was going to North Dakota to get one of those ninety-day divorces."

"And did he?"

"He left for a few weeks maybe. But by the next month, he was back, and we went on like before. Then, in March of last year, I received this letter from a lawyer in North Dakota saying my husband initiated divorce proceedings against me." Mrs. Dalrymple dabbed her eyes again. "So, I went to my brother-in-law, Charlie—he was my first lawyer—and asked him what I could do about it. He said he'd get an injunction ordering Walter to cease all divorce proceedings on account he was never a resident of North Dakota."

"You know this for a fact?"

"Of course I do. He was still living with the kids and me. Most days, anyway. You see, Walter runs several newspapers, two in Bloomfield and one in Morristown, and he publishes an insurance journal out of his office in New York. He travels some for business and might be gone one or two nights a week, but most days he's home at night."

Jenny's pen skimmed across the page as she recorded Mrs. Dalrymple's words. Without her stenography training, she'd be hard-pressed to keep up.

"So there was no basis for Walter establishing a residence in North Dakota in the months leading up to the alleged divorce?" Ben asked.

"No. That's why Charlie served him with the injunction."

"Do you have proof he was served?"

"Yes. Though now Walter claims he never saw it. Pretty convenient, if you ask me, now Charlie is dead."

"Other than Charlie, were there any other witnesses?"

"His clerk Miss Jeffries was there. But *she's* not about to confirm it, now is she?"

Ben tapped his thumb against the arm of his chair for a moment. "Well, Mrs. Dalrymple. If what you've told me is correct, I believe we have a good case for getting the North

Dakota divorce overturned. At the least, we should be able to have your husband tried for contempt for ignoring the injunction. Are you sure it's the route you wish to take? Your husband's infidelity is sufficient grounds for a divorce here in New Jersey if you prefer to dissolve the marriage yourself."

"No, Mr. Bennett, I do *not* wish to dissolve my marriage. I'll admit Walter is a cad. He's always been a cad, but I made vows to stay with him 'till death do us part,' and I'm not going to back out of it now. Besides, we have six children to raise. I *need* my husband, Mr. Bennett."

What the woman needed was a husband who wasn't a cad. Jenny couldn't see how forcing Walter back into the marriage would help anything, but she could understand the woman's desperation. She was glad now she'd made Ben listen to her story.

"Very well," Ben said. "I'll see what I can do. But I'm obligated to warn you, even if we do get the North Dakota divorce invalidated, we can't stop your husband from gaining a legal divorce if he decides to move to North Dakota or another western state with more lenient divorce laws."

"Oh, he wouldn't do that. He wouldn't leave behind his livelihood."

"Then I'll look into it. Do you have access to your brother-in-law's files on the case?"

"Yes. My sister kept all his files at her house."

"Good. Have her send over whatever she has on your case, and I'll get to work on it."

"Thank you, Mr. Bennet. I'd appreciate that." She rose and adjusted the tower of lace, ribbons, and feathers on her head.

Ben pushed to his feet, then gave her hat wide berth as he opened the door for her. Jenny intercepted one final glare from the woman before she turned to leave.

"Mark my words, Mr. Bennett," Mrs. Dalrymple said. "A woman in your office is nothing but trouble. You'll do yourself a favor by replacing that pretty, little typewriter of yours with a sensible male clerk. You might have to part with a few more dollars per week, but it'll be well worth the trouble you'll save yourself." With that, she sailed from the room, ribbons and feathers bobbing behind her.

"I'll keep your words under advisement, ma'am."

Jenny heard the tinge of humor in Ben's voice. When he stepped back into the room, the barest hint of a smile still toying with his lips, she threw him a glare of her own.

"You'll take it under advisement?" Jenny laced her words with just a touch of venom.

"You have to admit, she has a valid argument."

"How so?"

"Women in the office *are* trouble."

"Trouble? How have I been trouble?"

"Well, take Mrs. Dalrymple, for example. I'm pretty sure Johnny would never have let her past the outer office. I distinctly remember saying I was not to be bothered this afternoon."

"And Johnny would have lost you a client."

"A client whose case will probably prove more trouble than it's worth." Ben sank back down in his chair, arms bent behind his head, legs stretched out in front of him. He studied the tips of his crossed boots.

"How can you say that? Someone needs to help the poor woman."

Ben sighed. "It's a domestic dispute, and domestic disputes are always more trouble than they're worth. If she were suing to dissolve her marriage or pursuing an alienation of affection suit, I wouldn't even consider taking her on. As it is, I'm going to have to do some convincing to get Mr. Goddard's approval. He despises anything remotely associated with divorce."

"Oh." She hadn't known. "Well, that's hardly a basis on which to argue I've been trouble for the office."

"If that were all, Miss Westraven, then yes, I'd have little on which to base my argument. But then there's the law book incident."

Good heavens. Was he bringing that up again?

"I honestly don't understand you men's aversion to cleanliness. So I dusted and organized the law books. Is that really such a crime?"

"We hired you as a typewriter, Miss Westraven. Not a housekeeper."

"Then I think you'd be pleased to have both services for the price of one."

"We don't need nor want the cleaning services. Mr. Goddard has worked for twenty-five years to build a reputable, *established* practice. One afternoon with a duster and you have the place looking as newly minted as if he'd opened the office yesterday. What client is going to have confidence in a lawyer who appears to have just opened his doors?"

"I'd think your *female* clients would be appreciative of a lawyer's office where they would not have to soil their gloves or the hems of their skirts in order to receive legal advice."

Ben rolled his eyes to the ceiling but gave no other response.

"You have to admit my typewriting skills are impeccable."

"Indeed. In fact, we might find you irreplaceable were you equally as skilled at keeping your opinions on legal proceedings to yourself. And had you even tried to organize Mr. Goddard's desk as you did mine, you would have been out the door faster than you can type a paragraph, Miss Westraven."

Really. You'd think the man would be more appreciative. She was only trying to help when she'd written out her thoughts on the notes he'd asked her to type for his last case. And as for the desk, she'd only straightened things a bit. How he could find anything in that desk of his was more than she could fathom. Every pigeonhole was filled to overflowing with documents and papers of all sorts and sizes.

She raised her chin. "What you're describing are simple errors—misunderstandings, if you will—of how you and Mr. Goddard want things done. Hardly the type of 'trouble' Mrs. Dalrymple was describing."

"Ah, yes. *That* sort of trouble." Ben crossed his arms and studied her through half-closed eyes. "So are you telling me, Miss Westraven, the majority of men and women in an office situation are not capable of that sort of trouble?"

"Of course they're *capable*. I'm saying the majority are not so inclined. You cannot paint all people with the same broad brush based solely on their gender. Why, to say all female office workers are homewreckers like Miss Jeffries would be to say all men are cads like Mr. Dalrymple. Are all men cads, Mr. Bennett?"

A smile played at the corner of Ben's lips. "Of course, we are, Miss Westraven. I'm surprised you haven't learned that by now."

"Be serious. You don't truly believe all men are cads."

"I am serious. And I'll prove it to you." Ben rose from his chair and began pacing in front of her, arms clasped behind his back. "If all men are not cads, then why does society place such strictures on its unmarried daughters?"

Why indeed? She'd pondered that question often enough herself.

"Tell me, Miss Westraven." He turned to face her, dark eyes intent. She'd never seen him in the courtroom, but she could imagine how a witness might feel beneath that gaze.

"As a young, unattached female who has had a turn in society, were you ever allowed to attend a ball without a proper chaperone?"

She shook her head.

"The opera? With only an unattached male as an escort?" He held up a finger as she started to speak. "*Not* a relative, mind you."

She shook her head.

"A picnic?"

"No."

"A musicale?"

"No."

"A soiree?"

"No."

"Why would you say that is?"

"Because all *society* men are cads?"

He acknowledged her hit with a quick grin but continued his pacing.

"I say it's because society knows all men have a propensity to be cads. Therefore, it does whatever it can to protect its young daughters. That's why I believe Mrs. Dalrymple has a valid point. Young, unattached females in a man's world without the constraints of polite society can spell trouble."

"But the ballroom is nothing like the boardroom. In general, the social season's purpose is to present society's unmarried daughters and find them suitable mates. The business world is entirely different. The businessman is seeking to advance his business . . . serve his client . . . make his way in the world. His mind is not on the typewriter in the next room for anything more than how quickly she can type the last letter he dictated."

"So you're saying, Miss Westraven, that the business and social worlds never overlap? Do the men in your social circle never discuss business at society functions?"

Her mind flew to Mr. Fitzsimmons, who couldn't finish a quadrille without at least one reference to his gas and oil ventures. Oh, and hadn't Mr. Wyatt trapped her in a corner and droned on and on about celluloid at Mrs. Stuyvesant Fish's dinner party last season? Even Uncle Clarence's sole purpose in attending any social gathering was to further the City National Bank's interests.

Ben stopped in front of her. Bending toward her, he braced his hands on the arms of her chair. "And what do you know about the mind of a man? If he can think about business in the ballroom, is he not also capable of thinking of love in the office?"

He leaned so close she could smell the tangy scent of bay rum. She could see the golden flecks in his dark brown eyes. She licked her lips, trying desperately to focus on his last question and not on his mouth hovering a few inches from hers.

What would . . .

What if . . .

Her eyes drifted shut as Ben closed the distance between them, his lips meeting hers.

Mmmmm. They were soft and warm and delicious. But what she hadn't expected was the jolt coursing through her at his touch nor the tingle down her spine as his fingers cupped her neck, pulling her closer. She leaned into the kiss to explore all she was feeling, reaching up to tangle her fingers in his thick, soft hair.

"Jeanette Elizabeth Westraven!"

Wait. *Aunt Matilda?*

Why was Aunt Matilda's voice interrupting this perfectly splendid kiss? Ben sprang away, his face red and guilt-ridden, leaving her an unimpeded view of the doorway. Sure enough, there stood Aunt Matilda and Uncle Clarence, fairly shimmering with horror.

Drat! She was in for it now.

Chapter Two

She'd done it again. Drawn him in with her guileless blue eyes and mischievous smile until he forgot himself. Ever since that summer fifteen years ago when she and Ted had entered his life, Jenny'd been leading him into trouble.

Ben measured the anger in the faces of the couple standing in the doorway. He couldn't remember a single one of their scrapes ending well, and this would be no exception.

Not that Jenny was solely to blame. As usual, he'd been a willing participant. In fact, their kiss had been entirely his fault. Whatever the case, it was time to pay the piper—two very irate and powerful pipers.

"Uncle Clarence. Aunt Matilda. What are you doing here?"

The New York relatives. He'd wondered what had become of them but hadn't asked. He should have asked.

"The better question would be, what are *you* doing here? When Bethany told us where to find you, I never imagined . . . I would never have thought . . ." Jenny's aunt pressed a lacy scrap of cloth to her lips, apparently too overcome to continue.

"Could I get you a chair, Mrs. Westraven?"

"What we'd like, young man, is to know who you are and why you're taking liberties with our niece." Jenny's uncle glowered at him from beneath bushy gray brows. He was a force to be reckoned with for sure. President of City Bank and on the board of a slew of other businesses and charities, Clarence Westraven was one of the most powerful men in New York City.

"Now, Uncle Clarence. Surely you remember Mr. Bennett. Ben? Teddy's friend from our summers with Aunt Bethany? He and Teddy were at Harvard together."

No one he knew was better at taking a kernel of truth and stretching it in her favor. Yes, he and Ted had attended Harvard together, but they'd hardly run in the same circles. Ted wasn't to blame for that. Ben was. As a scholarship student barely making ends meet, Ben had never quite fit in with Ted's crowd of privileged sons of the nation's most wealthy families.

"That doesn't explain what we walked in on." Jenny's uncle wasn't backing down. Nor did Ben blame him.

"No, sir. What we were doing was entirely inappropriate. I take full blame. Your niece and I . . . what I mean is, I would like to . . ." What? Court her? He rubbed the back of his neck. He was bungling this badly, but he couldn't ask to court this man's niece when he was in the midst of a courtship with his boss's daughter. Besides, he didn't want to marry Jenny. He just wanted to kiss her. Very much, apparently. But marriage? No. Not that.

Jenny brushed past him and took her uncle's arm. "Maybe we should all sit down. Please, Aunt Matilda, Uncle Clarence, won't you have a seat?"

Reluctantly, the couple seated themselves in the chairs Ben and Mrs. Dalrymple had vacated. Jenny pulled her own chair from its place beside his desk and sat facing her relatives. Since there were no other chairs in the room, Ben leaned against the bookcase between the two windows and waited for Jenny to continue.

"You see, Aunt Matilda," Jenny's face took on a cherubic expression. "I took your advice after coming to stay with Aunt Bethany earlier this spring. Remember how you said I should study to improve myself while you and Uncle Clarence were abroad? Well, I took a course in stenography and typewriting at the Newark Business College."

"That was hardly the improvement I meant." Her aunt's lips could not purse any tighter.

"But think how useful it can be. I could type out your social schedule, guest lists, even your correspondence. And if Uncle Clarence should need to have some business documents drawn up or a letter typed this summer in Newport, he won't need to wait for his secretary to come up from the city. I will be right there to help him."

A glimmer of a smile played at the corners of the uncle's thick mustache.

"Don't be ridiculous." There were no smiles of any sort on Aunt Matilda's face. "I suggested you study to improve your skills in music and art while we were away. You know as well as I do you have no need for business skills."

"But that's where you're wrong. Once I learned them, I found I had all sorts of opportunities. For example, when I heard Mr. Bennett and his partner desperately needed the services of a typewriter, I couldn't help but offer my services. It wouldn't have been right. Haven't you always told me never to withhold help when it is in my power to give it?"

Well, this was a new spin. Since when had her working here had been a favor to him? Ben thought he was doing her a favor. The look of exasperation Aunt Matilda shot her niece told him she was not convinced either.

"That does nothing to explain the scene we walked in on."

A look of injured innocence crossed Jenny's face. "I don't know what it is you think you saw, but I was merely helping Mr. Bennett prepare for his court case on Monday. He asked me to play the part of the witness, though I must say"—she turned to look at him—"I think your intimidation tactic was a bit too intense. Surely, there's no need to lean in quite so close."

"Horsefeathers!" Clarence Westraven pushed to his feet. "I wasn't born yesterday, young lady, so cut the fal-de-ra. I know exactly what I saw, and I won't have it." He stopped a few feet from Ben, glowering. "You, sir, will keep your hands off my niece. She's not for the likes of you." He turned back to Jenny. "As for you, young lady, this nonsense ends now. Gather your things. You'll be returning to New York with us tonight."

"No." Jenny's response was low but firm.

"What?" Mr. Westraven's face deepened from red to purple.

"No. I don't want to return to New York. I'm happy right here in Newark with Aunt Bethany. I enjoy this job, and I'm not going to leave."

Jenny's aunt trilled a laugh, verging on hysteria. "Of course you'll leave it, child. You can't possibly believe we'd allow you to work. What would people think?"

"Hundreds of girls in this city have jobs."

"Poor immigrants, yes, whose livelihood depends on it. Why, the interest on your inheritance alone is worth—" Glancing Ben's direction, she firmed her lips. "You have a position to fill in society. A job is out of the question."

Jenny stood up, hands fisted at her sides, chin jutting in the air. "You can't make me return to the city."

"No," her uncle said, "but we can make sure no business in Newark will hire you."

"I already have a job, Uncle Clarence."

"Do you? Ask Mr. Bennett if you'll still have a job on Monday."

"Of course, I'll have a job." She turned her big blue eyes his way. "Tell him, Ben."

The room grew deadly silent. He heard the jangle of the telephone in the next room, the clatter of hooves on cobblestone outside, the pounding of his heart in his ears. There was no good way to say this.

He ran a finger under his collar and cleared his throat. "I'm sorry, Je—Miss Westraven. Your uncle's right. Without your family's consent, Mr. Goddard and I won't be able to keep you in our employ."

Had he shot a bullet through her heart he could not have killed her more effectively. The color drained from her face, the sparkle from her eyes—all the vibrant animation that made Jenny, *Jenny*, was gone, snuffed out like a candle in a windstorm.

Johnny poked his head in the door. "Mr. Goddard's on the phone for you, sir. Wants to know if you still plan to join them for dinner before the opera tonight."

The opera.

Nell.

Ben closed his eyes, pinching the bridge of his nose between his fingers. Could this day get any worse?

"We'll get out of your way." Ice laced Jenny's words.

"No! Jen . . . wait." He shot out a hand to detain her, grasping her by the sleeve. He turned to Johnny. "Tell Mr. Goddard I've been delayed. I'll do my best to make the opening curtain."

Jenny shrugged out of his grasp. "Really, Mr. Bennett, there's no need to stay on my account. I'll just gather my things."

"But . . . will I see you again?"

Her eyes met his—cold, lifeless, dead. "I'm sure I don't know, but I wouldn't think so."

She swept from the room without so much as a backward glance, her aunt and uncle in her wake.

THE SOPRANO'S VOICE WAS EVERYTHING THE CRITICS RAVED IT would be, yet Ben found no delight in the music. He couldn't shake the memory of the shuttered look in Jenny's eyes. Could he have kept her on as a typewriter girl?

He glanced at his boss clapping enthusiastically at the soprano's solo. No. Mr. Goddard would never employ a young woman in the face of her family's disapproval. He'd had no choice.

But he'd seen that shuttered look on Jenny before. And he hated it. That day had also ended badly.

He'd been fourteen that summer. Too old, in his mind, to be

bothered with Ted's troublesome little sister. He and Ted had spent their time pursuing manly interests like baseball and boxing matches, leaving Jenny to fend for herself. Then one day, she'd shown up on the streetcar they were taking to a cockfight, dressed in a pair of Ted's old knickers, hair tucked up in one of Ted's caps.

"I'm going with you," she'd told them. "And if you don't let me, I'll tell Aunt Bethany that you're the ones who took her bottle of elderberry wine."

They should've taken her home right then, but they hadn't wanted to miss the fight. He remembered laughing at her attempts to walk like a boy. And, if memory served him right, he'd even taught her how to spit.

At the cockpit, they'd squeezed their way through the crowd to positions bordering the ring. But in the excitement of the first fight, he and Ted lost track of Jenny. They were putting their penny bets on the second fight when the pit erupted. Roosters flew loose, flapping and squawking in every direction. Owners cursed and chased their prizefighters around the arena. Spectators ducked as the enraged birds pecked at anything within hitting distance. Then, above all the chaos, he heard a girl's scream.

Jenny. Across the melee, a mountain of a man held her aloft by her collar and shook her until her cap fell off. Long, blond curls cascaded across her shoulders.

"I'll teach you to mess with these cages," The man bellowed.

Unable to reach her through the roiling crowd, he'd yelled "SPCA" at the top of his lungs and pounded a fist into the stomach of the boy next to him. Fistfights broke out all around. He and Ted pushed and fought their way toward Jenny and reached her just as she sank her teeth into her captor's beefy arm. The man dropped her like a hot coal.

They made it to the door just as the police came, ending their adventure with a ride home in the paddy wagon. When word of their latest escapade reached the New York relatives, they sent a governess to collect Jenny. Ted told him later they sent Jenny abroad to boarding school. She never returned for summers with Aunt Bethany.

In fact, Ben's last childhood memory of Jenny was her white face at the carriage window, spiritless eyes staring into his as she drove away.

Thunderous applause jerked Ben back to the present. He stood and joined the ovation though he had little recollection of the last ten minutes of the performance.

Nell placed a gloved hand on his sleeve. "Wasn't that superb? Miss Scheff was amazing as Lucia."

"Yes." He mustered a smile. "Splendid."

"And now, sir." Nell tapped his arm with her fan. "Since you were unable to join us before the show, Father and I would like to take you to the Continental for a light supper."

"No need. This night's performance was treat enough."

"Nonsense, my boy." Mr. Goddard came to his daughter's side. "Of course, you'll join us. When was the last meal you ate today? I'm willing to wager it was breakfast."

Ben thought back over his day. He'd skipped dinner, having barely enough time to change into his evening clothes before the opera. Before that, he'd worked through the noon recess at court, polishing his closing arguments.

"You'd win that wager, sir. Maybe I will take you up on your offer."

They spent the cab ride discussing the finer points of the opera and comparing notes on the day's cases. It wasn't until Ben was making headway on a plate piled high with oysters, roast beef, and chicken croquettes that Mr. Goddard brought up the afternoon's events.

"Johnny told me you had several late visitors to the office. Anything I need to know?"

"A new client, perhaps. A domestic case." He shot a quick glance at Nell. "Might be best if we waited until Monday to discuss it."

She tipped her chin at him. "I'm the daughter of a lawyer, Mr. Bennett. Quite used to Father discussing his cases."

Maybe, but he knew Mr. Goddard would not look favorably upon discussing this particular case, fraught as it was with infidelity and divorce. "Surely you don't want us to monopolize the whole dinner rambling on and on about work."

"Yes, yes." Mr. Goddard speared an oyster. "It can wait until Monday. I'm not due in court until afternoon. I want to work out our approach to the Murphy case with you as well. With our new typewriter's help, we should at least be able to hammer out the initial correspondence."

Ben cleared his throat and picked at his chicken croquette, careful to avoid Mr. Goddard's eye. "I'm afraid we'll have to do without her services. At least until we can hire another."

"What? But Miss Westraven has been with us barely a month. I thought she was working out well. Except for that law book debacle, of course. Nothing we can't work through, however."

"Yes. Well, it appears her family was not in favor of her employment, after all."

"Didn't you tell me she was the orphaned niece of your grandmother's best friend? I assumed you had the woman's support when you hired her."

"Her maternal aunt, yes. What I didn't realize was the New York relations—her *paternal* relations—were not in favor of it. Did not know of it, in fact."

"New York relations? You mean New York City?" Mr. Goddard stared at him, fork poised halfway to his mouth. "Never tell me Miss Westraven is related to the Westravens of New York City!"

"Last I checked, yes."

Nell let out a gasp, followed by a high-pitched trill of laughter. "Mr. Bennett is jesting with us, Father. Surely he doesn't think we'll believe your typewriter is related to the banking mogul, Clarence Westraven!"

When Ben didn't respond, Nell's eyes grew wide. "Is she?"

He shrugged. "I believe she refers to him as Uncle Clarence."

"Good God." Mr. Goddard set his forkful of food back on his plate and drained his wine glass.

"You're serious," Nell said. "Mr. Bennett, if she truly is the Westraven's niece, she's an heiress, easily worth millions of dollars. Why in the world would she take a job as a typewriter girl?"

Good question. He'd given up trying to decipher the workings of Jenny's mind years ago.

He shrugged. "When she asked if I knew of any offices in need of a typewriter, I assumed she and her brother had suffered a reversal of fortunes. So many did, following the crash."

He should have known not to assume anything with Jenny.

"The gossip rags are going to have a heyday with this." Nell looked almost giddy at the thought.

"Not if we keep it to ourselves. The only ones who know about it are the three of us and Jenny's family."

"Well, I'm not going to say anything if that's what you're implying. But mark my words, it will come out. It always does. A servant will hear something and tell another servant, and before you know it, everything's in print for the whole world to see."

For Jenny's sake, he hoped Nell was wrong.

Chapter Three

"My daughter was right. You'll find she usually is." Mr. Goddard stepped into Ben's office and threw a newspaper on his desk.

"What's this?"

"One of those society rags. Go on. Read it."

Ben scanned the page to a paragraph outlined in ink.

Word has it yet another impoverished English lord is in town in search of an American heiress. As the house guest of one of our city's richest banking families, we can only assume he has set his eye on their fair niece. If so, he might be wise to ask the lady how she spent her time while her aunt and uncle were abroad this spring. Sources tell us the lively socialite masqueraded as a typewriter girl at a Newark law office, which begs the question: Are the family resources so strained the niece must now earn her living? Or were the charms of a certain bachelor lawyer the reason for the young lady's venture into the business world? An affirmative to either question would not bode well for the young viscount's matrimonial prospects.

Good Lord.

He looked up. "Did Nell read this?"

"Oh, yes. Who do you think gave it to me?"

"I take it she wasn't pleased."

"No. She wasn't. Thank goodness for you that the paper didn't choose to print your name."

His and Nell's courtship was still in the fledgling stages—too soon for her not to feel the threat of the subtle innuendos.

He read the paragraph through again. Poor Jenny. Though her name was never mentioned, anyone in her circles would know to whom the article referred.

"Will this cause her trouble, do you think?"

"Hard to say. Ten years ago, with Mrs. Astor at the helm of society, it might have been her death knell. But nowadays, with the Vanderbilts and the New York set continually pushing the line, who knows? Let's hope the family wasn't setting too much stock in the young English lord."

Ben threw the paper onto his desk. "How do these rags find their information?"

Mr. Goddard shrugged. "Disgruntled servants, indiscreet clerks . . . believe me, they're not above paying for their information and blackmailing the elite with what they dig up."

"You don't think Johnny . . ."

"No. He's a loyal fan of Miss Westraven. I wouldn't put it past some of those pals of his, though. Our office was a popular spot last month."

Yes. A typewriter girl of Jenny's spirit and beauty was a rarity in the Newark business scene. Johnny had enjoyed the status of sharing an office with such a paragon. Like Mr. Goddard, Ben doubted the boy was the one to rat on Jenny. But any number of the other clerks might have done so, if only to spite Johnny.

Mr. Goddard turned to leave, then stopped, looking back at Ben over his shoulder. "I forgot. Nell informed me over breakfast she would take on the responsibility of hiring our next typewriter girl."

Ben sighed. Looks like he'd need to work his way back into Miss Goddard's good graces.

~

BUT IT WASN'T MISS GODDARD WHO OCCUPIED BEN'S thoughts the remainder of the afternoon. Jenny's listless white face still haunted him. Would he see her again?

Granted, he played no part in her world, but for the last three months she'd played a large part in his.

Her absence created a void. That void was especially evident that evening as he walked the two blocks from the trolley station to Grandma's front door. The past four Tuesdays, he and Jenny had walked this path together, sharing the easy camaraderie of office mates and friends. But weeks before she came to work for him, her presence on Tuesdays had added a certain zest to his weekly meals with Grandma Janssen.

He was used to Jenny's Aunt Bethany being a part of his Tuesdays. As neighbors, she and Grandma Janssen ate many of their meals together. Still, he'd been surprised early in February to find Jenny as a dinner guest. He'd not seen her since the New York relatives whisked her away that long-ago August day.

She'd been a pretty child. She'd grown into a beautiful woman, poised and polished almost beyond recognition—until they began reminiscing. Then, the Jenny of old shone through. Her quick wit, her zest for life, her keen sense of adventure—all the traits that drew him as a boy were still there beneath her sophisticated veneer.

By the end of the evening, they'd fallen into the easy banter of lifelong friends, a friendship he'd become accustomed to these past three months. Would it be another ten years before they met again? Or had Friday been their last goodbye?

He climbed the steps to his grandmother's row house and let himself in.

"Hello," he called, mostly to let them know he was there. He knew he'd find the ladies in Grandma Janssen's front parlor, as he did every Tuesday.

"In here, dear," came Grandma's reply.

He left his hat and gloves on the entry table and headed for the parlor.

The two elderly ladies sat side-by-side on the red satin settee in the front bay window, taking full advantage of the late afternoon sun. Grandma Janssen worked her embroidery, some frippery destined to end up on a seat cushion or framed on the wall, though where she'd put this one was beyond him. Aunt Bethany plied her knitting needles at her usual rapid pace.

"Come on in, Lester. No need to stand in the doorway."

Grandma Janssen and Father were the only ones allowed to use that name. As if he had any say in the matter. They'd been the ones to name him Lester. Not much chance changing their minds now.

Threading carefully around furniture, he made his way to the ladies, giving them each a quick peck on the cheek before removing two heavily embroidered throw pillows and taking his seat in a tall wing-backed chair beside them.

A week ago, Jenny would have sat in the chair opposite him, a playful smile on her face as she noted his discomfort. He missed that smile.

"Have you had a good week?" Grandma Janssen tipped her head to one side, looking up at him over the frames of her gold-rimmed glasses.

"Yes. Except for losing our typewriter girl, of course." Might as well acknowledge the obvious. "I hope the New York relations didn't place any blame on you, Aunt Bethany."

Though she wasn't his aunt, he'd grown up calling her Aunt Bethany right alongside Jenny and Ted. As his grandmother's closest friend, she'd played the role of aunt in his life as much, if not more, than theirs.

She laughed at his question, her plump cheeks rounding. "Oh, they've blamed me for a fair share of Jenny's scrapes over the years. No hope of their stopping now."

"I would think they'd hold Jenny accountable for her own actions, now she's a grown woman."

Aunt Bethany's face sobered. "I imagine Jenny will suffer for this far more than I will." His expression must have mirrored his dismay because she was quick to add. "Oh, not physically, of course, but Matilda can be demanding. And Jenny can be very headstrong. Those two have been at odds since the beginning. Sometimes I wish . . ." Her voice trailed off. "But, never mind. Jenny will come through this scrape just fine. She always does."

"So you don't think we need to worry about the paragraph in *Town Topics*?"

A frown creased Aunt Bethany's forehead. "What paragraph is that, dear?"

She hadn't seen it. Not surprising. Grandma Janssen and Aunt Bethany weren't ones to take much stock in society's gossip. He drew his copy of the paper from his inner coat pocket and handed it to the women, pointing to the offending paragraph halfway down the page.

The two ladies bent over the paper in unison.

"Oh my." The quaver in Aunt Bethany's voice told him his concerns had not been unwarranted.

"It'll cause trouble, won't it?"

"Well, Clarence and Matilda will not be pleased. Especially Matilda. She hates anything that threatens the family's consequence."

"What a load of nonsense." Grandma Janssen folded the newspaper and handed it back to him. "I find it hard to believe sensible people would pay any mind to drivel like that. What can it hurt that the girl spent a few weeks in honest employment? I'm sure many of her peers have spent the last few months in pursuits far less profitable than that."

"Very true, dear." Aunt Bethany nodded and picked up her knitting. "But the rules and guidelines of high society have never been what you or I would consider sensible. Jenny won't have an easy time of it, I'm afraid, and I'm at least partly to blame. I should never have agreed to her helping out in your office, Ben, even for a short period of time. I had no idea the Westravens would be returning from Europe so early."

"If you ask me, the Westravens themselves are to blame for that." Grandma Bennett pointed her needle at the newspaper he'd set in his lap. "If they hadn't caused such a fuss, arousing all sorts of questions in the minds of their servants, no doubt, no one would be the wiser about how Jenny spent her vacation. They bring a lot of their drama on themselves by making such mountains out of molehills."

"Is there any way of knowing how Jenny is handling all this? Maybe I should pay her a call," Ben said.

"That's a splendid idea." Aunt Bethany beamed at him over her knitting needles. "Matilda keeps Thursdays as her reception day. You should run up and see her."

"It's not a splendid idea at all, Bethany. If Ben were to show up uninvited on the Westraven's doorstep, it would only add fuel to that nonsense about an attraction between the two of them. We'll simply have to wait until Jenny writes."

Ben didn't like the uncertainty of that option. What if she didn't write? What if her New York relatives decided to sever all connection between her and Aunt Bethany? But Grandma Janssen had a point. He could hardly show up at the Westraven's uninvited. Unless . . .

"We could go together. Surely, the gossips won't take exception to Jenny's aunt and an escort calling to see how Jenny is faring after her return home."

Aunt Bethany tipped her head to the side, lips pursed in consideration. "Yes. That would be just the solution. I'll admit I've been a bit uneasy about Jenny. A visit would set my mind at ease, and no one will question my bringing you along. We elderly ladies need our escorts," she said with a wink. "Are you free to go this Thursday?"

"I'll check my calendar. There's a matter I need to look into for a case I've taken on in the city. If you don't mind my mixing a little business with pleasure, I could handle that in the morning, and then make our afternoon call on Jenny."

"I may as well come along too, then," Grandma Janssen said. "Bethany and I can do a little shopping while you take care of your business."

Chapter Four

Two days later their hackney rolled to a stop in front of a massive limestone chateau. Jenny lives here? Though not the largest residence on the block, its polished ostentation was hard to reconcile with Jenny's down-to-earth friendliness.

He helped his two elderly companions from the carriage, paid the driver, then followed the ladies up the marble steps to the mansion's front door. At his knock, a butler in full livery opened the door. He took their cards and escorted them up a massive center staircase. Ben ran his gloved hand along the burnished mahogany banister, admiring the ornate carving on the spindles and the plush luxury of the Aubusson stair runner.

At the first floor landing, the butler led them into a spacious drawing room easily twice the size of Ben's entire bachelor apartment. The room, decorated in the French style in creams, blues, and golds, screamed femininity. And women—brightly dressed and trimmed with all manner of furbelows and gewgaws—were its primary occupants. Their high-pitched gabble reminded him of a flock of hens.

The few brave men in the room looked sadly out of place. A stout gentleman seated by the tea tray in the center of the room looked especially ridiculous. His girth perched precariously in one of the dainty Louix IV chairs scattered in small clusters throughout the room.

Ben's worry lifted some at the sight of the crowd. Aunt Bethany had explained that as Mrs. Westraven's first "At Home" after a trip abroad, her friends and acquaintances would be expected to call. Failure to do so was a sure sign they'd decided to cut Jenny for her behavior in Newark.

He scanned the room, locating Jenny in a group of women by the fireplace. Dressed in a frothy blue gown that clung to her curves and floated around her ankles, she looked as delicate and feminine as the room around her.

He shifted his weight from one foot to the other, wishing he could bolt. What was he doing here, anyway? Anyone could see she was perfectly fine.

She turned when the butler announced their names, her blue eyes widening as they caught and held his gaze.

And then she smiled.

Ah.

This was why he'd come. To see that smile—that curious mixture of innocence and mischief that never failed to draw him in, like a secret shared or a promise unspoken.

"Bethany. What a surprise." Matilda Westraven, resplendent in black and white, stepped in front of him, blocking any further view of her niece. "Mrs. Janssen. Mr. Bennett." Her manner was gracious if a bit reserved.

He bowed his greeting.

"What brings you to New York?"

"It's the spring weather, dear," came Aunt Bethany's vague response.

Before she could elucidate, Jenny glided up, grasping Aunt Bethany's hands in both of hers and pressing a kiss to her cheek.

"Aunt Bethany! What a wonderful surprise. Whatever are you doing in New York?"

"I was just telling your aunt, dear. It's the weather. I don't know why it is, but every spring I get a notion to travel. All winter long, I'm as content as can be to stay put, but once the trees start budding, it's all I can do not to climb on a train and go somewhere. Though, at my age, extended travel is out of the question. But the other night when I was telling Cordelia"—she nodded her head at Grandma Janssen—"how badly I wanted to go somewhere—anywhere—and Ben was there, as he always is on Tuesdays, talking about coming to the city on business, well, that's when I knew. Margaret and I would come with him and do some shopping. It was exactly what I needed to cure my travel bug." She pronounced the last with an air of one who had discovered the cure for typhus.

"And, of course," Grandma Jannsen added, taking Jenny's gloved hand and patting it, "we couldn't come to New York without stopping to see you, my dear."

"Oh, I'm so glad you did." Jenny caught his gaze again. "And you, Mr. Bennett. Thank you so much for bringing them."

He bowed. "My pleasure."

Jenny led the three of them from group to group, filling his head with names he would never remember. Or care to. The corpulent gentleman by the tea table turned out to be the Earl of Denbigh, father to the viscount alluded to in the *Town Topics* article.

He'd never met a titled gentleman and couldn't say he was impressed. Had he met the man on the street, he'd know no difference between him and the average Newark businessman. In fact, were one to put the earl in a butcher's apron, he'd be a dead ringer for Mr. Feldman in the shop up the street from his apartment.

Jenny handed Ben a cup of tea and begged him to take a seat before hurrying off to resume her duties as hostess. They'd left Grandma Janssen and Aunt Bethany in lively conversation with an old classmate on a chaise lounge by the window. Ben's group included a vivid young brunette, the British earl, and two matrons with their debutante daughters whose names he couldn't remember.

When he inadvertently caught the eye of one of them, she blushed and giggled into her teacup. Hoping to avoid further awkwardness, he turned to the earl.

"Are you enjoying your visit, sir—er, my lord?" He'd never "my lorded" anyone before. Doubted he would again.

"Well, the food's good at any rate."

He nodded, not knowing how else to respond, and the group lapsed into silence.

After a few minutes, one of the matrons took up the challenge. "Are you, by chance, related to the James Gordon Bennetts?"

"The newspaper family? Not that I'm aware. I believe my grandfather's family was from Albany."

"The John Bennetts?"

"No. Charles."

"And your grandmother's people?"

"She was a Wagner."

"Any relation to the Percy Wagners?"

"A distant cousin. Her father and Percy's father were second cousins."

"Oh. I see."

Yes. She probably did. Though thoroughly respectable, the branches he occupied on the family tree were firmly rooted in the lower middle in terms of wealth.

Within minutes, the matrons and their daughters excused themselves and moved along to greener pastures. Not that there were many alternatives. Apart from the English earl across from him, the only other man was a short, thin, fair-haired gentleman with a receding hairline. His handlebar mustache couldn't quite hide his prominent overbite. But judging by the number of young women buzzing around him, he must be rich indeed.

He turned from his perusal to meet the amused eyes of the brunette—Mrs. Gardner, was it?

"Sizing up your competition?"

"Am I competing?"

"You're not here to woo our fair Jenny?"

"I'm not here to woo anyone."

"Probably a good thing."

"Why? Have I so little to offer?" He knew that was a mistake the minute he said it.

She ran an appraising eye down his body. "Oh, you have plenty to offer as a man, Mr. Bennett. Just not so much as a husband." He felt his face heat at her boldness. He'd heard tales of the brazen behavior of some in high society but had never experienced it firsthand. Her frankness intimidated far more than it attracted.

"And that one?" He tipped his head toward the fair-headed man, hoping to deflect her attention. "He must be worth millions."

She laughed. "Oh, not nearly so much as that. In fact, monetarily speaking, I suspect his net worth isn't much more than yours."

"Yet *he's* good husband material?"

"Ah." She wagged a slim finger at him. "But he has something you haven't."

He cocked an eyebrow.

She glanced at the earl still occupied with the finger sandwiches and tea cakes on his overflowing plate and lowered her voice. "That's Viscount Parry, Lord Denbigh's only son. Any woman who marries him will someday be a countess."

Ben looked the man over again. Was Jenny really considering marrying him? Surely not.

"So, you see, Mr. Bennett," Mrs. Gardner said. "It's probably a good thing you've decided not to compete."

Was there a hint of a dare in that comment?

She leaned back in her chair and studied him through hooded eyes. "Tell me. If you're not here to woo our Jenny, why are you here?"

He gave a self-effacing shrug, "I'm merely an escort. My

grandmother and Jenny's aunt wanted a trip to the city, so I offered to bring them."

"Do you come to the city often?"

"Occasionally. On business."

"Oh? What type of business are you in?"

"Law."

A triumphant smirk lifted the corners of the woman's bright red lips. "A lawyer! From Newark?"

He bit back a curse. That confounded *Topics* article.

Schooling his face to remain neutral, he forced what he hoped was a degree of nonchalance into his answer. "Yes. Why do you ask?"

"Oh, no reason. Just curious. Does your office, by chance, have need of a typewriter girl?"

"Are you interested in the position, Mrs. Gardner?"

"No. But I may know someone who is." Her knowing gaze told him she was enjoying this tap dance far too much. Time to put an end to it.

"I'm afraid we already have a typewriter. Miss Spencer is quite competent and shows no sign of wishing to leave." He wasn't lying. Nell had proven as good as her word and supplied them with a new typewriter girl within days of Jenny's leaving. That the new girl was plain as last week's hash and just about as dull hadn't escaped his notice. But she was quite competent, so he anticipated she'd be with them for the long haul. "But if your friend is serious about finding a position, I'm sure there are offices in the city where she could apply."

"I'm sure you're right."

"And now if you'll excuse me, I believe my grandmother requires me." He stood and bowed, first to Lord Denbigh, then to Mrs. Gardner. "It's been a pleasure to meet both of you."

"Oh, believe me, Mr. Bennett," Mrs. Gardner said, "the pleasure has been all mine."

Her mocking laughter followed him across the room.

As he made his way to Grandma Janssen and Aunt Bethany,

he noticed Jenny had joined their group by the window. He almost checked his stride, not wanting to give the impudent Mrs. Gardner more fuel for her fire. But turning away from the group would be even more suspect, so he continued, taking a stand by Aunt Bethany's chair.

Grandma Janssen looked up at him. "Is it time we were going, dear?"

"We'll need to leave soon if we're to make the six o'clock train."

"Oh, must you? I've hardly had a chance to visit with you." Loneliness and a hint of vulnerability slipped through Jenny's social mask.

Aunt Bethany reached over and patted her arm. "We'll just have to come back."

"Please do. You have no idea how much I've missed our comfortable cozes over tea each evening."

"I've missed them too, dear. But now I know how easy a trip to the city can be, I'll be sure to come back. Really, I don't know when I've enjoyed a day more."

Jenny's eyes brightened, and for a moment, he thought she was going to cry. She blinked rapidly, then stood, pasting on a smile. "If you must be going, let me at least walk you out."

The four of them made their way across the room to say their goodbyes to Mrs. Westraven. Jennie fell in step beside him, giving him his first chance to speak privately.

"Are you doing all right?" He kept his voice low. "We saw the article in *Town Topics*."

"Yes, of course. I'm fine." The bleakness in her voice belied her words.

"I . . ." He wanted to apologize for that kiss, to assure himself somehow she was all right, but there wasn't time. "Could I see you sometime? In a more private setting?"

She took so long to respond he was afraid she would say no, but then she replied, "Come next Tuesday. Aunt Matilda makes her calls that day. I'll make an excuse not to go."

He gave a quick nod since they'd reached Mrs. Westraven who cut off any chance of further conversation. Within minutes, he was bundling Grandma and Aunt Bethany into the hired cab. Jumping into the coach behind them, he let out a sigh of relief. Today had gone better than he'd expected. As long as Mrs. Gardner kept her suspicions to herself.

Chapter Five

"I'm sorry, Lord Parry. I'm afraid we would not suit." Jenny injected the perfect amount of regret into her voice.

She was becoming quite good at this. Three refusals in as many days. Maybe she should feel more angst. According to Miss Pruitt, who taught Manners and Deportment at Madame DeLancey's, she most definitely should. In fact, her former teacher would be appalled she'd let matters come to this in the first place.

Jenny could almost hear her prim voice saying, "A lady of tact will discourage an unwanted suitor before he makes an offer so he does not humiliate himself with a proposal that may result in a refusal."

She'd been nothing but discouraging to all of them. She hadn't flirted, or smiled, or favored them with her attention. Yet, here was suitor number three, down on one knee, blinking in astonishment as if she'd answered him in Chinese. Honestly, his half-opened mouth did nothing to improve that overbite.

"I . . . I . . . I don't understand."

"Please, Lord Parry. Won't you take a seat?"

The man struggled to his feet and dropped onto the settee

next to her. She would have preferred he took the chair across from her, but at least now she didn't have a bird's-eye view of his pink scalp through his thinning hair.

"What I'm trying to say is this. I wouldn't make you a good wife."

Lord Parry brayed a laugh and took a vice-grip on her hand. "Maybe you should let me be the judge of that."

Jenny cringed. This was going to be more difficult than she thought.

"Truly. Uncle Clarence is always telling me I'm more trouble than I'm worth. And terribly expensive. Why I can run through my whole month's allowance in one day of shopping. And if it's not the shopping, then it's the gambling. Just last week, I lost $100 at Sally Gardner's card party."

Lord Parry paled a bit but kept clinging to her hand. Drat. The gambling ploy had worked like a charm on Mr. Van Clyde. Of course, Mr. Van Clyde was from a strait-laced New England Protestant family. Lord Parry, being English, was probably used to profligate women. Clearly, she needed another approach.

"And I suppose you'd want to live in England," she said with a sigh.

"Well, it *is* my home."

"But see, that's just it. I simply cannot abide England. So gray and damp. And the people don't even speak English. Well, not the way English should be spoken. I can hardly make out a word."

Lord Parry blinked. "Well, I daresay you'll adjust after a bit. And we could always winter on the continent, I suppose."

Goodness. How much money had Uncle Clarence offered the man? Such tenacity hinted at desperation.

"The fact is, Lord Parry, I cannot marry you because . . . because . . . well, really, I'm surprised Uncle Clarence didn't tell you . . ." She paused. Pulling her handkerchief from her pocket with her one free hand, she pressed it to her lips. "This is quite difficult for me to say, but . . . well, the doctors have left us little hope."

"You're not dying?"

"No. Worse. I'm . . . b–b–barren." She bowed her head and pulled her handkerchief up to hide her face. She wished she could blush on demand, but blushes were so contrary. They only came when you didn't want them.

"Oh."

They sat in silence for a moment.

"You are sure?"

"Quite."

"But, h—?"

"So you see, Lord Parry, it would be wrong of me to marry you. Your family title . . . I assume it's been in your family for years? How sad it would be for it to die with you. Or perhaps there's another to whom it would pass?"

Lord Parry was definitely pale now. He released her hand. "No. There's no one. No one acceptable at any rate. Quite right, Miss Westraven. Your uncle certainly should have informed me. I'm afraid, under the circumstances, I will have to withdraw my suit."

"I thought you might. We'll pretend this conversation never happened. And now, I promised my aunt I would help her with the guest list for her dinner next week. If you'll excuse me?"

He stood when she did and favored her with a bow. Head held high, she crossed the room at a dignified pace and let herself out without looking back. Once on the other side of the door, she let slip a pleased grin.

There. She'd refused another—no angst, no anger, no humiliation. She should give Miss Pruitt lessons. Not only had she turned down three unwanted suitors in three days, she'd left each with a keen sense of relief their suit had not prospered.

～

LESS THAN AN HOUR LATER, AUNT MATILDA KNOCKED AT HER bedroom door.

"You turned down Lord Parry." The accusation was out before her aunt was all the way into the room. "Child, what can you be thinking?"

Jenny set down the book she'd been reading. "I was thinking we wouldn't suit, and I told him as much."

"You do realize you turned down a viscount? The man is next in line for an earldom. You could have been a countess. Do you know how many girls dream of that opportunity?"

The dream was Aunt Matilda's, not hers. Ever since Consuelo Vanderbilt had married the Duke of Marlborough, Aunt Matilda had set her heart on Jenny's marrying into British nobility. The possibility seemed remote until her aunt and uncle had met the Earl and Countess of Denbigh during last year's London Season.

Aunt Matilda had cultivated that friendship as carefully as she did the prized orchids in her greenhouse. To have it all come to naught could not be pleasant. Jenny felt for her. She did. But not enough to sacrifice her future to become the wife of a balding bore with bad teeth.

"What on earth did you say to him? The Countess has been looking daggers at me for the past half hour. I would not be surprised if they pack up and leave before nightfall."

"I didn't say anything to offend. In fact, he seemed quite relieved to withdraw his suit."

"What did you say?"

"I told him I was barren."

"You *what?*" Aunt Matilda sank into the chair by Jenny's dressing table and dropped her head into her hand. "Please tell me you are not serious."

When Jenny didn't answer her, she looked up. "Do you realize what you've done? Don't you realize this news will be all over town in days? No one will want to marry you now."

"No one wants to marry *me*, anyway. They want to marry my money. Lord Parry and the others don't even know who I am."

Aunt Matilda shook her head. "True life is not like those pretty romances you read in your magazines and novels. Believe me, that type of emotion is short-lived and can lead you to make a disastrous marriage choice. The best marriages among our class are those that mutually benefit both parties. A wise business arrangement, if you will. From that, a love based on mutual respect and alliances can grow."

Can. Didn't mean it did. Aunt Matilda and Uncle Clarence's marriage was a prime example.

Jenny knew many of her set subscribed to Aunt Matilda's view of marriage. Take Sally Gardner. She'd happily married a much older and very wealthy man at the end of her first season with no thought of love. Now she spent her time looking for love outside of her marriage as did many of the young wives Jenny knew. But Jenny had been raised with far too much respect for the marriage vows to play that game. Besides if she ever married, she didn't want to be her husband's bankroll. She wanted to be his everything.

Aunt Matilda rose with a heavy sigh. "I don't know what we're going to do with you. You've effectively destroyed any hope for another offer any time soon. I've half a mind to wash my hands of you for good."

If only, but Jenny knew Aunt Matilda's sense of duty was far too ingrained for that.

"For now, you'd best stay in your room, at least until Lord and Lady Denbigh and their son leave. I'll have your dinner sent up and give the excuse you're not feeling well." She left, closing the door behind her with a firm click.

Jenny lay back against the bank of pillows flanking the head-board of her bed. Was it really so foolish to dream of love? Granted, few marriages she'd seen seemed to include it. But then, most she knew had been arranged according to Aunt Matilda's guidelines. But she knew of at least one that had been founded on love—the only one that mattered in her world.

She reached beneath her collar and pulled out a small gold locket. Clicking it open, she studied the faces inside—the woman with hair and eyes so much like hers, the man whose twinkling gray eyes reminded her of the love she'd once taken for granted.

She remembered the day she lost it all too well. She could almost feel the slick horsehair of the sofa she hid behind while the grownups talked. Smell again the cloying scent of too many perfumes in too small a space.

There'd been an accident. Mama and Papa were not coming home. Ever.

Over the horrified whispers about telescoping train cars and crushed metal, she could still hear Aunt Matilda's strident voice.

"Well, of course, we must take them in. Henry was Clarence's only brother. It is our duty to see they are brought up in a manner worthy of the Westraven name. Though, heaven knows, it won't be easy. Beatrice spoiled the two of them immensely. And Henry did nothing to stop her. He was so besotted. Nothing she did was wrong in his eyes."

"Such beautiful children," one of the ladies said. "Why, little Jenny looks just like an angel."

Aunt Matilda sniffed. "She might have the face of an angel, but she has the spirit of a hellion. A more spoiled little hoyden I've never met. If she hadn't been climbing that tree at the Bainbridge's on Tuesday and broken her arm . . . Well. I'm sure the Good Lord knows the number of our days, but Henry and Beatrice planned to stay at Niagra Falls until the end of the week. They should never have been on that train. But I know my duty, and I will do whatever it takes to raise her to be a proper lady."

Jenny rubbed absently at the spot where her arm had been broken. The pain of that break had been nothing compared to losing the two most important people in her life. She should never have allowed Rufus Bainbridge's bet that he could climb the highest in that tree to sway her. She should have kept her feet planted firmly on the ground like the rest of the girls. Her parents might still be alive if she had.

Instead, she and Ted soon learned the vast difference between being cherished as beloved blessings and being regarded as one's duty. Though she'd experienced six short years of the one and almost fifteen of the other, that unconditional, unmerited, unceasing love was what she longed for. Was it a pipe dream to believe she could have it again?

Jenny sighed and dropped the locket back beneath her collar. Maybe Aunt Matilda was serious this time. Maybe she finally would wash her hands of her. In six months, Jenny would turn twenty-one. At that point, the interest payment on her inheritance would come to her each month, instead of to her uncle.

The entirety would not be hers until she turned twenty-five, but the interest was enough to live on if she practiced economy. Up until three months ago, she'd planned to join Ted in Wyoming the minute she turned twenty-one.

She'd wanted to go with him two years ago when his tuberculosis diagnosis sent him out West. He'd been so sick and frail. No one believed he'd survive the journey. Oh, how she'd wanted to be the one to nurse him.

He was all she had.

But that was the year of her Come Out, and Aunt Matilda was not about to let her squander it. Uncle Clarence's secretary made the trip instead. And the Parkhursts, Uncle Clarence's good friends in Wyoming, had been the ones to nurse him.

Then last January, they'd received word he'd married the Parkhurst's only daughter. He'd set up a household with a wife. He had no need for a sister.

Since then, she'd been adrift. She didn't want to continue this empty social round of going from dinner party to ball to musical to opera performance, thinking of nothing more consequential than what she would wear or how she'd dress her hair.

She wanted to belong somewhere, to be a part of something

exciting, something meaningful. She'd thought she'd found that working at Ben's law office. She'd felt so alive. So needed.

Now even that had been taken away. She was a Westraven and an heiress, trapped in a life she didn't want.

But no one could force her to marry without love. She'd rather not marry at all.

Chapter Six

"*The grass is browning on the hills; No pale, belated flowers recall the astral fringes of the rills . . .*"

Jenny read the line for the fourth time in as many minutes. Oh, bother. If only she'd brought down *Life in the Mines* or *A Woman's Heart* to read. She simply couldn't concentrate on poetry, especially on a rainy day like today.

But she knew why she hadn't. She also knew her lack of concentration had little to do with the weather. Today was Tuesday. The day she'd told Ben he could visit. Honestly, she wasn't even sure why she told him he could come. It wasn't as if they had a future together regardless of how delicious that kiss had been. Their worlds were miles apart. Besides, he was courting Miss Goddard, and she knew for a fact any man who wanted a Miss Goddard was not the man for her. She'd learned that lesson years ago.

He probably wouldn't even come. Surely, he had better things to do than run into the city every week to see her. But if he were to come, she'd much rather he find her reading Whittier than a dime novel. Nell Goddard probably read Whittier all day, and Longfellow, and Poe. Or she did needlework or something equally ladylike and productive, like great-aunt Gertie who knitted industriously by the fire.

Jenny closed the book with a sigh and wandered over to look out the east window. A spate of rain pattered against the pane, dampening her spirits even more. She'd chosen to sit in the morning room today because it was usually much more intimate and cheery than the formal drawing-room, but even it felt gloomy. Besides, who would be foolish enough to pay calls on a day like this?

With the exception of Aunt Matilda, of course. She'd left for her calls at two o'clock sharp as she did every Tuesday, rain or shine, heat or snow. Nothing kept Aunt Matilda from her weekly ritual. The woman would probably be on her deathbed, and if it were a Tuesday, still rise to make her calls.

That she didn't make a fuss when Jenny excused herself from the weekly rounds proved how far Jenny must have slipped. She should never have told her suitors those lies about herself. As usual, she'd spoken without thinking, not considering what her careless words would do to her own reputation. No wonder Aunt Matilda was ready to wash her hands of her.

"A Mr. Bennett to see you," Felton intoned from the doorway.

She turned to see Ben standing behind Felton, derby in hand.

He came.

She couldn't stop an exuberant grin from spreading across her face. So much for calm sophistication and practiced indifference.

"Mr. Bennett. How wonderful of you to come and brighten our dreary day." At least she could sound poised and polished.

She introduced great-aunt Gertie, who continued to knit and purl, paying little heed to their visitor.

Ben bowed. "I'm pleased to meet you, Mrs. Vroon. Looks to me as if you've found a cozy spot to sit on this chilly day."

Aunt Gertie looked up with a nod. "I'm making them for those poor boys in the Philippines."

At Ben's puzzled glance, Jenny tapped her ear and murmured, "She's deaf. Quite, quite deaf."

"Oh." Ben turned back to Aunt Gertie and shouted, "Socks, I see? They're lovely. I'm sure the soldiers will be glad to have them."

Aunt Gertie beamed. Ben always could charm the ladies—young and old.

Jenny picked up her forsaken book from the settee and sat down, patting the empty space beside her. "Please, Mr. Bennett, won't you join me?"

Ben's thigh brushed hers as he sat. Goodness. This settee wasn't nearly this small the day she sat on it with the viscount.

He peeked at the cover of her book.

"Whittier? A little dull for you, isn't it? Have you forsaken your dime novels, then?"

"Oh, years ago."

"Hmmm. I could swear I overheard you and Johnny arguing just last month about whether Deadwood Dick or Frank Merri-well was the better hero."

Drat the man.

"Possibly." She kept her voice nonchalant. "Of course, I did read the dimes as a child, but I'd like to believe my literary tastes are more well-rounded now."

"Well, I applaud your ability to delve into poetry. I never could get a handle on it myself. Give me a dime novel any day. Or a biography or two. As for the Frank versus Dick debate, I'd have to agree with Johnny. Frank is the better hero."

"Oh, but how can you say that? Frank's adventures are not nearly as challenging."

"Throwing a ball that curves twice in flight isn't challenging?" The twinkle in Ben's eyes told her she hadn't fooled him for a minute with her polished airs. Why had she even tried? She'd never be anything like Nell Goddard, nor did she want to be. She might as well enjoy the debate.

"Throwing a baseball is nothing compared to fighting outlaws and Indians and discovering hidden gold."

"I seem to remember Frank finding treasure in the one where he's in Colorado hunting down those train robbers."

"Yes, but that's nothing like what Dick found in *The Phantom Miner*."

"But Dick is an outlaw. How can a true hero rob stagecoaches?"

"It's not because he wants to. He has no choice."

Ben frowned and shook his head. "Everyone has a choice. In fact, if Frank were in Dick's shoes, I'm sure he'd find a way out. After all, he's the 'typical American lad, as honest as he is brave.'"

Jenny couldn't help laughing at Ben's lofty manner. Ben joined in, laughter crinkling the corners of his eyes.

How she missed this.

She poured from the silver tea set Felton had left and handed Ben his cup.

"So, how is Johnny?"

"Desolate now that he can no longer boast an office with the prettiest typewriter girl on the block."

Jenny felt a flush creeping into her cheeks. Ben thought she was pretty?

"More than likely, he's just upset with all the extra work I left him. He never liked writing all those letters by hand."

"Oh, he's not overburdened. Miss Goddard hired us another typewriter after you left, but unfortunately for Johnny, this one doesn't draw in all the neighboring clerks the way you did. That honor now goes to the typewriter at the Mealy Bros. Accounting firm—a Miss Philpot, I believe."

Jenny didn't know what bothered her more—the fact she'd been replaced or the reminder that Miss Goddard still held a role in Ben's life while she did not.

"And your new typewriter girl? She's working out?"

"She's quite competent. And as far as I know, she hasn't tried to dust the law books."

Somehow she couldn't rise to the bait of his teasing. She knew she couldn't return to that life, but to hear they were all carrying on just fine without her made her current state all the more unbearable.

"Hey," Ben shifted closer, catching her gaze. "Are you all right?"

"Yes. Of course." Oh, who was she fooling? The words sounded hollow even to her. "I'm sorry. I'm a little blue-deviled is all. Must be the weather."

"I hope your aunt and uncle haven't been too hard on you." Ben set down his cup. He glanced over at Aunt Gertie, then back at her, his dark eyes troubled. "I . . . um . . . one reason I wanted to come today was . . . well, I feel I need to apologize for when I . . . when we . . ."

Oh.

Jenny felt her cheeks warm again. He was referring to the kiss. That very wonderful kiss. One she wouldn't mind repeating without an interruption. She let her gaze drift to his lips. Did he feel the same? Would he try again?

"Jenny, I should never have . . . I never meant . . ."

No. Apparently not.

He cleared his throat. "The truth is, I behaved badly and now with that article in *Town Topics* . . . well, what I mean is, I hope you haven't had to suffer for my actions."

She shook her head, setting her half-empty cup of tea next to Ben's. "If I'm suffering for anyone's actions, it's my own. Aunt Matilda has made that all too clear. She tells me if I don't amend my behavior, I'll end up without any marriage prospects entirely. I suppose she's right."

"Nonsense. What about the Englishman?"

"Gone. He and his parents left yesterday." Thank goodness. She'd grown tired of being confined to her room.

"Because you took a job?" Incredulity laced Ben's words.

"Oh. No. Because I turned him down." Among other things.

"I don't see why that would ruin your marriage prospects. A lady has a right to refuse a man's suit."

"Yes, but that's just it. I don't seem to be able to refuse anyone without saying the most outrageous things."

Laugh lines deepened at the corner of Ben's lips. They really were nice lips. And she really needed to quit focusing on them.

"Like what?"

"Like? Oh, well, like I'm addicted to gambling and . . . and cigarettes . . . and spending large sums of money."

"Are you?"

"No!" Jenny swatted him with a sofa pillow. "But Mr. Sanford doesn't know that, and he's sure to tell his mother. And once he tells her, he's as good as told all of society. True or not true, there's no taking it back."

"I thought your offer was from Lord Parry. How many outrageous refusals have you made?"

"Three." This week, anyway.

"Three? And you made up things like that to each of them?"
She nodded.

"Why?"

"It seemed the kind thing to do."

"The kind thing would have been to be honest."

"I don't see how my telling Mr. Van Clyde he smells like mothballs and reminds me of my late grandfather is kind. And if I told Mr. Sanford he's nothing but a mama's boy, or Lord Parry that he brays like a donkey when he laughs, would that have been kind?"

"I see your point. Maybe straight honesty is not what you're after. Maybe you should shoot for something in between— honesty that neither degrades you nor your suitor." He studied her for a minute through squinted eyes. "Tell you what, we'll practice."

"Three times in one week is not enough practice?"

"Not if you continue using all the wrong strategies. What you need is to find a good strategy and practice that. Here. You can try it on me. Pretend I'm a suitor for your hand."

"Why, Mr. Bennet, I had no idea you felt that way." Ugh. Now, she sounded like Sally Gardner.

"Hypothetically, of course."

"Of course." Though he needn't be so quick to remind her.

"So, I've asked for your hand in marriage, now what do you say?"

"Wait. You haven't asked me anything. If we're going to practice, you need to play your part."

He shot her a dark look. "Fine."

Dropping to one knee, he took her hand and looked soulfully into her eyes. "How's this?"

Good.

Too good.

"Better."

"Miss Westraven. Would you do me the honor of becoming my wife?" He was in exactly the same position, saying exactly the same words as the viscount two short days ago, so why did this feel so different? Those eyes of his could almost convince her he meant it, though she knew for a fact he didn't. She hadn't sat through a month of Tuesday dinners where he listed Nell Goddard's virtues to not know where his heart lay. Yet when the viscount held her hand, she hadn't felt a single flutter. Not one. Ben's touch unleashed a whole flock of them, starting in her fingers and traveling to her stomach.

She pulled her hand away. "This isn't going to work. I need to know your motivation."

"What do you mean?"

"Why are you asking to marry me?"

"For the same reason any man asks a woman to marry him. He wants to be married to her." Ben sounded exasperated.

"In my experience, men have all sorts of reasons. Lord Parry wanted to marry me because he has no money and needs to restore his estates in England. Mr. Sanford wanted to marry me because his mother told him he did, and Mr. Van Clyde wanted to marry me because . . . well, I have no idea. Maybe he owes my uncle a favor."

"You sell yourself short. Surely, each of these men also wanted you for yourself."

"I saw no indication of it. And I've seen no indication of it in you either, so don't think you can try that route. Here's an idea. You want to marry me because you need my money to open a law office of your own."

He shook his head. "Won't work. I'd never feel right living off my wife's money." Ben thought for a minute. "I know. I took advantage of your reputation by my actions the other day in my office and think it's only right I offer to marry you."

"Because of a kiss? This is the twentieth century. People kiss all the time without getting married."

"Your aunt and uncle don't believe that. Trust me, if I had been someone they wanted you to marry, they'd have had us engaged before the day was out."

He wasn't wrong. During the ride home from Newark, Aunt Matilda and Uncle Clarence had droned on and on about how she'd been so foolish as to get into "a compromising situation" with an entirely unsuitable young man.

"So, I've asked for your hand in marriage, now what do you say?"

She raised her chin and said in her most proper voice, "I'm sorry, Mr. Bennett. I'm afraid we will not suit."

"Why not?"

Jenny opened her mouth to speak, then shut it. She couldn't think of a single honest thing to say. Turning away, she picked up her cup of tea and took a swallow.

"You can't drink tea in the middle of a proposal."

"I'm thinking."

"You're stalling. And I'd appreciate it if you would stop so I could get off my knee. This floor isn't exactly comfortable."

She set down her teacup. "We would not suit Mr. Bennett because we're simply friends. We are not in love with each other."

"Good friends often make the best lovers."

Now she wanted her tea again. Not as a stalling tactic but because her mouth was suddenly as dry as the Sahara.

"You're like an older brother to me." Not true. She'd never felt all fluttery around Ted.

"Your aunt and uncle don't believe that."

They don't?

Oh. Right. The "compromising situation."

She tried again. "I'm not the type of wife you need. I don't know how to clean a house or cook. I've never so much as boiled a pot of water. The only housewifely thing I know how to do is pour a cup of tea."

"But I know for a fact you're a quick learner. I have no doubt if you wanted to become a model housekeeper, you'd learn to be one in record time."

He wasn't making this easy.

"Maybe. But even if I did, I'll only bring you trouble, remember? You and Ted have told me a thousand times. I rush into things without thinking, I talk too much, I'm reckless—"

Ben placed his gloved finger on her lips. "If you keep this up, you'll be back to telling those outrageous lies again. Give me an answer that's honest and kind but doesn't degrade yourself. And remember, my honor's at stake. It's my duty as a gentleman to marry you and restore your good name."

His duty? How she hated that word.

"Duty? Well, that's exactly why we won't suit. I don't want to marry someone who thinks marrying me is a *duty*. I want someone who believes I am a treasure. That I'm worth pursuing. . . worth fighting for . . . worth *dying* for. I want a man who, despite all my warts and failings and shortcomings, can't imagine living another day without me. That's how I want him to feel about me, and that's how I want to feel about him. And so, until I find a man like that, I won't marry anyone."

Something sparked deep in Ben's eyes. Respect? Relief? Regret? Had she made an utter fool of herself?

"Bravo, Miss Westraven." His voice came out low and soft. "I believe you've found the speech you can practice."

Chapter Seven

Asummons to Uncle Clarence's library was never good.
Early on Jenny learned such a summons meant Aunt
Matilda had reached the end of her rope and wanted Uncle
Clarence to mete out the required punishment. Sadly, Aunt
Matilda's rope was a short one.

In later days the library became more a command center
where Uncle Clarence and Aunt Matilda would strategize plans
before bringing her or Ted in to issue their orders.

Uncle Clarence's library was where she learned she was to go
to boarding school.

Uncle Clarence's library was also where she learned she
would be following boarding school with two years of finishing
school in France.

And Uncle Clarence's library was where she learned Ted's
failing health was actually tuberculosis and that he was moving
to a healthier climate out West in a last hope to save his life.

No. Uncle Clarence's library was never a place she wanted
to be.

She knocked at its heavy door of paneled rosewood, and at
Uncle Clarence's response, let herself in.

"You wished to speak with me, sir?"

"Yes, Jeanette. Please sit down."

The room was not unpleasant, though a bit too dark for her taste. As always, it smelled faintly of pipe smoke, leather, and varnish—a mixture that never failed to coil a spring of tension tight within. Taking in a long, slow breath, she made her way toward the high-backed leather chair opposite Uncle Clarence's desk.

Aunt Matilda sat in a similar chair off to the side of a wall of glass-enclosed books. Meeting Jenny's glance with a placid gaze, she sat with her back poker straight, hands clasped loosely in her lap.

So. Another planning session had ended. Where would their orders take her this time?

Jenny sat, assuming the same posture as Aunt Matilda. Those two years of finishing school hadn't been for naught. From a shelf above Uncle Clarence's desk, the bust of some Greek philosopher looked down his patrician nose at her. As a child, she'd thought the bust was Uncle Clarence. Wiser now, she realized the resemblance was merely a coincidence.

As usual, Uncle Clarence took his time to begin. She schooled herself to wait, watching the play of jewel tones across the shiny surface of the desk as light kaleidoscoped through the stained-glass transom above the room's large bay window.

Finally, he cleared his throat.

"Your aunt tells me that young lawyer has been calling on you."

"Be—Mr. Bennett? Yes, he accompanied his grandmother and Aunt Bethany to our At Home last week."

"Aunt Gertrude told us he was here again on Tuesday."

"Well, yes. He did drop by. He has business that brings him into the city on occasion."

"She told us he asked for your hand in marriage."

Oh. Insisting Ben get down on one knee probably hadn't been her smartest move. Apparently, Aunt Gertrude heard just well enough to be dangerous.

"No. I mean, we were . . ."

Uncle Clarence held up a hand. "No need to explain. She also told us you turned the young man down, as you have all your suitors. In this case, it was for the best. That's what your aunt and I want to discuss today. As you know, your father's will placed certain restrictions on your inheritance, the bulk of which you'll not receive until you turn twenty-five unless, of course, you are to marry before then to someone whom I, as your guardian, approve.

"Since you've had several offers of late, I thought it might be prudent for me to reiterate the conditions necessary for my approval." He fixed her with his steely gaze. "As I told you before your Come Out, your aunt and I are quite willing for you to pick someone of your own choosing, but we can in no way condone a match with someone beneath you in social standing. A gentleman can sometimes get away with marrying someone who is not his equal financially, but such an alliance never works well for a woman. You'll need a husband who is familiar with the pressures wealth brings. Someone who doesn't need to rely on the wealth you will bring to the marriage."

Unless he comes with a European title, of course.

Uncle Clarence paused as if waiting on a response.

"Yes, Uncle Clarence. Is there anything else?"

He studied her over the rims of his spectacles, as if not sure how to proceed. "Your aunt and I plan to leave for Newport early next month."

She knew that. Aunt Matilda and Uncle Clarence always spent their summers with the rest of New York's elite at their "cottage" in Newark, though how a small mansion of forty rooms ever came to be titled "cottage" she'd never know. She loved the ocean but wasn't looking forward to the steady diet of balls, picnics, musicals, and card parties that formed life there. Especially not this year. The gossip surrounding her bevy of spurned suitors was bound to follow her.

Uncle Clarence cleared his throat again. "After giving much thought to the matter, we've decided not to take you."

What? She glanced at her aunt. So Aunt Matilda wasn't looking forward to the social awkwardness any more than she. But where would she go? After the debacle at Aunt Bethany's, they weren't likely to send her there again.

"We've decided this summer might be the opportune time for you to visit Theodore."

Teddy! It took all her effort not to jump up and throw herself into Uncle Clarence's arms. Only the knowledge that such behavior would most likely cause him to rescind his decision kept her firmly rooted to her chair.

"I would love to visit Teddy and Grace," she said as calmly as possible. "When were you thinking I could leave?"

"Maybe as early as next week. Dr. Waite tells me of a young couple from Newark who is planning to migrate to Lander for the same reasons as Teddy. I've asked Dr. Waite to have them pay us a visit. If the wife proves a suitable companion for you, I see no reason why you can't accompany them."

Next week? Jenny couldn't stop a grin from spreading across her face. She didn't care if the wife turned out to be another Aunt Matilda. She'd be on that train come hell or high water.

Chapter Eight

Ben took a peek at what he could see of Nell's face beneath the brim of her hat. Frosty. Definitely, still frosty. What had he done to turn her to ice? This perfect spring day should have been ideal for a walk in the park, but Nell had hardly said three words to him since he picked her up.

Ben counted to ten, then counted to twenty. "Are you going to tell me what's bothering you?"

"Nothing's bothering me."

"Oh come on, Nell. You've given me the cold shoulder all afternoon."

"Have I?"

He lifted an eyebrow and waited. Nothing.

"Nell?"

"Fine. If you must know, I'm getting tired of seeing your name bandied about in newspapers."

"I thought we settled this. That *Town Topics* article didn't even mention my name. I'm guessing less than five people we know saw that article and fewer than that care."

"Well, that's where you're wrong. That might have been true with the first article, but with this second one, there's no mistaking it's you. I've had at least seven friends point it out to me since it came out on Thursday."

"What second article?"

"You haven't seen it?"

"You know I don't read those gossip rags."

"Well, maybe you should, now that your name keeps popping up."

"Is this about Jenny again?"

"Why? Is there another heiress you've been calling on I should know about? By all means, tell me. It's so unpleasant to find these things out through the papers."

"Don't be ridiculous. I haven't been 'calling on' anyone but you."

"That's not what the article said."

"Maybe you should let me read it. I can hardly defend myself if I don't know what it says."

Pressing her lips together, Nell reached into her reticule and pulled out a folded piece of newsprint, which she thrust into his hand. Once again, the offending paragraph was easy to locate, having been heavily outlined in ink.

"'Tinker, tailor, soldier, sailor . . . ,' or in this case should we say, 'viscount, lawyer, banker, scholar . . .' Who will claim the hand of New York's richest heiress? All four were seen paying their calls on the lady last week, but lest you think the handsome young newcomer, Mr. Bennett, has the advantage for having made two calls in a five-day span, you may rest easy. Miss W. appears to have turned all four away, choosing instead to leave our fair city for adventures out West. Maybe she's holding out for a cowboy."

She was leaving. He hadn't heard from her since his visit over a week ago. Hadn't expected to hear from her, of course, yet the thought of her leaving for good left him hollow.

"Well? Is it true?"

"I suppose so. She has a brother in Wyoming."

"What? No. Is it true you visited her twice in one week?"

"Well yes, but it's not what you think . . . not what the article insinuates anyway. Her great-aunt was worried about her . . . about how she left things when she returned to New York, and since I had business in the city last week, I escorted her and Grandma to visit Jenny. That's all."

"Twice?"

"Well, no. Jenny invited me back so we could talk in private." The frost was back in Nell's face. "She's a *friend*, Nell. I told you before, we spent all our summers together as kids. She's like a little sister to me. I was worried that the first article had caused her some trouble, and I needed to make sure she was fine."

A twinge of guilt pricked his conscience. Essentially, everything he'd said was true. Almost. Except . . . he'd never shared a kiss like that with his sister, or anyone else for that matter. Not even Nell.

But that was behind them. Jenny was leaving. Off to someplace out West to stir up more trouble, no doubt. But out of his life for sure. It was all for the best. A girl like Jenny didn't fit into his well-ordered world. But Nell did.

He took Nell's hands in both his own, catching her gaze and holding it. "Can we put all this behind us? Who cares what a gossip rag insinuates? You are the only one who has my interest . . . all of it. I've been looking forward to spending this day with you all week. And the weather's perfect. Can't we enjoy it?"

A glimmer of a smile fluttered, then vanished. She pulled her hands from his grasp. "I suppose we could, but if I ever see your name linked with hers again, it's going to take a lot more than some pretty talking to get yourself out of the trouble you'll be in."

He placed a hand over his heart. "Never again. I swear."

Ben returned to his lodgings that night, quite satisfied with the way the day turned out. Not only had Nell's mood improved, but she'd also thawed enough to invite him to dinner. A boon in several ways. First, it proved their relationship was well on its way toward its pre-Jenny status. Second, the Goddards employed an excellent cook.

All in all, he'd come through this trouble with Jenny far better than any time before. Nell might not have Jenny's classic beauty and a mouth that simply begged to be kissed, but she was the type of wife he needed. If he was ever going to win Father's approval, he needed a wife far more grounded than the mercurial Jenny. Nell was pretty, sensible, and practical. She would never lead him into scrapes. In short, she was the perfect wife for an up-and-coming lawyer.

He settled into his favorite easy chair and picked up a book. Yes. This was the life he needed—calm and quiet.

A soft knock interrupted his thoughts. Mrs. Battleby must have heard him come in. He considered ignoring her but knew she wasn't going away. Might as well get it over with.

Sure enough, his landlady stood on the threshold, her face wreathed with concern.

"I'm so sorry to bother you so late, Mr. Bennett, but this telegram came while you were out. I thought you should have it right away." She held out an envelope. His eye caught on the black edging.

He took the letter and scanned the postmark. South Dakota. No. Dear God, not Father. But something deep inside him knew. His life was about to change forever.

Chapter Nine

Apleasant breeze wafted through the open window of the stage bringing with it the sharp scent of sage. Thank goodness the day was warm enough for them to tie back the leather flaps that covered the stage windows.

Jenny followed the flight of a large bird—a hawk maybe—hanging low in the sky, seemingly suspended above them. Her heart soared.

Like that bird, she was free. Free of conventions. Free of society schedules. Free of everyone else's expectations. But most of all, free of Aunt Matilda and her endless lists of dos and don'ts.

Jenny learned early on that she'd never measure up to the high standards of the Aunt Matilda's in this world. And it wasn't that she hadn't tried. Her first year at boarding school, she'd been determined to start fresh, prove Aunt Matilda wrong. She set her sights on Madame DeLancey's Star Pupil Award given each year to the girl most proficient in all areas of training. How diligent she'd been. For eight and a half months, she'd missed skating parties, picnics, birthday gatherings, and trips into town to stay behind and practice her scales or verb conjugations. Languages were her nemesis since she was years behind the other students who had grown up speaking German and French. But she was so close. In all other classroom subjects, she was top of the class. She might not have been quite as skilled in the arts of music and dancing as her rival Cecily Lamoreux, who had been star pupil two years running, but she felt sure her scores in the academic subjects would put her in the lead.

Then came Lucerne. Madame DeLancey had chosen a trip to Lucerne as a final outing at the end of the school term. Those students who were in the running for Star Pupil were expected to attend a lecture by Professor Brauer on the "Dying Lion" in the afternoon, followed by the organ performance at the Hofkirche in the evening. The other girls were taking the steamer to Vitznau to take the cog railway up the Rigi. Jenny watched in envy as her closest friends, Louisa Silverthorne and Ann Margaret Boulier, packed their bags to leave for the steamer. Not only were they taking the rail to the top of the mountain, but they were also staying overnight to watch the sunrise the next morning.

She watched them leave, then trudged down the hallway of the hotel toward where her group was meeting. As she turned a corner, she saw two of her teachers walking just ahead of her, deep in conversation. She paid them little mind until she heard the words "star pupil" and "Jeanette." Were they talking about her? Had she finally won the prize? She crept closer.

"Jeanette Westraven?" Fraulein Luttgen gave a short laugh. "You can't truly believe Jeanette Westraven will be our star pupil."

"Why would she not? She is the top student in all subjects."

Jenny smiled. Mademoiselle Jarreau had always been her favorite of all her teachers.

"Ah. But Madame's Star Pupil must be far more than clever. She must also be refined and poised—a perfect lady. Jeanette has a recklessness to her. An overabundance of what you would call *joie de vivre*. If you think Madame will choose passion over poise, you do not know Madame. Mark my words, Cecily Lamoreux will be our star pupil."

Jenny didn't wait to hear more. She turned and sprinted the other direction chasing the girls headed toward the Rigi. She reached the dock minutes before the steamer left and was welcomed with open arms by Louise and Ann Margaret. What followed was one of the best adventures of her school days, and the sunrise the next morning was spectacular. As she watched the sun turn the clouds a brilliant orange and slowly gild the peaks and lakes surrounding her, she vowed never to miss another sunrise experience chasing someone else's expectations. She was made for sunrises on mountaintops, not lectures and organ music. Aunt Matilda's approval just wasn't worth it.

Today was a sunrise moment. Like a heroine from a dime novel, she was on a stagecoach—a stagecoach!—in the middle of Wyoming, heading straight for new adventures. Who knew what lay beyond that next hilltop? That outcropping ahead was perfect for an ambush.

What would it be like to be held up by road agents? The leader would be young and handsome, of course, his dark eyes dangerous yet compelling behind his black mask. He would be ever so polite as he asked her to hand over her valuables. He might even flirt with her.

She wouldn't bat an eye at giving him her money and jewels. Except . . . her locket and chain were all she had left of her parents.

And, if they stole her valuables, they'd most likely steal from the Skivingtons as well. That wouldn't do. Though she'd known them less than a week, the couple Dr. Waite recommended to Uncle Clarence had quickly become her best friends.

No road agents, then. But a band of Indians would be divine. Wouldn't it be amazing to see Indians in their natural setting? She could almost picture them atop that rocky cliff, headdresses blowing in the wind, war paint striping their faces.

She turned to Maddie Skivington. "Do you think we'll see any Indians?"

She was answered by a rumbling chuckle from the stage's fourth passenger, an elderly gentleman who'd been dozing in his seat since they'd all climbed aboard in Rawlins.

"If you're looking to see Injuns out here, Missy, you're about thirty years too late." He yawned and stretched, then pushed back the wide brim of his Western hat, revealing a pair of twinkling gray eyes.

"Name's Willoughby, by the way," he said, leaning forward with a big, beefy hand outstretched. "Cyrus Willoughby. Most folks call me Cy."

His grip was strong and calloused, and though his three-piece suit looked as eastern as Rob's, she guessed from his hat and boots she might well be meeting her first cowboy.

"You folks must be new to these parts. What brings y'all out this way? Besides Injuns, of course." Mr. Willoughby shot Jenny a grin. She grinned back, liking the gentle humor she saw in his eyes.

Before she could answer, the coach swerved, sliding them all to the left. Outside her open window, she saw the lead mules of yet another freight train. They'd passed several today, the wagons piled high with bundles of fleece.

Clouds of dust billowed through the open window, sending Rob into a coughing spasm and covering their clothes with yet another layer of dust. Thank goodness she'd worn her simplest waist and a sensible black skirt this morning.

Maddie was the first to recover. "My husband's health has been delicate of late. Our doctor suggested he spend time in the dry Western air." Irony laced her words.

"A lunger, are ya?" Cy nodded his understanding. "Well, I've heard tell our air can cure ya, if the wind don't kill ya first." He broke off mid-chuckle after glancing Maddie's way. "Sorry, ma'am. Didn't mean nothing by that, I swear. The wife always tells me I've got the tact of a bull in a field full of heifers. I'm sure your man will get along mighty well out here."

"Just like Teddy." Jen reached over and squeezed Maddie's hand, hating the pain she saw in her new friend's eyes. Turning to Mr. Willoughby, she asked, "Do you live near Lander? You might know my brother. Ted Westraven? He's a banker there."

"Westraven? Is he the young man who married Parkhurst's daughter a few months ago?"

"That's him. You know him?"

"Well, we ain't exactly met, but you can't help but notice when a young man marries the daughter of the richest man in town. It was quite a shindig, let me tell you. Didn't take the groom for a lunger, though."

"Oh, Teddy's ever so much better now. But when he first came west, he was even worse off than Mr. Skivington."

"Thanks, Jenny. I appreciate your vote of confidence." Rob was carefully tucking his handkerchief back into his pocket, but she didn't miss the hint of sarcasm in his tone.

"Well, it's true," she said. "When Ted made this trip two years ago, he was so weak he could barely sit up. Dr. Waite didn't think he'd survive it." Her throat grew thick at the memory. She'd been so sure she'd lose him. Her only brother and the only person in the world who accepted her for who she was.

It was Maddie's turn to squeeze her hand. "Don't mind Rob. He always gets testy when he's tired."

This final phase of their travel had been grueling. Unlike the plush accommodations of their private Pullman car, the stagecoach was cramped, the seats hard. They'd rocked and lurched and careened over every stone and rut in the road. And they still had a full day's travel ahead of them. She could imagine the toll it was taking on Rob.

He winked, letting her know he wasn't serious, and turned back to Mr. Willoughby. "Are you a rancher by chance?"

The man nodded. "Been ranching purt' near all my life. Grew up on a ranch in Texas before I went off to fight the Yanks.

Came out West after the war and tried my hand at mining first, but I've been back at ranching for more than twenty years now."

"Cattle or sheep?" Rob asked.

"Well now, I've always worked with cattle, though I know many near Lander who've been real successful with sheep. Don't care much for the critters myself. Eat the grass down to nothing and stupid as the day is long." Willoughby shook his head. "Takes just one of 'em to take some fool notion to step off a cliff or something, and the whole durn herd'll follow him. Now cows aren't the smartest either, but they've got sheep beat all to pieces. No sir, don't know why anyone would want to take on sheep."

A wry smile lifted the corners of Rob's mouth. "I met a man on the train in Nebraska who thought *sheep* ranching might be the thing for me. My doctor says I need to make a change. I'm a jeweler by trade, but he tells me I need to find a job outdoors."

The rancher stared at Rob for a minute before bursting out in loud guffaws. His laugh was so infectious, Jenny and the others couldn't help laughing with him.

"I've gone and done it again." Cy wheezed, wiping his eyes with a large red handkerchief. "Stuck my foot right square in my mouth. Wife always tells me I'd be much better off if I didn't talk at all. She's right, ya know." He winked across at her and Maddie. "She always is."

Sobering, the man stroked his bushy gray mustache and studied Rob. "You know, your man on the train just might be right. Much as I hate the critters myself, sheep could be the best thing for ya. Ya don't need much to get started—couple thousand sheep, a wagon, a few dogs—and you're in business. And it'll get ya outdoors, all right."

Hooves pounded outside the window, drawing Jenny's attention. She blinked. Had her imagination conjured up this as well? A dime novel hero atop a spotted mustang galloped toward them —hair, mane, fringe, and tail flowing from the pair. His gaze caught hers as the man drew abreast. Then, with a wave of one gauntleted hand, he flew past.

Holding onto her hat, she stuck her head out the open window, following the man's progress until he topped the next rise and was gone.

"Who was that?" she asked as she sank back into her seat.

"Looked like Sparrowhawk to me," Mr. Willoughby said. "Runs a road ranch up on Crook's Creek. It'll be our supper stop if we keep the time we're making."

"Sparrowhawk. Is that an Indian name?"

"English, I think. Though no one knows much about him. Showed up in these parts 'bout a year ago. The Harrises took him on and now he purt' near runs the place. Pretty tight-lipped, though. Folks say he used to be an Indian fighter, but I don't hold much stock in that. Couldn'a been more'n a lad in short pants during the last Indian battles."

Jenny watched the cloud of dust disappear over another rise in the far distance, but the man's image stayed emblazoned in her mind. Such beauty. Such freedom. Would the man himself be as untamed as he looked? Their supper stop could not come soon enough.

THREE HOURS LATER, THEY REACHED THE STATION AT CROOK'S Gap. The stage had been climbing steadily since its last stop, following a narrow stream. It now traveled along a high plateau with low, rolling hills flanking each side.

As the coach slowed, Jenny saw a cluster of log buildings—a crude stable and corral on one side of the road, a long, rambling log house with a dirt roof on the other.

"I recommend you part with the fifty cents it'll take to get a meal here," Cy said, as he hobbled out of the coach after Rob. "It'll be well worth your money."

Jenny eyed the modest building in front of her. Aunt Matilda would be aghast at the crudeness of their traveling accommodations, but then, Aunt Matilda wasn't here, was she? Besides, Cy had said that paragon on horseback would be here. She hurried out of the stagecoach after Maddie.

Ducking into the ranch house's dim, cool interior, she spied colorful wool rugs on a clean-swept dirt floor. The room was long and narrow. A table covered with an oilcloth ran its entire length. At the far end, two overstuffed, leather armchairs flanked a stone fireplace.

"Welcome, folks."

Jenny turned to see the Bill Cody look-alike step through the doorway leading to the next room. Sparrowhawk.

"Grab yourselves a seat," he said, his voice strong and deep. "Supper will be out in a minute."

He was almost as impressive up close as he'd been on horseback. Green eyes stood out in a face darkened by the sun, his wavy brown hair flowed to his shoulders. He'd removed his large western hat but still wore the thigh-high riding boots and spurs. A long jacket and bandana completed his outfit. But unlike the real Buffalo Bill, this man was no more than thirty. Her breath hitched as he caught her eye, and she felt herself blush. Goodness. She hadn't reacted to a man like this since, well, since . . . Ben. But Ben was back east. The West held her future.

Cy scurried to the table. "I'm telling you folks, you're in for a treat tonight. Sadie's one of the best cooks in the county."

Sadie? Was she Sparrowhawk's wife? Suddenly the beef stew and biscuits he'd placed on the table lost their appeal.

"Who's Sadie?"

Bless Maddie for asking.

"Sadie Harris. She and her husband own this place. Though Sparrowhawk runs it, she does the cooking. Be sure you save room for dessert. Her apple pie is the best in the county."

Jenny suddenly felt quite charitable toward the invisible Sadie and was soon agreeing with the others that the beef was as savory and tender as any she'd had, the biscuits the flakiest she'd ever tried. She'd just dipped her fork into the famous apple pie when the beat of hooves and jangle of spurs announced the arrival of more guests.

Within minutes, a trio of grimy young cowboys burst through the doorway and headed for the rough plank forming a crude bar along the far wall.

"Sparrowhawk," one of them yelled.

The man stepped out of the kitchen, carrying a coffee pot.

"Get me something to drink, will ya? Ya got any whiskey?"

"If it's a saloon you want, Jake, you'd better head to Rongis. You know we don't serve liquor here."

The young man he called Jake straddled a bar stool. "Give me coffee then, but I want it black as sin, hot as heck, and stirred with a pistol."

His companions hooted their approval, but Sparrowhawk never blinked an eye. Taking a tin cup from a hook on the wall, he set it on the bar, filled it with coffee, then pulled a pistol from his belt.

Holding it just above the cup, he growled, "You want some smoke in it?"

Oh, this was as good as watching a play. Jenny exchanged an excited glance with Maddie, who seemed as intrigued as she.

Jake took a sip of coffee before replying. "Naw just wanted to see if you were still packing that thing."

Keeping a steely eye on Jake, Sparrowhawk holstered the pistol. "Oh, I'll be packing as long as the likes of you keep coming around."

"Hear that, boys?" Jake looked at his companions. "If I didn't know better, I'd say we wasn't welcome at this here eating establishment."

"If you're here to eat, Jake, you know what to do. Show me your money, and I'll see you get a plate. In the meantime, I have other customers."

Three pairs of eyes turned their way. A shudder coursed through her as the young men gave her and Maddie the once over. She turned her attention to her pie, hoping they'd soon lose interest.

The room fell deadly silent. Then, she heard the thud of boots hitting the dirt floor and the jangle of spurs.

"Well, well, what have we here?"

One of the men stopped right behind her chair. So close, she could see the mud caked on his boots, smell a day's worth or more of sweat on his skin. Maddie raised her napkin to her nose.

As he leaned in, she saw it was the one Sparrowhawk had called Jake. "Aren't ya going to introduce me to your friends here, Cy?"

Cy gave the young man a measured stare. "If you'll mind your manners, Jake. This here's Mr. Rob Skivington, a jeweler from New Jer—."

"Jeweler, huh?" Jake leaned even closer. Jenny felt his breath on the back of her neck. "I don't know much about jewelry, but I sure do like the looks of these two jewels." To her horror, he reached out a grimy finger and pulled a lock of her hair from beneath her hat. "This here one's like spun gold."

Jenny jerked away, but he seemed undeterred, turning instead to study Maddie, whose glare alone should have withered him on the spot.

"And this other one, well, I can't tell exactly, but she looks a bit like topaz. If you'd get yourself a ruby-haired one, Jeweler, you'd have a fine collection."

Rob lunged to his feet, but before he could come around the table, Sparrowhawk grabbed Jake by the back of the collar and hauled him away.

"You're so stupid, Jake, you couldn't spot a goat in a herd a sheep. You've just treated two respectable ladies like a couple of dance hall girls. Mistakes like that could kill you." He gestured to Rob, who stood on the other side of the table, face dark, hands balled into fists. "Take the advice my mother gave me. If you don't have enough sense to know the difference, treat *all* women like ladies." He shoved Jake toward the bar. "Now, your coffee's getting cold, and these ladies have a stage to catch. Make your apologies and let them be."

Jake backed away, hands held high. "Sorry, sir . . . ladies," he said with mock humility. "Just being friendly." Turning, he swaggered back to the bar where his cohorts chortled and slapped him on the shoulder.

Maddie jumped to her feet and intercepted Rob before he could follow him. Grasping him tightly by the arm, she murmured something in his ear.

Rob threw another smoldering look but allowed Maddie to turn him toward the door.

A whistle from the driver confirmed the stage was ready to leave. Jenny caught Sparrowhawk's eye on her. Daring to walk over to him, she laid a hand on his arm.

"Thank you. That was wonderful."

His eyes crinkled in a slow smile, and he covered her hand with his, releasing a flutter of sensation in the pit of her belly. "It's been a pleasure to serve you, miss. I'm sorry you had to witness that. I promise few men in Wyoming are as rude as those scallywags."

"I'm sure you're right." Breaking free from the mesmerizing spell of his gaze, she reluctantly pulled her hand from his grasp and followed Cy to the stage.

"Wasn't he magnificent?" she said, once they'd all settled back into their seats and the stage was underway. She stroked the soft kid leather on her right glove. His arm had been rock hard, and his touch electric. What would it have been like to touch him without the glove?

Another low, rumbling chuckle erupted from Cy. "Well now, I dunno as I'd call him magnificent, but that Sparrowhawk's a smooth one. I'll give him that."

"Maybe they'd shown more respect if you'd told them I was a sheep rancher instead of a jeweler." Rob's color was still high.

"Now, don't think I didn't think of that, cuz I did, but in this case, I figured it was the lesser of two evils. Those McCreedys are a bad lot. They've been ranching here twenty years or more and think they run the place. Been a lot of bad blood between them and the sheep ranchers in this area for years. Not as bad as the trouble out in Johnson County, but close.

"Besides, the McCreedy outfit ain't just mean, they're dangerous. Rumor has it a couple of 'em are members of the Wild Bunch Gang hiding out after that train robbery last spring." He shook his head. "I know it don't seem that way, but the deal back there could'a been a whole lot worse."

Outlaws masquerading as cowboys? Cattle ranchers battling sheepmen? Oh, this western adventure was turning out exactly like her dime novels. Jenny couldn't wait to see what tomorrow would bring.

Chapter Ten

"I regret to inform you," five words no one wanted to see at the start of a telegram, especially one edged in black.

"Of course, you have to go, Ben," Nell had said when he'd shown her and her father the telegram the next day. "He's your father."

What Nell hadn't understood, and probably never would, was that he hardly knew his father. Hadn't seen him in almost fourteen years.

"Your family lives in the Black Hills, isn't that right?" Mr. Goddard had asked.

"My father's family does, yes. In Lead." He didn't consider them his family, though Letty and Lucas were his half-siblings. He hadn't wanted to come. Didn't see the point. But somehow, he'd allowed Nell and Mr. Goddard to persuade him, and now here he was within ten miles of a place and people he'd never wanted see again.

How different this trip was from that first one. He stared out the train window into the darkness at his own face staring back at him in the reflection caused by the gaslight behind him. The face of a grown man now, but inside he could still feel the excitement of that ten-year-old boy. How naïve he'd been. How unprepared for what lay ahead.

The details of that day were still crystal clear. Funny how some memories were like that. After years of waiting, he'd finally come West to be with Father. He'd been sitting in the kitchen of his father's boarding house munching on the housekeeper Nora's gingerbread cookies. Her children, Baby Lukas and four-year-old Letty, played together on the floor.

"My son Roy will be home from school any minute, now," Nora had told him. "You two are about the same age. I'm sure you will get along first-rate."

He remembered being rigged out in that ridiculous Little Lord Fauntleroy suit Grandma Janssen made him. They were all the rage with mothers in the East at the time, but the black velvet and wide lace collars were the bane of every boy he knew. Mrs. Spicer, the mother of the family he'd traveled with to South Dakota, had insisted he wear it.

"Your father will be so proud of what a fine-looking young man you are," she'd said.

He didn't see how a collar as big as a tablecloth was going to make anyone proud, but he'd done what he was told. He should have known better. When Roy came home from school, he took one look and said, "He's nothing but a sissy boy!"

Ben wanted to pummel him right then and there but held back, not wanting to disappoint Father on his first day. He settled for making faces at Roy, who made faces right back.

What happened next was still painful. When Father finally came in, little Letty went running into his arms calling, "Papa's home. Papa's home."

Everything slowed.

Papa? Why was the housekeeper's daughter calling *his* father Papa? The truth set in when Father pulled Nora close, giving her a kiss on the cheek and saying, "How's my favorite girl?"

Father had married another wife and made himself a whole new family. And no one bothered to tell him. No wonder Father hadn't sent for him before. He didn't need another son. He already had two.

This was all swirling through his mind when Father turned to greet him. Amusement shown from his eyes as he looked him over. "Good thing we got you out here when we did, son. Your Grandma's just about made a girl out of you."

He'd fled to the bedroom where Nora had put his trunk, not wanting them to see him cry. It was bad enough to be replaced. He didn't need them laughing at him, too.

Father came in later and apologized, but Ben wanted nothing more than to go home from then on. He never fit in with his father's new family. And he and Roy hated each other. Roy called him Little Lord Lester, and they fought nearly every day.

Somehow, he believed if he beat Roy in a fight, his father would no longer think he was a girl. But Roy was a good head taller and twenty pounds heavier. He hadn't stood a chance.

Though Father had been adamant about having him stay, the fighting finally wore him down. One night, when he'd come in with yet another busted lip and swollen eye, Father had sat him down, disappointment evident in his voice. "Maybe it's best you went back to your grandmother, son. If you stay here, you're liable to get yourself killed."

He'd vowed then and there to make Father proud of him. To make him glad he had him as a son. He'd thrown himself into his studies, climbing to the top of his class. As he grew physically, he got into sports. He made captain of the football team by his junior year. He graduated high school with honors and earned a scholarship to Harvard.

But letters from his father became fewer and farther between. He heard nothing from him when he graduated cum laude from Harvard, nor when he passed the bar in both New York and New Jersey. And his father never again came east for a visit.

Ben's plan had been to visit him once he made full partnership with Goddard. Surely then, he'd have earned his respect, but now it was all for naught.

The train slowed as it came into the station, and Ben disembarked. He'd sent a telegram ahead but wasn't sure anyone would be there to greet him. As he stepped onto the platform, a woman's voice called his name. Turning, he saw two women dressed in black walking his way. He recognized one as Nora. The younger of the two must be Letty, all grown up.

They stopped a few feet from him. Nora looked him over, gloved hands pressed to her lips, tears forming in the corners of her eyes.

"Oh, Lester," she said, her voice tremulous. "I would know you anywhere. You look just like your father."

Ben swallowed hard. This was going to be more difficult than he'd imagined.

"Hello, Nora. Letty. Please, call me Ben."

Nora studied him for a minute more, then nodded. "Very well, Ben. Best come along, now. You must be exhausted from all your traveling. We have a room ready for you at the boarding house. I'm so glad you came."

If only he could say the same.

THIS WASN'T HOW IT WAS SUPPOSED TO END. NOT HERE. NOT now. Not when he still had so much to prove . . . to himself . . . and to the man in the coffin the undertaker was lowering to its final resting place. Ben closed his eyes, wishing he could close his ears as well to block out Letty's quiet sobs, Nora's louder sniffles, and the finality of the minister's words, "Ashes to ashes, dust to dust."

It couldn't be over. Just weeks ago, Father had been in prime condition for a man in his fifties, stronger than most thirty-year-olds. He'd had all the time in the world, or so he'd thought, to mend their relationship . . . to prove his worth.

No hope of that now. Everything he'd worked to build these past fourteen years was wiped away by the stroke of one burning timber.

Because, of course, Lester Owen Bennett, Sr., had died a hero —making his name and reputation all the more impossible to live up to. The fire that had swept through downtown Lead last week, destroying more than forty businesses and houses, and threatening the Bennett family's livelihood, had actually spared them their hotel and boarding house, but not their father.

As captain of the Lead Volunteer Fire Department, Lester Bennett Sr. had fought the fire with the vigor of ten men, or so everyone told him. His father's last act was to rush into the home of Mrs. Abernathy, an elderly neighbor whom they'd all thought was trapped inside. There was never a chance for anyone to tell him she was safe at a friend's house three doors down. The roof collapsed seconds after he entered, its huge center beam striking him as it fell, removing any chance of his leaving the house alive.

Beside him, Letty stood up. The minister had stopped speaking. Ben pushed to his feet as Letty and Nora stepped closer to the grave, each dropping the small bouquets they'd held throughout the ceremony down onto the coffin. Roy and Lucas moved forward next. Roy reached over to support his mother who was now sobbing openly into a black handkerchief. Ben held back. As usual, he was the odd man out.

Letty, ever vigilant on his behalf, turned and beckoned him to a spot between her and Lucas. Not wanting to cause a scene, he stepped forward, ignoring the glare Lucas shot him. So here they stood, Lester Bennett's three children, joined as awkwardly at his death as they'd ever been in his life. But none of that mattered now that Father was gone. He wasn't part of this life. He never had been. And, without Father, he never would be.

Nora stepped away first, letting Roy lead her down the steep path to the waiting carriages. Letty and Lucas followed close behind. Ben watched them go. Somehow, he couldn't accept it was over. The other guests filed past him as they came to pay their last respects. Still, he lingered.

A hand clasped his shoulder, and he turned to a tall, middle-aged gentleman whose keen blue eyes peered at him through gold-rimmed spectacles.

"I'm sorry for your loss, son." The man reached out a hand. "Lester, isn't it? Your father told me all about you. I'm C.J. Foster."

"Of course, Mr. Foster." His father's lawyer. He recognized the name from the telegram he'd received, urging him to come for the funeral. "Call me Ben." He'd quit being Lester about the time he realized he'd never measure up to the name.

The lawyer's left eyebrow lifted a fraction at his request. "I'm glad you were able to make the funeral, Ben. I'm sure your family is happy to have you here."

Maybe Nora and Letty were happy to see him, but Roy and Lucas had shown no sign of pleasure. Nor had he expected them to. Ben turned from the grave, picking his way around gravestones and down the steep path. Mr. Foster fell in beside him.

"Frankly, Mr. Foster, without your telegram, I probably wouldn't have come. You have to know our family has never been close."

A troubled frown crossed the man's face. "I do. I also know it wasn't what your father wanted."

Ben shrugged. His father had no one to blame for the rift but himself. But no use dwelling on old wounds. Not anymore. Best to leave that all buried on the hilltop.

"Will you be staying in Lead for a while?"

Ben shook his head. "I need to get back to my practice." No reason to tell him Mr. Goddard had offered him extended time off. A week was all he was prepared to give.

"I'll be at your stepmother's for the reading of the will in the morning. Can I at least ask you not to make travel plans until after that?"

Blast. He'd forgotten about the will. He supposed Father had left him something. He *was* his eldest son. Hopefully, something easy to transport. Cash would be best. Whatever it was, he could tell from what Mr. Foster wasn't saying, it would take more time than he wanted to give.

They reached the line of carriages where the others waited for him.

Ben sighed. "All right, Mr. Foster. I'll postpone my travel plans until after the reading."

Chapter Eleven

Jenny poked her head out the window of the stage as it rolled to a stop. Soon she'd see Teddy. If only her legs were as eager to move as the rest of her.

Cy and Rob climbed out first. Jenny stretched her legs as much as she could in the cramped space, then hobbled after Maddie, thankful Rob's arm of support kept her from collapsing onto the boardwalk as she stepped from the coach. She stood a minute, letting blood rush back into her feet.

So this was Lander.

They stood in front of a small brick building labeled STAGE OFFICE. A strange wooden tower perched atop its roof. Ahead, the business section of the town stretched along a single main road. Though unpaved, the road was wide and boasted many large buildings, some several stories high. One might be the bank where Teddy worked.

The town sat in a pretty valley and was bustling with activity even this early in the day. In the distance, the Wind River Mountains gleamed blue and white. She couldn't wait to explore it all —the town, the mountains, all this great, wide, expansive space.

"Jenny."

Turning, she saw her brother jump down out of a stylish buggy. Forgetting all propriety, she ran to meet him.

He wrapped her in a bone-crushing hug, and she hugged back just as hard. When he'd left New York two years ago, so weak, so skeletal, she truly believed she'd never see him again—in this life anyway.

"Don't tell me you're crying."

She pulled out of his arms, swiping her eyes with her gloved fingers. "Of course, I'm crying. Look at you—so healthy and strong. Oh, Teddy, it's wonderful."

He grinned. "The air out here has been exactly what the doctor ordered. But look at you." He held her at arm's length. "If I hadn't seen all these wild curls peeking out from beneath your fashionable hat," he said as he tweaked at a tendril at the edge of her cheek, "I'd have driven right by thinking this sophisticated young woman couldn't possibly be my kid sister."

"Don't you poke fun at my curls, mister. Yours would be just as bad if you didn't crop them so short."

"Theodore." A soft, cultured voice broke into their teasing. A fashionable young woman stood behind them, twirling her parasol.

Ted turned and stretched out a hand. "Darling, I'm sorry. I didn't mean to leave you behind. Come meet my sister. Jenny, this is Grace."

Dark waves peeping beneath the brim of a fashionable hat, dark eyes hooded in haughty beauty—the girl was a Dana Charles Gibson drawing come to life. And she was Teddy's wife.

"Oh, Teddy. She's every bit as lovely as you said she was." She drew Grace into an embrace but let go as soon as she realized the girl was not hugging back. Oh, dear. Aunt Matilda was always telling her she was far too demonstrative. "I'm so pleased to finally meet you. I've always wanted a sister."

Grace favored her with a cool nod.

Ted threw an arm across each of their shoulders, pulling them both close. "My two favorite girls, together at last."

Grace was the first to break free. "Theodore, we *really* must be going. Mother is waiting."

"Of course." Arm still across Jenny's shoulder, Teddy turned her, so they were facing the growing pile of luggage at the edge of the boardwalk. "Lead me to your bags, sis, and we'll be on our way."

"Oh, but you haven't met the Skivingtons yet." She drew Teddy over to where Maddie stood, watching the men unload the luggage. "They were the most wonderful travel companions a girl could ask for. Maddie, this is my brother, Ted, and his wife, Grace. Teddy, this is Mrs. Skivington, and her husband Rob." She nodded toward where Rob was pulling a satchel off the top of the stagecoach. "Oh, and this is Mr. Willoughby." She turned toward the older gentleman. "But maybe you know him already?"

Cy reached over to shake Teddy's hand. "Well now, I don't believe we've had the privilege. But I know your father-in-law and your pretty little wife quite well. Call me Cy."

Rob climbed down to join them. "We've met through correspondence, at least." The two men shook hands. "Thank you for taking the time to answer my questions."

"And thank you for bringing my little sister to us. I'm sorry to hear you're a fellow TB sufferer, but Dr. Waite's prescription was dead-on for me. I'm sure it'll hold true for you."

Grace placed her hand on Teddy's arm.

He glanced at her. "My wife has a previous engagement, so we can't stay, but feel free to stop by the bank to see me if you want to hear how I found the cure."

"Thank you. I will. Would you like some help with Jenny's trunks?"

"Trunks?" Teddy's blue eyes twinkled. "How much luggage are we talking about here, sis?"

"Well, there's my valise and those bandboxes, and my two trunks . . ."

"Isn't this box yours also?" Maddie said.

"Oh yes, of course. I had Lucy pack my furs in that. Oh, and that little handbag over there, but I think that's all."

"All? Did you bring everything you owned?"

"Of course not. But it was difficult to know what to pack. And I'm sure before the day is out, I'll think of something I wished I'd packed but didn't. I always do."

Teddy shook his head. "We'll take the valise and handbag for now. I'll send Martin around with the wagon for the rest later. Ready?"

She turned to Maddie. "When will I see you again?"

"We plan to stay at the Fremont Hotel for a few days. You can call on me there."

"I will." Jenny gave her a quick hug, surprised by the tears that sprang to her eyes as she pulled Maddie close. Strange that a friendship of so short a duration could feel like the closest she'd ever had.

But she would see her soon, and in the meantime, she had Teddy. With a final wave to Rob and Cy, she followed her brother and his wife to the buggy.

"So here's where you've been hiding." Jenny stepped through the outer door of a small upstairs sitting room onto a sleeping porch that ran along the house's entire backside. Teddy reclined on a chaise lounge, book in hand.

He looked up as she approached. "Well, look who finally woke up."

"I know. I can't believe I slept for almost twenty-four hours."

"Twenty-four is nothing. I slept an entire week after I arrived."

"Yes. But you had an excuse." Jenny dropped onto the plush cushions of a wicker rocker and looked around. A full iron bed and bed-stand sat at the opposite end of the porch, flanked by a large bearskin rug. In between her and the bed, up against the porch railing, stood a roll-top desk cluttered with papers and a typewriter. A soft breeze wafted through the full-length screens, filling the air with the subtle scent of lilacs.

"This is lovely," she said. "Is this your office or your bedroom?"

"A little of both, I guess. After taking the fresh air cure, I find I prefer to sleep in the open whenever possible."

Did Grace sleep here with him? Somehow she couldn't picture it of her prim sister-in-law, but she knew better than to voice so intimate a question.

She got up to inspect the typewriter.

"Oh, you have a Remington. Mind if I try it?"

"Help yourself. Grace's father bought it, thinking I might use it when I work from home, but I'm so slow, it's easier to write the letters by hand and have our clerk type them up when I go into the office."

"Do you have a letter ready now? I could type it for you."

"Don't tell me DeLancey's School for Young Ladies offered business courses."

"No, but they should have." Jenny rummaged through the papers on the desk until she found a blank sheet of stationery. Rolling it into the machine, she took a seat in the desk chair, fingers poised over the keys. She turned to look at Ted, who regarded her with amusement. "Go on. Dictate a letter."

"You're not joking, are you?"

"Not at all. To whom should I address it?"

"All right. Have it your way." Ted stood and plucked an envelope off the desk. "Mr. E.E. Murane, Wyoming Bank Bldg., Caspar, Wyoming—Dear Sir, It has come to my attention . . ." He started off slowly, but as Jenny quickly typed his words, he picked up his pace. By the end of the letter, he was dictating faster than Ben or Mr. Goddard ever had, but Jenny found herself well able to keep up. When he finished, she pulled the paper from the typewriter and scanned its contents. No errors. She hadn't lost her touch.

She handed it to Ted, not even trying to keep the satisfaction from showing on her face. "Well, what do you think?"

He let out a low whistle. "Where in the world did you learn to type?"

"The Newark School of Business. You know I spent the winter and spring with Aunt Bethany, right? Remember her cook's daughter, Mary?"

"The one you were always leading into trouble?"

"I never got her in trouble."

"How about the time you taught her to make mud pies, and the two of you covered the kitchen in muck trying to bake them in the oven? Or that day, you convinced her to sled down the hill behind the school and onto the ice on Rucker's Pond? Aunt Bethany and Mrs. O'Reilly about had heart palpitations when they discovered where you had been. Or the time . . ."

"Well, never mind. Obviously, you remember Mary O'Reilly. Anyway, she was taking some courses at the Newark School of Business and thought it might be fun if I joined her."

"She thought, or *you* thought?"

"We *both* thought. And as it turns out, I'm quite good. I took a course in typewriting and one in stenography and finished at the top of both classes."

"So that's what the brouhaha was about with Aunt Matilda? You attending business school?"

"Not exactly. I think Aunt Matilda and Uncle Clarence were more upset about my getting a job."

Ted let out a hoot of laughter. "You got a job? Who in his right mind would have hired you?"

She'd forgotten how annoying an older brother could be. "You remember Mrs. Janssen's grandson?"

"Ben? Sure. What does he have to do with anything? Oh, don't tell me you tricked him into giving you a job."

"I didn't trick anyone."

"Why else would he have hired you? The Ben I know is

smarter than that. In fact, last I remember, he was buried in law books at Harvard. I suppose he's graduated by now."

"Yes. He's now a junior partner of the Goddard law firm in Newark. And I was their typewriter girl."

"You convinced him you needed a job?"

"Not *needed*, necessarily. *They* needed a typewriter, and I offered to help."

"But he must have known Uncle Clarence and Aunt Matilda would never stand for it."

"He may have assumed they were out of the picture."

"Why would he assume that?"

"How should I know? Maybe because I was living with Aunt Bethany and taking business courses? Whatever the reason, he assumed it."

"And you did nothing to set him straight."

"Of course not. I wanted that job."

Ted groaned and dropped his head into his hands, shaking it back and forth.

"I don't know why everyone is making such a fuss over it. Uncle Clarence works. *You* work. Why shouldn't I?"

"Because, little sister, you're not simply a Westraven. You're a *female* Westraven. From the moment you were born, your sole purpose in life was to be pretty and pleasing and pampered. Pretty you have in spades. It's the pleasing aspect that still needs some work."

Jenny grabbed a small pillow off the rocker beside her and threw it at Ted's head. He ducked, and the pillow sailed past, striking a potted fern on the windowsill behind him.

"See what I mean?"

"That's so unfair. Why should my life be dictated for me simply because I was born a girl? Why should you men have all the freedom?"

Ted snorted. "You think I'm free? Our lack of freedom doesn't come from whether we're male or female. It comes from being born *Westraven*. From the moment I was born, I was destined to go into banking. I can no more choose a different destiny than you can."

She'd never thought of it that way. "You don't like banking?"

He shrugged. "It's all right, I guess. For a job. I don't know it'd be my first choice, though."

"If you could choose—anything at all—what would you do?"

Ted looked out the windows on the west end of the porch, so quiet she began to wonder if he'd heard her question.

"I don't know." He stood up and walked toward the windows. "But whatever it was, I'd make sure I was doing it somewhere out there." He gestured toward the bank of mountains, blue in the distance.

"The Wind River Mountains?"

"The Winds, yes, or farther west—the Tetons, Yellowstone. You should see them, Jenny. So magnificent, so wild . . ." He turned from the window, a half-smile on his lips. "Maybe I'm lucky I got TB. Otherwise, I'd never have seen this. Those mountains saved my life. In a way, you could say my disease set me free. I know one thing. I may still work in banking, but I'll never work in New York City again for as long as I live."

Jenny joined him at the windows, draping an arm around his waist. She gazed at the distant mountain range, drawing a deep breath of the cool, cleansing air—the air that saved him. She felt the draw in those mountains too. She longed to see them up close.

"Take me with you next time you camp, would you? You said you go often during the summer months. Will you take me?"

"Theodore? Theodore?" A voice called from within the house.

"We're out here," he called back.

Grace stepped onto the porch, lovely in a dinner gown of peach and lace. "Mother and Daddy will be here in less than thirty minutes. You aren't even dressed."

"I'm sorry, darling. Jenny and I got to talking and lost track of time." He turned back to Jenny, apology in his eyes. "I forgot to mention we're having dinner guests. Will you be able to manage in time?"

"Of course."

"I'll send Molly to help you dress," Grace said, as Jenny passed her in the doorway. "But do hurry. Mother hates to be kept waiting."

~

"AH, HERE SHE IS. I TOLD YOU SHE WOULDN'T BE LONG." TED held out a hand as Jenny stepped into the parlor thirty minutes later. "Come meet my in-laws, Mr. and Mrs. Parkhurst."

Jenny smiled at the distinguished gentleman with the full gray beard who stood next to Teddy at the fireplace, then turned to greet Grace's mother, a lady of delicate frame sitting ramrod straight on the settee beside her daughter.

"I'm so pleased to finally meet you. Teddy has told me so much about you in his letters."

Mrs. Parkhurst inclined her head, then motioned Jenny toward the empty chair on her right. "There was no need to rush through your toilette on our account, dear. We would have been content to wait until your maid had a chance to help you with your hair."

Jenny felt the nape of her neck for stray locks, wishing the room's sole mirror didn't rest above the fireplace out of her line of vision. Her hair had looked lovely when she left her room five minutes ago, but her unruly curls often had a mind of their own. She glanced at Grace's tidy pompadour and Mrs. Parkhurst's even tighter topknot.

"Oh, you musn't blame Molly," she said. "She did a wonderful job, given what she had to work with. I'm sure my own Lucy could not have done better."

"Your maid did not travel with you?"

"No. Aunt Matilda will need her to help with house guests in Newport far more than I'll need her here."

"You may be surprised, dear. Our social calendar may not be on par with a summer in Newport, but we still have plenty of functions where you'll want to look your best."

Jenny smoothed the trim at her waist. Did she not look her best? Granted, this dress was not her finest, but she hadn't felt the need to be too fancy for a simple dinner at home. A favorite in blush pink satin under an overskirt of ecru netting and lace, she loved the beaded trim of pink and gold lining the collar and waist and accenting the skirt.

"Dinner is served," Ted's man, Deavers, intoned from the doorway.

As the others left the room, Jenny took a moment to glance at her reflection in the mirror above the mantel. Though certainly curlier than either Grace's or Mrs. Parkhurst's, her hair looked much the same as when she'd left her room. Ted took her arm at the parlor door and bent to whisper in her ear.

"Don't let Mother Parkhurst get to you. It's just her way. You look as lovely as ever."

Dear Teddy. He always knew what to say.

He drew her chair for her when they entered the dining room, and she was soon settled between him and Mr. Parkhurst. She breathed in the heady fragrance of the bowl of potato soup Deavers placed in front of her. Goodness. How long had it been since she last ate? She'd had a cold luncheon when she'd arrived yesterday but then slept straight through dinner, breakfast, and today's luncheon. No wonder she wanted to attack this bowl of soup like a dog attacking a bone.

"Being just family tonight, I hope you don't mind that we dine more casually?" Grace said from her seat at the end of the table.

"Not at all. I prefer casual to formal any day." Jenny took a spoonful of soup, savoring its warm, creamy lusciousness.

"My dear, you really must speak with your cook," Mrs. Parkhurst said to Grace. "This soup has sat far too long. It's tepid at best and much too salty."

"I'm sorry, Mother. Would you like me to send yours back?"

"Oh, no. Don't go to any trouble on my account. I only fear Jeanette will find us quite backward. I'm sure she's used to dinners cooked by the finest of French chefs."

"Please. Call me Jenny. And I think the soup is delicious." She sent Grace a reassuring smile. "Besides, I've had a week of travel fare. Anything you serve tonight will no doubt taste like pure ambrosia in comparison."

Mrs. Parkhurst shuddered. "Yes, traveling is horrid. I simply refuse to eat when we travel."

Then she must not travel often. Or very far. The trip from New York had taken almost four days, and as hungry as she was now, Jenny couldn't imagine not eating for a full four days.

"Mr. Parkhurst and the others on the city council are pushing for a railroad spur between Rawlins and us," Mrs. Parkhurst continued. "Hopefully soon, we'll no longer be subject to stopping for refreshment at those atrocious stage stops."

"Oh, I wouldn't have missed that stage ride for the world. It was just as I imagined travel in the West would be."

"Really?" Ted turned to her, a twinkle in his eye. "That's not what you said when I picked you up yesterday. I believe your words went something like, 'If I ever have to ride in that bone-crusher again, please kill me first.'"

"Well, maybe the ride could have been shorter. But dinner at Harris' Road Ranch almost made up for it."

"Why's that?"

"I met my first genuine Wyoming cowboys."

"And you were enthralled."

"Well." She wrinkled her nose. "They were much ruder than I'd imagined. And dirtier and smellier, but the manager of the road ranch was magnificent."

"Let me guess. Sparrowhawk?"

"How'd you know?"

"Oh, Nick has a way of impressing the ladies. Even Grace is quite in awe of him."

"I am no such thing," Grace colored rosily. "He may be hand-some enough in a rough sort of way, but I like my gentlemen far more refined."

"Good thing for me, because I'm certainly no match for Nick in the manliness department."

"You know him?"

"Sure. When he's not managing the road ranch, he hires out as a hunting guide. He's babysat me on more excursions than I'd care to admit. Was my nursemaid and lifesaver on some of my early ones."

"And you'll take me on your next excursion, won't you? Say you will."

"Hunting?" Mrs. Parkhurst's voice was thick with shock, her fork poised halfway to her mouth. "Heavens, child. Why ever would you want to do that?"

"Teddy's written about his hunting adventures so often. I've dreamed for years of coming out here and seeing it all for myself."

"Are you sure it's the mountains you want to see and not the hunting guide?" Ted teased.

Now it was Jenny's turn to blush. "Of course, it's the moun-tains. I told you that long before I met Mr. Sparrowhawk."

"Well, I suppose we could arrange something while you're here. Sometime in late summer or early fall perhaps?"

"Oh, Teddy, that would be—"

"Will you be staying that long?" Grace broke in.

Wouldn't she? Uncle Clarence had mentioned no return trip. In fact, she was certain Aunt Matilda and Uncle Clarence had washed their hands of her, finally giving her what she'd always wanted—a chance for her and Ted to be together again.

Except now that he had a wife, maybe she wasn't welcome. She looked at Teddy, voicing the question with her eyes.

"You're welcome to stay as long as you wish," he said. "You know you'll always have a home with us."

"Yes, of course, but will she *want* to stay that long? Surely our poor entertainments will pale in comparison to what she's used to." Grace's voice took a decidedly sarcastic tone.

"Oh, no. This is exactly where I want to be. If I never attend another ball or stuffy dinner party, I will die happy. I can't wait to experience my first rodeo, meet my first Indian, and see a working ranch. I want to feel the spray from Old Faithful, smell the sulfur fields, and hike the Grand Tetons. I want to hear an elk bugle and a wolf howl. I want to experience it all!"

Mrs. Parkhurst sniffed. "Goodness, child. We're not nearly as uncivilized as that. You'll find yourself spending far more time at those 'stuffy' dinner parties, as you call them than you will hobnobbing with cowboys and Indians. Take a few sight-seeing trips if you must, but if you have any amount of intelligence under all that hair of yours, you'll return East in the fall. Whatever dust you kicked up back there will have settled by then, and at your age, you can no longer afford to wait before choosing a husband. You'll find little husband material out here."

Jenny blinked back the tears that threatened. She would *not* let this woman make her cry. But a few things were abundantly clear. First, the Parkhursts knew far too much about her intimate history. Second, despite her frail appearance, Mrs. Parkhurst was cut from the same cloth as her aunt. But most obvious of all was the fact neither Mrs. Parkhurst nor her daughter had any intention of Jenny calling Lander, Wyoming, home. That last cut worst of all.

Chapter Twelve

Ben stood at the parlor window of Nora's boarding house, looking out at the charred remains of what used to be a thriving business section. The town of Lead had grown tremendously since his only visit fourteen years ago, but he thought he recognized the framework of what once had been Murphy's Furniture store. Across from that, where Jenkins' drug store should have stood, lay only a pile of smoldering rubble.

It was a wonder, really, the fire had spared both this building and the Bennett Hotel, a lone sentinel at the southeast edge of the business district. Between the hotel and the boarding house lay approximately six fire-ravaged blocks, including almost the entire business district and several residential blocks.

The blackened shell of a four-story brick edifice rose in the distance. Men and horses swarmed across the debris, pulling down charred timbers and hauling away wagons filled with rubbish and ashes. Farther off, the framework for a new building was already going up. That the businessmen of Lead were so quick to rebuild after such a disaster was impressive and a testament to their tenacity.

He turned as the door opened behind him. Letty came into the room, wiping her hands on her apron.

"Any sign of him?" She asked.

"No." He turned back to the window. "It's early yet."

She came to stand at his side. "It's so hard to look at all the damage." Tears thickened her voice.

"We don't have to watch."

"No, it's all right. I'm glad to see them working. The sooner they rebuild, the sooner . . ." Her words trailed off.

The sooner, what? This would all be over? That wasn't happening. She'd never have Father back.

He strode to the sofa. As he'd hoped, she followed, taking a seat beside him.

He stretched out his legs and laid his head back, tracing the familiar pattern in the ceiling tiles above him. This room and the rest of the boarding house brought back so many memories—none good. He wished this meeting with Mr. Foster was over and done so he could be on his way.

Turning his head, he studied his sister's profile. He wouldn't mind getting to know her a little better. She'd grown into a pretty young woman with her mother's placid nature. Even as a child, she could bring a sense of calm to his soul. She was the one bright memory from those dark days. Too bad her brothers weren't more like her.

"Will Roy be at this meeting, or does he have to work?" he asked.

The constant rumble beneath his feet confirmed the stamp mills remained unaffected by the downtown fire. The fire brigades from both Lead and Deadwood had made sure of that. They'd sacrificed several buildings to dynamite, he'd heard, but their efforts had saved the town's largest employer.

"He works second shift, so he'll be here. Lucas should be along soon too."

At sixteen, Lucas should be in school, but Ben had no say in the doings of his youngest half-sibling. Nor did he want any. As if on cue, a door slammed at the back of the house, and the sound of male voices wafted down the hallway.

"Oh, here they are now." Letty turned toward the doorway, a welcoming smile on her face. Ben went back to studying ceiling tiles.

"I thought you'd be long gone by now."

Ben turned his head slightly to look at his stepbrother, acknowledging his sneer with the mere lift of an eyebrow.

They were progressing. There'd been a time the two of them couldn't be in the same room without throwing punches. This visit, they'd been content to pummel each other with words.

The door knocker sounded. A few minutes later, Nora entered the room, followed by Mr. Foster, who carried a bulky leather satchel. Ben came to his feet while Nora settled herself into a wing chair by the fireplace. Mr. Foster took a seat across from her and pulled out a stack of papers.

Dropping back into his place on the sofa, Ben contemplated the lawyer. Yesterday, the man hadn't seemed the type to wax eloquent. He hoped that was the case. He was in no mood for legal jargon today. If Foster kept it short, he might be able to make the 2:30 train to Chicago.

The lawyer cleared his throat and glanced over at Roy and Lucas, who lounged in the doorway.

"Gentlemen, please. Join us." He gestured to an elegant chaise lounge to the left of the sofa.

The brothers exchanged a look, then all but sprinted into the room, making a beeline for the empty seat on the sofa next to Letty. Lucas, being lighter on his feet, won the prize, leaving Roy to perch uncomfortably on the lounge's dainty edge. Any other time the sight of his burly stepbrother in such a feminine pose would have sparked a comment, but Ben held his tongue. The sooner they started, the sooner they'd be done.

A slight smile twitched the corner of the lawyer's mouth. He cleared his throat again. "I'd like to thank each of you for being here today. I'll try to keep this as brief as possible." His gaze caught Ben's over the gold rims of his glasses. "First, I'll read through the will in its entirety. Then, if any of you have questions, I'll do my best to answer them."

He shuffled a few papers and adjusted his glasses. "I, Lester Owen Bennett, Sr., being of sound mind and body do hereby make my last will and testament as follows: To my wife, Nora Elaine Bennett, I leave the boarding house at 229 Pearl Street in Lead, South Dakota, the property and all its furnishings. To her son, Roy Yvonne Dupree, I leave my gold watch."

Ben glanced over to where Roy sat, eyes trained on the floor. Yvonne? What he would have given to know that middle name fourteen years ago.

With an effort, he turned his attention back to Foster. ". . . Leticia Ellen Bennett, I leave my entire library. To my son, Lucas Reginald Bennett, I leave my Winchester rifle and my Colt .44 pistol." The lawyer paused briefly. "The remainder of all my real and personal property of every name and nature of which I die possessed, I leave to my eldest son, Lester Owen Bennett, Jr."

Chapter Thirteen

A half-muttered curse slipped into the silence. For a moment, Ben thought he might have uttered the word himself, for it was certainly on his mind. A shocked "Roy!" from Nora set his mind at ease.

Still. Lester Owen Bennett, Jr.—that was he. Had the women not been in the room, he'd have echoed Roy's sentiments with gusto.

Instead, he clenched his jaw and looked over at Mr. Foster. "What does that entail precisely—all his real and personal property—the hotel?"

Letting out a full string of curses this time, Roy plowed to his feet and began pacing between the fireplace and the sofa.

"Roy," Nora said. "Please. Sit down."

"Sit down? Seriously? I can't believe you're willing to sit there and take this. Of all the ass-backwards things he could have done, this one takes the cake. And I'm not talking about me here. I'm just the stepson. I didn't need or want anything from the old man. But his own flesh and blood? You know Letty and Adam had plans for the mercantile. Library, my ass. A few shelves full of old books is more like it! And what about Lucas? Pa never would have bought that ranch without his pushing for it. And the mine? Hell, Ben doesn't know a mine from a hole in the ground."

Hole in the ground? Good one. But still. A mine . . . a hotel . . . a ranch . . . a mercantile. This was more complicated than he'd anticipated. Ben glanced at Letty. Her hands were clenched so tightly in her lap, her knuckles showed white. Two bright spots of color bloomed on each cheek. Was she as angry as her step-brother or merely embarrassed by his actions? There was little doubt what Lucas felt. His face mirrored Roy's stormy one.

"I'm sure Lester had his reasons," Nora interjected weakly.

Roy let out a snort. "What sort of reasoning would leave everything a man worked for in his life to a snively-nosed, sissy boy who doesn't know a gold nugget from a plug nickel, or a prime steer from a mule? I doubt Ben knows the meaning of the word 'work.' It's like pissing everything Pa built into the wind."

"Hey!" Ben was on his feet, fists balled. Twelve years of school plus four years of college, not to mention the hours he spent studying for the bar exam—that wasn't work? Fourteen-hour days with back-to-back court sessions and no time for lunch, nights burrowing through law books trying to build a case—that wasn't work? Who did this two-bit miner think he was anyway? He'd like to thrust those words right down Roy's throat.

"Stop it." Letty pushed between them, tears streaming down her face. "Stop it. You WILL NOT fight over this. I don't care if Pa left me nothing but his books. I wouldn't care if he left me nothing at all. He's gone, and nothing he could have left me can change that. But I will not stand by and let you two fight. He hated that. You know he did. I hate it . . ." Her words trailed off into heart-wrenching sobs.

Ben unclenched his fist and pulled her into his arms, letting her tears soak his jacket. Truth be told, he hated it too but didn't know how to stop it. He'd thought they'd grown past it, but two days with Roy and they were acting like ten-year-olds again, ready to punch each other at the least provocation.

"Hush, now," he said. "We'll behave. I promise." The glare he sent Roy over Letty's shoulder dared him to contradict.

Nora came over and laid a hand on Roy's arm. "Maybe it would be best if we left Ben alone with Mr. Foster for a while," she said.

Letty pulled away, wiping her eyes with the sleeve of her shirtwaist. Ben offered her his handkerchief.

"Fine." Roy spat the words. "I have to get to work anyway. But don't think you've heard the last of me. I'll protect the rights of my family if it's the last thing I do."

"In case you've forgotten," Ben said through clenched teeth. "They're my family too."

"Yeah? And exactly how much time have you spent with 'your' family in the past fourteen years? I can answer that. None. You know nothing about any of us. You don't even know your own father's business interests. Just because Letty and Lucas share your blood doesn't make you family. Not in my book anyway. I've been their older brother all these years, and I'll continue to look out for them. Come on, Lucas. I've had about all I can stand of lawyers for one day."

With a smirk thrown in Ben's direction, Lucas shoved to his feet and sauntered out the door on Roy's heels. Letty and Nora soon followed suit, leaving Ben with Mr. Foster.

Ben dropped to his seat on the couch, raking a hand through his hair. "Sorry about that. Our family dynamics are anything but pretty."

Mr. Foster shrugged. "I've seen worse."

"Oh, we've been worse. Believe me. So, fill me in. I knew Father owned the hotel. Roy mentioned a mercantile, a ranch, and a mine. Is that about it?"

"You really don't know your father's businesses, do you?"

"We've had very little contact over the past fourteen years, sir. Frankly, I'm as surprised as Roy by his decision to name me as the major heir to his assets. Is there something I'm missing here? His death was unexpected. How old is his will?"

"This version was updated as recently as last December. I

assure you, your father had every intention of wording it as he did." Mr. Foster rocked back in his chair, steepled his fingers, and studied Ben for a minute.

"Before we discuss your father's remaining assets," he said, "perhaps I should explain how your father obtained his wealth. Maybe that will give a clearer picture of his intentions.

"I arrived in Lead back in '83 and rented a room at this very boarding house while I was establishing my practice. During that time, your father and I struck up a friendship. One evening, he asked me to help him make his will 'all tight and legal' as he put it. At that time, the will had one bequest. He left everything to you. Letty was just a little thing, and Lucas had just been born. When I questioned why he'd made no mention of Nora and their children in his will, he told me this story.

"Your father's family made their fortune manufacturing guns and ammunition during the Civil War. After the war, they invested heavily in the railroads, for a while increasing their wealth. Your father took over the family business after your grandfather's death, and his future looked bright until the Panic hit in '73. All his investments dried up overnight, and the economy became so bad, your father was forced to sell his munitions factory." Mr. Foster pulled a pipe from his pocket and began to pour tobacco from a small pouch into its bowl. He glanced up at Ben. "You don't mind if I smoke, do you?"

Ben shook his head. He watched Mr. Foster light his pipe and take a slow draw, then just as slowly blow the smoke out. Clearly, the man was in no hurry.

"Things would have been quite bleak for your family," Mr. Foster finally continued, "if your maternal grandfather hadn't died about then, leaving a substantial amount of money to you and your mother. Though nothing like the fortune your family had once known, it was enough to allow your father to make a fresh start.

"In the spring of '74, news hit the papers of the discovery of gold in the Black Hills. Your father believed this was his chance to recoup the family losses, so he set off for South Dakota soon after you were born, hoping to make a home here for you and your mother." Mr. Foster took another slow drag on his pipe. "Well, you know how those dreams ended."

Yes. His mother died a year later of typhoid fever, and his father never sent for him. Grandma Janssen became his only family.

"From what I understand, your mother's death nearly crushed your father, but he was more determined than ever to make a go of it in the gold business. Unfortunately, by the time he arrived in South Dakota, all the placer mines had already been claimed. He moved with the crowd to Lead when news of the Homestake discovery spread. Miners began looking for promising veins of ore rather than gold in the streams. About this time, he met Peter and Nora Dupree and their baby, Roy. I think spending time with the three of them helped assuage some of the loneliness he was feeling for his own wife and child."

Ben shifted in his seat. Seemed to him, Father could have had him with him by then if he'd wanted. Apparently, it was easier to find a new family than send for the one he already had.

"Peter had just bought the property this house is on and planned to build a boarding house. Your father also invested in land in Lead, but his plans were larger than Peter's. In early June of 1877, he erected a four-story frame building he named the Miner's Hotel and began a thriving business.

"But he never gave up his dream of finding gold. He and Peter spent all their spare moments scouring creeks and valleys around Lead, finally locating a promising area along Squaw creek near the base of Bald Mountain. They bought two adjoining claims and began the dangerous job of quartz mining. I say dangerous because a year later, Peter lost his life in an explosion gone terribly wrong.

"Your father always blamed himself for Peter's death. He bought out Peter's share of the mine to support Nora and Roy, even though all tests showed the gold they'd found there was impossible to separate from the ore. The double tragedy—the loss of your mother and then Peter—brought your father and Nora together. A year later, they married."

And Father and Grandmother had never told him any of this. If they had, that terrible summer of '85 never would have happened. As it was, the family lawyer knew more about Ben's family history than he did.

Ben swallowed his bitterness and tried to focus.

" . . . with the discovery of new chlorination processes in the early nineties, the Bald Mountain mine became viable, and in the last ten years, your father's initial investment has proved quite profitable."

"So, the mine is operational?"

"Not only operating but turning a healthy profit. Your father invested in several hotels in Deadwood, a mercantile in Terraville, and a ranch northeast of Lead with its proceeds. All told, your father's estate is worth somewhere in the neighborhood of $1,000,000."

A million dollars? Ben Bennett, the scholarship kid from Newark, had a father who was a millionaire? And no one ever mentioned it?

"But how . . . why . . . ? I don't understand. Why am *I* the sole heir?"

"Don't you see? The money your father invested in the mine . . . in his first hotel . . . that was yours—your inheritance from your maternal grandfather. Your father had no intention of keeping it for himself. Everything he did, he did for you."

This was all too much. Pushing to his feet, Ben paced the perimeter of the room, coming to a halt by the window. He stared blankly out. Everything his father did had been for him? Nothing about that phrase rang true. It spoke of love, sacrifice. If his father had truly loved him, he wouldn't have left him money. He would have made him part of his life. As it was, his million-dollar legacy felt like a pair of golden handcuffs. One thing was certain. He wouldn't be catching that 2:30 train.

Chapter Fourteen

Jenny stifled a sigh and pushed an oyster around her plate with her fork, breaking Madame Delancey's number one dinner-hour rule—never play with your food. Not that she cared. Tonight would mark her third dinner party since arriving in Lander. Three! In less than ten days!

Yet the mountains remained as far off as ever, and she hadn't come within walking distance of a working ranch. She might not have minded if the company had been more stimulating. She was quickly learning, as exclusive as the social scene might be in New York City or Newport, it was far more exclusive in a small town like Lander. In fact, the Parkhursts only seemed to mingle socially with one other family—their hosts of the evening—the Joneses.

Daniel Jones was a director of Mr. Parkhurst's bank and its largest stockholder. The Parkhursts had invited the Jones family to a dinner in her honor last week. There she'd met Mr. Jones, his wife Minerva, and their daughter Stella, who happened to be Grace's best friend. They'd met again to celebrate Mr. Jones's birthday and then today to honor the visit of Monsieur Dumont, a French gentleman the Joneses had met on a visit to the Conti-

"

nent the previous winter. Three dinner parties in one week, all with the same family.

Not only was Jenny bored, she was lonely. Neither Grace nor Stella seemed interested in being friends with her. To make matters worse, the Skivingtons left town yesterday to become sheepherders out on the open range. She didn't know when she would see them again. It was the right thing for Rob's health and the entire reason they'd come to this area, but still. The thought of life in Lander without Maddie made her want to cry.

How many times in the past two weeks had she wished she were back in Newark, working at the law office with Ben and spending Tuesday dinners with him at Aunt Bethany's? She knew a large part of that longing had to do with that interrupted kiss and the attraction that sizzled between her and Ben. Well, it sizzled for her at least. Other than kissing her, Ben had shown no other indication that the attraction was mutual. Had he truly wanted to pursue her, he could have done so at their last meeting rather than calling their kiss a big mistake. No, Ben and Newark were in the past and needed to stay there. She needed to quit woolgathering and find a way to thrive in the here and now. She forced herself to focus on the conversation at the table.

"I shall never forget that masked ball we attended at Rue la Boète. It was magical," Mrs. Jones was saying. Their hostess had spent the first ten minutes of the meal reminiscing with Monsieur over each dinner, ball, and opera they'd attended while in Paris.

Jenny longed to converse with the young man seated on her right. Will Dickinson was a friend of Ted's who seemed quite personable, but she'd only had a chance to exchange a few words with him before dinner was announced. Unfortunately, the small dinner party's other guests were politely silent, content to let their hostess do all the talking.

"Stella," Mrs. Jones continued, hardly stopping for breath, "speak with Monsieur Dumont in French the way you did last winter."

"*Oui, Maman*," Stella set down her wine glass and gazed up at the Frenchman through fluttering lashes.

Mrs. Jones favored her daughter with a smile. "Stella received top honors in school in both French and Latin. Her teacher told us she is a natural for languages."

Stella was a pretty girl, tall with hair a shade darker than Grace's and deep blue eyes. Personally, Jenny thought her nose a trifle long, but it could be because she had a habit of looking down it at other people—Jenny in particular.

"It's delightful to have you at our table at last, Monsieur," Stella continued in French. "I hope you will find America to your liking." Stella's vocabulary was impeccable, but Jenny noticed her accent made the Frenchman wince several times.

But the Frenchman did not lack in charm. "*Oui, Mademoiselle*," he responded. "I find your country charming. And beautiful hostesses such as yourself and your maman make it more so. But for the sake of the others, we shall continue in English, no?"

Mrs. Jones placed a hand on her heart. "It's like being back in France again to hear you two speak. Tell me, Monsieur, have you seen Lord and Lady Crestfield since our visit last January? They were such a lovely couple."

Jenny caught herself in the middle of a yawn, snapping her lips shut and praying no one else had noticed. She glanced across the table and found Monsieur Dumont's eyes on her.

He gave her a slow wink before answering, "*Non*. They, like you, stayed only for the Season. But enough about past company. I'm sure our company tonight will prove every bit as delightful."

Mrs. Jones turned to follow the direction of Monsieur's gaze, and Jenny felt the heat creep from her shoulders to her forehead. Some days she quite hated her fair skin.

Unexpectedly, Grace saved her from the lady's scrutiny.

"Were you able to attend the Exposition Universelle before coming to America, Monsieur Dumont?" she said. "I've heard it is magnificent."

"*Oui*. I've had the pleasure to go several times, and it is as you say. *Magnifique*. Everyone is talking about the moving sidewalks and stairs. And our Ferris Wheel is the largest in the world—much taller than the one at the Chicago World's Fair. To ride it at night with the Palace of Electricity and the Eiffel Tower all lit up is . . . magical." He paused. "But you must come to Paris and see for yourself. I cannot do it justice."

"Oh, I hope to. Maybe this fall. My husband and I have talked of a belated honeymoon trip to Europe. What do you think, Theodore? Wouldn't it be delightful if we could make it in time to see the Exposition?"

Ted shifted in his seat. "This fall may not be the best time to go."

"Nonsense," Mrs. Parkhurst broke in. "Fall is a wonderful time to be in Paris. As Mr. Parkhurst told you at your wedding, he will be more than happy to cover your responsibilities at work so his daughter and son-in-law can have their honeymoon trip." She spoke as if she had settled the matter.

From the set of Ted's jaw and the way he tore into his next bite of meat, Jenny knew the matter was far from settled.

She hurried to change the subject. "But what of your travels in our country, Monsieur? Mrs. Jones tells me you have been to Yellowstone. I've heard the natural wonders there are every bit as magnificent as all the scientific wonders at the Exposition."

He lifted his glass in a salute. "I must agree, Mademoiselle. The park is also *magnifique*. I have seen nothing like it in France."

"There is nothing like it anywhere," Ted said.

"Did you see the Grand Canyon of the Yellowstone River?"

"*Oui*. And the Upper and Lower Falls and the Mammoth Hot Springs and all the geysers. But surely you, living so close, have seen these also?"

"Not yet. Like you, I've only recently arrived in Lander. Did you see any wildlife?"

Monsieur Dumont nodded. "The elk and moose and antelope. Oh, and the *Aigle chauve*. How do you say? The large bird, the . . ." He furrowed his brow, tapping his index finger to his mustache. Then shook his head. "I do not know the English name."

"Bald eagle." Jenny supplied.

"Yes. That is it. *Parlez-vous francais?*"

"*Oui, Monsieur.* But tell me of the geysers. Is it true you can set your watch to Old Faithful?"

The Frenchman tipped his head to the side and grinned broadly. "Every hour, like clockwork. The fountain reaches sixty feet in the air. We sat on the porch of the hotel and watched it blow time after time. In the moonlight, it is as magical as the lights of Paris."

"Oh, I simply must see it. Teddy, can we plan a trip there soon? It would be a shame to be so close to all those wonders and not see them."

Her brother gave a short laugh and shrugged. "If you're talking to me, Jenny, you'd better use English. You forget I don't speak French as well as you."

Oh mercy, had she and the Monsieur been conversing in French? Jenny glanced at the other guests. Across the table, Stella paused with her fork suspended halfway to her mouth, her lips forming a perfect O. Jenny turned her head to find Mrs. Jones staring at her as if she'd sprouted two noses.

She was so used to dinnertime at Madame DeLancey's, where they'd been forced to switch languages throughout the meal to improve their vocabulary and diction. Partway through each meal Madame would switch to speaking French or German or Italian, and all the girls would comply or remain silent. She'd never been good at silence, so after the first few weeks, she'd learned to switch with the best of them.

When Monsieur Dumont had spoken to her in French, her switch must have clicked automatically. How rude she must seem.

"You've been holding out on us, Miss Westraven. I had no

idea you also spoke French." Mrs. Jones' words were dipped in ice.

"*Comme un ange*." Monsieur Dumont kissed his fingers at her.

"Jenny went to boarding school in Switzerland and finishing school in Paris," Teddy said. "Uncle Clarence would have been sorely disappointed if she'd come home unable to speak all the European languages after six years abroad."

His comment elicited a polite laugh from several of the dinner guests, but Grace's stare spiked daggers, and Mrs. Parkhurst's mouth settled in a disapproving line.

Did they think she'd upstaged Stella on purpose? What a show-off she must seem. Oh, why couldn't she learn to keep her mouth shut?

"Forgive me," she said. "I got carried away with our topic and forgot we were speaking French."

"But so enchantingly, I'm sure we all agree there is nothing to forgive," Monsieur Dumont replied.

Jenny could tell the ladies, at least, were not in agreement. Thankfully, Teddy steered the conversation back to the Frenchman's fishing expedition on Yellowstone Lake, and the focus was no longer on her. For the rest of the meal, she spoke only when spoken to, which meant she didn't speak at all.

After everyone finished the last of the plum pudding, Mrs. Jones rose and said, "We'll leave you men to your cigars and your talk about bank futures while we women enjoy a comfortable coze in the parlor."

Jenny's stomach knotted. She hated these times alone with the ladies. If only Mr. Jones and Mr. Parkhurst did not enjoy their cigars quite so much.

Slowly, she followed the others to the parlor and was soon ensconced on a small couch between Mrs. Jones and Mrs. Parkhurst while Grace and Stella sat, heads together, whispering, on a velvet settee near the window. A militant glint sparked in each of the older ladies' eyes. Jenny braced herself.

"Is that a Worth dress you're wearing?" Mrs. Jones's voice sounded deceptively sweet.

"Yes, ma'am." Jenny ran her hand across the pale blue silk. Aunt Matilda had brought this one back with her this year.

"I had no idea you were so familiar with the Continent, my dear. But having seen your dress, I should have known. Worth is so distinctive, is he not? And now that I think of it, I do believe we met your aunt and uncle on our visit to London in December. They were guests of the Earl of Denbigh if I recall." She tapped her index finger to the side of her nose. "And yet I don't remember meeting you there."

"No. I did not care to go abroad this year."

"You didn't *care* to go abroad." Mrs. Jones had the same look on her face as Aunt Matilda the day she told her she didn't care for caviar. "My. Your aunt and uncle must be very indulgent. But perhaps your matrimonial plans are already settled. I did hear talk of a match between their niece and the Earl's heir? Unless . . . were they speaking of a cousin perhaps?"

"No, ma'am. I'm their only niece."

"Have I been remiss? Should I be congratulating you on your upcoming nuptials?"

"No, ma'am." Jenny shifted in her seat and glanced across at Grace and Stella. She cleared her throat. "On further acquaintance, Lord Parry and I decided we did not suit."

"La," Mrs. Jones continued. "If an earl's heir does not suit, one can only wonder who would? Surely, no one in our lowly company tonight would dare compete."

Jenny fingered her locket, choosing her words carefully. "A man's title and station aren't nearly as important to me as his character and heart. If he loves me and I love him, his status or pocketbook will not matter."

Mrs. Parkhurst's laugh was not a pretty one. "Youth. Full of romantic foolishness. You've been reading too many silly novels if you ask me. You know, my dear, love won't buy you Worth gowns or trips to Europe. You may think you can live without all that now, but a few years of making-do with last season's fashions and your husband's waning attentions, and you'll soon be singing another tune."

Thankfully, the men chose that moment to rejoin them, and Jenny was spared further lectures. Mrs. Jones bustled to greet the men as they came through the door, hurrying Monsieur Dumont over to the settee, where Stella received him like a queen bestowing favors. Mrs. Parkhurst joined her husband and Mr. Jones by the fireplace.

"You look like you could use a friend."

Jenny looked up into the friendly hazel eyes of Will Dickinson.

"Oh. I was hoping I'd get a chance to know you better. Will you join me, Mr. Dickinson?" She patted the couch beside her.

"Only if you call me Will," he said, taking the seat Mrs. Jones had vacated. "Mr. Dickinson is, and always will be, my father."

Will's sandy blond hair grew in a cowlick over his forehead. That, along with the freckles scattered across the bridge of his nose, gave him the look of a grown-up little boy. She liked him already. "All right, Will it is. I'm so glad you came tonight. I haven't had a chance to meet many of Ted's friends yet."

"Ah. That's because most times, we average town folk don't get asked to mix with the royals. The only reason I was invited tonight was to even out the seating."

"I don't believe that. Ted tells me you're one of his best friends."

"Ted's a sport. But I was speaking of Mrs. Jones and Mrs. Parkhurst. A word of advice? If you're going to spend time with the Joneses, you'd best let Princess Stella keep the throne. Any attempt to usurp it will be met with the utmost disfavor."

"I wasn't trying to usurp anything. I was hoping we could be friends."

Will shook his head. "If you're trying to get into that particular Girls' Club, you're out of luck. They stopped taking members years ago."

"But Grace is my sister-in-law. You'd think she'd be willing to make room for one more."

"And risk having to share both her husband and her best friend? Oh, no, no, no. Grace has never had to share anything. She's not about to start with you."

Really? Could the reason Grace remained distant be jealousy?

"Don't despair. I know someone who'll be your friend," Will said.

"Who?"

"My sister, Sara."

Jenny thought back over the ladies she'd met so far. Other than the dinner parties with the Joneses, she'd been to a Ladies Aide meeting with Grace and Mrs. Parkhurst, but she didn't remember a Sara. "Have I met her?"

"No. But you met my two older sisters, Emma and Julia."

"Oh, were they your sisters? I remember them. Emma was our hostess, and Julia had that sweet little baby." If Sara was anything like the rest of her siblings, she was sure to like her.

Will nodded. "Sara's been out at the home ranch helping cook for the roundup. But she'll be back in time for the ice cream social on Friday. Will you be going?"

"Oh, I hope so. Anything but another dinner party." She glanced around to be sure Mrs. Parkhurst and Mrs. Jones had not heard her, then lowered her voice a notch. "Forgive me. I know that sounds rude, but I'm so anxious to experience something different. I've been to a million dinner parties, but I've never been to an ice cream social. What do you do there?"

"Well, you eat ice cream."

Jenny swatted his arm. "What else?"

"The town band will be playing. You don't want to miss it. They've been practicing for weeks. Mr. Murdoch even dusted off his old trombone. Oh, and I think the Ladies Aide will be raffling off a quilt."

"That's right. We were working on it at the meeting. Well then, if there's to be ice cream AND Mr. Murdoch's trombone

AND your sister, who is guaranteed to be my new best friend, then I simply must go. Now, I know we've just met, but what's going on between you and Stella?"

"What do you mean?"

"Don't try to deny it. You can't keep your eyes off the settee, and I don't think Monsieur Dumont's the one drawing your attention, so it must be Stella."

Will's face turned a dull red. "You're imagining things."

"Am I? Am I also imagining she looks at you every time you aren't looking at her?"

Will's glance immediately sought out the occupants of the settee. "She does?"

"So there *is* something between you."

Will's face darkened. "Not anymore. Back when Ted and Grace were courting, we spent a lot of time together. I had hopes that . . . well, I was obviously fooling myself. Ever since she returned from Europe, it's like we've never even met. Apparently, without a title or a foreign accent, I don't stand a chance."

"Are you sure?"

"You've seen her tonight. It's been all 'Monsieur' this and 'Monsieur' that."

"But she's been watching us like a hawk."

"You're imagining things."

"I don't think so. Play along with me, and we'll see what she does." She leaned closer to Will, looking up at him through her lashes. "Pretend like I'm the most fascinating woman in the room."

"You're wasting your time. She won't even notice," he said but kept his eyes trained on her face.

Jenny gave a lilting laugh and placed her hand on Will's upper arm. "Now, as subtly as you can, glance over there and tell me what she's doing."

An echoing trill from across the room told her what she wanted to know even before Will replied, "Now she's all over that Frenchman."

Jenny tightened her grip on Will's arm. "Is she touching his arm?"

"Yes!"

"Like I'm touching yours?"

He nodded.

"Then it's working. Now, lean in and whisper something in my ear. But whatever you do, don't look at her."

Will leaned a little closer but narrowed his eyes at her. "What do you mean it's working?"

"Don't glower. Remember? I'm the most fascinating woman in the room."

Will continued to frown. "I don't like playing games."

Jenny smiled deep enough to ensure her dimples were showing, then tilted her head to the side and began twirling a curl at the base of her ear. "If you want to win the Princess, you have to play the game. Believe me, *she's* played this game before. Now, lean closer and whisper something in my ear. It doesn't matter what. Just look like you're saying something intimate."

Will leaned over and whispered, "Mary had a little lamb, its fleece as white as snow."

Jenny didn't have to fake a laugh this time.

"And everywhere that Mary went, that lamb was sure to go. It followed her to--"

"Mr. Dickinson, we're forming a foursome to play a round of whist. Would you care to join us?" Stella stood a few feet from their sofa, her lips curved in a winsome smile.

Seems Grace wasn't the only one who didn't like to share. Monsieur Dumont, who'd followed her over, sank onto the couch next to Jenny.

"Ah, the enchanting Mademoiselle Westraven," he said. "While the others play cards, you must speak to me in French and tell me why it is you spent so much time in my country, and we never met."

"But I was planning on your being a part of our foursome, Monsieur." Stella's lips pursed into a pretty pout.

He waved her away. *"Non*, Monsieur Westraven can have my place. I am quite content where I am."

"And I'm quite comfortable as well," Will said, leaning back on the couch, arms crossed. "Maybe Mr. Parkhurst or your father would be willing to be your fourth."

If Stella were able to incinerate objects with her eyes, Jenny would be nothing but a heap of ash between the two gentlemen. *You'll learn it's best to let Princess Stella keep the throne.* Oh, dear.

She turned to Will. "You should play. That way, you won't feel left out if Monsieur Dumont and I are speaking French." She widened her eyes at him, praying he could read her mind. They'd worked so hard to bring Stella around. Surely he wasn't going to miss this opportunity.

He seemed to hesitate, then nodded. "All right. I guess I could play one hand. But I'll see you on Friday?"

"I'll be there."

JENNY CLOSED HER EYES, RELISHING THE FEEL OF THE BRUSH through her long curls. What a relief to lose the hairpins. Unlike her own maid, Lucy, who was often impatient with her mess of curls, Grace's Molly had a gentle touch and, so far, an immeasurable amount of patience when it came to dressing and undressing Jenny's hair.

Jenny sighed and let the tension slip from her neck and shoulders. Who knew a simple dinner party in a small town in Wyoming would be as fraught with social disaster as any of Mrs. Astor's gatherings of New York's Five Hundred? Judging from her progress so far, Jenny was more likely to meet Mrs. Astor's approval than she ever would Mrs. Jones's and Mrs. Parkhurst's.

"Did you need me, Mum?" Molly's low voice broke into her thoughts.

Jenny opened her eyes to see her sister-in-law in the doorway of her bedroom. She was dressed in a red silk wrapper. Her hair hung in a long dark braid down her back.

"No, Molly. Go ahead with what you were doing. I'm here to speak with Jenny." Her voice sounded none too friendly.

Tension raced back into Jenny's shoulders.

"Theodore says he won't say anything to you, but I find I simply cannot sleep without speaking my mind." She stepped a few feet into the room. "I'm appalled, absolutely appalled, by your behavior tonight. I've never seen anyone put herself out there the way you did. Showing off in French to Monsieur Dumont. Practically throwing yourself at poor Will on the couch. You were an embarrassment to both your brother and me."

If her mild flirting had embarrassed Grace, she'd hate to see what the girl would think if she ever saw Sally Gardner, New York City's most accomplished flirt, in action.

But Grace wasn't finished. "Honestly, watching you tonight, I'm not a bit surprised Aunt Matilda and Uncle Clarence didn't want you with them in Newport. No man wants to marry a woman who always needs to be the center of attention."

That was both unfair and untrue. "I've had plenty of offers."

"And yet here I am, almost a full year younger than you, and six months married, while you . . . are not."

She hadn't known it was a competition. Jenny shrugged. "You were simply lucky enough to find the man you loved before I did. What of it?"

"You'll never find a husband if you continue to behave so shamefully. The only reason you're living with us is because there simply is nowhere else for you to go." Grace stepped closer and leaned in, so her eyes were on a level with Jenny's. "Let me make myself clear," she continued, her voice low and even. "If you do anything, *anything* to smear the honor of my family's name or that of your brother's, I'll see you're sent back to Aunt Matilda so fast it will make your head spin. Count on it." She spat the last words with all the venom she could muster, then spun and stalked from the room.

Jenny clenched her jaw, swallowing hard against the lump in her throat. She would not cry in front of Molly.

"Miss, I—"

She could hear the sympathy in Molly's voice and cut her off. "Just braid my hair, Molly, and then you can go."

"Yes, miss."

Once in bed, Jenny let the tears flow. Silent tears in the darkness just like all the times before. The years had passed, but her circumstances hadn't changed. She was still the girl no one wanted.

Chapter Fifteen

Ben sidestepped his mount around a gopher hole. The past six weeks had gone better than he'd expected. And today, Lucas agreed to join his visit to Father's ranch. Granted, his little brother galloped up ahead, but the fact he'd agreed to come at all was a victory.

Lucas had sneered when he saw Ben's horse that morning. The name above the bay's stall read Firecracker, but the liveryman simply called him Cracker, his fire having gone out years ago. Ben had hired him a few times for trips he'd made to Father's various holdings. He was slow, plodding, reliable—just the type of horse he needed.

Lucas was not impressed.

Didn't matter. Lucas was never impressed. No use killing himself on a horse he couldn't handle in a futile effort to win the boy's approval.

At Cracker's slower gait, Ben was able to relax and drink in the morning. Waving grassland stretched as far as his eye could see. Dawn had put on a show in shades of coral and melon shortly after they left Lead. The colors soon faded, leaving behind a pristine blue sky and a cacophony of birdsong.

Ahead, Lucas pulled his horse to a halt. Impatience etched every fiber of the boy's body.

"Can't you get him to go any faster? At this rate, we won't make it to the ranch before supper."

"Last I knew, it didn't take all day to travel sixteen miles, even at a walk. We have plenty of time."

"Can't you at least *try* to make him trot?"

Ben prodded Cracker's flanks. The horse cantered a couple of steps but soon fell back into his plodding gait. Lucas groaned, kicked his horse into a canter, and took off again. No matter. As long as he stayed within sight.

Visiting the ranch was Ben's final stop in his tour of Father's properties. He'd purposefully saved it for last, like saving the best dish on the plate to be the last flavor he savored. None of the visits had been onerous. His father had made sound investments and hired capable managers.

The hotels in Lead and Deadwood were clean, profitable establishments that ran like well-oiled machines. Ben could see no reason to make any changes at this point. Lord knows, his employees knew the business far better than he did.

The small mercantile in Terraville wasn't as profitable as the hotels, but he understood his father's motivation for it. At least he thought he did. The manager, Adam Youngfield, was a friend of Letty's. A very special friend, from what he could tell. Most likely, Father saw that purchase as an investment in his daughter's future.

The mine was the only sore point. The mining expert Mr. Foster referred him to believed the mine was on the verge of playing out. Ben would sell it today if it weren't for Roy. He knew nothing about the ins and outs of mining. Had no desire to learn. He even had a prospective buyer, and his gut told him if he waited, he'd end up stuck with a dying mine.

But after the initial blowup at the reading of Father's will, the animosity between him and Roy had quieted. Selling the mine might cause things to boil over again.

For Father's sake, he was trying to get along with his family. Letty and Nora's gentle natures made them easy to like. Lucas, on the other hand, lived under a perpetual dark cloud. Ben wasn't sure he'd ever seen his kid brother without a scowl. He hoped this outing would be an opportunity to get beneath the boy's angry surface.

Up ahead, Lucas slowed again, so Ben urged Cracker into a semi-canter to catch up to him.

"I forgot to ask," he said, as he ambled up beside the boy, "what type of water supply does the ranch have?"

"Coon Creek runs along the western edge of the ranch, and father drilled a couple of wells. Oh, and the upper ranch has a small lake."

"How many acres are we talking here?"

"Pa said close to a thousand acres all told."

Ben let out a low whistle. He was learning his father didn't go small in his investments.

"How long has your family owned it?"

Lucas shot him a sharp look. Drat. He'd done it again. He didn't know if he'd ever get past this feeling of being on the outside looking in.

"Pa bought it the summer I turned ten."

Ah, yes. He remembered ten. At ten, his yearning also led toward all things western—wild horses and gunfights and life on the open range. He devoured every dime novel he could find with a western theme. In his mind, if his father wasn't the original Deadwood Dick, he was at least the man's best friend.

"Letty tells me you've spent all your summers at the ranch since Father bought it. Why aren't you there now?"

The scowl was back. "Ma needs me at home, with Pa gone and all." His voice broke a little on those last words, and he looked away, jaw clenched. Maybe he'd been too harsh about Lucas' black moods.

Ben cleared his throat. "Seems like you could still spend some of your time out here if you'd like."

Lucas shrugged. "Maybe."

He'd talk to Nora when they got home. Sure, Lucas helped out around the boarding house and hotel, but it wasn't as if they couldn't get along without him. Time at the ranch had to be better for him than hanging around the bars of Lead with Roy.

"What time do you think we'll be at the ranch?"

Lucas gave Ben's horse a disdainful eye. "At this pace? Probably 'nother hour. But when we get to the next rise, we should be able to see it."

Sure enough, when they reached the top of the bluff, Lucas pointed out a cluster of dark specks far on the horizon. Anticipation shot through Ben, surprising him. Maybe his childhood dreams hadn't dissipated completely.

"My reports say we own almost sixty head of horses in addition to all the cows. Why so many?"

Lucas shrugged. "Each hand has a string of five or six. Not every horse is used every day."

"You have a string of your own?"

"I have my favorites."

"Are any easier to ride than the others?"

"None as broken down as the one you're on if that's what you're asking."

"You don't think there are any I could ride?"

Lucas pursed his lips a minute. "If I was you, I'd choose Cochise. He's a big black. Seems a bit fiery to look at, but get a saddle on him and he's as calm and gentle as lake water."

"Cochise, huh? Thanks, I'll remember that."

"I'm going to ride on ahead. Just keep heading toward those buildings. You can't miss it. See you 'round dark," the boy taunted. Then, spurring his horse, he took off in a cloud of dust.

Well, it wasn't much, but they'd exchanged more words this trip than they had the entire six weeks Ben had been in South Dakota. It was a start.

～

He arrived at the ranch in plenty of time to go over finances with Mr. Rutledge, the ranch foreman, and take a tour of the ranch house and outbuildings before the men came in for their midday meal.

Dinner was a fast, furious event. Mrs. Rutledge and her oldest daughter passed around platters of smoked elk and fried prairie chicken, bowls heaped high with creamy mashed potatoes, jugs of cold milk, loaves of freshly baked bread, stewed plums, and strawberry preserves. The men said little, attacking the food like a hoard of locusts. Within minutes, the serving platters and bowls were empty, and the men were on their feet and back out the door.

"Reno plans to break a few wild horses this afternoon. Would you like to watch?" Mr. Rutledge asked.

"Would I!" This was just the type of excitement he was hoping to see.

By the time they reached the pole corral, Reno already had a lariat around a good-looking blue roan and was letting him run in wide circles around the outer edges of the pen. The other cowboys lined the exterior, leaning forearms against the pole railings. Only Lucas perched atop the upper railing, face radiating excitement.

"We call this one Storm," Mr. Rutledge said. "He's a strong one and pretty darn wild, but once he's broke, he'll make a great cow horse."

Reno shortened the length of his lariat, slowly drawing the colt to him, all the while humming a sing-song sort of chant.

"What's that he's saying?"

"That's Reno's horse-breaking song. He's a half breed Lakota Sioux. Says his people have always used it to calm their horses." Mr. Rutledge shrugged. "Seems to work. Haven't seen a horse yet that Reno couldn't handle."

The cowboy brought the horse to a halt. Gently, he stroked its neck, nose, and ears, all the while singing his low-pitched song. Storm trembled under his touch, then grew still. The pair stood that way for close to five minutes, Reno stroking and singing, the horse alternately shying and prancing, then stilling again under Reno's touch. Finally, Reno eased a hackamore rope around Storm's nose and neck and motioned Jed in with the saddle.

The colt tensed and skittered backward when Jed laid the blanket and saddle on his back, but Reno continued to stroke and sing while Jed buckled and cinched the saddle in place. Then the two men stepped back, giving the colt some rope. Storm took off, bucking and kicking out his back heels as he raced around the corral. Ben saw the whites of his eyes and sweat running in rivulets down his chest as he ran by their side of the pen.

After several laps around the corral, Storm slowed to a trot, then a walk. Slowly, Reno circled closer and closer until once again, he stood in front of the colt, stroking and singing. As the horse quieted, Reno loosened the lariat and handed the end of it to Jed. Wrapping the hackamore rope around his wrist, Reno put a foot into the stirrup and eased into the saddle. He nodded to Jed, who pulled the lariat free and jumped clear.

Storm erupted, twisting, bucking, leaping, hopping. He slammed into the poles on the opposite side of the ring, then twisted and ran their direction, pure terror in his eyes. Ben released his hold on the top rail and stepped back a foot.

Reno whipped around like a bundle of rags but never lost his seat. After a few minutes, Storm slowed and finally came to a halt in the center of the corral, trembling and sweating. Reno kicked at the colt's sides, and he took a tentative step forward. Ben caught himself holding his breath, waiting for Storm to erupt again.

Instead, the colt let Reno ride him in a slow circle. After two rotations, the cowboy nodded to Jed, who opened the gate. Storm took off like quicksilver, past the outbuildings, and onto the open range until the two were a mere speck in the distance.

Ten minutes later, they were back. Instead of terror, calm settled in the young colt's eyes as if he'd been carrying a rider all his life.

Reno took the saddle and hackamore off Storm and released him into the pen with the other horses. By the time the supper bell rang, Reno had saddle-broke two colts and was working on halter-breaking a third. Ben and Lucas stayed at the corral the entire afternoon.

After Reno took the second colt, a bay named Andy, for his solo ride on the prairie, he let Lucas ride him. The colt bucked at the new rider, but Lucas handled him easily. He and Reno spent the afternoon working together on the third colt, Lucas doing the actual work while Reno told him what to do. Ben didn't think he'd ever seen Lucas so happy.

"Lucas seems to enjoy working with the horses," he said to Mr. Rutledge as they headed for the main house.

"Yep. The boy's a natural and learning from the best. I'm sorry he couldn't come help us this summer."

"Did he tell you why?"

"Said his Ma needed him at home."

"Yeah. He said as much to me as well, but I think it's an excuse. From what I can tell, Nora'd be happier seeing him doing what he enjoys."

Mr. Rutledge shook his head. "Been awful rough on the kid, losing his Pa the way he did. He purt' near hero-worshiped the man. Not that he didn't have reason. Your Pa was one of the best men I knew. I still can't believe he's gone."

He'd heard those words or something like them from just about everyone these past six weeks. Lester Bennett, Sr. set the bar pretty high. Try as he might, Ben had yet to reach it.

Chapter Sixteen

The next morning, Ben looked over the band of horses in the corral. Which was Cochise? The only black he saw was a wild-looking stallion who threw back his head and skittered to the other side of the pen as soon as Ben came near. He'd never handle a horse like that, no matter what Lucas said.

Mr. Rutledge walked over. "See a horse you'd like to ride today?"

Ben shrugged. "Lucas told me I should ride Cochise."

Mr. Rutledge looked skeptical. "You do much riding?"

"Of streetcars."

Mr. Rutledge nodded. "Stay away from Cochise, then. He's part of Reno's string, and far as I know, Reno's the only man who can ride him. I'm thinking Ellie's the mount for you. She's a great cow horse, but so tame my daughter can ride her."

"She's the one I'll take, then."

"Good. I'll have Jed saddle her up." Mr. Rutledge started toward the barn, calling back over his shoulder. "You might want to steer clear of your brother's advice from here on out."

Ben let out a harsh laugh and looked back at the big black. Cochise tossed his head, snorted, and stamped a foot at him.

"Calm as lake water, my eye. Lake Erie in a thunderstorm

more like." Ben shook his head. Guess yesterday's rapport was all a facade. He'd had his suspicions. The truth stung a little, though.

Ellie was a pretty little seal-brown mare with a star on her forehead. Lucas sneered when he saw Ben riding her.

"Whatcha wanna ride a girl's horse for?" The boy sat astride a fiery gray gelding that looked ready to break loose the instant Lucas let up on the rein. "Guess she's better than Cracker, but barely. Try to keep up, will you?" He wheeled his mount and headed to the front next to Reno.

They trailed a small herd of cows and calves that needed to join the rest of the herd at the summer range. For the most part, they simply rode along beside the herd. Every now and then, a straggler broke loose, but Ben found himself with plenty of time to sit back and enjoy the ride.

Ellie was indeed a good cow horse. She could cut off a wandering cow before Ben even thought to react. He learned to let her have her head.

Jenny would love a day like this. He could almost picture her, riding by his side, throwing herself full-tilt into the life of a cowgirl. No one he knew took to new adventures with as much joy as Jenny. He wished she were here. Which was crazy. If he was wishing for anyone, it should be Nell, but somehow he couldn't picture Nell out here. Nell was the perfect wife for a lawyer, even the perfect wife for a judge, but a rancher's wife was another thing altogether. Good thing he had no intentions of being a rancher.

And he needed to quit thinking of Jenny. Seemed like she was on his mind a lot these days. More than she should be, considering their paths weren't likely to cross again. He guessed it was because of all those childhood memories where he and she and Ted had played at being cowboys.

And because she was beautiful and bewitching and . . . so not his. He should never have kissed her. He still wasn't sure why he had. One minute they were having a light-hearted debate. The next, he was leaning in to capture those oh-so-tempting lips of hers. And Jenny, true to form, had responded. Oh, how she had responded. Probably a good thing they were interrupted.

He was committed to Nell and his life back in Newark. Once he got things settled here, he'd be heading back. It was the life he knew and the life he'd chosen. Sure, he'd enjoy a day or two of playing cowboy, even the chance to kiss a beautiful woman who was way out of his league, but in the end, Newark with Nell was where he belonged.

Soon, they reached the upper ranch, which was little more than a corral and bunkhouse. Off in the distance, he glimpsed the white roof of a chuckwagon. Cattle spread out as far as his eye could see. A cowboy waved as they headed their herd in his direction.

"That's Judson," Mr. Rutledge said. "He's in charge of the men up here."

Judson was a short, wiry man a little older than Ben with a firm handshake and an honest face. He introduced Ben to the Mexican cook, Chaco, who stirred a big stew pot by the chuckwagon. A dutch oven full of biscuits sat off to the side.

"Saddle up," Judson said, "and I'll show you around."

By the time they returned, Lucas and several cowboys had already formed a line for the food. Ben, Mr. Rutledge, and Judson fell in behind.

"You have any trouble with that storm last week?" Mr. Rutledge asked Judson.

"A little. Lightning strike started a night stampede with one of the upper bands, but Leroy and Chase were able to head them off before they got to Clay's Canyon. Had a few stragglers, but I think we've managed to round them all up by now."

A commotion at the head of the line drew Ben's attention. Lucas and another young cowboy, Trace, stood toe-to-toe, glaring at each other. Trace held a large donut high above his head.

"You thieving rotter. That's my donut, and you know it." Lucas shouted.

"If it's yours, what's it doing in my hand?"

Lucas swiped at the cowhand's arm, sending the donut flying.

"Why you—" Trace shoved Lucas backward.

Lucas surged forward, throwing Trace to the ground. Their two bodies became a whirling mass as each boy struggled to remain on top. Mr. Rutledge, who'd headed to the front of the line as soon as the fight broke out, yanked Lucas up by his collar. Trace jumped to his feet and would have come after Lucas if Judson hadn't grabbed both of his arms and locked them behind his back.

"Enough!" Mr. Rutledge roared. "You both know the rules about fighting. If you're going to wrangle over a bit of food, you can go without dinner. Trace, saddle up and head out. You'll be working with Greg and Lars until I tell you otherwise. And Lucas, get on over to the stream. Wash off and cool down." He released his hold on Lucas and, when the boy didn't move, gave him a push. "Move."

Ben followed Lucas to the stream. Once there, he dipped his handkerchief in the water and handed it to his brother.

Lucas' lip had a nasty cut and was swelling up like a boil. Otherwise, other than being covered with dirt, the boy didn't look much worse for wear.

"What the tarnation were you thinking, fighting over a donut? You're smarter than that."

"Trace has been asking for it since we got here."

"I don't care. You can't go around hitting people. I've been talking to Mr. Rutledge about your coming back to work here this summer. Do you think he wants to hire someone who can't keep a cool head on his shoulders?"

Lucas whirled on him, face red. "Who said I wanted to work here? I told you, Ma needs me at home. You may own this ranch and everything else Pa had, but you don't own me. So don't try to tell me what to do."

He stalked to where his horse stood ground-tied next to the

chuckwagon and flung himself into the saddle. Wheeling the horse around, he took off toward the home ranch.

Ben blew out a long breath. Reno stood a few yards off, arms folded across his chest, dark eyes studying him.

"Is he always like this?"

Reno was slow to answer. "Lucas always have short fuse, but he never fight before."

"Why doesn't he want to work on the ranch? Letty told me he loved it out here."

Reno's gaze followed the dust cloud in the distance that marked Lucas' progress. "He like young colt when he takes saddle for first time. When Storm kick out, it isn't because he mean. He scared. Everything he ever know since the day he born is changing. Lucas fight against change."

Change, huh? There'd been plenty of that in Lucas's life lately.

"So what should I do?"

The old cowboy shrugged a shoulder. "It take time. Teach him to trust you. To understand change can be good thing."

Teach Lucas to trust him? Ha! There wasn't enough time in the world for that to happen.

BY THE TIME BEN REACHED THE HOME RANCH, LUCAS HAD already headed out. Just as well. A quiet ride home would be nice. Give him time to think, without the presence of the thundercloud that was his little brother.

"You remember how to get back?" Mr. Rutledge asked.

"Shouldn't be a problem. It's a pretty straight shot. Once I hit the foothills, I'll take the road toward Central City."

The foreman nodded. "Come back any time," he said. "And tell your kid brother, he's welcome to his old job. But he'll need to control that temper of his to keep it."

"I appreciate that. I hope he takes you up on it."

"He's a good kid. Just going through a rough time."

With a wave to Mr. Rutledge, Ben guided Cracker onto the road that followed Spearfish Canyon into the hills.

While he rode, he thought about what Reno had said. He'd been younger than Lucas by a few years that summer he'd lost Father. Of course, Father hadn't actually died, but the loss was just as devastating in a sense. Angry? Heck, he'd initiated a fight with Roy practically every day. In his mind, he wouldn't have lost his father if it hadn't been for Roy.

And now? All his plans to somehow earn a place in his father's life again were for nothing. Father was gone. The best he could hope now was to take his father's legacy and care for his family the way he'd have wanted. That meant somehow helping Lucas.

Get him to trust you.

Right. How in tarnation was he supposed to do that?

He could almost hear Grandma Janssen's voice, "Have you prayed about it, Lester?" She'd always been a champion for prayer.

He'd been one too, years ago, especially after Father's betrayal. He'd felt like God was the only father he had left and turned to him often. But as the years went by and life got busier, he'd fallen out of the habit. Maybe it was time to begin again. He lifted his eyes to the blue expanse above him. "Lord, I could use a little help here."

He took a bend in the road and there, tied in a strand of cottonwoods, stood Lucas' big bay. After the prayer he'd just spoken, he knew he had to stop.

He tied Cracker beside Jasper and headed through the trees. Lucas sat on the bank of the nearby river dropping cottonwood leaves into the water. He glanced sideways as Ben sat down beside him.

"Cracker must want to get home. I didn't expect you to make it by here till sundown. Or maybe sometime next week."

"He's slow, but he's not that bad."

Lucas grunted.

Silent minutes ticked by. Ben cleared his throat.

"Help me understand something. Why are you so against working at the ranch? Mind you, I'm not trying to control you or anything. I just thought you liked working there. Mr. Rutledge says you have talent.

Lucas said nothing, just kept tossing leaves into the water.

"Letty tells me Father planned for you to run the ranch someday."

"Yeah. But that's not gonna happen now, is it?" Anger simmered beneath his words.

"Why not? If it was Father's plan, I'd be more than willing to follow it. But you're barely sixteen. You're not ready yet, and if you don't take advantage of working there when you can, you never will be."

"I know a heck of a lot more about ranching than you. I'll bet you don't even know the difference between a cow and a steer. You can't stay on a real horse to save your life, yet guess who owns the ranch? Little Lord Lester, the pretty boy lawyer."

"What did you call me?"

"Sorry. *Ben*." He ground out the word. Surging to his feet, Lucas strode down the bank a ways before turning, red-faced, fists clenched. "You couldn't even keep Pa's name. And yet, he gives everything to *you*? I don't get it."

Ben stood up. "Trust me, I don't understand it either. But I'll tell you this. I'm going to do my best to do what I think Father would have wanted for this family. With God's help, that is."

"God? You're bringing God into this?" Lucas let out a string of words no sixteen-year-old had any business knowing, let alone saying.

"Hey, watch it. Father would tan your hide if he heard you now. He was a God-fearing man."

"Yeah? And what good did that do him?" Lucas swallowed hard, then looked away, blinking rapidly. "Why'd he have to die that way?" His voice was tight, tortured.

A sympathetic lump formed in Ben's throat. "I don't know. Some things in this life are a mystery. My Grandma Janssen used to say, 'God's ways are not our ways.'"

The words felt inadequate the minute they left his mouth. He could tell from his brother's face that he wasn't buying it.

"Well, if that's *His* way, letting a man die for trying to save a neighbor, then I want nothing to do with him." Lucas stalked off through the trees.

Ben didn't try to follow. Why should he? Lucas didn't want him. He wanted his father. And try as he might, Ben would never be their father.

Moments later, hoofbeats pounded off down the road. With a heavy exhale, Ben headed up the bank. Looked like he was back to playing catch up. He mounted his horse and gave a kick to get him started, but instead of ambling forward, Cracker erupted in a side hop, then threw his hind legs in the air.

If he hadn't seen for himself Cracker's familiar brown hide, he'd have thought someone had exchanged his quiet hack for Cochise. Half in the saddle and half off, Ben grabbed for the reins and missed. Another wild buck had him flying through the air, heels over head, landing with a thud on his upper back. His head slammed into hard ground.

Ben struggled to breathe. He hadn't landed this hard since Billy "the train" Bunson blindsided him during the annual Yale/Harvard game his sophomore year. Mocking laughter sifted through the haze in his brain. He blinked, trying to clear his vision.

Lucas? Sure enough, the boy sat on his horse a few yards away.

"You should'a seen your face," he crowed. "Believe me, it was worth coming back for. And Cracker? I have to hand it to the fellow. He has more fire left than I thought. What could possibly have gotten into him? Must be one of life's mysteries, I guess." With another jeering laugh, Lucas wheeled his horse and cantered off.

Son of a monkey, that boy deserved a thrashing. And he'd be more than happy to give him one once he caught up with him. But for now, all he could manage was to lie in the dirt and gawp like a landed trout.

After a minute or two, Ben rolled over and pushed to his feet. His vision blurred. Bending over, he closed his eyes until the world stopped spinning. His head pounded from where he'd hit it. He gingerly fingered the knot forming there.

His hat had landed in the dirt a few feet away. He whacked it against his leg to get the dust off and looked around for Cracker, who was nowhere in sight.

He gave a low whistle hoping the horse would respond. No answering whinny or snort. The road to Central City veered off to the left and wound up into the hills through groves of cottonwood and ash.

With any luck, Cracker would have followed it. He didn't think the horse would run far due to his earlier disinclination to run at all, but then he would have bet his right arm Cracker couldn't buck as he had either.

About a quarter-mile up the road, he found the horse cropping grass in a small meadow. He inched toward him, but Cracker didn't spook.

"Come on, boy. Let's take a look at your saddle."

Lifting it off Cracker's back, he peeled back the blanket. Sure enough, three large cockleburs stuck to its underside—the oldest schoolboy trick in the world. Well, if Lucas wanted to act like a child, he'd treat him like one. This last prank was the final straw.

Chapter Seventeen

"Someone's got his eye on you," Sara Dickinsen said, tilting her head toward a group of officers standing beside the grandstand. Their corporal stared brazenly in their direction.

"What makes you think he's not looking at you?" Jenny knew she looked her best today. She loved her white lawn dress with its panels of tiny tucks and bands of Valencia lace. In honor of the nation's birthday, she'd paired it with a hat of navy satin braid wreathed with American Beauty roses. Molly had arranged her curls artfully beneath the hat that drooped ever so slightly over her eyes.

But Sara also presented a pretty picture. She wore her rich red hair in a braid down her back and paired her own white lawn with a straw boater and a jaunty red, white, and blue bow.

"No, it's you. I saw him during the ball game, watching every move you made."

Jenny shrugged. She'd noticed him too. At first glance, his dark eyes and hair had reminded her of Ben, but a closer look showed he was not nearly as handsome or as personable. She had no interest in encouraging such brash behavior. She turned away.

"After the trouncing our boys just gave them, I'm surprised

they aren't running back to Fort Washakie with their tails between their legs."

Sara giggled. "Will played well, didn't he?"

"Splendidly. You should be proud. Sadly, my brother never made it off first base."

True to his word, Will had introduced her to his sister at the ice cream social, and Jenny recognized at once a kindred spirit. Since that night, she and Sara had been inseparable.

"When do they start the horse racing?" she asked.

"It'll be a few hours yet."

"So what shall we do in the meantime?"

She and Sara strolled arm-in-arm toward Main Street. Sara twirled her sunshade. "All this sun is making me thirsty. Let's go over to Pa's store for some lemonade."

"Lemonade it is, then."

A crowd gathered in front of Noble and Lane's. As she and Sara drew closer, Jenny saw the tips of eagle feathers bouncing above the audience's heads. A drum thrummed in rhythm to a sing-song chant.

"What's that?"

Sara shrugged. "The Shoshone do a dance here every year."

"Oh, let's stop and see them."

"Are you sure? Their dance goes on forever, and it's so hot today."

Jenny wasn't about to miss her first real Indians. "Tell you what. You go along to the mercantile and get us some lemonade. I'll be along in a few minutes. I promise."

Sara hesitated. "Maybe I should stay with you. Mrs. Parkhurst said—"

"Never mind Mrs. Parkhurst. I'll be fine. I see Cy Willoughby. I'll go stand with him for a few minutes and then be right along."

"All right, I'll save you a seat."

Jenny wove her way through the groups of standing spectators until she reached Cy's side. He grinned when he saw her. "Still looking for your Injuns?"

She nodded, fascinated by the scene in front of her. Seven dancers leaped and gyrated in time to the beat, at times crouching low, at others, reaching arms and bodies toward the sky. Jenny had never seen so much naked flesh on grown men. Her eyes riveted to the play of muscles on their bare chests, arms, and legs.

One dancer wore a full headdress of eagle's feathers and a breastplate of ivory bones. Another, bare to the waist, had beaded and fringed leather leggings. Two more wore only beaded jackets and loincloths.

"What do you think?" Cy asked.

"It's wonderful. What type of dance is it?"

"Some call it the wolf dance. Each dancer tells his own story of a hunt or battle he's been in. Kinda' like a group of old soldiers sitting around reliving their glory days."

It ended all too soon. The crowd dispersed, but Jenny stood rooted to her spot, reluctant to leave the experience.

"Well, little missy," Cy said. "Have you had your fill of Injuns now?"

"Oh, no. I want to see so much more. I want to see how they live. I want to know what they eat. Do you think I could learn their language?"

Cy laughed, shaking his head. "You do beat all. But if you're serious, tell you what I'll do. The Missus wants me to take her over to the Mission School this week to help Mrs. Roberts. If you'd like, you can ride along. I'll even drive you by some tepees on the way."

Squealing, Jenny threw her arms around her friend. "Yes, please. I'd love to go. Just tell me when, and I'll be ready."

Cy returned her squeeze. "Well, now. If word gets 'round a trip to the Indian reservation will win a hug from a pretty lady, we'll have the men lining their buggies up in droves. I'd best be off, though. I'm supposed to judge some of the events out at the Roundup. But I'll send round to let you know what day next week. Probably Wednesday or Thursday."

She waved him off, then turned toward the Lander Mercantile. But as she headed up Main Street, she realized Lannigan's saloon stood between her and Sara. A group of soldiers gathered in the doorway and, by the sounds of it, were already well under the influence of the establishment's hardest brew. Among them, she recognized the corporal who had stared so rudely during the baseball game.

She'd either have to step down off the boardwalk into the dust of the street or try to make her way through them somehow. She slowed, weighing her choices.

"Hey, pretty lady," one of them called. "Wanna come over and give *me* a hug?"

Drat. Not caring if she looked cowardly, she whirled around, hoping to catch Cy before he got too far, and ran right into a wall of flesh, encased in buttery soft leather.

She looked up into mesmerizing green eyes. Familiar green eyes.

"Mr. Sparrowhawk."

Amusement sparked in the green depths as he glanced to where her bare hand splayed against his chest, softly stroking his buckskin coat.

"Oh. I'm sorry." She pulled back as if she'd touched a hot plate. Where were her gloves? She must have misplaced them when she took them off to eat those roasted peanuts at the game.

"No need to apologize. Could I be of assistance?"

"Yes. I mean, I'm not sure if you remember me, but we have met, not formally, I guess, but—"

"I remember." The way he said it sent a delicious shiver down her spine.

"I'm Jenny Westraven. You know my brother, Ted?"

His smile broadened. "Ted Westraven's sister? Then I'm very pleased to meet you. He's told me all about you. Can I escort you somewhere?"

"To the mercantile, if you would." With him by her side, she could brave a whole army of soldiers. "I'm to meet my friend there. I hope it's not out of your way."

"Not at all. I'm headed to the livery." He tucked her hand into the crook of his arm and confidently strode forward, making a path for them through the ranks of soldiers.

Heat rose up the back of her neck as ten or more pairs of eyes watched them walk by. She lifted her chin. Let them look.

As they left the men behind, she peeked at her escort from under the brim of her hat.

"Do you make a habit of rescuing damsels in distress, Mr. Sparrowhawk? Or are you merely my personal guardian angel?"

"Oh, I'm no angel." His grin bordered on wickedness. "Just lucky, I guess."

"Lucky?"

"To be the one who escorts you, rather than those poor blokes back there who can only dream."

Her blush returned.

"Are you in town for the day, or are you staying a while?"

"Just today. I'm competing in some of the Roundup events.

"Oh? Which ones?"

"Bronco busting and the wild horse race."

"That sounds dangerous."

"Not if you know what you're doing."

"And do you?"

"Absolutely."

She loved confidence in a man.

"You'll come cheer me on?"

"Absolutely." She parroted.

He laughed and pulled to a stop. "Well, Miss Westraven, I believe this is your destination." Surprised, Jenny looked up to see they stood before the Lander Mercantile's large glass windows. Sara waved from a table inside.

"I need to grab my horse and head out for the competition, but it's been a pleasure to walk with you."

"The pleasure is all mine, Mr. Sparrowhawk. Thank you for coming to my rescue . . . again."

From the corner of her eye, she could see Sara gesticulating wildly and pointing her direction. She turned slightly, trying to block her friend's antics from Mr. Sparrowhawk's view.

"Jeanette. I didn't expect to find you here."

Suddenly Sara's sign language made perfect sense. Mrs. Parkhurst bustled up the boardwalk, Grace by her side.

"I'm meeting Sara." She pointed to where her friend was once again demurely sipping her lemonade.

"I thought the two of you already *were* together."

"Yes, but we got separated at the Indian dance."

Mrs. Parkhurst's sour expression told her that wasn't welcome information. Her penetrating gaze zeroed in on the man standing beside her.

"Have the three of you met?" Ignoring the frosty shake of Mrs. Parkhurst's head, Jenny plunged ahead. "Mr. Sparrowhawk, allow me to introduce Mrs. Parkhurst and her daughter, Mrs. Grace Westraven, my sister-in-law."

Mr. Sparrowhawk bowed. "It's a pleasure to meet you, Mrs. Parkhurst. I already know your lovely daughter."

Mrs. Parkhurst granted him an almost imperceptible nod.

"And now I must go. Shall I see you at the Roundup?"

"We wouldn't miss it," Jenny answered for the three of them.

With a tip of his hat, he strode off up the street.

"Just pin it so it won't drag," Jenny said. "I'll have Molly sew it on later."

She stood in the ladies' retiring room of Coulter's Opera

House with Sara kneeling at her feet, trying to repair the bottom flounce of her dress. Her favorite lawn dress had wilted considerably over the day, the material around the hem now more gray than white due to the fairgrounds' dust. Jenny didn't care. She only wanted it repaired enough so she could continue dancing.

She couldn't remember when she'd spent a more fun-filled day. She and the entire Dickinsen clan had cheered from the grandstand while Ted and Will competed against each other in the buggy races. Ted's grays won the day, but Will won his own first-place ribbon in the quarter-mile. After the races, Jenny finally got to see cowboys in action.

Bronco busting, calf roping, and bulldogging filled the afternoon, with trick riding and roping exhibitions between the events. Sparrowhawk won first place in both his contests.

Fireworks closed the show, then the crowd migrated to the opera house for the dance. Jenny hadn't sat still since the music began. She'd waltzed with Will, two-stepped with Ted, and even danced a staid minuet with Mr. Parkhurst. She'd romped through a polka with Cy and finally relented and joined the lancers with the rude corporal. That last had been a mistake. One of the other officers in their set had stumbled, coming down squarely on her dress and nearly ripping off the entire bottom flounce.

Thankfully, Sara carried pins in her reticule, or the evening's fun might have been over for her.

"How's it looking?"

"It still droops a little in the middle."

"Never mind how it looks. Just so I don't trip over it. I promised your cowboy I'd dance the next quadrille with him."

Sara sniffed. "He's not *my* cowboy."

"Don't be mean. Clearly, he's smitten."

Charlie Green worked for Sara's brother-in-law, Tom Peterson. The ranch hand had been following her around like a lost puppy all evening.

"I don't waste my time on cowboys."

"Yet, you didn't mind dancing with Ray Hornecker."

"That's different. Ray is a rancher's son, not a cowboy."

"They all look the same to me when they're wrestling steers." They left the ladies' room and headed back toward the ballroom. "I'll tell you one cowboy I wouldn't mind spending time with. Mr. Sparrowhawk. Wasn't he magnificent today?"

Sara wrinkled her nose. "He puts on a good show, but isn't he a little old?"

"Old! You should have seen the potential husbands Uncle Clarence picked for me. Mr. Sparrowhawk's a child compared to some of them."

"Still. He has to be as old as Julia's husband Tom, maybe even as old as my brother-in-law Drew."

"And they're what? Seven, eight years older than us? That's not so old."

Sara shrugged.

"You have to admit he's handsome," Jenny said.

"I'll admit he has a way with the ladies. Even Stella and Grace fell under his spell at one time."

"They did? What happened?"

"Your brother happened for one. Though I think Stella was the more interested of the two. Mr. Jones put an end to that by taking her abroad. Ever since she got back, all Stella will talk about are her European beaus."

"I thought she and Will were an item before that European tour."

"Oh, Will's had a crush on Stella ever since grade school. She'll throw him a bone now and again, but only if there's no one else in the picture. I wish he'd wise up."

As they re-entered the ballroom, a thrill shot through Jenny. The night just got a whole lot more interesting, for there, talking to Will and Ted stood Sparrowhawk. He no longer wore his chaps and had slicked his long hair back into a ponytail. Still. He stood out from the rest with canvas pants tucked into knee-high boots and a simple white shirt paired with a black vest, no jacket.

He glanced up and caught her staring. His gaze lassoed her as easily as he'd caught his wild horse today. She threaded her way through the crowd until she reached his side.

"Sparrowhawk, have you met my sister?" Ted asked.

"I've had the pleasure, yes." The timbre of his voice reminded her of their earlier encounter. She could almost feel the softness of leather, the play of muscle beneath her palm again. She held his gaze.

"We're organizing a fishing excursion to Graves Lake," Ted said. "Sparrowhawk says he'll guide us. Are you still interested in camping out? We'll probably go for ten days at least."

"And you'll take me with you?"

"I don't see why not. Sara too, if she'd like. Drew thinks he can talk Emma into coming as a chaperone."

"Oh, Teddy. Yes." She would have thrown her arms around her brother's neck if they hadn't been in such a public place. "Sara, say you'll go. It'll be such fun."

"I wouldn't miss it. I've been begging Will to let me tag along on one of these for years. I'll finally get to prove to him he's not the best fisherman in the family."

"We'll see about that," Will said.

"We'll plan for the first of August, then, Sparrowhawk. If anything changes, I'll write and let you know."

The man nodded, then bowed to Jenny. "Now that business is settled, would you do me the honor of this dance, Miss Westraven?"

Jenny could do little more than nod.

Where was her poise? Her hard-earned sophistication? She, a veteran of numerous seasons both in New York and abroad, found herself tongue-tied by a mere cowboy. And when he pulled her into his arms for the waltz, she could think of nothing other than his hand against her waist and his warm breath stirring the curls on her forehead. Honestly, she could do better than this. She'd danced with dukes, for heaven's sake.

She took a deep breath and let her finishing school training come to the fore.

"You were quite impressive at the Roundup today. I thought for sure that wild bronco would throw you on its first jump."

"Naw, just lucky with the horse I drew. Old Steamboat's more show than danger. After you've ridden him once, you pretty much can tell which way he's going to buck."

A modest man. She liked that. "And the wild horse race? Were you just lucky there?"

"Anyone will tell you winning a wild horse race is nothing *but* luck."

"But even you have to admit, you have a way with horses."

"Maybe. I've always believed you tame a horse the same way you woo a woman."

She wasn't sure she liked his analogy. "Really? How is that?"

"You get them to want what you want."

"You think you can make any woman want whatever you want?"

A slow smile played along the corners of his mustache. "I don't *think*, Miss Westraven. I know."

So much for modesty. She had a sudden urge to take him down a notch.

"Try me. What is it you want?"

"I want to kiss those pretty, little lips of yours."

She missed a step and would have tripped if he hadn't caught her close, supporting her until her feet found the rhythm again.

"Don't look so surprised. Surely you've been around men enough to know what's on their minds."

"And you think you can get me to want that too?"

"I already have. Never underestimate the power of sugges-tion. Just my mentioning a kiss has you thinking about it. You're a beautiful woman. Chances are you've been kissed before. And if the men were worth their salt, one or two of them have shown you how delightful kissing can be."

Her mind flew to Ben's warm lips on hers. A kiss like that? Yes, she wouldn't mind repeating that.

Her gaze dropped from Sparrowhawk's green eyes to his full lips, partially hidden beneath his thick mustache and goatee. How would it feel to kiss a man with facial hair? Would it feel scratchy or as soft and silky as it looked? Would his kiss be anything like Ben's?

She licked her lower lip. Why was it suddenly so warm in here?

"Now you're wondering what it would be like to kiss me. Would it be just as good? Better?" His voice purred in her ear. Was she really that easy to read?

Oh. He was good. Too good.

"Admit it. You want that kiss as much as I do now."

"I certainly do not."

He bent his head until his lips were barely touching her left ear. "Liar."

The music came to an end, and she pulled out of his arms, choosing to ignore his last comment.

"You're looking a little overheated, Miss Westraven," Sparrowhawk said, tucking her arm into his. "Would you care to take a stroll on the balcony and cool off?"

The promise in his hypnotic green gaze warned her if she accepted his invitation, he had no intention of allowing her to cool off. She was half tempted to agree. Had he not been so sure of himself, she probably would have. As it was, she found it hard to break the grip of his gaze.

Thankfully, she caught sight of Charlie, making a beeline her way. "I'm sorry, Mr. Sparrowhawk, I'll have to decline. I've promised this next dance to Mr. Green."

"Another time, then," he said with a bow. The dratted man didn't even give her the satisfaction of looking disappointed.

As she took her position in the quadrille, she watched his

progress as he wove his way through the crowd to the ballroom's exit. That man was trouble. If she were wise, she'd avoid him at all costs.

At the door, he turned and caught her watching him. He winked and blew her a kiss before slipping out into the night. Oh yes, trouble with a capital T. And she'd never yet been able to steer clear of trouble.

Chapter Eighteen

The first few stars were glimmering before Ben made it back to Nora's boarding house. The hike to Central City took nearly three hours. Once there, he'd exchanged the lame Cracker for another hired mount before riding the last two miles home. The proprietor of the Central City livery promised to care for Cracker's lame knee until he could return for her.

The seven-mile journey home, most of it on foot, gave him plenty of time to build a strong case of grievances against Lucas. Instead of cooling his temper, each step of the way, each additional blister to his feet, each throbbing pain at the back of his head, fanned the flame within. His little brother needed a lesson, and he was more than willing to give it.

Letty must have seen the murderous intent in his eyes because she was oddly reticent when he asked about Lucas.

"He came home, didn't he?"

"Yes, several hours ago. But he went out again."

"Do you know where?"

She shook her head. Ben had a pretty good idea. Lucas had taken to hanging out at the bars with Roy and his mining crew at the end of the second shift. He'd probably find them both at O'Donnell's. He'd never liked Lucas mixing with that crowd but hadn't wanted to interfere. Well, that was going to change. Lots of things were changing for that little brother of his.

He shoved his hat back on his head and turned for the door. Letty stepped in front of him.

"Don't you want some supper? You look all worn down. Why don't you rest and eat a bit before going out again?"

"I'll rest after I've seen Lucas." He tried to push past her, but she stopped him with a hand on his chest.

"Promise me you won't hurt him, Ben. He's just a kid."

He steeled his heart against the pleading in her brown eyes —eyes so much like Father's. "Sorry, Letty. That *kid* tried to kill me today and just about succeeded. I'm not making any promises."

He pushed on by and slammed the door on his way out, in no mood to lollycoddle Lucas anymore. His path took him through the burned section of downtown. Construction scaffolding still blocked the majority of the sidewalks. When the breeze blew, the faint odor of charred wood mingled with the fresh scent of newly-cut pine boards. He turned off of Main onto Bleeker and headed up Hill Street.

The bars were hopping tonight. The tinny sound of piano music and raucous laughter spilled from the doorways of the establishments he passed. He caught the word *O'Donnell's* on a sign two doors down and ducked inside. Smoke saturated the room.

Sure enough, Lucas sat beside Roy in a far corner deep in a game of cards. Both brothers had their backs to him so he could approach without notice. He wove his way between tables, dodging barmaids and drunken patrons. When he reached their table, he grabbed Lucas by the back of his collar.

The boy let out a surprised yelp as he pulled him to his feet.

"Didn't think I'd let you off that easy, did you?" He gave Lucas a shake.

Roy surged to his feet. "What the heck are you doing? Get your hands off my kid brother."

"Not this time. I have a score to settle with *my* kid brother, and if you're wise, you'll stay out of my way."

"Like heck, I will. Let him go."

Ben ignored Roy. Still holding onto Lucas' collar, he pushed the boy toward the door.

Roy forged ahead of them, cutting them off.

"I said, stay out of this."

"And if I don't?" Roy stood with his legs spread wide and his arms folded.

"Then I guess I'll have to teach you both a lesson."

As Ben anticipated, Roy threw his head back in a laugh. In a flash, Ben launched Lucas into him, using the weight of his body to push both of them through the doorway.

"Fight! Fight!"

The bar's patrons erupted, flowing out the door after Roy, carrying Ben with them. He found himself surrounded by a circle of miners and facing a jeering Roy.

"You think you can fight me? Come on, Little Lord Lester. Let's see what you got."

Those three words transported Ben back fourteen years to the schoolyard and back streets of Lead where he and Roy fought, Roy's circle of friends egging them on. He'd never stood a chance back then. But tonight might be different.

Then he'd been an under-sized, inexperienced boy. And though he still didn't have Roy's height and girth, he did have a grown man's body, and the experience of countless boxing matches fought in the intramural boxing clubs of Harvard. He might not be a Corbett or Fitzsimmons, but he was quick and had learned to use that quickness to his advantage.

Roy opened with a roundhouse punch that would have floored him in the old days. Ben ducked and wove out of his reach. He eluded a second punch, then feinted and countered with a swing that clipped Roy on his jaw. Angered, Roy came at him swinging both arms, but Ben once again slipped out of his reach. Frustration built in Roy's eyes and Ben couldn't help grinning. Big mistake. Roy let out a roar and rushed him, wrapping him in a bear hug and sending him crashing to the ground.

For the second time today, the back of Ben's head slammed into the dirt. He blinked against the stars blurring his vision, and gradually focused on Roy straddled on top of him, one beefy fist raised. It hit like a sledgehammer, the second fist following right behind. Ben was back in the schoolyard again, helpless to stop the blows. He threw up his arms. Through a fog of pain, he heard Roy taunt.

"Not so funny now, is it Little Lester?"

Something inside him snapped. All the built-up anger of the day, all the years of never being able to best Roy, coursed through his body like an electric current. With strength he didn't know he possessed, Ben planted his feet and bucked his torso, knocking Roy off balance. He followed Roy's falling weight with his own, flipping him on his back and taking his turn on top.

Trapping Roy's arms with his legs, Ben let his fury fly in a flurry of punches to Roy's head. The smack of flesh against flesh was so satisfying. His knuckles were slick with Roy's blood, yet he kept punching, relentlessly firing blow after blow.

His mind didn't register Roy was unconscious until two of the miner's caught his arms and pulled him off.

"You trying to kill him?" one man asked.

He wiped at the blood trickling down his forehead, focusing on Roy's battered body. He lay still. Too still.

God. What had he done?

Looking up, he saw Lucas tight against the circle of men. The look on his face brought to mind Storm trapped against the far side of the pole corral, eyes white with fear.

"You gonna beat on me now?" Lucas' voice was high and shaky.

Ben looked down at his bloody hands and shook his head. He heard his own voice, distant and tired. So tired.

"No," he said. "I'm done. I'm . . . done."

Turning, he stumbled off into the night.

Chapter Nineteen

Ben sat at the desk in his bedroom, toying with two letters. He'd meant what he'd said last night. He was done. He'd tried. He had. But what his father asked was impossible. And he'd failed.

Again.

He didn't need the disappointment he saw in Letty's eyes when he got home to tell him that.

He ran his fingers across the bruises on his knuckles. Imagine what she'd say when she saw what he'd done to Roy. He was pretty sure she thought he'd received the worse end of the deal, as he had every time before. But it didn't matter. He was done trying. As soon as he tied up loose ends with Mr. Foster, he was leaving. The only question was where he'd go.

He felt like playing the childhood game of eeny-meeny with the two letters in front of him. One was from Nell, full of news from Newark. It came about a week ago, and he had yet to reply. A new name had entered her letters. Joshua Pinkert. Ben knew the man. A junior lawyer with the Bennington and Bartley firm, Pinkert would probably jump at the chance to take Ben's place at Goddard's. And from the number of times Nell mentioned Mr.

Pinkert, Ben suspected she was warning him the man would be more than willing to take his place in her life as well.

He should be worried. Should have packed his bags and bought a one-way ticket home the day he received Nell's letter. But he hadn't. Somehow the full partnership . . . Nell . . . Newark . . . none of it appealed.

He picked up the second letter, studying its return address. Lander, Wyoming. Ted had written about a month ago, offering his and Jenny's condolences on the death of Ben's father. Word must have reached them through Grandma Janssen and Aunt Bethany.

If you get the chance while you're still in the West, you should come to Lander, the letter read. *The hunting and fishing in the Winds is some of the best around. We could have some of those adventures we dreamed about when we were kids.*

Why did Lander entice when Newark did not? One simple word.

Adventure.

Other than that short trip to the ranch, when was the last time he'd had an adventure? Seemed like the past ten years had been nothing but work. And somehow, that ranch visit had ignited all his childhood dreams.

Yes, Ted's invitation tempted him. So did the vision of an angel face with vivid blue eyes and soft-as-cream lips.

He was a fool. Jenny wasn't for him. He didn't fit in her world, and she wasn't a part of his plans for the future. Yet, truthfully, he didn't need a game of eeny-meeny to tell him where he wanted to go. What would it hurt to extend his time away by a week or two? Goddard had told him to take as long as he needed. He stuck the two letters back in the pocket of his traveling secretary and pushed to his feet. He'd stop by the train station on his way to Mr. Foster's.

~

"ARE YOU SURE THIS IS WHAT YOU WANT?" THE LAWYER pushed the papers across his desk for Ben to sign. "You know it's not what your father intended."

"Maybe not. But I feel in my gut it's the right thing to do. And if I don't do it now, it may be too late." He read through the papers, then signed away his ownership of the mine. With every stroke of the pen, the weight on his shoulders grew a little lighter.

"Your leaving like this isn't what your father wanted, either." Mr. Foster speared him with that direct gaze of his.

Ben gave a harsh laugh. "You might be surprised. I believe the last time Roy and I came to blows, *he* was the one who sent me packing."

"You were a child then. He did what he thought was best."

"And I'm doing what I think is best now. I don't need to stick around Lead for Father's businesses to run like clockwork. And if there's a problem, you know where to reach me."

Ben pushed to his feet, holding out a hand to Mr. Foster. "I appreciate all you've done for my father and for our family. Keep an eye on Letty and Nora for me, will you? If they need anything —anything at all—you'll let me know?"

"Of course. And Lucas and Roy?"

Ben shrugged. "I expect they'll take care of themselves." He turned toward the door, then turned back. "He *is* going to be all right? I didn't hurt him too badly?"

"He's pretty beat up, but he'll survive. The doctor said there'd be no permanent damage. You're lucky there were plenty of witnesses to testify he threw the first punch, or you might have found yourself on the ugly end of the law."

Lucky? Ha. He certainly didn't feel lucky. He gave the lawyer a parting nod, then headed out the door. He couldn't leave this town fast enough.

Chapter Twenty

"And this is the shop where our young men are taught carpentry skills." Superintendent Fallcourt opened the door to a one-room stone building and led Jenny, Cy, and Mrs. Willoughby inside.

Jenny stepped into the empty room, its cool interior a glad relief from the hot July wind. Sawdust lingered in the air.

"This building was added within the last year and is quite well equipped. I believe it will be a much needed asset in training our men for future employment."

Cy ran a hand across the stones in the wall. "Whoever built this did a mighty fine job. Looks to be made of much better material than the main buildings."

Fallcourt didn't appear too pleased by the comparison. A distinguished-looking gentleman with silver hair and a trim build, he'd conducted their tour with the proprietary air of someone who'd reigned here for years, though Cy had told her he'd only been at the Government School a few months.

Frankly, Jenny didn't like this school nearly as much as the Mission School for Girls run by Reverend Roberts. Though much larger, with three big brick buildings and many smaller outbuildings and shops, this one looked and felt like an institution. It sat on acres of open, barren prairie surrounded by barbed-wire fencing. The Mission School, with its white picket fence and strand of trees, was far more welcoming.

But she was glad the Willoughbys brought her along today. She'd accompanied Mrs. Willoughby to the mission school several times and now wanted to see other parts of the reservation. She was also determined someday to visit one of the Indian teepees she'd seen on their drives.

"Are there any children in residence this summer?" she asked.

"The majority will not be here until September, but we do have two crews of young men who work the farm during the summer and a small crew of girls who help in the kitchen and gardens." He led the way out the back door of the shop. "The garden, farm, and livestock provide the majority of the school's support, so it's imperative we have adequate help during the summer."

Across the barnyard, Jenny could see a large garden. Three or four girls in white pinafores bent over hoes between tall rows of corn. As they entered the barnyard, a small boy came running out of the hen house, chickens squawking at his heels.

"Slow down there, Willie." Mr. Fallcourt held out his arm to stop the boy as he barreled their way. "You must learn to walk, not run. Otherwise, you endanger others."

Willie hung his close-cropped head and dragged the toe of his boot in the dirt.

"Why were you in the hen house? Did Mrs. Pickering send you for eggs?"

The boy shook his head, continuing to look at the ground.

Mr. Fallcourt lifted the boy's chin with his forefinger. "If someone is addressing you, you should look them in the eye. And if Mrs. Pickering did not send you for eggs, then you need to stay away from the chickens. Scared chickens won't lay eggs."

The boy looked at Mr. Fallcourt with wide brown eyes but said not a word. The superintendent sighed.

"Surely this isn't Willie Yellow Bear," Mrs. Willoughby said. "I would think he'd still be far too young for school."

"Indeed, it is Willie Yellow Bear. He's just turned five. Normally, I would not have taken him on until fall, but his uncle is the foreman of our work crew and asked if he might stay. Apparently, his mother is not well?"

"Ah, yes. She hasn't been since her last baby. Still, I wouldn't have thought Willie was five already." Mrs. Willoughby shook her head.

"Is he related to Alice Yellow Bear?" Jenny asked. Alice was one of her favorites at the Mission.

"Her younger brother, I believe."

She squatted to eye-level with the child. Something in the boy's face, the tilt of his eyes maybe, reminded her of Alice.

"Hello, Willie. I'm a friend of your sister's. I'm pleased to meet you."

The boy stared at her with solemn dark eyes. What was it the Mission girls had taught her? Oh, yes.

"*Pehnaho*, Willie. *Dei*'." She pointed to herself and repeated. "*Dei*'"

Willie's face split into a toothless grin. He opened his mouth as if to reply.

"Willie," Mr. Fallcourt barked.

The boy snapped his lips shut and dropped his gaze again.

"I must ask you not speak to him in Shoshone, Miss Westraven," the superintendent said. "The students here are strictly forbidden to talk in their native language. For an adult to encourage him in that way is confusing."

Forbidden? Jenny rose to her feet. "But at the Mission—"

"Yes. I understand they are far more lenient there, but studies have shown that complete immersion in their new culture allows them to learn our language at a more rapid pace."

"What about homesickness?"

Mr. Fallcourt shrugged. "That will pass once he learns to leave his old ways behind." He watched the boy's meandering progress toward the school's kitchen and shook his head. "I'm afraid the lad's already been a bit of a troublemaker, small as he is. He never says much but is behind all sorts of pranks and mischief. The others have taken to calling him 'Little Ghost.' A few weeks ago, our boys were awakened in the middle of the night by an unearthly howling. They were sure it was a ghost, but no one wanted to leave his bed to investigate. This continued for several nights until someone finally told the house mother. She stayed up the next night until the howling commenced, and upon further investigation, found Willie's bed empty. They discovered him on the roof over the kitchen porch, howling at the moon."

They all chuckled at the story, but Jenny couldn't help but feel indignant on Willie's behalf. What did they expect? They'd taken away his voice! She remembered those early days at Madame DeLancey's. She'd not been forbidden to speak English, but there were times in the classroom or at the dinner table when all the girls were required to speak only French or German. One night, early in her stay, she'd purposely spilled her milk during the French portion of the meal simply to ensure she was not invisible. No wonder Willie howled.

They finished their tour of the school grounds and were heading toward the Willoughby's carriage when Willie came running around the corner of the main building, clutching something in his hand. He skidded to a stop in front of Jenny and held it out to her. Stooping, she reached for the mud-covered object.

"Oh, it's my reticule. I must have dropped it by the barn. Thank you, Willie."

She took it, mud and all then released it with a scream. Something had moved inside!

"What's the matter, dear?" Mrs. Willoughby asked.

"I . . . I'm not sure." As she bent to pick it up, the bag flipped on its side. She jumped back. What in the world?

Cy reached down and snagged it, then released the tie

around the neck of the bag. Looking in, he let out a chortle. Squatting, he turned the bag over and shook it a little. A brownish lump spilled out onto the ground. Big round eyes blinked up at them.

A toad.

She let out a breath and gave a shaky laugh.

Mr. Fallcourt frowned. "Willie, come here."

She looked at Willie's bewildered face. "I don't believe he meant any harm."

Mr. Fallcourt ignored her. "Hands," he barked. Slowly, Willie held out his tiny brown hands as the superintendent pulled a small riding crop from his pocket.

"No!" Jenny launched herself between them. She heard a thud as the whip hit her skirt. The heavy broadcloth deflected most of the blow, but Willie's skin would not have been so fortunate.

"Miss Westraven!" Mr. Fallcourt sounded horrified. "That was foolhardy. You could have been hurt."

She turned toward him, livid. "And Willie wouldn't? Look at him. He has no idea why you're angry. He simply wanted to give me a treasure. It's not his fault I scream at toads rather than delight in them as he does."

A muscle twitched along Mr. Fallcourt's jawline as he glared down at her. With obvious effort, he swallowed, then gave a short, stiff bow. "Very well, Miss Westraven" He stepped around her to address Willie. "Pick up your toad and take it back to where you found it. I will not punish you this time, but should you ever pull a prank like this again, I will."

Willie scooped up the toad and made a beeline for the barn. An awkward silence ensued.

"Well, now," Cy spoke first. He held out a hand to the superintendent. "Thank you for your time today. It was mighty fine to meet you and hear your plans for the school. We'll look forward to seeing them come about."

"Thank you, Mr. Willoughby. You and your wife are welcome to visit anytime."

Jenny noticed he didn't include her in that invitation. Cy turned to help his wife into the buggy. Before she could follow, Mr. Fallcourt blocked her way.

"Miss Westraven, a moment, please?" He drew her aside. "If you visit again, please keep in mind I am the one in charge here. I gave into you just now because you are young and, understandably, soft-hearted. But I will not be told how to run my school. I trained under Captain Pratt at Carlisle and have twenty-five-years' experience. My method of discipline is proven and effective. I cannot have you undermining my authority in front of the students. Have I made myself clear?"

"Quite clear." The man was a tyrant. "Thank you, Mr. Fallcourt. Today's visit has been *most* enlightening." She let the chill in her tone relay her displeasure. Chin up, she swept past him and allowed Cy to hand her into the buggy. If Mr. Fallcourt thought she'd do nothing the next time she saw a child mistreated, he didn't know her at all.

BY THE TIME THE WILLOUGHBYS DROPPED HER OFF AT HOME, Jenny had put the odious Mr. Fallcourt from her mind. No one stayed angry with Cy around.

Trailing her hat behind her by its ribbons, she headed up the stairs to her bedroom, anxious to wash off the grime and dirt of the day. Her mind wandered, as it often did of late, to the Independence Day dance and a pair of mocking green eyes. She'd see Sparrowhawk soon. Was he thinking of her too?

Men's voices filtered down the hallway from Ted's sun porch. Maybe Will had stopped by for a visit.

Changing course, she walked through the sitting room and out onto the porch. Teddy reclined on his chaise lounge. Another man stood with his back to her, looking out over the

Wind River Mountains much as she had her first day in Wyoming.

But instead of the tall man with sandy blonde hair she'd expected, this gentleman was shorter, with broad shoulders and crisp, dark hair that curled around his collar.

"Ben?"

He turned, familiar brown eyes twinkling a welcome.

"It *is* you!" She hadn't realized until that moment how much she'd missed him.

She closed the distance between them, hands outstretched. She might have hugged him if they'd been alone. "It's so good to see you again. But when . . . how . . .?"

He laughed, taking her hands in his. "It's good to see you too, Jen. I take it Ted didn't tell you I was coming?"

"He never breathed a word."

"You're looking well."

She flushed, realizing they were still holding hands. She gave his hands a quick squeeze and let go. "Oh no," she brushed back a stray curl. "I'm all windblown and covered in dirt, but you . . ." His skin was tanned as if he'd spent many hours in the sun. If anything, he was even more handsome. "Has Mr. Goddard taken to conducting business outside?"

"I didn't come from Newark, Jenny. I've spent the last few months in South Dakota."

"Oh, that's right." His father. She laid a hand on his arm. "Aunt Bethany wrote to tell us about your father. I'm so sorry."

"Thank you." His expression, so open and happy a few minutes ago, took on a shuttered look.

Jenny hastened to change the subject. "But what brings you to Lander?"

"Well, Ted wrote and promised me a Western adventure. But had I known how grueling two-and-a-half days on the roof of a stage would be, I might never have come."

"You rode on the roof? Oh! You men always have all the fun."

"Hardly fun. Just a lot of sun, wind, and dirt."

"Try riding inside. If you open the windows, you're covered in dirt. If you close them, you can't breathe. And the shaking! I've never been so sore in all my life." Jenny sank into the wicker rocker beside Ted's lounge.

Picking up Ted's desk chair, Ben brought it over and straddled the seat, resting his arms across its high back. His dark gaze settled on Jenny. "So, tell me. What scrapes have you been in lately?"

"None, of course. Right, Teddy?"

"Not yet."

"Not yet? What's that supposed to mean?"

"It's been three months. I'm guessing you're due."

"I'm not five anymore. I'm perfectly capable of staying out of trouble for longer than three months. Tell him, Ben. Was I any trouble when I worked for you?"

"I thought we had this discussion already." The glint in his eye brought to mind that fateful day in his office and their remarkable kiss. Jenny felt her cheeks heat under his gaze.

Best to keep the conversation on track. "Be honest now. I made your life easier as your typewriter girl. You know I did."

"Oh, I wouldn't go that far, but I admit you were excellent on the typewriter."

"See?" she turned to her brother. "I told you I was good."

Ted shook his head. "What I don't understand is why you hired her in the first place."

"Simple. As her boss, I got to tell her what to do."

Teddy laughed. "And she did it?"

Ben gave a mournful shake of his head. "Only when she wanted to."

Jenny pushed to her feet and headed for the door. "You two may continue to poke fun at my expense, but I don't have to stay and listen." She looked back at Ben when she reached the doorway. "Are you staying for dinner?"

"Yes, and Ted tells me we'll be off on a fishing excursion soon. Plenty of time for the two of us to continue teasing you."

She stuck her tongue out at him. She couldn't help it. Something in his teasing reverted her to their childhood days. His laugh followed her down the hallway.

So, he was going on their fishing trip. Of course he was. Ted had promised him adventure. He couldn't leave him out of the first adventure they'd had all summer.

She liked Ben, and she liked the thought of the three of them having another adventure. Just like old times. But the thought of his coming on this particular adventure left her unsettled.

She knew why, of course. She'd been daydreaming of green eyes and flowing brown locks since the Fourth of July dance. Still, at night, sometimes her real dreams included a certain pair of dark eyes and a delicious kiss. If a girl didn't feel unsettled at the thought of spending time with both those men together, well, she simply wasn't human.

Chapter Twenty-One

He didn't like the man. Ben's gaze narrowed on Sparrowhawk, who stood next to the supply wagon talking with Ted and Will. Their fishing party had left Lander in the early hours just before sunrise, all on horseback except for Drew and Emma Johnson, who drove the large field wagon containing their tents and food.

From the moment he'd laid eyes on their guide, with his flowing locks and carefully sculpted goatee, something about him rubbed Ben wrong. Could be his Western swagger reminded him too much of Roy. Or the fact he stuck to Jenny's side like a burr on a dog's back. But something about him rang false.

His outfit, for one. Who did he think he fooled with his mountain man get-up? He couldn't be much more than thirty—yet he dressed like Buffalo Bill's long lost brother.

Ben poked a stick at the logs in the campfire, sending a shower of sparks into the air.

"Careful there. You'll ruin my masterpiece." Rob Skivington shot him a grin, then used his own fire stick to steady the log Ben had poked, keeping it from tumbling down onto another.

Now *this* man he liked. He was down-to-earth, genuine. He was . . . Newark.

When they'd found the Skivington's sheep camp late that afternoon, Jenny and Maddie Skivington had flown into each other's arms, with all the crying, hugging, and squealing such a reunion always required of women. Now they sat on a bench across from him, heads together, talking and laughing like a couple of schoolgirls.

On Sparrowhawk's instruction, they'd pitched their camp in a small clearing just over the ridge from the Skivington's sheep wagon. At first, Ben had wondered at the distance, but once Rob drove in his flock to bed down for the night, he understood.

Fifteen hundred bleating, baaing, restless bodies filled the open space around the sheep wagon, leaving its canvas top a lone oasis in the midst of a living mass of smelly gray wool. He was quick to appreciate Sparrowhawk had also pitched their tents upwind of the sheep. No doubt the guide knew his business.

Didn't mean he had to like him.

The three men finished their conversation and drifted over to the fire. Will and Ted upended a couple of logs and used them as seats, while Sparrowhawk dropped cross-legged onto the dirt next to the women.

Was he the only one who noticed how the man brushed a hand along Jenny's leg on the way down? He jabbed at the fire again, causing one well-burnt log to crumble into coals, their red heat slowly cooling to black.

"Ran into a mutual acquaintance of ours a few weeks back, Sparrowhawk," Rob said.

"Oh? Who would that be?"

"That cowboy Jake and his cronies."

"You mean the McCreedy bunch? How in the world did you meet them?" Drew Johnson asked.

"They were part of our welcoming committee when we stopped at Harris' Road Ranch on the way into Lander."

"Not a friendly committee, I take it?" Emma said.

"But Mr. Sparrowhawk took care of them in no time. He was magnificent." Jenny and Sparrowhawk exchanged smiles.

Magnificent, huh?

"You ran into them out here?" Sparrowhawk asked.

"Yep. Said they were hunting a mountain lion. Would it be likely they'd trail a cat this far north?"

Sparrowhawk shrugged. "It's possible if their dogs had a fresh trail. Mountain lions cover a lot of territory."

Rob tilted his head, absently pulling on his beard. "I don't remember them having any dogs. Rosie would have put up a fuss if they had. Could they have been hunting without them?"

"Maybe. Wouldn't do 'em much good, though. Sometimes you can track a cat in the winter if there's snow on the ground, but even then, you'd probably need a dog to flush 'em out. A mountain lion's like a ghost. You won't see it unless it wants you to." Sparrowhawk stretched out a leg and leaned back against the side of the women's bench, inching even closer to Jenny. "I'm guessing if you saw Jake this far north without any hunting dogs, he was making an excuse to get out of work at the ranch."

"Is there a bounty for mountain lion?" Ted asked.

"Three dollars, same as wolves."

Ted turned to Rob. "Have you seen any sign of one? I'd love to get a shot at it."

"Our camp tender saw a few tracks at our last campsite. And we had a kill a couple of nights ago that wasn't like a coyote's. Rosie set up a terrible fuss, and the sheep were sure spooked. But all I found was a pool of blood and a trail in the grass like the body'd been dragged." Rob looked over at Sparrowhawk. "What do you think?"

"Could'a been a lion. Like I said, they're ghosts. Only time you'll hear them is when a female's in heat. Now there's a scream that'll curdle your blood."

Rob and Maddie exchanged a glance across the fire. "Like a woman screaming in mortal agony?" he asked.

"You've heard one? Recently?" Sara's voice came out squeaky. She looked behind her into the dark as if she expected a scream to start up at any minute.

"Months ago." Maddie shuddered. "Thank goodness, we've never heard it again."

"Oh, I'd love to hear it." Jenny's eyes glowed in the firelight. "I hope we see all kinds of wildlife on this trip. I'd love to see a herd of elk or antelope. Maybe a mountain lion or a wolf. Or a bear. Do they have bear in these mountains, Mr. Sparrowhawk?"

"If you see a bear, we'll all be hearing that blood-curdling scream," Will said, prompting a laugh from Ted.

"There are a few bear around. Not many," Sparrowhawk said. "With a party our size, we'll probably never see them. You might happen upon one if you're out hunting alone. Most likely, though, they'll hear us long before we see them and run off."

"Have you ever had to fight off a bear?" Jenny asked.

Sparrowhawk smoothed a hand over his mustache and down his goatee. "No. I've known a few who did, though."

"You've known someone who survived a bear attack?" Jenny's eyes were wide.

Sparrowhawk shook his head. "I've known a few who didn't."

The group fell silent.

Firelight flickered over Sparrowhawk and the women. Was it Ben's imagination, or was their guide now leaning against Jenny's legs? He glanced at Ted to see if he noticed, but he was busy threading a new fly for his fishing kit. Figures. Ted was single-minded when it came to hunting and fishing.

"There's no need to worry, Miss Westraven. I'm here to keep you safe from predators. If you follow my instructions, there'll be nothing to fear." Sparrowhawk's right hand slipped beneath the folds of Jenny's riding skirt. Jenny's eyes widened, telling Ben the man had made contact. The mongrel. Giving the fire a sharp poke, he sent a burning log rolling toward Sparrowhawk's outstretched boot. Quick as a cat, the man pulled his leg out of the way and sat upright.

"Oops. Sorry," Ben said.

He caught Sparrowhawk's gaze and held it. The guide quirked a brow and kicked the log back toward the fire with the heel of his boot, but Ben noticed he made no effort to return to his previous position against Jenny's legs.

Predators, indeed. The only predator Jenny needed to worry about was the one right beside her.

Chapter Twenty-Two

"Are you sure there's one in there?"

"Trust me, Jen. They're there."

Jenny peered into the brown depths pooling beneath the rock she and Ben were perched upon. She couldn't see anything other than rocks lying beneath the surface. "And you'll catch them with that worm? You don't need a fly?"

"There's not a fish on the face of the earth that will pass up the chance of a fat, juicy worm for dinner. Your brother may have finesse in his fishing, but I've brought in my share of trout with just a pole and a worm. Watch."

Ben dropped his bait into the deep, quiet waters at the base of the rock, inches from where the rest of the stream went rushing down the mountain. Jen caught the barest flicker of a shadow before Ben flicked his wrist and pulled a writhing trout from the water.

"See? A worm will do the trick every time."

"He's not very big." The fish's speckled body barely spanned Ben's hand.

"He's big enough for the pan. Give me a few minutes to catch five or six like him, and I'll have more than enough to contribute to whatever the others catch."

Early that morning, Sparrowhawk had led Will, Ted, and Sara on a fishing excursion to a nearby lake. Jenny chose not to join them, wanting to spend time with Maddie. She wasn't a bit sorry, either. She, Ben, and the Johnsons had followed the sheep out to pasture, learning first-hand how Maddie and Rob spent their days.

Her imagination had pictured Rob and Maddie, like the sheepherders of some pastoral painting, looking out over a flock of fifty or so sheep quietly scattered across a grassy meadow. The reality of a herd of 1500 was far noisier, smellier, and dirtier than she'd anticipated, but she wouldn't have missed it for the world.

She and Maddie spent the morning catching up. She told Maddie about Grace and the Parkhursts and her visits to the Indian schools. Much as she loved Sara, she'd missed Maddie's gentle wisdom.

After a picnic lunch, the sun grew warm, and conversation lagged. Drew pillowed his head on one of the many rocks in the area and promptly fell asleep. At the same time, Maddie and Emma discussed recipes and household tips they'd found in Maddie's magazine. When Rob offered Ben his fishing pole and told him of this nearby stream, Jenny had jumped at the opportunity to follow along, eager for a chance to explore.

Ben pulled a second trout from the stream and added it to his stringer.

"He's not much bigger than your first one."

Ben shrugged. "Mountain trout rarely grow big. The winters are too cold."

"When do I get a turn?"

"You mean they taught fishing at your fancy finishing school? And here I thought it was all music and dancing."

"You know very well where I learned to fish. At Cousin Harland's, right along with you and Ted."

"I remember fishing with Ted, but all I remember from you was your falling into the pond and running home crying to Aunt Edna."

"I was eight years old. Of course I cried. Besides, I didn't fall. I jumped in, and that was entirely your fault."

"My fault? I wasn't even there."

"Exactly. When Aunt Edna told you to take me fishing, you and Ted rowed me out to that rock in the middle of the cow pond and left me there while you explored upstream. How was I supposed to get out of there if I hadn't jumped in?"

"We'd have come back for you."

"Sure, you would."

Ben chuckled.

Jenny grinned at him. This was nice, like the old days at Mr. Goddard's law office. Like Tuesday night dinners at Aunt Bethany's. She hadn't realized how much she'd missed Ben until now.

"Face it. You're not giving me a turn because you know I'll catch the biggest fish, like the year I won the fishing contest."

"You can't call what you did fishing. Cousin Harland baited your hook and let you hold a pole. You happened to get one on your line but screamed so much when you saw it, Cousin Harland had to reel it in. If you ask me, Harland won the contest. You just held a pole."

"That does it." She reached over and grabbed the fishing rod. "From now on, we're taking turns. We'll fish for one hour, and the person with the largest fish wins the prize."

"What prize?"

"The prize of being the best. Whoever wins gets the satisfaction of seeing the other one bow to her—"

"You mean, him."

". . . and proclaim her the Champion Fisherwoman—"

"Man."

"Of . . . what did Rob call this creek?"

"Brown's Creek."

"Of Brown's Creek."

"And you'll bait your own hook?"

Jenny looked at the tin can full of grubworms Ben had

scraped from the moist earth under a rotting log. The thought of touching one turned her stomach, but she wasn't letting Ben get the better of her.

"I will bait my own hook."

He handed her the can of worms. "They're all yours."

Trying her best not to shudder, Jenny reached in and grabbed the first worm she could find. As quickly as she could, she speared the hook through its body and wiped her fingers on the rock.

"You might want to fasten that worm a little better."

"It looks like it's on there just fine to me."

"Suit yourself." Ben held up both hands. "Just thought you might want a few tips. No skin off my nose if you lose all your worms to the water."

She hesitated. He might have a point. "So show me."

Ben took her hook and bent the worm so the hook could pass through its body a second time. "That'll hold it better and keep the fish from stealing it."

It also got Ben touching her worm instead of her, but she wasn't about to mention it.

"Thank you." She leaned over the water's edge and dropped the hook into the deep area just below the rock where Ben had fished earlier. "Come on, fishies. Take the bait."

Ben stretched back on the rock beside her, hands hooked behind his head. She jiggled her rod a bit, scanning the water for shadows. Ben's fish hadn't taken this long.

Wait. Was that a bite?

She waited until she felt another tiny pull on her line before bringing it up. Nothing but an empty hook.

"What happened?"

"You didn't set the hook."

"I pulled it up as soon as I felt something."

"It's more of a flick than a pull." Ben sat up. "Here. Let me show you."

He pulled another worm from the can and quickly baited her

hook. Handing her the rod, he wrapped his arm around her, guiding her hand as she dropped the line back in the water. This was better. A worm on her hook she didn't have to touch, and Ben's arm around her. Very nice.

She leaned into him, noticing he didn't back away.

"There. Do you feel that?"

She most certainly did.

Oh. Did he mean a fish? Ben's hand closed around hers, and he jerked on the rod with a flick of his wrist. The pull on the other end intensified.

"Did we get one?"

"Pull it up and see."

She pulled up the rod but almost lost hold of it when the writhing body of a trout hit the surface of the water.

"Careful there." Ben reached out to grab the line, unhooking their catch and holding it up for her to see. It was twice as big as any Ben had caught.

"I knew I could catch a bigger one than you." She couldn't help crowing, just a bit.

"Hold on, now. You didn't catch this one. You didn't put the bait on, you didn't set the hook, and you didn't bring it in." He ticked his points off on his fingers, one by one. "If anyone gets credit for this fish, it should be me."

"That's not fair. I helped catch it. You know I did."

Ben grinned. "See? It's Cousin Harland all over again."

Leave it to Ben to take the fun out of a perfectly delightful catch. "Fine." She held out her hand. "I'll do this one on my own. No more tips from you."

He handed over the fishing rod with a slight bow. "Here you are. From here on out, my lips are sealed."

She dug into the bait can, pulled out a worm, and jabbed it onto her line, careful to hook it twice like Ben had shown her. It wasn't so bad if you didn't allow yourself to think about it. Hopping off the boulder, she set off down the stream.

"Where're you headed?" Ben had already stretched out on the boulder again. He pushed himself up onto his elbows.

She held up a finger to silence him. "I thought your lips were sealed."

He chuckled. "Suit yourself. Be careful you don't fall in." With that, he lay down and closed his eyes.

Jenny walked along the rushing stream, looking for deeper water. She finally found what she wanted twenty yards downstream—a deep, quiet pool on the backside of a row of boulders, sheltered by a line of willows. Perfect, if it weren't on the other side of the stream. But if she could make her way onto that large boulder in the middle, surely she could reach the pool with her line.

The stream ran fast, but not deep. Hiking her skirt up with one hand and holding her rod out for balance with the other, she carefully picked her way across the rocks to the boulder. Once there, she laid her rod across its rocky top and pulled herself up. It wasn't as wide as she'd anticipated, but she needn't be here long.

She cast into the quiet depths below the willows and breathed a prayer. Minutes passed. Then a gentle tug. She flicked her wrist, and silver flashed as the trout broke the water. Jenny squealed as the trout jumped, almost pulling her and the rod into the water. She wasn't about to let it get away.

"Sit down! I'm coming to help."

She glanced over at the bank to see Ben running her way. No. She would do this on her own. Planting her feet, she pulled again. The fish arced out of the water straight toward her, causing her to duck back. This time she really was falling.

She braced herself for icy water and hit solid flesh instead. Ben wrapped his arms around her, holding her above the current. All would have been well if she hadn't still been clutching the fishing pole. The weight of the trout threw it in a pendulum around them. She heard a slap and a grunt. Ben loosened his grip on her, and she slid knee-deep into the water. She looked up to see Ben and the fish, cheek to cheek, both wearing identical expressions—eyes bulging, mouths gaping. She dissolved in laughter.

"You look . . . you look . . ." She barely registered the frigid water pulling at her skirts and seeping down her boots. "If you could see your face!" She bent over, gasping for breath.

Ben grabbed the pole from her and tried to untangle himself. The fish, played out, hung limply from the line, but one glance at its gaping mouth sent her back into paroxysms of laughter. By this time, tears were streaming down her face. She struggled to stay upright.

Ben grabbed her around the waist, lifting her with one arm like a sack of wheat. At the water's edge, he dropped her in a heap. She lay there a few minutes trying, with little success, to gain control. The minute she thought she'd finished, she'd remember Ben and the fish, cheek-to-cheek, and begin again. Finally, she rolled over and sat up, pushing back her curls.

Ben stood over her, holding the pole and fish. She swiped away the tears pooling under her lashes.

"You have to admit it was funny," she said.

"Do I? Let's slap you in the face with a trout and see how funny you find it." But Ben grinned in spite of his testy words, then reached out a hand and helped her to her feet. He held up the fish. "He's a beauty, though. I'd say he's close to three pounds."

"The biggest one today, right?"

"So far. I'll have my work cut out for me if I'm going to beat you."

Jenny checked the watch on her shirtwaist. "No time for that. We said the largest fish caught within an hour, and it's been an hour. We'll count the one you said I *didn't* catch as yours."

"That's the way you're going to play it, is it? All right. I'll concede the victory this time, but only because I've had about all the excitement I can take for the day. Why in the world did you stand up on that boulder? You could have killed yourself if your head hit a rock."

"I'd have probably done more damage to my backside than anything. Nevertheless, thank you for catching me." Now she'd won, she could afford to be magnanimous. She tilted her head. "Well? I'm waiting."

Ben wrinkled his brow. "For what?"

"My prize. I'm the winner. I get the prize."

"Very well." He bent at the waist in an elaborate bow. "I bow to you, Oh Champion Fisherwoman of Brown's Creek. Satisfied?"

She gave him a regal nod and held out her hand for him to kiss. His lips brushed softly against her hand, making her realize what a fright she was. In the excitement of the fall and all her laughter, her hair had fallen from its pins so it was more down than up. Her skirt and petticoats were a sodden mess, clinging to her thighs and calves.

She pulled at the heavy broadcloth. "I suppose we should head back to camp to get out of our wet clothes."

Though Ben's were hardly wet. Because of his knee-high boots, other than a few places on his trousers and shirt, he was none the worse for wear.

"It'll be rough walking all that way in that skirt. If you'd rather, you could wrap up in my duster. It may be a bit big, but it'll cover you until your clothes dry. Shouldn't take too long with this sunshine and dry air."

"Oh, yes. Let's do that." She wasn't ready for the afternoon to end, and the thought of a thirty-minute walk in wet, heavy skirts did not appeal.

They headed back to the first boulder where they'd left their things. Once there, Ben handed her his duster then went to the water's edge, where he pulled up his string of fish.

"I'll head downstream and clean these while you change. If you spread your skirt out on those bushes, I'm sure it'll dry in no time."

"Thank you."

She pulled off her boots first, tipping them over so the water could run out. How good it felt to be out of those soggy woolen socks. She stood, relishing the feel of soft grass between her toes. Next, she stepped out of her skirt and petticoat and pulled Ben's duster around her. Designed to fall at Ben's calves, its length brushed her ankles.

She wished the coat had a belt, but beggars weren't choosers. She wrung as much water from her clothes as she could, then spread her skirt, socks, and petticoat over the bushes before scrambling atop the boulder.

She leaned back on its flat surface, basking in the sun's warmth on her face and toes. Eyes closed, she let the sound of the rushing water soothe her.

This was living. She never wanted to go back to Lander.

BEN FOUND A FLAT ROCK WHERE HE GUTTED AND CLEANED THE fish. Not his favorite part of fishing, but well worth it for the taste of fresh trout grilled on an open fire. He wrapped the four they'd caught in ferns he found by the creek and set them in his creel.

They might not bring in as big a catch as the others, but what they had was respectable given the amount of effort.

On his part anyway. Jenny certainly put forth the effort. He shook his head at the memory of her teetering atop the boulder. That girl couldn't even fish without causing trouble.

She was a good sport, though. No other woman he knew would have dissolved into laughter after being dropped into that icy water. Nell wouldn't have spoken to him for a week. But then, Nell wouldn't have gone fishing in the first place.

He packed his fishing kit and headed upstream, letting out a quick holler to warn Jenny, just in case. As he rounded the corner, he saw her perched atop the boulder, bright curls cascading down her back and bare toes peeping from beneath his duster. He wasn't prepared for what the sight of those bare feet would do to his thoughts.

Swallowing hard, he tore his gaze from the enticing view of a disheveled Jenny, forcing his mind to other images. A pile of fish guts did the trick.

"Aren't you coming up?" She patted the surface of the rock beside her.

He climbed up, careful to keep a proper distance between them.

"Isn't this glorious?" She swept her hand in an arc, indicating the stream, the aspens, the sunshine.

He kept his eyes trained on her face.

Yes.

Glorious.

"Wouldn't it be wonderful to build a cabin over there in that open area and live here always?"

He could almost picture it, nestled against the rocky backdrop, Jenny in the doorway welcoming him home.

Hold on. *Jenny* in the doorway? Shouldn't he be picturing Nell? Imagine living year-round with Jenny and her penchant for trouble. He should be shuddering in his boots. Except . . . he wasn't.

"You'd be bored within a week's time."

"How can you say that? How could anyone be bored with all this? I never want to leave."

"Admit it. You were bored after about an hour with the sheep."

"No, I wasn't. Not really. It's just . . . I've been waiting all summer for Ted to bring me to the mountains. I want to explore everything. Think of the fun we'd have missed if we'd stayed in the pasture. Oh, and Ben," she laid a hand on his thigh, sending a jolt of heat down his leg. Did she have any idea what her touch did to him? "Promise me you'll keep our adventure secret. This part of it, at least." She glanced toward her skirt, hanging on the bush behind them and pulled his duster close around her body. She must have noticed her bare feet were sticking out because a flush crept up her cheeks, and she tucked her legs beneath her.

"Sounds like the promise I make at the end of all our adventures. At least the ones where we don't get caught."

Her dimples came out at that one, and he was tempted to reach out and poke a finger into one of them, the way he did when they were younger, and he'd wanted to hear her squeal.

"Should I be afraid of your turning to blackmail?"

"I do own a fair amount of your secrets."

"At this point, it's probably safe to tell the majority of them, but this one . . . ." She let the words trail off. "Not that we've done anything to be ashamed of, but if Grace or Mrs. Parkhurst were to get wind of the fact I sat unchaperoned with a man, even one I have no romantic interest in whatsoever, with only a duster to cover me. Well. No more adventures for me. And I'm barely getting started on the things I want to do out here. I don't want this to be my last camping excursion. And I'd love to see a ranch —a real working ranch during a roundup. Not an exhibition like they had on the 4th, but the real thing, with branding and everything. But if Mrs. Parkhurst should hear about this?"

She didn't continue. She didn't have to. He'd only met Mrs. Parkhurst once, but from what he'd seen, she was cut from the same cloth as Jenny's Aunt Matilda. Neither woman had a clue how to handle the whirlwind that was Jenny, though they both believed it their God-given duty to try. He hoped they'd be unsuccessful in changing her—at least too much.

"Did I tell you I own a cattle ranch?" Now, why had he blurted that out? But he knew why. To see those blue eyes of hers as they were now—wide, sparkling, and fastened on him as if he were suddenly the most interesting man in the world. He wasn't going to lie. That 'no romantic interest whatsoever' had stung a little. None? Whatsoever? Unless he was mistaken, they *had* shared a kiss.

"Ben Bennett. You bought a ranch and didn't tell me?"

"I *inherited* a ranch as part of my father's estate. Yes, ma'am. You're looking at the owner of the Flying B Ranch, 960 acres of the best cattle country in western South Dakota, at least that's what my ranch manager tells me."

"Is that where you lived before you came here?"

"No. I lived with my step-family in Lead. But I visited the ranch. I didn't see a roundup, but I did see one of the cowhands break a wild horse. Oh, and I got to help drive some cattle."

"And you haven't told me this until now?"

"It hasn't come up."

"Come up? If I owned a cattle ranch, I'd bring it up. Hello." She reached her hand out as if to shake his hand. "I'm Jenny Westraven, and by the way, I own a ranch. Yep. Jenny Westraven, ranch owner, that's me."

He laughed. "I'll keep that in mind next time I introduce myself."

"Was it as wonderful as we always dreamed it would be when you and me and Ted were kids? All we ever wanted was to head out West and be cowboys. Remember how you and Ted spent that whole summer trying to ride Cousin Harland's ornery old mule? You'd have contests to see who could hold on the longest without getting bucked off."

"And you got mad because we wouldn't let you try, so you went out to the pasture and climbed onto one of Aunt Edna's cows. Only what you didn't know was Harland had put the cows in that far pasture to spend time with his stud bull." He could remember him and Ted running toward the sounds of Jenny's screams and the terror he'd felt when they'd arrived to see her flying high in the air off the back of a cow and straight into the path of an angry bull. They'd leaped the fence, shouting and waving their arms to distract the bull, but in the end, Cousin Harland saved the day by throwing a rope around the bull's neck and pulling him to a stop.

"Your cousin was my hero that day, though I admit, I had a bit of a crush on him all summer. I was determined to grow up and marry a cowboy, and, yes, Harland was merely a farmer, but he was very handy with a rope. I figured he was about as close as I would get to a cowboy in New Jersey."

"Well, he's married to someone else now and has three children. I'm afraid he didn't wait for you."

Jenny heaved a sigh. "The good ones always go first." Then she chuckled. "I'd forgotten all about riding that old cow. Why is it all your memories of me are so unflattering?"

"Not all of them." The words slipped out before he could catch them. It was the truth, though. Especially this memory. This moment. He turned to see her gazing at him in surprise, a slight flush staining her cheeks. She was beautiful.

So beautiful.

His gaze dropped to her soft red lips. He couldn't help but lean in closer.

What was he doing? This was Jenny. Jenny! A woman with no romantic interest in him whatsoever. So why did he have this desire to pull her into his arms and taste her once again?

Think fish guts, Ben.

Picking up a twig from the rock beside him, he broke off small pieces, tossing them one by one into the stream below.

"So why aren't you still there?" Jenny's voice broke into his thoughts.

"Where?"

"On your ranch. Or with your step-family."

His mind flashed to the events of his last night in Lead.

He picked up another stick, larger this time, and heaved it into the stream. "I'd rather not talk about it."

After a few moments of silence, he glanced over to find Jenny studying him like a specimen under a microscope.

"What?"

"I just realized something. I know nothing whatsoever about your family, other than Grandma Janssen, of course. You used to brag about your father all the time, tell us how someday you were going out West to live with him. It's *all* you ever talked about that first summer we met.

"Ted and I always figured you were making up stories. Kind of like we did when we pretended our parents weren't really dead —that someday they would come for us and it would all be like it was before. But yours wasn't a story. That next summer, when we came to Aunt Bethany's, you were gone. Grandma Janssen said you'd gone to live with your father."

Ben studied the water bubbling and crashing over rocks below them. He didn't want to think about that summer.

"That was the longest summer I ever spent at Aunt Bethany's because Ted got all ball crazy and would go off to play baseball, and I had to spend all my time with Mary O'Reilly. Not that she's not nice enough, but she has about as much aptitude for adventures as a turnip. All she ever wanted to do was play house and dress up her dolls." Jenny made a face. "But then the next summer, you were back, and you never mentioned your father again." She fell silent, still eyeing him dubiously.

"Your point?"

"My point is, I always thought I knew everything there is to know about you, but now I realize I don't. I don't know anything about your father and your family in South Dakota. I didn't even know you had a stepfamily. It's like a whole side of your life I know nothing about."

He heaved a sigh. "It's not some deep, dark secret or anything. They've just never been a big part of my life."

"Why not?"

"My mother died when I was a baby. Shortly after, my father got gold fever and went out to South Dakota along with half the country back then. But unlike most, he stayed there and made his fortune."

"He struck gold?"

"No. His mine didn't even turn a profit until the past five years or so. He made most of his money through other ventures —hotels, boarding houses . . . and ranching."

"So why didn't you live with him?"

He shrugged. "I was too young at first. You can't work a mine and care for a baby at the same time. And Grandma Janssen wasn't willing to leave Newark. So he left me with her with the idea that when I got old enough, I'd come and join him. He came back to visit some. Those visits were the highlights of my childhood. Each year I'd think . . . this time . . . this time I'll go back with him, but for one reason or another, that never happened.

"Then, the summer after I turned ten, he sent for me." He hated thinking about that summer but somehow felt compelled to continue. "I'd caught the measles that winter and been pretty sick. Maybe they thought they'd lose me. I remember Grandma saying it would be healthier for me to live out West. All I know for certain was I was glad I got sick."

"Why didn't you stay?"

He blew out another heavy sigh. "It's complicated."

"We've got time."

He forked his fingers through his hair. How could he find the words to describe the disillusionment of that summer? "I didn't have a father like all the other kids—at least not one that hung around. So I had this dream of how it would be. In my mind, my father lived in this little cabin up in the woods next to his mine, and every day he'd go into that mine hoping to make enough money that someday I could come be with him.

"I pictured myself living at the mine with him. Maybe cooking for him, though how I thought I would do that, I don't know. I was a kid. I didn't even know how to boil water. But I had this whole scene imagined in my mind of how I'd go down in the mine with him and help him, and at the end of the day, he'd clap me on the back and say, 'Son, I don't know how I managed without you.'" Ben swallowed hard. Had his voice just cracked? He couldn't bring himself to look at Jenny. Instead, he gazed off down the stream and continued on.

"Well, reality isn't anything like our dreams, but at ten, I wasn't prepared to learn that. When I got to South Dakota, I found out my father didn't live in a little cabin next to his mine. He lived in a huge boarding house in town and spent most of his days managing his hotels and other properties. I never even saw his mine that summer. And he wasn't living all alone. He'd remarried . . . had a stepson the same age as me and two other kids—my half brother and sister—Lucas and Letty."

"You didn't know this?"

He missled a rock across the stream, striking the trunk of a pine on the other side. "Everyone seems to think I *should* have known, but somehow I'd missed that bit of information. They got married when I was pretty young, so maybe everyone just assumed I knew. I knew *about* them, of course. Father mentioned their names all the time in his letters, but I thought they were simply his housekeeper and her kids. I had no idea they were his family."

He stole a glance at Jenny, who sat with her knees tucked up under her chin, arms wrapped around her legs, staring out across the water. In his over-sized duster, she looked more like his childhood playmate and less like the sophisticated debutante she'd become.

She turned to meet his gaze, blue eyes solemn. "I know what that's like . . . when the dream meets reality. It's hard enough to handle as an adult. I can't imagine what it must have been like as a child."

"Yeah. Well, I didn't handle it well at all. I was so angry . . . at my father, at this new family, but especially at Roy, my stepbrother, who I felt had taken my place. I hated him, and believe me, the feeling was mutual. I can't begin to tell you how many fist fights the two of us had that summer. Finally, Father sat me down and told me he was sending me back to Grandma's. Said it would be best for all of us."

"He sent you away? That's so unfair!"

"No. He was right. If I'd stayed, with all that anger, Roy and I would have ended up killing each other."

She gave him a half-smile and shook her head. "And this time?"

"This time wasn't much better, though at first, we acted like adults. It didn't help that my father made me his sole heir. Of all the lame-brained ways to handle a family rift, that one tops them all. Oh, we limped along for a while. I thought maybe we could make a go of it . . . learn to live with each other, but then Lucas pulled this schoolboy prank, and I lost my temper. When Roy came between us, we were back to being ten-year-olds all over again."

She reached up and traced the nearly-healed scar on his cheekbone, featherlight. "Is that how you got this?"

"'Fraid so. I knew then it wasn't going to work out any better than it had fourteen years ago . . . that I needed to do what my father had done. Get *me* out of the picture. So I left. It's not like I need to live there in order to supervise Father's properties. He hired good managers. They practically run everything themselves."

"But what about your family?"

"They're fine." He thought about Lucas, so young and lost and angry. "They will be anyway. Besides, I'm not the one they need. They need my father, but . . . he's gone."

Silence stretched around them. He tossed a few more twigs into the stream and watched the current take them.

"What now? Will you go back to Newark?"

"Eventually. I want to see and do out some things out here first."

"And Mr. Goddard?"

"Gave me a leave of absence, time to sort things out with my inheritance and all. I have until the first of the year to decide if I'll go back."

Jenny's eyes widened. "You might not?"

He shrugged. "I don't know yet."

"Well, wherever you decide to stay, they'll be lucky to have you. You're the best lawyer I know."

He looked down at her, so earnest, so full of confidence on his behalf. "Thank you."

She tilted her head. "For what?"

"For . . . everything. For spending the afternoon with me. For listening. For believing in me."

She reached out and placed her hand over his. "Always. I'll always believe in you. You know that, right? Friends for life?"

The urge to kiss her came back in spades, and this time he didn't try to squelch it. Instead, he leaned forward and brushed his lips against hers, ever so softly. He'd meant it to be the briefest of kisses, a quick touch and then done, but once there, his lips lingered. Slowly, he traced the contours of her mouth with his tongue. Her lips parted, and he leaned in closer. She tasted of sunshine and laughter and everything Jenny. He reached up to trace the velvet soft skin by her ear just as she tore her lips from his.

"They're coming," she gasped.

Before his mind registered what she'd said, she'd vaulted off the rock and disappeared with her clothes into the thicket of alders that lined the stream.

Then he heard it. Tinkling sheep bells and voices calling their names. He slid off the rock and gathered his kit and fishing rod. With a quick glance at the alders, he headed toward the voices and gave an answering shout. With any luck, he could stall them. Give Jenny time to dress.

A few seconds later, he met Maddie and Emma on the path.

"We thought you might be close," Maddie said. "But, where's Jenny? Isn't she still with you?"

"She got pretty wet trying to bring in a trout earlier. She's up the creek a ways drying off. I expect she'll be along soon." In these situations, he'd learned to stick as close to the truth as possible. "I'll be glad to wait for her and bring her along when she's ready."

"Oh, no. You go on along with the men. We'll wait," Emma said. "I've already been lax in my duties. Mrs. Parkhurst would throw a fit to know I let Jenny spend an entire afternoon unchaperoned. I'm sure she'd have nothing to worry about. You two are such old friends."

Old friends who apparently liked to kiss. Too much. But Emma didn't need to know that. No one did. Especially not Mrs. Parkhurst. And from here on out, he needed to keep his distance from Jenny Westraven. That was the only sure way to keep them both out of trouble.

Chapter Twenty-Three

Two days later, Ben stood on the bank of a mountain lake, watching dawn break across the ridge of peaks on the far side of the water. A wall of shadows inched its way down the face of the serrated gray rocks as the sun rose behind him.

He breathed in the crisp mountain air and slowly released it, the quiet weaving a spell of peace around him.

Their group had camped the previous night beneath the tall branches of a pine forest that reached the edge of this sparkling blue lake. Surely there was no bed in existence to rival a bed of fragrant pine needles. He'd slept better last night than he had in months.

He didn't know why, but he felt God here. It was as if, away from the bustle of the city and the hectic hum of everyday life, he could finally hear Him speak. Feel His presence. Despite the fact he'd failed miserably with his family. Despite the kiss that never should've happened. Despite his confusion about where he should go, what he should do. He felt at peace. No matter what the future brought, for this moment, at this time, he was meant to be here.

"Was there ever a more beautiful morning?"

Ben turned to see Jenny walking toward him, swinging an

empty pail. Her golden curls shone like a halo in the bright morning sun. They'd barely spoken since the kiss. She'd arrived back at camp with Maddie and Emma shortly after he had, hair and skirt in place. Since then, they hadn't been alone. He knew he needed to apologize . . . again . . . but didn't know how to bring it up.

Taking the coward's path, he ignored the issue. "Need more water?"

"No, I'm off to pick some berries. I saw some bushes back by the trail where we came in yesterday. I thought they'd be my contribution to breakfast."

Will and Ted had left early to fish the streams that fed into the lake, promising them mountain trout for breakfast. Drew and Sparrowhawk had followed shortly after with their rifles, in search of something more substantial to feed the group for dinner. He could already smell the bacon and potatoes Emma and Sara were frying back at camp. Maybe he should pitch in as well.

"I'll help you if you'd like. Have you developed a taste for mountain berries?"

Jenny flushed a little. "Not really, but I heard Mr. Sparrowhawk say he'd love to have some cackleberries for breakfast."

Oh. The mission to pick berries soured a little, but since he'd committed, he followed her up the path.

They reached a thicket of silver-colored bushes laden with bright red berries. "I don't know what cackleberries are," she said. "But these are the only berries I've seen."

"Are you sure they're safe to eat?"

"Yes. Maddie had some like these near their camp, and she told me she made them into jam."

He pulled what looked like a ripe berry off the bush and took a small bite. "Pretty tart if you ask me."

Jenny popped one into her mouth. "This one's sweet." She chewed for a minute, then puckered. "No, wait, maybe not."

"So do we pick them or let them be?"

"Let's pick some anyway," she said. "Maybe Emma will know how to sweeten them."

They worked in silence, their harvest slow due to the sharp thorns protruding from the bushes. He should say something. Clear the air. They couldn't just go on ignoring that kiss.

"Oh, Ben. Come and see." Ben peeked around the bush, expecting to see her entranced by a patch of wildflowers or maybe a chipmunk. Instead, his heart stuttered at the sight of her on her knees, hand outstretched toward a baby bear.

"Jen. No! Stay ba—"

A roar smothered his words of warning. The mother bear hovered no more than fifteen yards away, clawing at the ground and popping her teeth. Jenny screamed and staggered to her feet.

"Don't move!" He called. "Don't even breathe."

With a shout, he charged around the bushes waving his arms, hoping to distract the bear's attention. He picked up the half-full berry bucket and threw it with all his might. Berries scattered in all directions as the pail glanced off the bear's shoulder and hit the ground.

Instead of retreating, the mother bear came closer, stopping only ten feet away. Her cub scampered over beside her. With a low, menacing growl, Mama Bear swung her huge front paw, kicking up dirt and leaves. Ben searched the ground for a rock, a stick, anything he could throw. Maybe if he was threatening enough, she would leave, now her cub was safe.

Off to the side, Jenny slowly backed up, but her foot caught on the hem of her dress. Her arms flailed as she struggled for balance, drawing the bear's attention. The animal rose on its back feet, roaring and pawing the air, then dropped and ran straight at her. Jenny let out a piercing scream and turned to run.

Without thinking, Ben launched himself, tackling Jenny to the ground. Using his body as a shield, he braced himself. He felt his heart pounding in time with Jenny's as timed slowed. He could smell the dank, rancid odor of the bear, a smell he would forever after associate with fear. Then the first blow hit, so powerful it almost turned him over.

The growling was in his ear now, the heat of the animal's breath tickling the bare flesh on his neck. He steeled himself. Please, God. Let me stay strong.

As the bear's teeth closed around his ear, he heard a sharp crack. Searing, ripping pain tore through his shoulder, then the bear's full weight fell on him. He struggled to take in air, managing only short, quick breaths as he tried in vain to push against it. If he could barely breathe, he could only imagine what Jenny must be feeling, pinned beneath both his weight and the bear's.

A shout, the sound of running feet, and then, blessedly, someone pulled the suffocating weight from on top of him, and he was able to roll to the side. As if in a fog, he watched Sparrowhawk put down his rifle and bend over Jenny's inert body.

Why was she so still? Sparrowhawk turned her over and lifted her into his arms. Her head lolled back against his shoulder, her skin paperwhite against the leather of the guide's jacket. Oh, God. Had he suffocated her?

"Is she breathing?" He heard someone ask, then realized that desperate, strangled voice was his.

Drew came into focus then. Kneeling, he placed two fingers against the translucent skin of Jenny's throat.

"She's alive," he said. "I think she just fainted."

Ben closed his eyes and let out a pent-up breath.

Someone screaming Jenny's name brought him back to the scene. Sara came running through the trees, followed closely by her sister.

"What happened? We heard shots. Oh, merciful heavens, she's not dead?"

"No. Fainted. She's starting to come around."

Sure enough, Jenny's eyelashes fluttered. A faint flush of color came back into her cheeks as she looked up into Sparrowhawk's face.

"Wha—what happened?"

"You and Ben were attacked by a bear," Drew said. "But we shot him in time. At least, Sparrowhawk did. My shot went wide, but Nick's dropped him like a stone."

Jenny smiled up at Sparrowhawk, like the sunrise bursting through clouds. "You saved me," she said in a voice rich with wonder.

Her words hit like a blow to the gut.

Had he done nothing?

Well, to be honest, he hadn't done much. In fact, if Sparrowhawk and Drew hadn't happened along, he and Jenny might both be dead. It was Cousin Harland and the bull all over again. The man with the skills saved the day, and he ended up the fool.

He pushed to his feet. Something wet trickled down his cheek, and he brushed it away. Good Lord, he wasn't crying, was he? He looked down at his fingers, struggling to come to terms with what he saw. Red. Sticky. *Blood.* Where had that—? And then it hit him.

Pain.

Deep. Penetrating. Up his left shoulder and across his neck. His right ear burned, and his head pounded. Why hadn't he noticed it before?

"Ben!" Jenny screamed his name. Five faces with varying degrees of shock and horror looked at him.

"Good God, man. You're a bloody mess," Drew said, coming toward him. "Sit down before you fall down." He grabbed him by the arm and led him to a nearby rock, forcing him to sit. "Someone get a blanket. I think he's going into shock."

The ringing in his head that had been a constant since they rolled the bear off him intensified as the pain increased. The world around him spun and pitched him forward into darkness.

~

Jenny paced outside Drew and Emma's tent. She couldn't shake the image of Ben's face, webbed in trails of blood. And when he'd slumped forward, unconscious, the back of his jacket was solid crimson.

It was all her fault.

How could she have been so foolish? She knew a mother bear was most ferocious when she thought her cubs were threatened. Yet when she'd spied that cub by the bushes, all she wanted was to get closer.

Now Ben could be dying.

When would she ever learn to think before she acted? How many more people had to get hurt because of her? She swiped a tear with the back of her hand. She couldn't imagine a world without Ben in it. He had to live. He had to. Please, God? Though why she thought God would listen to her now when he never had before, was beyond her. Still. It didn't hurt to try. She'd try anything, do anything if only Ben would live.

Emma stepped out of the tent with a bowl of bloody water. Seeing Jenny, she set the bowl on the ground and came over and wrapped her in her arms.

"Have you been out here this whole time?" she asked. "After the shock you had, you should be resting."

"I couldn't. Not without knowing how Ben is doing. Oh, Emma. Please, please tell me he's going to be all right."

Emma pulled a handkerchief from her sleeve and wiped at Jenny's tears. "He's going to be fine. Thankfully, Sparrowhawk killed the bear quickly and stopped the attack in time. He's got several ugly scratches and some bite marks, but we're going to get him stitched up, and you'll see. He'll be up and around in no time."

She slumped in relief. "Can I see him?"

"That's probably not a good idea. Drew gave him enough whiskey to put an Irishman under the table. He's talking kind of crazy right now. Give him time to sleep it off, and then we'll see."

A crash and a low moan came from inside the tent. Emma turned, worry lines creasing her forehead.

"Are you sure there's nothing I can do to help?"

"No, honey. Drew and Mr. Sparrowhawk can handle it, but I need to get back in there with some fresh water." She patted Jenny's cheek. "You go lie down. I promise. Ben's going to be all right."

Turning, Jenny made her way slowly back to her own tent. But once there, she couldn't rest. Instead, she went over to the washbasin and looked at herself in the small mirror she and Sara had hung there. As she suspected, she was a mess—face streaked with dirt and tears, leaves and twigs caught in her riotous mess of curls. Glad for something to do, she poured cold water into the basin and splashed it on her face.

She wanted to wash away all of it—the dirt, the mess, but most of all, the memory of those terrifying moments when she thought they were both going to die. Hands trembling, she splashed the cold water against her face, again and again, but still the horror of those moments—those dark, mind-numbing moments where she couldn't move, couldn't breathe—haunted her. What must it have been like for Ben, feeling his flesh torn and mauled? The sound of his moans echoed through her mind.

Two days ago when they'd sat by that mountain stream, sharing that sweet and way-too-short kiss, life had seemed so simple. These mountains were beautiful and full of promise. Now everything seemed tainted. Ben was hurt. And it was all her fault. Once again, her thoughtless actions had hurt someone she deeply cared about. Would she never learn to think before she acted?

She couldn't do this. She couldn't stay in this tent alone. Scrubbing her face dry with a towel, she quickly changed into a clean shirtwaist, her fingers fumbling with the buttons. After what seemed an eternity, she finally accomplished the task and turned back toward the mirror to survey her hair. Putting it to rights would take forever, and she had to get out of this tent. She pulled a few leaves and twigs from the mess, then turned to go. She doubted the others would care.

She found the group by the campfire, eating breakfast. Sara saw her first and rushed to her side, brushing back a few of her curls and cupping her face.

"Jenny, honey. Are you sure you should be up already? You are still so pale."

"I can't rest. All I can think of are the whuffing sounds of that bear—" A tremor rocked her body.

Sara wrapped an arm around her shoulders and led her to the makeshift bench by the fire. "Sit here. I'll get you some coffee. Do you think you could eat some breakfast?"

Jenny started to shake her head, but the smell of bacon, fried potatoes, and fish made her stomach rumble. "Well, maybe . . . but only a small plate."

Will and Ted had returned with a long string of fish shortly after the encounter with the bear. After seeing the dead bear and hearing the story, Ted had pulled her into his arms and held her for a long time. Neither had said anything, but she knew he'd been as shaken as she.

Now, he and Will and Sparrowhawk sat across the fire from her, each working on a heaping plate of food.

"Drew tells us Ben is going to be fine," Ted said.

Jenny nodded.

"You both had a close call there. I still can't believe you'd be so fluff-headed as to get between a cub and its mother."

Will elbowed Ted in the ribs. "What he's trying to say, with such brotherly concern is, didn't you hear anything Sparrowhawk told us about mother bears?"

"I didn't think about its having a mother. It was so cute, just sitting there looking at me. All I wanted to do was get a closer look, and before I had time to think at all, the mother was already running at me." Jen shuddered again. "If Ben hadn't been there . . . and you, Mr. Sparrowhawk . . ." Her throat closed around her words. She blinked rapidly to keep the tears at bay.

Sara pushed a coffee cup into her hands and gave her shoulder a squeeze. "We're all fortunate the incident ended as it did."

"What made you decide to pick buffalo berries anyway?" Apparently, Ted wasn't ready to let the topic slide. "Have you ever tasted one? They're sour as all get out."

"I didn't know what type of berry they were. I heard some of you saying how you'd like cackleberries for breakfast. I thought maybe those were what you meant."

"Cackleberries?" Ted held his fork suspended in mid-air, mouth agape. Then he looked at Will and let out a guffaw.

"What? What did I say?"

Sparrowhawk cleared his throat and smoothed his mustache and goatee with his thumb and forefinger. A flush stained his cheeks. "Um. Cackleberries ain't berries, Miss Westbrook."

"They're not?"

"No," Sara said, a smile in her voice. "It's a term the cowboys around here use for eggs."

"Eggs? How do you get eggs from cackleberries? Oh. Cackle. Like a chicken." She hung her head. Why was she always making such foolish mistakes? And this one? This one almost cost Ben his life!

Ted must have realized her discomfort because he put his plate down and came over to sit beside her on the bench. Wrapping his arm around her shoulders, he pulled her close. "Hey, don't be so hard on yourself. Look at me." With a finger to her chin, he turned her face to his. "You're not to blame for this. It's all part of the danger of coming on these trips. If you're going to blame anyone, blame me for allowing you to come out here. The important thing is, you're safe, and Ben is going to be all right."

She nodded, trying to take his words to heart.

"Speaking of Ben—" Drew walked up to the campfire, took a seat on the up-turned log Ted had vacated, and looked around the circle. "I think we need to make some decisions on what to do next. Ben's wounds aren't life-threatening, but he has a pretty deep gash on his left shoulder and came close to having his right ear torn off. We got him patched up for now, but he needs some stitches. Now Emma can stitch him up. Growing up on a ranch, she's had plenty of practice, but she's worried about infection. She thinks our best bet is to take him by wagon back to the Skivington's camp. She says Mrs. Skivington has enough medical supplies to run her own hospital.

"Emma knows for sure she has carbolic acid and morphine. Both would make the process a lot better for Ben. I got him plenty liquored up--which should keep him comfortable until we can get back to the sheep camp, but we need to leave right away. I wanted to check with the rest of you to make sure you're all right with Emma and me taking the wagon--at least until tomorrow."

"Do you think we all should go? See he gets to a doctor?" Ted asked.

"I don't see the need. It would be a lot quicker for the three of us to go without trying to pack up the whole outfit. Besides, he's pretty adamant about not wanting anyone to change their plans on his account."

"Maybe I should go with you," Jenny said.

Drew looked at her over the top of his coffee cup. "That's up to you. I know today's been rough on you, too. If you'd rather not stay, I understand."

Sparrowhawk caught her gaze from across the fire. "If you're wanting to leave because of your fears, I can understand that, but I don't recommend it. The best way to fight your fears is to face them head-on. Like falling off a horse, if you don't get right back on, you may never ride again."

She wasn't afraid. That wasn't it. Jenny let her gaze drift to the mountain range to their west. Wind River Peak was so close, and she had so wanted to climb it with the others. But Ben had wanted to as well. How selfish would it be for her to leave him in his pain and go merrily on, especially when he was missing out because of her?

Besides, she wouldn't mind spending some time alone with Ben. They'd had no time to talk about that kiss. Again, a kiss so delicious, so promising . . . and interrupted far too soon. He'd initiated both kisses, so clearly, he had to have feelings for her. Surely, he didn't still think their kissing was a mistake.

She looked back at Drew. "Can I let you know?"

He pushed to his feet. "Sure. But don't take too long. I'd like to be on our way within the half-hour."

~

"TA RA RA BOOM DE AY"

The slurred notes from a strong baritone voice slightly off-key met Jenny as she headed back toward her tent after breakfast.

Was that Ben? How much whiskey had they given him? Still. If he was singing, he was awake.

A quick glance around assured her everyone was busy. Drew and Emma were over at the wagon, packing the supplies they'd need for their overnight trip. The others were gathered around the fire down by the chuckwagon. If she were to return to the sheep camp with the Johnsons and Ben, she'd need to pack her things, but if Ben was awake maybe she should stop in and see him first.

Turning quickly, she headed up the path to the Johnson's tent and slipped inside. Ben lay on his stomach on a cot in the middle of the room, head cradled on his arms, singing at the top of his lungs.

"A smart and stylish girl you see,
Belle of good society
Not too strict but rather free
Yet as right as right can be!"

He was bare to the waist and drunk as a lord. She shouldn't be in here. Her gaze lingered on the muscles on his back and shoulders before it snagged on the swath of gauze covering his left shoulder. Four red stripes bled through the material, giving testimony to what lay beneath. Drew had said one claw mark went so deep, he could see the bone.

She shuddered and looked away, her gaze traveling to the bandages covering his head. A pad of bandages cupped his right ear, held in place by bands of cotton that wrapped around his head. He looked like a victim of war.

She took a step closer, calling his name.

"Ta ra ra Boon de ay"

He belted out the chorus with gusto.

She reached out and touched a hand to his bare shoulder. He jumped and turned his head, his gaze lifting no higher than the bottom of her skirt. She snatched her hand back.

"Come to give me more pain, Nurse Emma?"

She squatted down, so they were eye-level. "It's not Emma."

A foolish grin creased his face. "Ah. Jenny. Beautiful Jenny. Don't be fooled, boys," He turned his head to the other side of the tent as if he were speaking to an imaginary crowd. "She may look like an angel, but she's trouble with a capital T." His gaze returned to hers. She resisted the urge to brush back the hair that fell across his bandage and into his eyes. He narrowed his eyes at her. "You shouldn't be here."

"I--I know, but I wanted . . . I *needed* to see you. Oh, Ben. I'm so sorry. I needed to see for myself how you're doing."

He shook his head. "Not good. Not good. Got mauled by a bear, you know."

"Yes. I know."

"Saving our Jenny. Always the way, you know. She gets in trouble, and I get hurt."

She wanted to argue the fact, but the truth was he often took the worst of their adventures. But this. This had been the worst. She should be the one on that cot—her flesh torn and bleeding. Instead, she had only a few bruises from where she hit the ground when Ben tackled her. She gave in to temptation and reached out and brushed the lock of hair from his eyes, letting her fingers linger. "I wanted to thank you and to let you know I'm going to stay right by your side until you get better. I'm going back to the sheep camp with you and the Johnsons."

He blinked. "Don't bother."

"It's not a bother, Ben. I want to. You saved my life. It's the least I can do."

He gave a harsh laugh. "I didn't save your life. Leatherstocking saved your life. Don't you know the guy with the skills always wins the day? If you want to pledge your undying loyalty and gratitude to someone, better save it for him."

"But Ben. You're hurt so badly. And it's all my fault."

"Of course, it's your fault, sweetheart. It always is. Didn't you hear what I said earlier? You get in trouble, and I get hurt. But not anymore." He gave his head an emphatic shake. "I figured it out. If I stay away from you, I won't get hurt." He grinned at her as if he'd suddenly discovered radium or something.

"Don't be ridiculous."

"I'm never ri--ri--ridicuwous. Except when I'm drunk." He squinted up at her. "Do you think I might be drunk?"

"Oh, most definitely."

"Thought so. Doesn't matter, though. I've made up my mind. Stay away from Jenny, and all will be well. Besides, who needs Jenny when they've got Nell? Hey, that rhymes." Another silly grin split his face. "Stay away from Jenny, and all will be well. Who needs Jenny when they've got Nell?" He continued in a sing-song voice. "Nell, Nell, Nell."

He buried his face in his arms again and broke into song.

"Never lived a queen so fair,

With my Nelly life I'd share,

By her side I know no care,

My Nelly, my own."

Oh, he was impossible. Jenny stood and, with a flounce of her skirts, headed for the door of the tent, but before she could exit, Emma pulled back the flap and stepped in.

"Jenny. What are you doing here?"

"I wanted to talk to Ben, but talking to a drunk man is about as profitable as having a conversation with a pig."

Emma gave a rueful smile. "Using whiskey as pain relief has its disadvantages, to be sure. Have you decided what you're going to do?"

Jenny glanced at Ben, who was still humming his song. Any charitable feelings she had for the man had vanished at *"who needs Jenny when they have Nell."* He was just like the Aunt Matildas and Madame Delanceys of this world. When it came right down to it, he would choose milk toast and safety over someone like her.

"I believe I'll stay here." She paused. "Unless you think you need me."

"No. Maddie and I are plenty capable of handling the nursing duties. And after we get him stitched up, there's little to do other than let him heal. If you feel up to it, stay. There's no reason for you to miss out on the rest of the excursion."

Emma was right. Nothing held her to Ben. Once again, their kiss was just a passing impulse to him. He'd made that fact perfectly clear with his silly chant. She could continue this adventure without him and enjoy herself with a clear conscience.

"Thank you. I believe I will."

Chapter Twenty-Four

Ben was going to die! The bear slashed at him with razor-sharp claws, teeth bared. Latching into his scalp, it flung him back and forth like a child's stuffed toy. Jenny tried to scream, but no sound came out. Arms and legs pinned beneath her like a bug on a corkboard, she struggled in vain to move.

Silently, she screamed his name. Over and over. Then, with a jerk, she woke. Heart pounding, she stared into the dark, her eyes finally focusing on the canvas above her. Sara's deep, even breathing rose from the cot next to hers.

Heaving a sigh, she pushed back the sweaty curls plastered to her face and sat up. This could not continue.

For the second time tonight, she'd woken from the same nightmare. Understandable after the day's events, but unacceptable, nonetheless. The walls of the tent closed in on her, suffocating, binding. She pushed back the panic.

Slowly, so as not to wake Sara, she felt her way to the end of the cot where she stored her bag. She pulled off her sweaty nightgown, glad for the relief of cool air against her skin. Relief quickly gave way to shivers as she dug in her bag for her riding skirt and jacket. Pulling them on over her bare skin, she stuffed her feet into her French silk slippers. She might look ridiculous, but she couldn't take the time to lace on her boots. She needed to get out of this tent. Now.

With a quick glance at Sara's cot, Jenny pushed back the tent flap and stopped short. Eerie shadows danced in the moonlight, sending a chill down her spine. What if there were another bear? Fear trapped her in the doorway.

Honestly, this could not continue. She forced herself back to her bag, where she dug under the clothes until her hand connected with the cold metal of her .46-caliber pistol. Checking the safety, she dropped it into the large side pocket on her skirt. There. That should give her the courage she needed to escape this tent.

She made her way through the pines toward the open space next to the lake, glad for the almost full moon lighting the trail. Stepping out from amongst the trees, she threw her head back to inhale deep lungsful of the cool night air. The stars hung heavy in the sky above her.

Ahead, moonlight made a path across the water. This was peace, pure and simple, and beauty so breathtaking, it brought tears to her eyes. If only that peace would infiltrate her soul.

Ben's words prodded at a sore that never quite healed. *Who needs Jenny when they can have Nell?* She'd heard that message in various forms all her life. *She might have the face of an angel, but she has the spirit of a hellion,* and *the star pupil must be refined and poised. If you think Madame will choose passion over poise, you do not know Madame.*

She didn't mind so much that the Aunt Matildas and Madames of this world felt she didn't measure up, but Ben? Two days ago, by the stream, everything had seemed so perfect. They had laughed and talked, *really* talked, and then that kiss. She could almost feel Ben's lips on hers, exploring, tasting, setting every one of her senses alive. If only they hadn't been interrupted again. No. If only they'd never kissed at all. Because those kisses made her hope, made her think that maybe Ben would choose her. She should have known better.

He'd told her his plan. That second dinner at Aunt Bethany's, he'd told her how he wanted to be full partner in a law firm before he was thirty. How Mr. Goddard had all but promised it to him, along with his daughter. How Nell would be the perfect lawyer's wife. How she had connections and decorum and an impeccable reputation. In short, Nell Goddard was Cecily Lamoreux all over again. And she . . . well, she was not. Oh, she might try and even succeed for a time, but at some point, she'd act without thinking, let her emotions take over, and just like today, Ben would end up paying the price.

A stick cracked to her left, and she spun, gun drawn.

"Whoa, there. Careful."

She could see him now, in the shadow of a boulder at the water's edge. Hands raised. Stance wary. The glowing red tip of a cigarette dangled from between his fingers.

Sparrowhawk.

"Sorry if I startled you," he said, his voice low and gentle, "but I'd appreciate if you'd put down that gun."

"Oh." She brought down her arm, letting the pistol dangle from her fingertip. "I-I'm sorry. I didn't expect anyone to be awake. The safety's on if it makes you feel any better."

"What would make me feel better is knowing you can handle one of those."

Jenny shrugged. "I'm not nearly the shot you are, but I might manage to scare off a bear."

He dropped the stub of his cigarette and ground it into the dirt with the boot of his heel. Walking toward her, he held out his hand. "Mind if I see it?"

She handed it to him and watched as he examined it in the moonlight.

"Looks like a dueling pistol. French?"

She nodded. "A brother of a friend of mine bought them for us when he realized his sister and I were determined to ride bicycles all over the French countryside."

"You're full of surprises, Miss Westraven. But why aren't you asleep?"

"It's that horrid bear. Every time I close my eyes, I see him—ripping, tearing, clawing." A shudder wracked through her. Crossing her arms, she hugged herself tightly, hoping to stave off the tremors that threatened.

Sparrowhawk reached out and stroked her cheek, releasing tremors of another kind. They stood for a moment in silence, only the murmur of a nearby stream that fed into the lake broke the still of the night.

"I'm not usually such a coward," she said, her voice little more than a whisper.

"You're no coward. Any other lady I know would have high-tailed it off this mountain long ago."

"Don't think I wasn't tempted." She took a few steps closer to the lake, her eyes on its moonlit path. "Will I ever get past this? The nightmares? The fear?"

"In time. It's only the first night." He came up beside her and took hold of her hand. "I've had some practice calming nightmares in young ladies. Should I try my methods on you?"

His thumb traced slow circles on her skin.

"What . . . what kind of methods?"

"Well, the young lady of my experience always responded best when I held her on my lap and stroked her hair."

Jenny pulled her hand from his. Surely he wasn't suggesting . .
.

"Then I'd sing her favorite song. Goes something like this. 'Wynken, Blynken and Nod one night sailed off in a wooden shoe . . .'" He sang in a rich baritone.

Jenny laughed, wishing now she hadn't been so hasty to release his hand. "How old is this young lady? Three?"

"Four-and-a-half. The last time I saw her, anyway. She's almost six now."

"Someone close to you?"

"Yes. My da . . . dear niece. Little Etta Mae."

"You miss her."

He looked out over the water. "Yes."

"Where is she now?"

"Montana."

"Is all your family there?"

"All that's left. There were five of us at one time. Now there's only me and my younger sister, Anna Marie."

"And the others?"

"All gone."

So much loss. She knew the pain of loss. And the bond it created with an only sibling.

"It must be hard for the two of you to be so far apart," she said.

He shrugged. "I think I miss the kids most of all."

"Kids?"

"Etta Mae and her brothers. The baby was born a year ago June."

"So you've never met him?"

"Not yet."

"Why did you leave them?"

"There were more opportunities here. Anna Marie has always had a taste for the finer things in life." Bitterness laced his words. "I knew if I were to keep her happy, I needed to make more money than I could in Billings."

"But isn't that her husband's job?"

"Her husband . . . died . . . shortly before I came here."

"Oh, how sad." To lose her husband and only brother in so short a time. "You must find a way to go to her, or if not, bring them all here. You're the only family she has. And to be so far away . . ." She let the words trail off. "I'm sorry. I know it's not that easy. I wanted desperately to be with Ted when he was so sick, yet it took two years before I could join him."

"You're very passionate about family."

"Yes."

Reaching out, his fingers cupped her chin, turning her face

toward his. "A woman with passion is a beautiful thing." Finally. Someone who found value in passion. In the moonlight, his eyes were dark, searching. "Tell me, Miss Westraven, do you ever wonder what would have happened if you'd taken me up on my offer that night of the dance?"

The pad of his thumb traced the outline of her mouth. She swallowed, her lips burning under his touch.

"I do," His voice was soft as velvet. "Seems to me fate has given us another chance. You . . . me . . . the moonlight." He leaned in until his lips hovered mere inches from hers. "What will you choose this time, Miss Westraven?" He murmured. "Passion? Or propriety?"

Passion. Oh, most definitely, passion. Reaching up, she ran her finger along his mustache and down his goatee. Was it wrong to want to kiss this man when she'd shared a kiss with Ben just two days before? But Ben wanted nothing to do with a girl who chased sunrises. He wanted propriety. He wanted Nell. She didn't need a man like that.

"Jenny? Are you out here?"

Slowly, she dropped her hand and stepped back.

Sara emerged from the shadows of the pines. "There you are. I was worried when I saw your empty bed." She stopped short. "Oh. Mr. Sparrowhawk. I didn't see you there."

He gave a slight bow.

"I'm sorry, Sara. I couldn't sleep. Nightmares. The bear . . ." She shook her head against the memory.

"You poor dear. You should have woken me."

"No use both of us not sleeping."

"Well, I'm awake now, and I know exactly what you need." She turned to Sparrowhawk. "Is there still a kettle of hot water by the fire?"

"Should be."

"Good. I have some chamomile tea in the tent. Come. We'll have you relaxed in no time."

She took Jenny's hand and led her toward the trees. Jenny glanced back over her shoulder.

"Good night, Mr. Sparrowhawk.

"Good night, Miss Westraven. Pleasant dreams."

The low timbre of his voice brought to mind soft whiskers and fiery touches. Pleasant dreams indeed. Could be his nightmare-soothing methods worked on girls of all ages.

Chapter Twenty-Five

For the first time in three days, Ben woke with a clear head. Clear head but a fuzzy tongue. He sat up and swung his legs over the side of the cot, bracing his head in his hand as a fresh wave of dizziness hit. So. The laudanum cobwebs hadn't completely cleared.

He reached for the tin pitcher sitting on the camp table by his bed, wincing as the skin in his left shoulder stretched against his stitches. He downed a cup of cold water and poured another before taking a quick inventory of his injuries. A dull ache radiated from his right ear, but the sharp, burning pain in his left shoulder had lessened considerably. Good thing he'd refused the dose of laudanum Mrs. Skivington tried to give him last night.

The pain hadn't been great enough to risk the strange dreams brought on by the medicine.

Oh, those dreams. Jenny lying on the rocky ground beneath him, white and lifeless. Jenny's disembodied head floating around the inside of his tent—tears swimming in her crystal blue eyes. Jenny, lips lush and inviting, drawing closer and closer, until the very moment he expected their lips to touch, she vanished in a vapor.

Jenny.

Always Jenny.

And a bear the size of Montana.

He shuddered at the memories, whether real or imagined—the bear's musky smell, its hot breath against his neck, the low menacing growls, the sharp claws. Worse was the memory of the vicelike jaws wrapped around his head. The scabs he felt when he ran his hand through his hair, and the pain in his right ear confirmed at least *that* memory was real.

"You're up."

Mrs. Skivington pushed through the tent flap, tray of food in hand. Was that bacon he smelled? His stomach rumbled at the thought. Anything would be better than that god-awful broth she'd been spooning down him for the last three days.

As she bustled past to set the tray on the table, he pulled his blanket around his bare back and shoulders, holding it close at the neck, so it covered his front as well. Silly of him to be so modest. After all, she'd been the one to clean and stitch his wounds and change his dressings several times a day. But now, head clear of whiskey and laudanum, he felt the need to be civilized.

She removed the cover from the plate and turned to him with a smile. "I thought you might be feeling better this morning after you refused the laudanum last night, so I took a chance and fixed you a proper breakfast. Do you think your stomach can handle it? I have some oatmeal back at the wagon if you'd prefer."

He eyed the plate heaped with scrambled eggs, toast, and yes, two slices of bacon. "This looks great."

"Better than the stew I've been giving you? Be honest. Did it taste as bad as it smelled?"

"Worse. You mean, you fed it to me and never tasted it?"

Amusement filled her eyes. "I couldn't get past the smell. Trust me. If you hadn't lost so much blood, I never would have fed it to you, but Mr. Johnson brought the organ meat from that bear and said to make sure we got it down you somehow. He said it would speed up your recovery, and looking at you this morning, he may have been right."

Ben bit into his first slice of bacon, savoring the burst of flavor on his tongue. How could pig taste so wonderful and bear so nasty? He chased the flavor with a swig of rich, creamy milk. Wiping his mouth, he grinned at Mrs. Skivington. "I'll forgive you if you continue to feed me meals like this one."

But the idea of having eaten a part of the bear that bit him wasn't horrible. It felt right somehow—sort of a you-hurt-me-I-eat-your-heart justice.

Mrs. Skivington scurried around his tent, tidying up. She reminded him of a pretty little wren with her bright eyes and quick movements. When he laid his fork on his empty plate, she came and stood by his cot.

"Would you mind if I take a look at your stitches this morning? You could keep the blanket wrapped around you if you'd like."

"No. Go ahead. I do appreciate all you and Mrs. Johnson did to fix me up."

She pushed his hair away from his right ear with cool, gentle fingers. "We were a bit worried about this ear. When I first saw it, I wasn't sure we'd be able to save it, but it's looking quite good now."

She peeled back the bandage on his shoulder. "And these are, too. No sign of redness or infection. Let me just put some more of this ointment on the stitches, and I'll leave you be."

She opened a jar of gooey, grayish-brown ointment and slathered it on his stitches. It smelled pungent, earthy.

"What's that?"

"I have no idea. Emma gave it to me. She said her family has been using it for years. They get it from the Indians, I guess, and it aids in healing and fighting infection. I'm thinking I need to get a jar of my own to add to our medicine chest because it sure has worked wonders on your gashes."

She finished replacing the bandages on his left shoulder, then gave him a light tap. "All done. Now, if you feel strong enough, you're welcome to join us in the pasture. The walk may feel a little long, but you'll have plenty of time to rest before you'd need to walk back."

"I may do that. Thank you."

"Don't feel you have to if you're not up to it. But it might do you good to get out in the fresh air."

She picked up his tray of dirty dishes and headed to the doorway, looking back before pushing through the tent flap. "Do you need me to send Rob to help you get dressed? That shoulder might prove a problem."

"I think I can manage. Thanks."

"All right. See you in a bit."

BEN SPENT THE NEXT TWO DAYS HELPING THE SKIVINGTONS with their sheep, growing stronger each day. Late in the afternoon of the third day, they trailed the band back into camp to find the hunting party had returned. The group seemed happy, and maybe a little surprised, to see him up and about as if they thought he'd still be languishing on his cot after almost a week.

"Oh, you're looking so good," Emma Johnson said. She pulled his head down to look at his right ear. "See?" she called over to Maddie. "I told you my expertise in mending Drew's trousers would come in handy."

"I'm mighty glad for torn trousers then. I owe you and Maddie a huge debt for all you did for me."

"Pshaw. I'm just glad our efforts were successful. You are far too handsome a man to go through life with only one ear." She gave his good shoulder a quick pat and went off to help Maddie with supper.

The only one not pleased to see him was Jenny. She met his gaze with a frostiness he'd never seen in her eyes before, their blue taking on the tint of a high mountain glacier. She responded to his smile of greeting with the barest of nods as she led her horse to where Sparrowhawk was tethering the others.

Apparently, that hazy conversation he remembered between him and Jenny wasn't a figment of his drug-induced imagination. Were the tears he remembered real as well? Blast it. What had he said to her?

Her relationship with Sparrowhawk had certainly deepened since the last time he saw them. He watched their easy laughter as the two stood side by side next to the horses, his gut clenching a little when she laid a hand on Sparrowhawk's arm and smiled up at him in that teasing way of hers.

After supper, he headed down to the stream gurgling through the pines at the camp's southern base. On this last night in the mountains, he wanted some time alone to drink in the quiet and beauty he'd come to love up here.

Halfway down the path, he came upon Jenny heading back from the stream, a bucket of water in each hand. With a regal nod worthy of Queen Victoria herself, she moved to the side just as he moved to let her pass. They stepped back again in tandem, continuing their awkward dance.

"Allow me," he said with exaggerated politeness. He stepped off the trail and motioned for her to pass. With a lift of her pretty little chin and not so much as a thank you, she swept by.

Oh, for Pete's sake.

"Jen, wait."

She stopped but did not turn.

"Can we talk?"

"I should think we've done all the talking we need to by now, Mr. Bennet."

Mr. Bennet? He hadn't heard her call him that since their office days and never in so frosty a tone.

"Look. I know I might have said some stupid things the night the bear mauled me, but whatever I said, I never meant to hurt you."

"Hurt me? What makes you think you could hurt me?" She

turned to look at him with eyes so cold they made ice chips seem toasty. "There's no need to apologize on my account."

He leaped in front of her as she started back up the path. "Wait. Can't we talk this out?"

Letting out a huff, she set her buckets down, sloshing water over the tops of his boots. "*I* have nothing to say, but if you want to talk, go right ahead." She crossed her arms and glared at him. If he didn't get his words out quickly, she'd probably start tapping her foot at him.

"I'm just . . . why are you acting this way?"

"What way?" Sure enough, the foot started tapping.

"*This* way." He pointed at her stance. "Like you can't stand to be near me."

"I'm only doing what you asked. You told me to stay out of your life, so I am."

"Jenny, I was in a lot of pain that night and drunk off my gourd. I guess I said a lot of crazy things."

"You don't remember?"

He raked a hand through his hair and blew out a breath. "A little. It's kind of fuzzy."

"Well then, let me refresh your memory: 'Stay away from Jenny, and all will be well. Who needs Jenny when they've got Nell?'" She said in a singsong voice.

Oh, boy. "I *said* that?"

"No, Ben, you didn't say it . . . you *sang* it . . . at the top of your lungs . . . over and over and over."

No wonder she was spitting daggers at him.

"You know I didn't mean it."

"No, I don't know. I understand you were drunk and not thinking clearly, but those thoughts had to come from some-where. Haven't you ever heard the saying, *In vino veritas?* Besides, you're right. I *am* trouble. And for some reason, whenever we're together, you get the worst of it. So, I've decided to do as you asked. I'll stay away from you, and 'all will be well.'"

"But that's not what I want."

She heaved a sigh. "What *do* you want, Ben?"

"I want us to be friends, like before. Can't we just be friends?"

She drew a shaky breath. "No. I don't believe we can. We try, but then something always happens. You kiss me, or I kiss you. Then everything gets all muddied, and disaster strikes." She reached up to cup his cheek with the palm of her hand, the look in her eyes much softer now. "Much as I love you, Ben, and I do . . . as a dear childhood friend . . . I can never just be your friend . . . and we can never be more than friends. I can never be the type of woman you need, no matter how hard I try. What's more, I don't want to be, so it's better if we go our separate ways." She dropped her hand, leaving a cold void in its wake. "You need to accept it, Ben. You're a very dear part of my past, but I can't be a part of your future. And you're not part of mine. So, do us both a favor. When you get back to Lander, write to Nell and tell her you're coming home."

He watched her leave until he could no longer see her through the trees, then slowly worked his way down the path to the stream. Once there, he picked up a rock and hurled it across the water at the trunk of an aspen on the opposite side. It landed with a satisfying thunk. He slammed another and another, not stopping until dusk turned to full dark. Finally, he turned and trudged up the path to his tent, the ache in his shoulder a mere shadow of the one in his heart.

Chapter Twenty-Six

"When will I see you again?" Jenny looked up at Nick through her lashes.

He'd pulled her into a narrow alley behind the livery while the others were unloading the wagon. Jenny's back pressed against the warm bricks of the livery's back wall. Nick propped his shoulder on the wall beside her, effectively blocking her from the view of anyone on the street.

"That's just it, sweetheart. I don't know. I'll be driving Harris' steers to the rail yard in Caspar next week. Then I'll be tied up at the road ranch for a while. Maybe October?"

October! That was two months away.

"Hey, now." He lifted her chin, running the pad of his thumb along her cheek. A delicious shiver coursed through her. "I'll write you. I promise."

She shook her head. "Ted would never allow it."

"Who says he has to know? We cowboys have ways of getting around the post."

"How?"

"Your brother isn't the first to disapprove of a cowboy as a suitor. Lucky for us some folks in this town take pity on us poor cowboys. Do you know Mrs. Stacia Allen?"

"The milliner?"

He nodded. "Word has it she has a soft spot for lovers and an even softer spot for cowboys. You drop by her store by the end of the week, and I promise she'll have something for you."

Did he consider them lovers? They'd been spending a lot of time together this past week, talking, flirting, but neither of them had said a word about love. Their relationship, if it could be called a relationship, was too new for her to know her feelings, but she knew she didn't want whatever was between them to end. Not until she'd had time to explore it. From the moment she'd first laid eyes on him, he'd reminded her of the heroes she'd dreamed of in her childhood fantasies. The more she got to know him, the more he lived up to those fantasies. And the fact neither Mrs. Parkhurst nor Aunt Matilda would approve? So much the better.

"And if I want to write you back?"

"Take it to Stacia. She'll see it gets to me, and no one will be the wiser."

"I wish this trip never had to end." After the excitement of the last few weeks, she couldn't imagine going back to the way things were before—the stuffy dinner parties, Grace's icy disapproval, and months without Nick anywhere around. Letter writing seemed so, well, tame. "We should ask Ted to hire you again next month. He's been wanting to hunt big-horned sheep. I'm sure we could find some others who would like to go, and we could . . ."

But he was already shaking his head.

"I'm sorry, sweetheart." He tucked a curl behind her ear, his fingers lingering on her earlobe, making it difficult for her to concentrate. "I gave Mr. Harris my word I'd help him through the fall. I can't go back on that. Besides, I need the money he's promised me if I'm ever going to bring Anna Marie and the kids out here."

Of course. It would be selfish to monopolize his time when his sister and her children were counting on him.

"This is it, then? Goodbye?" She glanced up to see his eyes leveled on her mouth. Something somersaulted in her lower belly at the intensity of his gaze. Maybe, finally, he'd kiss her. She ran her tongue along her bottom lip.

She'd been wanting this kiss for days, hoping to finally cancel out the memory of both of Ben's kisses. Those kisses still haunted her, and she needed to let them go. Ben didn't want her. He wanted Nell. And she wanted—oh, how she wanted—to forget everything about his kisses.

She drew herself up on her tiptoes, bringing her mouth so close to Nick's that their breath mingled. Still, he made no move to bridge the gap. Fine, then. She reached up and pulled his mouth down to hers, letting her lips barely graze his, his mustache silky soft against her skin.

At her touch, his mouth came down on hers, hard and demanding. His hands roamed her body, pulling her against him so tight she couldn't move. A sharp gasp penetrated Jenny's senses. She tore her mouth from Nick's, her eyes snagging on a flash of blue silk as it disappeared around the corner.

Had someone seen them kissing?

Unaware of her distraction, Nick continued to kiss her neck, her cheek, her ear, all the while holding her in his vise-like embrace. Trapped and suffocating, she struggled in his hold until she managed to get her arms between them.

"Nick." She pushed against his chest with all her might. "Nick!"

He stared at her, eyes dark, breath ragged.

"I . . . I think someone might have seen us. I need to get back. My brother . . ." She let the words trail off.

He put a finger on her lips. "You worry too much, sweetheart. No one will notice if we're gone a little longer." He bent to kiss her again, but she pushed away. He looked so hurt, she almost relented. But if someone had seen them . . .

"I should go."

Finally, he stepped back. "All right. Let's go then."

"No. I mean, it's best if we're not seen together. Give me five minutes before coming back."

With a quick wave, she dashed around the corner of the livery. Their group was still occupied at the wagon, and no one noticed her come out of the alley. She scanned each dress in the crowd. Grace was wearing russet, and Mrs. Parkhurst was garbed in her usual dove gray. Emma and Sara were dressed as she was in dark, serviceable riding skirts. No blue silk to be seen.

Had she imagined it? She went to stand by Sara, who was helping her sister sort luggage.

"Where have you been?"

"I'll tell you later. Did anyone notice I was gone?"

Sara shook her head. "They've all been too busy showing off the bearskin and unloading the wagon." She dropped her voice to a near whisper. "Does this have anything to do with Sparrowhawk?"

"Shhh. Later." But she couldn't stop the heat from building in her neck and cheeks.

"Aha, it does. All right, I'll wait, but I'll want every detail."

Jenny wasn't sure she wanted to share the details. Everything had happened so fast. Only one thing was certain. Sparrowhawk's kiss did nothing to eradicate Ben's. If anything, it made Ben's seem all the sweeter.

Chapter Twenty-Seven

Ben slammed the door to his room and flung himself into the corner armchair, mind reeling from what he'd just witnessed.

Sparrowhawk and Jenny.

In an alley.

Kissing.

Not a mere peck on the cheek either.

At first, he thought he'd stumbled across some cowboy taking his pleasure with a dance hall girl . . . until he spied the deep green riding skirt and the curly blond braid whose tip swung just to the narrowing of that tiny waist. He knew that skirt, that braid, those curves. Hadn't his eyes strayed to them over and over on their six-hour ride down the mountain?

He dropped his head into his hands, rubbing at his eyes as if the scrubbing could erase the image emblazoned there.

Sparrowhawk and Jenny.

How long had this been going on? Just last week, *he* had been the recipient of her kisses. Did that moment by the stream mean so little to her?

He leaped to his feet, hands clenched as he paced the room. No. She wasn't that fickle. This was his fault. Those things he'd said to her after the bear attack. He'd pushed her away.

He stopped at the washstand and studied himself in the mirror. There'd been logic in his decision, right? Did he want to spend the rest of his life pulling Jenny out of scrapes? Sure, she was beautiful. Yes, he couldn't get her out of his mind. But she was trouble. Through and through.

The kiss he'd just witnessed proved that. What was she thinking letting a man kiss her on a public street? Well, alleyway, anyway. But that was Jenny. She never considered the consequences, just flew straight ahead into whatever life brought, seizing the moment with both hands, living each moment to its fullest.

He loved that about her.

He looked himself in the eyes again and groaned.

No. That wasn't true. Not fully. He loved *everything* about her. He loved *her*.

That was the problem. Jenny in no way fit into the life he'd envisioned for himself. The one he'd worked so hard to attain. He had a plan. Lawyer by age 23, full partnership by age 28, judge by age 35. After that, maybe politics. He was well on his way to full partnership, and Nell was his ticket. He knew full well that should he decide to end his courtship with Nell, he could kiss his job with Goddard goodbye. But how could he marry Nell now, knowing Jenny was the one he loved? And how would the fireball that was Jenny in any way fit into the staid New Jersey law community?

No, Jenny wasn't what he needed, not if he were to stick to his plan, but God help him, she was what he wanted. Had been since the day he met her. She'd stepped out of her uncle's fancy carriage looking like an angel in a lacy white dress, golden curls flowing down her back, and challenged him, then and there, to a foot race. Two hours later, looking more like a tarnished angel with a tear in the knee of her stocking and a smudge of dirt on her nose, she'd climbed into his treehouse and told him the sign that read "No Girls Allowed" would have to go. He'd been hooked ever since. He'd been a fool not to see it.

He turned from the mirror and raked a hand through his hair, allowing the scene in the alleyway to play through his mind once again. Jenny with another man. The thought made his stomach roil. He wanted to punch the guy, but what right did he have?

Sparrowhawk was only doing what he had done . . . twice. He knew exactly how soft those lips were, how sweet they tasted, how absolutely right she felt in his arms. At least Sparrowhawk was being honest with her. *He* wasn't kissing Jenny while telling himself he didn't want her. *He* wasn't kissing her while still in a courtship with another.

Ben sank onto the edge of his bed, the throbbing in his left shoulder, reminding him of the mess he'd made of things. When had everything become so muddled? A week ago, he'd stood by that mountain lake, so sure he was exactly where God wanted him. Now he wasn't sure of anything other than seeing that kiss had slain him.

Have you prayed about it, son?

Grandma Janssen's voice again. But the last time he took her advice, he'd ended up with a burr in his saddle and bloody fists.

No. He wouldn't blame God for that fistfight.

And he couldn't blame Jenny for turning to someone else when he pushed her away.

I can't be a part of your future, Ben. Her words rankled. Had she meant that? Other than the fact she allowed him to kiss her . . . twice, he had no idea how she really felt about him. At the time, he had agreed with her. She wasn't a part of the future he'd planned either, but now he wasn't so sure. The drive behind that plan had died when Father did, but if he was being totally honest, it had begun to fade that day last February when he'd come to Aunt Bethany's for dinner and rediscovered Jenny.

And now it might be too late. Or was it? He could stay. He could fight for her. But he'd have to fight smart. Right now, she wouldn't even talk to him. But if he took it slow, earned his way back into her life, maybe he still had a chance. And if, in the end, he lost her to Sparrowhawk, so be it. At least he'd know he tried.

But he'd do things right this time. No more lying to her or to himself. No more trying to hold on to something he no longer wanted. He walked over and pulled a clean sheet of paper and fountain pen from his desk drawer. He had a letter to write to Nell that was long overdue.

~

"So you've decided to stay?" Ted rocked back in his chair, hands clasped behind his head, legs stretched in front of him, looking more like the carefree man of fortune than a hardworking banker. "I knew the West would claim you if you gave her a try."

He studied Ben through half-closed eyes. "Or is it something, or should I say, some*one* else that keeps you here?" His eyes twinkled as he spoke, but Ben refused to take the bait.

"You're right. This place beats Newark, hands down. The mountains, fresh air, all the hunting and fishing. Besides, with my business interests in South Dakota, it only makes sense I stay close. At least for now."

"And Matthews will take you on? Could be a great opportunity. He's been looking for a partner since I've been here, and in a few years, who knows? He may let you buy out his practice. He's been the town's most prominent lawyer for years, so you shouldn't have trouble finding clients."

Ben nodded. "Could be fun practicing western law for a change."

"I expect it's not much different from law in the east."

"Maybe not. Though I never had to defend any cattle rustlers back in Jersey."

Ted chuckled. "Oh now, cattle rustling's not that far removed from embezzlement or corporate takeovers. Are you keeping your room at Mrs. Kavenaugh's?"

"For a while. The room's comfortable, and the meals are good . . . most days."

"Does she still serve liver and onions every Wednesday?" Ted had been the one to recommend Mrs. Kavenaugh's boarding house, having lived there himself before marrying Grace.

"And some God-awful hash on Saturdays."

"Ah yes, the hash. All the week's leftovers thrown in a pot whether they go together or not." Ted gave an exaggerated shudder. "Tell you what. You have an open invitation to dinner at my house every Wednesday and Saturday for as long as you live at Mrs. Kavenaugh's. It's the least I can do for a friend."

Perfect. Ted's invitation was just the advantage he needed. Two nights a week in Jenny's company was two nights more than Sparrowhawk would have.

"I may take you up on that."

"You'd better. I'm counting on you to even out the numbers. Being the lone rooster in a house full of hens isn't as appealing as it seems. See you tomorrow night, then?"

"As long as hash isn't on the menu, I'll be there."

Chapter Twenty-Eight

My Dearest Jenny,
*   I hope you won't take offense to my using your given name.*
I know we have not known each other for long, but I feel as if my soul
has known you forever. The way my heart leaped in my chest on our first
meeting told me it recognized its mate immediately. Do you remember
that day?

Oh, yes, but she couldn't believe Nick did. Jenny flung herself onto her bed, propping herself up by her elbows to read his latest letter. She'd received two thick letters each time she'd visited Mrs. Stacia Allen's shop. Today's letter had been tucked in with the delivery of a hat she'd purchased when she'd dropped off her last letter to him.

At first, she'd thought courting through letter-writing would be tame, but Nick's letters were proving her wrong. He wrote to her every night at the end of the day, sending a full packet each time he arrived at a town with a post office. His early letters had described the cattle drive, sleeping at night by an open fire, and little adventures along the way. She'd liked his humor and the glimpses he gave her into his everyday life. It was like reading one of the dime novels she'd loved as a young girl, except this real live hero was pursuing her. Lately, his letters had become more intimate, sharing his goals, his dreams, his heart. But this letter was shaping up to be by far his best.

I couldn't believe the beauty of the woman who walked into my road ranch that day, like an angel dropped from heaven. And to think I can now call her my dear friend. I cherish every moment we were together, from that very first meeting to the night we met in the moonlight after the bear attack. How beautiful you were that night. So brave. So lovely. I've never known a woman who could go through such an ordeal and still have the courage to face her fears with nothing more than a loaded pistol. I admire your passion and sense of adventure. You are like a blazing flame in a world of paltry candles.

Who was this man, and where had he been all her life? He admired her passion? No one had ever said that to her. Unlike all the others, here, at last, was someone who didn't want to change her.

Forgive me if I am too bold, but I am hoping you feel the same about me as I do of you. When I lay in my bedroll at night struggling to stay warm, I have only to pull up the memory of that kiss we shared, and I'm warmed through and through.

Jenny flushed. A frisson of the discomfort she'd felt during those last minutes in his embrace resurfaced—his iron grip, the suffocating helplessness that almost overwhelmed her. If only she could remember that kiss as fondly as he did. This was the second time he'd brought it up. She almost wished it had never happened. What had gone wrong? The kiss had started well enough, much like the kisses she shared with Ben. But between Nick's intensity and her fear of being caught, all she remembered now was her desire for it to end.

She shook off the memory. Surely, the next time would be better. She knew him better now. He'd shared his heart with her.

I've told you about my next endeavor, to build a ranch of my own down here on the Sweetwater. I have the land. Next week, with the help of a few of my friends, I plan to start work on a small cabin. Soon, I hope to send for my sister and her children, but in all honesty, I find that all these dreams are now starting to include the presence of a certain angel by my side. Am I getting ahead of myself when I say my house would not be a home without you in it? Please tell me I haven't overstepped. If I have, I will never mention such things again. But you were made for this life, Jenny. Imagine the adventures we could have together.

Maybe his soul did know hers. It was almost as if he had looked into her innermost being and pulled out all her secret hopes and dreams. Jenny flipped onto her back and stared up at the silk canopy above her bed. She could picture it. A pretty log cabin surrounded by the hills and the sage. She and Nick riding horses together, chasing down cows, building a life, and someday a family out on the open range. How perfect that would be.

But did she love him? How did you know? She loved the idea of him. That was a fact. His very essence screamed adventure and romance. Best of all, he loved her just as she was. He thought her passionate nature was beautiful, not something to be suppressed. And the more letters he wrote, the more she was coming to like and admire the man behind the words.

Maybe the idea wasn't so farfetched. She clutched his letter close to her breast. Was it an impossible thought? Marrying Nick? She couldn't stay with Ted indefinitely. Not a day went by without either Grace or Mrs. Parkhurst making that perfectly clear. But she didn't want to go back east. And, although Aunt Matilda and Uncle Clarence had returned from Newport weeks ago, neither had made any mention of her coming back there. In fact, after her birthday in September, Uncle Clarence had started sending the interest payments from her inheritance to Teddy. She knew because he'd opened an account for her to draw from at his bank.

Of course, that money would cease to come to Teddy or to her if she were to marry Nick. Uncle Clarence would never give his permission for her to marry a mere cowboy. If an up-and-coming young lawyer like Ben wasn't good enough for Uncle Clarence, a lowly ranch hand surely wouldn't measure up. Aunt Matilda would be aghast at the mere thought. Which, honestly, only made Nick all the more attractive.

But what if Nick was counting on her to bring some money into their marriage? Surely, after all the time he'd spent with Ted before she arrived, he knew their family had money. Maybe that was why he was pursuing her. His plans to build a ranch and bring his sister and her family to live with him would go much faster if he had money. Maybe he was just like all her suitors back home.

The thought was more depressing than she expected, but it made sense. Why else would he be pursuing her with such urgency? Well then, she'd tell him. In her very next letter, she'd make it perfectly clear that if they were to marry, she'd be bringing no money with her. If that changed his tune, then at least she would know.

"Jenny? Are you up here?"

She catapulted off the bed, shoving Nick's letter under a stack of handkerchiefs in her bureau drawer.

Sara peeked her head around the door. "You're not ready to go? I was running so late, I expected you to be downstairs waiting for me."

And she would have been, had Deavers not delivered her new hat from Mrs. Stacia Allen's just when she was ready to walk out the door of her bedroom.

Sara caught sight of the box and scattered tissue paper on the bed. "Another new hat? Didn't you buy one just last week?"

So far, she'd bought a new hat each time she'd taken a letter to Mrs. Stacia Allen's. Buying the hats wasn't necessary, but it seemed the least she could do. Clearly, though, she needed to keep her future purchases to items like gloves or handkerchiefs. A new hat every week was an extravagance even Teddy was sure to notice.

"Ohhh." Sara pulled the hat out of the box. "This one is gorgeous. That deep blue velvet will look wonderful with your new pelisse."

"Which is precisely why I had to have it, even though I just ordered the straw boater. But I've run right through my pin money for the month, so you must hold me accountable. No more hats!"

Though she shared most secrets with Sara, she hadn't told her about her correspondence with Nick. Somehow keeping the letters to herself made them all the more intimate.

"Are you going to wear the boater today?"

"It would be more practical, don't you think?"

"As if you owned anything practical," Sara teased. "But yes, save the blue one for a special occasion. Maybe when a certain young lawyer is in attendance."

Ever since the bear incident, Sara had been pairing her and Ben—in *her* mind at least. "It's all so romantic," she'd say. "How can you not fall in love with the man who threw himself in front of a bear for you?"

Sara couldn't, or wouldn't, accept that she and Ben were simply friends. Actually, not even friends after their trip to the mountains. She'd been surprised when Ted told her Ben was going to stay in Lander for a while to be closer to his family in South Dakota. After his drunken confession that morning in the tent, she'd thought for sure he'd be on the next train back to Nell. She almost wished he had. It didn't help that he was constantly underfoot these days. Granted, Lander's social scene was limited. She was bound to run into him on occasion. But as Teddy's best friend, he was in and out of this house as if he lived here, staying for dinner two or more times a week. Try as she might to hold him at arm's length, he'd invariably draw her into his conversation with some anecdote or opinion until they were back to their old ways of sparring and teasing.

But Sara didn't know about Nick and his letters. Nick had just told her he wanted a future with her. Ben never had. Nick called her passion beautiful. Ben wanted the prim and proper Nell.

The sound of wagon wheels on gravel drew Sara's attention from the hat to the window.

"Oh. There's Mrs. Willoughby now," Sara said. "Are you ready?"

"Yes. If I can find my gloves."

Sara picked up a pair from the bureau and threw them Jenny's way.

"Anything else I can do for you?"

Jenny laughed and followed her friend out the door.

~

"IF YOU PUT YOUR FINGERS ON THESE THREE BLACK KEYS, SEE, like this," Jenny placed the girl's fingers on the three keys above middle C. "I'll teach you a song."

She held the girl on her lap. Lottie, they called her. She was new to the Mission school. Today she'd met them at the door with a finger in her mouth and a frown in her eyes.

A little mite, the sleeves of her school-issued hickory dress hung several inches below her wrists. Jenny had to roll them up to allow her the freedom to play on the piano.

"Now listen to the notes," Jenny put her own fingers atop the girl's tiny ones and gently pressed them down. "Hot Cross Buns . . ." She sang as she played, "hot cross buns, one a penny, two a penny, hot cross buns."

The girl twisted in Jenny's lap to gaze up at her face, brown eyes wide, questioning. "Did you like that? Should we try again?"

Lottie didn't answer. Probably couldn't answer. Like Willie at the government school, she'd been robbed of the ability to speak the minute her family dropped her off. At least here, the older girls were allowed to translate for her until English became more familiar.

"Let's try it again, shall we?" Jenny guided the small fingers through the simple tune again.

Jenny had enjoyed her first visits to the Mission school with the Willoughbys so much, she'd volunteered to come back weekly and teach the girls piano. Sara started coming too to help in the kitchen. Like her work in the law office, Jenny loved being part of something that mattered, something more than just a round of dinner parties and social events. Ted might believe her sole purpose as a Westraven woman was to be pretty and pampered, but she'd always wanted to be part of something bigger. Now that Aunt Matilda wasn't controlling every hour of her day, she was determined to do what she wanted. For now, that meant teaching piano.

Normally she didn't teach the younger girls. Her students were all fifth-year girls and above. But Lottie had followed her and her first student out to the chapel where the upright Steinway was housed and hadn't gone back when the first girl went away. She watched with wide-eyed concentration as Jenny worked her way through the afternoon's pupils. So when her four o'clock student, Alice Yellow Bear, hadn't shown up, Jenny pulled Lottie onto her lap.

"Do you think you can play it on your own now?"

Lottie turned her solemn sloe-eyed gaze on Jenny again. What was she thinking, her forehead all wrinkled like that?

"Try it. On your own." Jenny tapped the girl's tiny ring finger still poised above the top key. Tentatively, Lottie tapped out the song, slow but accurate.

When she finished, Jenny pulled the girl close against her and dropped a kiss on her blue-black braid. "What a clever girl you are! You did that all by yourself."

Jenny glanced at the watch pinned to her lapel. If Alice didn't come soon, she'd miss her entire lesson. It wasn't like her to be late.

She swung the piano stool to the side and stood up, letting Lottie slide to the floor but keeping hold of her small hand. Together, they walked to where Jenny's last student had left the door ajar.

Peeping out, she scanned the empty yard between her and the larger brick school building. No sign of anyone. Except there. By the back door, two girls sat huddled together, arms around each other's waists. Jenny recognized the blond braids of Reverend Robert's second-oldest, Marion. Marion and Alice were inseparable friends, so she was sure the girl sitting next to her must be Alice. Whatever were they doing? Marion's lesson was to follow Alice's, so usually the two arrived together, but if they didn't hurry, there'd be no time left for either of them.

Before she could call them, they got to their feet and started walking her way. Finally. Yet, instead of coming to the chapel, they veered off toward the small cabin next door disappearing inside.

Well.

Pulling Lottie onto her hip, Jenny followed them. The wind whipped at her skirts, tangling them around her legs, making her glad she'd left her hat in the Mission parlor.

Coming to the cabin, she tapped on the door. "Come in," a woman's voice called from within.

She pushed the door open and stepped into a small kitchen. Miss Whitney, the school's missionary teacher, stood at the center table kneading a loaf of bread. In front of her sat the two girls in two straight-backed chairs. Alice's face was streaked with tears and dirt. Marion had her arm around her friend's shoulder.

"I'm sorry," Jenny said. "I don't mean to intrude, but Alice and Marion are late for their lesson. I saw them come here and wanted to make sure everything was all right."

"Of course. Please have a seat . . . Miss Westraven, is it?" Miss Whitney gestured one floured hand toward a rocker that sat by the window next to the woodstove. A sewing basket sat on the floor next to it.

"Please, call me Jenny." She settled into the rocker, pulling Lottie onto her lap.

She and Miss Whitney had met early on, but since then, she'd seen little of her. The schoolgirls did their classroom work in the morning, so Miss Whitney spent her afternoons here in her cabin while the girls worked their shifts in the kitchen, laundry, and sewing rooms.

"I'm sorry the girls missed their lessons." She glanced over at them. "I'm wondering if they'll tell us the reason?"

Alice looked down at the floor. Marion patted her shoulder, then looked up at Miss Whitney.

"She's upset about the news. She heard Papa telling Mama about Lewis."

"Ah. He's a relative, is he not?"

Alice nodded. "Her uncle."

"Oh, Miss Whitney." For the first time since Jenny'd entered the cabin, Alice spoke up, her voice almost a wail. "They won't send him to Laramie, will they?"

Miss Whitney's mouth firmed into a grim line. "I don't know." She was quiet for a moment. Then, with a sigh, she continued. "What I do know is Reverend Coolidge and Reverend Roberts will do everything they can to see that doesn't happen. I also know your uncle wouldn't want you to spend time crying over him."

"But I don't want to play music today," Alice glanced over at Jenny sheepishly. "I don't have any music in here." She placed a fist across her chest above her heart.

"Oh, honey. You don't have to have a lesson today." Jenny said. "If it's all right with Miss Whitney, why don't you and Marion take Lottie down to the mud village and show her how to make a teepee or a horse."

A favorite free-time activity for the girls was creating objects out of mud from the banks of Trout Creek. In a sloping area not far from the school, they'd created a miniature Indian village. When Jenny first saw it, she'd been amazed at the intricate detail the girls had molded into each figure.

"I think that's an excellent idea," Miss Whitney said. "Run along now but be sure to get cleaned up in time for supper."

The two girls slid off the bench, taking Lottie's hand. Soon they were skipping down the path to the creek bed. Miss Whitney shook her head as she watched them go.

"If only all their troubles could be so easily forgotten."

"So what's in Laramie?"

"The State Prison."

"Goodness. What has her uncle done?"

Miss Whitney fixed her with a hard stare. "It's not so much what he's done as what they're accusing him of doing."

Well, naturally. Innocent until proven guilty. She knew that. She'd hadn't worked in a law office for two months for nothing.

"What is he accused of?"

Miss Whitney continued to knead her dough, silent for so long, Jenny wondered if she'd heard her. Finally, the teacher sighed. "Lewis took a wife last year . . . the Indian way. She's very young. In fact, she was a student here until last spring—probably should have returned this fall. The superintendent filed charges against Lewis when he learned she was pregnant."

"Why is that a crime?"

"Because of her age. And the fact they were never married the white man's way."

"But aren't most couples on the reservation married the traditional way?"

"The older ones, yes. But the agent and superintendent encourage the younger ones to get a license and marry before a judge or a pastor."

"And because he chose not to, he's guilty of a crime that can put him in state prison? What did they charge him with?"

Miss Whitney firmed her lips and kept her gaze focused on her dough. "It's an ugly word. One I'd rather not repeat. I'd certainly never heard it used before I came out here. Suffice it to say, it doesn't apply to Lewis. If Wyoming hadn't raised the age of consent a few years ago, the superintendent wouldn't have a case."

"Surely a competent lawyer will get him acquitted."

"I doubt he'll be given a competent lawyer." Miss Whitney's tone had a bitter pitch to it. She pounded the dough with greater fervor. "I've yet to see any court-appointed attorney get a not-guilty verdict for any of his Indian clients."

"Are you saying the courts are corrupt?"

"I'm saying white justice and red justice are two entirely different things." Miss Whitney gave the dough one last vicious punch before transferring it to a loaf pan and covering it with a dishtowel. She turned to Jenny. "Let's talk of something else. Would you like a cup of tea? I was about to pour myself one."

"Yes. Thank you."

As Miss Whitney busied herself at the stove, Jenny took a look around the cozy, two-room cabin. The furniture was simple but adequate. Miss Whitney was not given to excessive decoration, but a colorful quilt and red throw rugs added splashes of color within the cabin's dim interior.

Would the cabin Nick build look something like this? The rooms were so small. In fact, her bedroom suite in New York was bigger than this entire cabin. Mrs. Willoughby said Miss Whitney also came from a well-to-do family back east. Yet, she seemed quite at home in these humble surroundings.

Would she make the transition to a simpler life as easily? One thing was sure. She'd need a lot more training in the kitchen to be anywhere near as capable as Miss Whitney seemed to be. She wouldn't know the first thing about baking a loaf of bread, or anything else for that matter. She could brew and serve a cup of tea, but somehow she couldn't picture Nick sitting down with her for afternoon tea.

Miss Whitney handed her a teacup. "Would you like some sugar?"

"Yes, please."

"I have some shortbread if you'd like."

She went to her cupboard and pulled out a tin. Placing four cookies on a small plate, she offered them to Jenny.

"Thank you. These are delicious." And another area where Miss Whitney excelled, but she didn't.

The teacher smiled at Jenny over the rim of her cup.

"I'm glad you stopped by. We haven't had the chance to become acquainted."

"No. We're always so busy with the children."

"Do you enjoy teaching piano?"

"Very much. I've never taught before, but the girls are so sweet and so interested in learning."

"Yes, music has always been a favorite, but with Miss Drescher getting married last summer, Mrs. Roberts and I simply haven't had time to teach it this year. I know Mrs. Roberts was especially pleased Marion would have a chance to take lessons from you. It's a skill she wants each of her daughters to have. She did well teaching Elinor herself, but now with the three younger ones and the school growing, well . . ." She shrugged. "We can't do it all, can we?"

"Maybe I shouldn't have been so quick to let Marion run off and play."

Miss Whitney shook her head. "I doubt she'd have gained much today. She and Alice are such good friends, and Marion has a tender heart. If Alice is struggling, then Marion will struggle too."

"Do you really believe her uncle will be sent to prison?"

"I've seen it happen before. And it's such a shame. Lewis is a good young man. He supports his wife's blind grandmother as well as his sister and her children. It will be hard on the whole family if he has to spend time in jail. And I can't help but feel it's all due to spite. Especially coming so close on the heels of that letter."

"What letter?"

"Didn't you hear about Willie?"

"Willie Yellow Bear? No. What happened?"

"I'm surprised Mrs. Willoughby hasn't told you. I heard the story from Reverend Coolidge, who teaches at the Government school during the week. Seems as if it all started with a goose."

"A goose!"

"A nice, fat goose the superintendent was raising to feed a special delegation from Washington that's due to visit the week before Thanksgiving. Apparently, Willie got bored one day and decided to go hunting. He made himself a slingshot, and by the time they found him, he'd taken down several chickens. Worst of all, he'd killed the goose. The superintendent had been pampering and feeding that bird all fall, and when he saw it lying dead at Willie's feet, I'm afraid he lost his temper.

"He hauled Willie off to the lockup—not the school's lockup—but the Agency jail where they house adult criminals. He left Willie there for the night with only a tray of bread and water for company."

"Oh, the poor thing." Jenny pictured the small boy huddled in the dark, scared and alone.

"He admitted later he regretted his choice, but Willie is so naughty, and the usual punishments have had no effect on him. I'm sure the man was at his wit's end and not thinking clearly on account of the goose. At any rate, Willie did not end up spending the night there. In fact, he showed up at the agent's quarters around 8 o'clock that evening, crying and clutching his arm. Turns out, he somehow managed to climb up to a spot above the doorway where he noticed some loose bricks. He pried them out until he had a hole large enough to slip through but somehow lost his balance on the way out and fell, breaking his arm.

"The agent sent for the doctor right away, and they were able to set it. In fact, by the time I saw Willie about a week later, he was running around, with a cast on his arm, but in all other regards his usual lively self. Reverend Coolidge says the superintendent was full of remorse. If only the matter could have ended there. But Lewis wrote a letter of complaint to the Commissioner of Indian Affairs, and they sent out an Inspector to investigate.

"Both Superintendent Fallcourt and the agent were reprimanded and the event written up in their permanent records. The superintendent has been hoping for a promotion to a position within the Office of Indian Affairs, but with this report, I'm sure he feels his prospects have diminished."

"You think he may have retaliated by having Lewis arrested?"

"Oh, I don't know. Now you say it out loud, it does seem far-fetched. But I can't help feeling something isn't as it should be."

Jenny thought of her own encounter with Superintendent Fallcourt. Granted, the man was arrogant and high-handed. She hadn't liked him, but she wasn't sure that was enough to accuse him of something like this. Still, for Willie's sake, and Alice's, shouldn't someone look into it?

"Who is Lewis' counsel?"

"He probably doesn't have one yet. They only took him into custody last night. The court will have to appoint someone."

"But if Lewis chooses, he can hire his own lawyer, right?"

"I doubt he would know anyone, and he certainly wouldn't have the money to hire any of the ones who take the larger cases in Lander."

But she knew a lawyer—one who rarely lost a case—one who could name his price in one of the largest cities back east. If anyone could get Lewis out of this charge, Ben could. But would he? Could she even ask it of him? Ever since the bear incident, she'd done her best to put distance between them. Asking a favor was the last thing she wanted. But maybe, for Willie and Alice, she could set aside her pride.

"THERE'S A LADY TO SEE YOU."

Ben looked up from the stack of papers on his desk. His clerk, Eustace Frye, stood in the doorway. Judging from the goofy grin on his face, the lady in question was young and attractive.

Ben stifled a groan. "Miss Jones again?"

"Not this time. This one says she needs to engage your services." Frye waggled his eyebrows.

Well, that was a new approach. Over the past month, the foyer of his law office had resembled the front room of Mrs. Stacia Allen's Ladies Emporium. So far, all the single ladies in town, or their matchmaking mamas, had found a reason to pay him a visit.

Apparently, Mrs. Parkhurst spread the word he was a bachelor who'd recently inherited a fortune. Since then, he'd been invited to more dinners, concerts, and card parties than he cared to count. Miss Stella Jones had been most persistent, dropping by his office two to three times a week.

He should be flattered. Stella was lovely, cultured, the daughter of an influential man and . . . not what he wanted. The one he wanted would barely talk to him.

"Shall I send her in?"

He gave a short nod and returned to his papers, looking up when he heard the rustle of a woman's skirts.

"Jenny?"

He drank in the sight of her. Her dress brought out the blue of her eyes and accentuated her curves. With great effort, he tore his gaze from the swell of white lace at her breast, lingering for a fraction on her lips, and settling on her hat. Her hat was safe.

She reached up and touched the ribbons adorning the brim. "Is something amiss? Please tell me I don't resemble Mrs. Dalrymple."

"No. No. It's lovely. You're lovely. Charming, in fact." Good Lord, he was babbling like a haberdasher. Where was his poise? This was Jenny, for Pete's sake.

Dredging up his most professional manner, he stood. "Please. Come in."

He started around the desk to pull out a chair but found Frye had beat him to it, leaving him with nothing to do but usher the man out the door and shut it on his impudent face.

He returned to his desk, took a calming breath, and sat. "So . . . to what do I owe this pleasure?"

But she wasn't looking at him. She perused the room, giving

him the chance to admire the creamy flesh of her throat, the curve of her cheek.

"I like what you've done with the place," she said. "It's cozy. Comfortable. A lot like your office back in Newark." Her gaze strayed to his cluttered desk. A dimple played at one corner of her mouth. "I could tidy things for you if you'd like."

How long had it been since she'd favored him with those dimples? Far too long.

"Hmmmm." He pretended to consider. "Maybe not. But if you have time later, I could dictate a letter or two."

She leaned forward. "You have no idea how wonderful that sounds. I can never get Teddy to let me help him with his correspondence. And he has his own Remington right at home. I'm afraid if I don't practice, I'll lose everything I learned."

"Ted would have both our hides if I made you my typewriter girl again. Look at the trouble it caused last time."

She shrugged. "It got me a trip out here, which was just what I wanted."

He had a feeling she got what she wanted more often than was good for her.

"So, what is it you want now?"

A slight flush stained her cheeks. "I beg your pardon?"

"Sorry, but this isn't a social call, is it?"

"Oh. That. Yes. I mean, no." She folded her hands primly in her lap and cleared her throat. "I need your legal advice."

He quirked an eyebrow. "Trouble?"

"No." Indignation radiated from every pore of her body. "Why is it you and Teddy always assume I'm in trouble?"

He let his left eyebrow do his talking for him. Lifting it a quarter of an inch higher, he simply sat and waited. The trick always served him well in the courtroom.

But Jenny was a lot tougher than his average witness. Rather than faltering, she dug in, crossing her arms across her body, mirroring his lifted eyebrow with one of her own.

They held their impasse for several seconds before he gave

in. "Fine. Forgive me for assuming something so terribly outrageous." He folded his hands on the desk in front of him, summoning his best imitation of the serious Mr. Goddard. "Since you, most obviously, have no need for legal advice on your own behalf, how may I be of service?"

Her left dimple played hide-and-seek on her cheek, gone before he could fully attest to its presence.

"I'm here on behalf of a friend. Well, not really a friend. More of a friend of a friend, I guess. He's the uncle of one of my piano students."

"At the Indian school?"

"Yes."

"And he has a legal question?"

"He's in the county jail."

Oh. "If he's committed a crime, I'm sure he'll be assigned legal counsel through the Office of Indian Affairs."

"From what I understand, their counsel will be less than adequate at best. And he's done nothing wrong."

"Jenny, every criminal since Cain has claimed innocence."

"Yes, but even Miss Whitney—she's a teacher at the school —even she thinks he's been wrongly charged. She thinks he may have been put in jail out of spite. Couldn't you at least investigate?"

No. He didn't have the time nor the inclination to chase across the county on a case that didn't concern him. He drew a deep breath, his gaze snagging on Jenny's blue eyes. Drat. There wasn't a man alive who could resist the plea in those blue eyes.

He stifled a groan. "What's he accused of?"

Jenny looked away. "I'm not entirely sure. Miss Whitney wouldn't tell me the actual charge. It has something to do with the fact his wife is too young, and they never officially married, in the white way, that is. And now his wife is pregnant."

Good Lord. Was she talking statutory rape? He raked a hand through his hair. Now he knew for sure he didn't want to get involved.

He started to shake his head, but Jenny held up a hand to stop him. "Don't decide right away. Please, Ben? At least come with me to the reservation to meet his wife and hear her side of the story. Then, if you still don't think you can help him, I'll understand. But I know when you hear the whole story, you'll think it's wrong too. I know you'll want to help him."

He knew no such thing, but what she asked was tempting. He'd been trying for weeks to find a way to spend time with her. Here was his chance. A trip to the reservation and back could take an entire day.

"All right. If Ted approves, I'll ride out to the reservation with you. But I'm not making any promises."

Chapter Twenty-Nine

He received Ted's approval with the stipulation Jenny's friend Sara ride along.

"It's not that I don't trust you," Ted said. "But Grace's mother would have my head if I didn't make sure Jen acted with the strictest propriety."

Ben was tempted to tell him propriety in the West wasn't nearly as strict as it was back in New York City, but held his tongue. No use jeopardizing what little advantage he had. Instead, he rented a buggy with a narrow front seat and a small rear-facing seat in the back. Jenny could never face rear in a vehicle without getting nauseous, so as he anticipated, she took the front seat next to him. Sara sat in back.

Not that the seating arrangement hampered the girls' ability to visit. The two talked non-stop from the moment they left Lander until they reached the Mission School. He may as well have been a hired coachman.

His only advantage was the seat was so narrow, Jenny had no choice but to sit close enough to touch him. She didn't pull away, which he took as a good sign. Unless, of course, she didn't notice. In which case, it wasn't a good sign at all.

They stopped at the girls' school to trade Sara for Miss

Whitney, who promised to guide them to Lewis Yellow Bear's village. He deduced Miss Whitney and Jenny were not as well acquainted, because after the initial greetings, Jenny fell silent.

He studied her profile, drinking in her beauty. The wind had whipped roses into her cheeks and brightened her nose. He leaned over and tucked the lap robe more firmly around her, pulling her even closer.

"Are you warm enough? The wind has a bite to it today."

"Yes, of course. I'm fine." A flush crept up her neck, deepening the color in her cheeks. Ah, she noticed.

If Miss Whitney hadn't been with them, he'd have been tempted to put his arm around her. Maybe even steal a kiss. Guess Ted wasn't entirely wrong about the need for propriety.

"Yellow Bear's encampment should be just over this ridge," Miss Whitney said.

Sure enough, as the buggy topped the next rise, he saw a cluster of canvas tepees next to a modest log structure. Smoke curled from the tops of each dwelling, signaling the camp was occupied.

Jenny's hand gripped his arm. "Oh, Ben. Wouldn't it be wonderful—"

"No."

"You don't even know what I was going to say."

"Sure, I do. You were going to say, 'wouldn't it be wonderful to live in a tepee?'"

"Fine." Her pretty little lips pouted. "But don't you think it would be wonderful? Not for forever, of course, but think of it— like sleeping out under the stars, only better. Can't you imagine it?"

"Sure. Cold and crowded and . . . " The wind blew a whiff of smoke their direction, the acrid tang causing his eyes to burn. "And smoky and smelly."

Miss Whitney laughed. "That's the sagebrush they use for their fires. It's more plentiful than wood in this country and cheaper than coal, but it definitely has a strong odor."

Jenny wasn't amused. She crossed her arms and sent him a glare. "Since when did you become such a pessimist?"

"I prefer to think of myself as a realist."

"Hmmph. You haven't always been this way. Remember Geronimo?"

How could he forget the summer of Geronimo? He, Ted, and Jenny had spent their entire vacation reenacting Indian battles and vying for the privilege of playing Geronimo. Even Jenny had her turn, though he and Ted had scorned the idea of a girl playing the part of the great Indian chief. But more often than not, the role of Geronimo fell his way.

They'd begged and begged to spend a night out in the tepee they'd constructed from sticks and blankets until Grandma Janssen and Aunt Bethany finally relented. That night was the highlight of his summer.

"I was what? Eleven? At some point, Jenny, we all grow up and realize the difference between fantasy and reality." His voice sounded harsh even to him.

The surprise in her eyes faded to a mixture of understanding and pity. Great. He should never have bared his soul to her that day by the stream. The last thing he wanted from Jenny was pity. Besides, he didn't want to think about his family right now and all the ways he had failed them. Not today.

"How is your family? Have you heard from them?"

She wasn't going to let this go, was she? "They're fine. Letty writes every so often, and Mr. Foster keeps me informed on all the business issues." They were doing just fine without him. Better than fine, just as he'd expected.

He slapped the reins, bringing the buggy into camp at a gallop, barely missing a bony dog lying in the dirt in front of one of the tepees. Ben pulled to a quick stop, but neither woman remarked on his reckless driving. Hopping down, he helped them descend from the buggy.

Miss Whitney led the way to a tepee a little ways apart from the others.

"Hello, Blind Woman," she called as they approached. "I know it sounds disrespectful," she said over her shoulder, "but that is what everyone calls her. I don't even know if she would respond to her given name anymore."

A girl, round with child, stepped out through a flap in the teepee. She looked young. Too young. The face of a girl on the body of a woman.

"*Hao*, Bridget," Miss Whitney said. "Is your grandmother home?"

The girl nodded and gestured for them to follow her inside. The interior was light and roomy, warmer than he'd imagined. Bed pallets, covered with animal skins and bright woven blankets, lined the white canvas walls. A wizened old woman sat by the fire pit in the center where a fire crackled, thick black smoke rising in a plume toward a hole in the teepee's roof. The pungent odor of the burning sage almost overpowered.

Despite her stomach's girth, the girl sank gracefully to a seat beside her grandmother and motioned for them to sit. The older woman rubbed a piece of wet rawhide back and forth across a stick pounded into the dirt floor. When they sat, she stilled and turned her sightless eyes in their direction, tilting her head to the side.

"I've brought some visitors," Miss Whitney said. "Miss Westraven and Mr. Bennet. Mr. Bennet is a lawyer who would like to help Lewis if he can."

Bridget turned to her grandmother and said a few rapid words in Shoshone. "*Aishe, aishe.*" The old woman spoke in a low melodic voice. She stretched a hand in their direction.

Bridget looked at him. "She would like to shake your hand. To say thank you."

Ben reached out, and she took his hand in both of hers, stroking and patting and nodding her head. Her fingers were gnarled, and he noticed the fingertips on several of her fingers were cut off at the last knuckle.

"Can she speak any English?" he asked Miss Whitney.

"No, but Bridget can interpret."

He hesitated. "Is there no one else? The questions I need to ask—" He trailed off, not knowing how to word what he needed to say. Good Lord. He hadn't thought this through. How did one begin an interrogation with only the alleged victim as an interpreter and two unmarried females as witnesses?

Miss Whitney seemed to understand his quandary.

"Bridget," she said in a schoolmarm's voice. "Mr. Bennett needs to speak with your grandmother in private if he's going to help Lewis. Is your husband's sister around? Could she interpret?"

The girl turned solemn brown eyes his direction and gave a slow nod. Rising, she left the tepee to return a few minutes later with another woman, whom he guessed to be at least fifteen years Bridget's senior. Miss Whitney introduced her as Lewis's sister, Yvette.

"Would you ladies excuse us for a moment?"

"Of course. Bridget can show us around the encampment. Miss Westraven is most eager to explore."

As the three women left, Jenny caught Ben's eye, a decided question in her own. He was certain Jenny didn't understand the exact nature of the charges. Women of her station were kept protected from the world's sordidness by their menfolk. He wasn't looking forward to the interrogation from her that was sure to come.

He turned back to Yvette. "You are Lewis' sister?"

She nodded.

"You understand the charges against him?"

She nodded again.

"I know you can probably answer the questions I'm about to ask, but I need to hear the answers from Bridget's guardian—her grandmother. Will you interpret for us?"

Once more, a nod.

"Good. Please ask her how long Lewis and her granddaughter have been together."

The women spoke, and then Yvette answered him in English. "About two years."

Two years! Bridget looked barely older than the girls he'd seen playing in the schoolyard at the Mission. Two years ago, she would surely have been in their number. He began to see the superintendent's side of the issue.

"And how old is your brother?"

Yvette looked puzzled by his question.

"Is he older or younger than you?"

"Younger."

"By how much?"

She held up five fingers, which would still give him roughly ten years on Bridget. A man, by anyone's standards—certainly a man in terms of the law.

"Does he consider himself married to Bridget?" The two women spoke back and forth for a few minutes before Yvette answered.

"They are not married in the white way. They have no papers, but they moved in together—not last summer, but the summer before. It is the Indian way. They ask Mr. Harlow, the agent, if they can be married in the white way also, but he say Bridget is too young. They ask him twice, but still, he say, too young."

"So even though the agent told him Bridget was too young, your brother pursued her?"

Yvette shrugged. "They were already together."

"Reverend Roberts tells me your brother has been married before."

"Yes."

"What happened to his first wife?"

"She died. She and her baby both died three summers ago."

"And when did he begin to court Bridget? Ask the Blind Woman."

She spoke once more with the older woman, then turned to him. "Two summers ago."

"Did he ever force himself upon her? Do anything to her she did not want him to do?"

More words back and forth. The old woman shook her head vigorously and spoke with great vehemence. Yvette interpreted.

"Lewis is a good boy. A good provider. Bridget, she love her husband. She only want him to come back. She does not understand why they take him to jail. He is a good boy. The Blind Woman asks that you talk to the superintendent and the agent. Tell them Lewis is a good boy. They need to let him go."

He sighed. "Tell her I will do my best."

Yvette relayed his message to the grandmother, but he could tell by the resignation in her eyes, she had little hope his best would be good enough.

He left the tepee in search of Jenny and Miss Whitney but had only gone a few steps before he felt a touch on his arm. Bridget crept out from beside the tepee as if she'd been lying in wait for him.

"Please. You will help us? Yes?"

"I'll do what I can."

"It's not his fault." She hung her head, dragging the toe of her moccasin back and forth in the dirt. "He wanted to wait. To ask the agent again for permission, but I didn't want to. I moved all my things and grandmother's things into his tepee one day when he was out hunting. He could not move them back without shaming me. He did not want to shame me." She looked up at him then, brown eyes fierce. "It is my fault, not his. Tell them." She laid a protective hand across her abdomen as if to remind him not only her interests were at stake.

He wanted to groan his frustration. Instead, he repeated, "I'll do what I can."

He hoped his words didn't sound as empty as they felt.

∼

He went alone to visit Lewis Yellow-Bear. Much as he wanted to spend time with Jenny, the county jail was no place for a lady. She was none too happy with him, but though she pleaded and pouted, neither he nor Ted would allow it.

The day was cold, and since the courthouse sat on the edge of town, he elected to ride rather than walk. The jail resided in the left-wing and upper level of the Fremont County courthouse, a three-story redbrick structure built in the classical style. Sunlight glinted off the green tin of its hipped roof as he approached.

If it weren't for the wind, the day might almost be pleasant. But this was Wyoming. Wind was a constant. Today's variety bit through his overcoat with a ferocity that warned winter wasn't far away.

He tethered his mount in the lean-to next to the jailer's quarters. The jailer's ample wife waved to him from where she hung out the day's laundry. He waved back. Rumor had it some in the county committed crimes simply to have a chance to eat Mrs. Robinson's famous pies every day. Having sampled a slice on a previous visit, he could almost believe it.

He found the deputy sheriff, Chet Robinson, in his office, feet up, whittling on a block of wood and spitting tobacco into a nearby spittoon. He glanced up as Ben walked in.

"Ya here to see Carmichael? What happened? Didn't Matthews get enough out'a him yesterday?"

"Actually, I'm here to talk to Lewis Yellow-Bear. I understand you have him in custody."

"The Injun?" Robinson shot a stream of tobacco into the spittoon, then studied Ben as if he'd suddenly sprouted an extra nose. "What'cha wasting your time with that one for? Tell ya what ya should do. See if Nate Clements will take ya on. They brought him in last night for shooting that no-good sheepherder, Flynn. Nate's real popular around here and everyone knows Flynn was a drunk and a mean one at that. Getting Nate off on a self-defense charge would be as easy as shooting fish in a barrel and would make you real popular too."

Ben crossed his arms. "Yellow-Bear's wife asked me to represent him. I'd like to talk to him."

Robinson snorted. "Wife? If she was his wife then he wouldn't be in here, now would he?"

Ben didn't reply, simply stared at the man until he pushed to his feet. "Suit yourself. Ain't my funeral." He grabbed a ring of keys off a hook by the door.

Ben followed Robinson out the door and waited while he unlocked a steel door at the entrance to the stairwell. He led the way up three flights of stairs, where he unlocked a second steel door. A whiff of foul air tainted with body odor and urine greeted Ben as he stepped onto the men's cellblock. This upper floor was vented only by two small, grated windows.

Robinson handed Ben a straight-backed wooden chair from inside the door and gestured down the long corridor. "Yellow-Bear's cell is the one on the end. If ya decide he's not worth the effort, Nate's in cell three. I'll be back in half an hour to get ya."

With that, he clanged the metal door shut. The key turned in the lock, and Robinson's footsteps faded away. Picking up the chair by its top rung, Ben began the uncomfortable walk down the cell block. The inmate in the first cell snored loudly. Inmate number two acknowledged his presence with a baleful glare. Nate, in cell three, gave him a cheerful grin and wave. For a murderer, the man seemed plenty relaxed. Guess he shared Robinson's optimism about his situation.

Mr. Matthews' client sat in the next cell. Ben had been in to see the man before. As Ben made his way past, Carmichael came over to the bars and called out. "Ole Matthews told me you were new to these parts, but I never took you for an Injun-lover."

Ben ignored him, but Carmichael continued. "Good luck getting that one to talk. If you get tired of jawing away to yourself down there, you can come on back and visit with us. We ain't too particular, right, boys?"

Nate laughed. The other two kept their silence. Well, the sullen one anyway. The snoring inmate was none too quiet.

Ben passed three empty cells, finally reaching the end. He straddled the chair, peering into the cell's dusky interior. Yellow-Bear sat on the floor next to his narrow iron cot, head resting on his knees. A curtain of long, stringy black hair shielded his face.

Ben cleared his throat.

No response.

"Yellow-Bear?"

The man didn't move a muscle.

Ben pressed on. "The Blind Woman and Bridget asked me to come talk to you."

Yellow-Bear raised his head, and Ben looked into a stony face with eyes as black and fathomless as a well at midnight.

"Bridget would like me to represent you at your trial. I need to know if you agree."

Yellow-Bear shook his head. "We have no money for lawyers. Tell her to save the money for the baby."

"I'm not asking for your money. Friends of your wife and family have offered to pay my fee." He didn't tell Yellow-Bear he had no intention of letting Jenny pay him. He'd take the case pro-bono. He was probably as big a fool as Robinson thought him, but somehow he couldn't let it go. Not after visiting the Blind Woman and meeting Bridget.

"Tell these 'friends' you speak of to spend their money on helping my wife and baby for the next five years. They'll need it more than I do."

The man spoke better English than Ben anticipated and had a much better grasp of his situation than his wife did. But Ben wasn't giving up. "I'm sure they'll do everything possible for your wife should the need arise, but won't you allow them to help in this way, too? Wouldn't it be better for you to go free and to care for your wife and child yourself?"

Yellow-Bear leaned forward, face intent. "I will not be going free. I'm not in this cell because I decided to take a wife the

Indian way. I'm in this cell because I decided to use the White Man's education against him. I write letters—lots of letters. This is the only way they found to keep me quiet."

"There is such a thing as justice."

"In your world, maybe. Not mine."

Ben realized now what it was he saw, or didn't see, in Yellow-Bear's eyes. Hope. He searched their depths and found nothing.

He tried again. "Robinson tells me you'll be traveling to Laramie tomorrow. When is your trial?"

"A week from Tuesday."

Not much time. He stood and picked up his chair. "I'll see you in Laramie, then."

Yellow-Bear shrugged and dropped his head back down.

As Ben walked up the cell block, Yellow-Bear's words, an echo of what Robinson had told him earlier, rang in his ears. No one—not Robinson, not Matthews, not Yellow-Bear—thought he had a snowball's chance in hell of succeeding with this case. So why couldn't he let it go? This wasn't about Jenny anymore, and he knew it.

His mind flashed to a memory of Grandma Janssen taking his face between her hands one day when he'd come home from school sporting yet another black eye.

"Oh, Lester," she'd said. "Must you fight every little injustice you see?"

Apparently so, because tomorrow he'd be on that stage to Laramie.

Chapter Thirty

He found both Miss Stella Jones and Jenny waiting for him back at his office. He assumed Jenny was waiting for him. At the moment, she appeared more interested in the new typewriter they'd purchased for Mr. Frye. She bent over the machine, affording him a delicious view of her backside. He let his gaze linger a moment before tearing it away to greet Miss Jones.

He bowed her direction. "What a pleasure to see you again, Miss Jones."

"Ben!" Jenny turned, face glowing. "Mr. Frye was showing me his Underwood 2. It's so much nicer than the Remington in Mr. Goddard's office. It has a front strike like the one I used in training. I was showing Mr. Frye how it works."

Ben suspected Frye knew how to use all the components of the Underwood as well as Jenny did but decided not to spoil the man's fun. Though married, Mr. Frye clearly gained more pleasure from the influx of female visitors than Ben ever had.

He turned back to Miss Jones.

"I assume you're here to see me? Would you care to step into my office?"

"Oh, no." She said, casting a swift glance at Jenny. "Miss Westraven was here before me. I'll wait."

Jenny, once again engrossed in the typewriter, called back over her shoulder. "No need to wait for me. Ben and I have a case to discuss, which could take some time. You two go ahead."

Miss Jones sat even straighter in her chair if that were possible.

"No, please. I insist." Her words carried a hint of venom.

He didn't know what Jenny had done to make an enemy of Miss Jones, but enemy she was, and none too happy about his and Jenny's casual relationship. He needed to diffuse the situation.

"Miss Westraven is right. Our business could take some time." Gauging the storm clouds gathering in Miss Jones' eyes, he pulled out his pocket watch and gave it a once over. "And since it's getting rather late, maybe we should reschedule. Mr. Frye, could you find Miss Westraven a spot on my calendar? Maybe the week after next, since I'll be out of town for a few days?"

He had Jenny's attention now. She spun from the typewriter, eyes wide, a protest forming on her lips. Before she could voice it, he casually reached up and pulled on his right ear lobe.

He knew the minute their childhood signal registered. Formal Jenny kicked in.

"Of course, Mr. Bennett. I'd be happy to reschedule. You two go ahead. Our business can wait until you get back."

With a toss of her head, Miss Jones preceded Ben into his office. When he turned to close the door, Jenny caught his eye and winked.

Well, that worked better than he'd expected. He led Miss Jones to a chair.

"Now, Miss Jones, what can I do for you?"

She leaned forward, reaching out to tap his arm. "What you can do is reaccept Ted's invitation to the concert tonight. I was so disappointed to hear you had canceled."

Ah, the concert. Anna Held was visiting the opera house tonight. Lander had been abuzz with excitement for weeks.

Originally, he'd accepted Ted's invitation hoping Jenny would be in their party, but when he learned Jenny would attend the concert with the Dickensons, the lure of the evening paled. He'd excused himself even before he knew he'd be traveling tomorrow, citing the need to work.

He summoned a regretful smile. "I'm sorry. I have a case to prepare. I won't have time for the concert tonight."

Her lips formed a moue of distaste. "You men are always so wrapped up in your work. Surely one night off won't hurt."

"Any other night, yes. But I leave town first thing tomorrow and need to prepare before I go. I owe my client that much." He didn't tell her his client was Yellow Bear. Somehow, he knew without asking what her response to that would be.

After vaguely promising to come to dinner sometime after he returned, he ushered her from his office. Thank goodness, Jenny had also left, forestalling any complications. He'd drop by Ted's to talk with her later.

HER SCENT PERMEATED HIS CONSCIOUSNESS LONG BEFORE HER presence did—lilies with a hint of spice. Ben glanced up from his law books to find her in the doorway, a vision in rose and gold, the silk of her gown hugging her in just the right places, the satin of her bare white shoulders begging his touch.

"How'd you get in? Frye locked up hours ago." His voice came out more gruffly than he intended, but she didn't seem to notice.

She dimpled, flashing him the roguish grin that so often led to trouble—for him anyway. A large brass key dangled from her gloved fingertips.

"Top right drawer under the blotter just like in Mr. Goddard's office. Really, Ben, you are far too predictable." Jenny floated across the floor and sank into the chair on the opposite side of the desk, setting the key halfway between them. "I took the liberty of taking it when Mr. Frye was distracted with your calendar because, for all your ear-pulling and empty promises, I knew you wouldn't make it by to see me tonight."

He opened his mouth to protest, but she stopped him with the lift of a finger. "Admit it. You have no idea the time."

He glanced at the window. Dark. He assumed from her evening dress, she was either heading to the concert or returning from it, but as early as it got dark these days, he had no way of knowing which. He was tempted to pull out his pocket watch, but she would only crow in triumph if he did.

"Come on. Admit it. If I hadn't stopped by, you would have been lost in your law books until well after midnight, at which point you'd have stumbled home to bed and boarded that stage tomorrow morning without giving me another thought."

He leaned back in his chair and crossed his arms. "I would have come to see you."

"Oh? And when might that be? It's well past eleven now. Did you plan to show up at Teddy's after midnight and expect him to let you in?"

She had a point, but if it were really that late, what was she doing here?

She wagged a gloved finger at him. "I know what you're thinking, but I've got it taken care of. The Dickensons are next door at Scott's, eating desserts. Sara and I stepped out to use the ladies' room. She's waiting for me at the bottom of the steps. In a few minutes, we will both return together, and no one will be the wiser. But that means we don't have much time, so tell me quickly. You met with Yellow Bear today and agreed to represent him, right? That's why you're leaving in the morning?"

Ben nodded. "His trial is a week from Tuesday in Laramie."

"So soon? That's barely enough time to prepare a case."

"I know."

She shrugged. "No matter. I know you'll represent him brilliantly."

"Jenny, you've got to know there's almost no chance he won't do time for this."

Her forehead furrowed. "Why? You don't seriously think he's guilty of . . . of . . . that awful crime."

"Not in intent, no. But by the letter of the law, yes. He and Bridget have been living together openly for almost two years. She's not quite seventeen and is clearly with child. They're not married in the eyes of the law. He's guilty."

"Ben Bennett, he most certainly is not. If he is guilty of . . . of *that*, then almost the entire reservation is guilty. He married Bridget the same way his father and his father's father married their wives. What he did has nothing to do with . . . with . . . what they are accusing him of. She was the one who pursued him. She'll tell you that herself."

"But the law clearly states consent has no weight if the girl is underage. The age of consent in Wyoming is now 18. Back when Yellow Bear's father found his bride, the age was 10. Things have changed."

"But aren't Indians under their own jurisdiction? Why should the white man's laws have any effect on him?"

"Because . . . what he's accused of . . ." He hesitated to name the crime since she wouldn't. "Is a major crime, like murder, and therefore falls under federal jurisdiction."

"Then, the laws are unfair."

"The laws aren't the problem. They're good laws, put in place to protect the innocent and weak. Wyoming, and almost all the other states, raised the age of consent to protect young girls from being forced into prostitution." He raked a hand through his hair and blew out a breath. He could not believe he was having this conversation with her. "The problem is how men use the law. When you've been in this business even for a little while, you come to understand the same laws designed to shield the weak can be used as billy clubs by the powerful."

"But you love the law."

"No. I love justice. They're not always the same."

Jenny rose and came around to his side of the desk. She stroked back a lock of his hair, then rested her palm against his cheek. "That's one of the things I love about you, Ben. You always fight for what you believe is right. And that's the reason I know you're the best man to represent Yellow Bear."

Even through her glove, her touch ignited a firestorm. It took all the self-control he could muster not to reach up and pull her down onto his lap.

And what was that she'd said? About loving him?

Before he could respond, she made her way to the door in a swish of silk and lace. Looking back over her shoulder, she said, "I made that appointment to see you, so when you return, expect to present me with a full report. Safe travels, Ben."

And she was gone, leaving behind the scent of her perfume, the fire of her touch, and the certain knowledge he'd be unable to accomplish anything the rest of the night.

Chapter Thirty-One

Jenny fingered the silky corset in black and pink brocade on display at Mrs. Stacia Allen's. So pretty with its rows of baby pink ribbon threaded through the black lace. Would Nick like to see her in this? She smiled, hugging close the secret she'd held for the past three weeks. She was going to be Nick's bride.

No one knew yet. Not even Sara. Nick wanted her to keep it secret until he had a chance to come to Lander and talk to Ted. But Thanksgiving was a mere ten days away. Nick had promised to come.

Soon. Very soon. The whole world would know. She'd finally found a man who loved her for herself alone. How worried she'd been waiting for his reply to her letter where she explained how she'd lose her inheritance the day they married. The moment she read his reply, she knew she'd found The One.

Darling, your money means nothing to me. In fact, I'm glad you'll be coming to our marriage without it. I want to be the one who provides for your every need.

No one had ever dismissed her millions so easily. Even now he was working on finishing the cabin where they'd live. Yes, it was only a modest, two-room cabin, but he was building it just for her. Besides if Maddie and Rob could be happy in a sheep-herder's wagon, she could be content in a cabin.

"Are you thinking of buying this, dear? I had it shipped in straight from Paris."

Mrs. Allen had finished her business with her previous customers and now stood at Jenny's side, her ample bosom swathed in layers of white lace, much like the samples she had on display.

"It is lovely," Jenny replied. "Yes, I believe I will." After all, she hadn't lost her inheritance yet. She might as well spend her money while she still had it.

Mrs. Allen smiled. "The minute I took this one from the box, I knew you would like it. Have you seen the new selection of gloves?"

"No. But I don't need gloves at the moment." She didn't mind buying the corset, but she had to be firm. She'd bought something, big or small, every time she walked in the door, which had been as often as two to three times a week in the last month alone. Mrs. Allen had been repaid ten times over for her postmistress services.

Jenny watched her wrap the corset in tissue, cover it with brown paper, and tie it with twine. The shopkeeper had always been discreet in passing on Nick's letters, but Jenny was certain she hadn't seen her slip one into the package this time.

"Are you sure you don't have anything else for me?" Jenny asked.

Mrs. Allen gave a sympathetic smile. "No, dear. That's all I have. Maybe next time."

But there hadn't been a letter last time either. Or the time before that. This wasn't like Nick at all. In fact, during those early weeks of their correspondence she'd almost been embar-rassed by the amount of letters she received. Yet now, for almost two weeks, there'd been nothing.

She glanced around the empty store. "You're sure?"

"Quite." Mrs. Allen's smile tempered.

"I don't understand. You sent on my last letter?"

"Of course. I wouldn't let it worry you too much, dearie. The ranching life can get very busy."

"Yes." But something felt off. A group of ladies came in, silencing any further discussion.

Jenny left the shop, making her slow way home. The day had started so fine, but now the glorious November sunshine grated on her mood. Could Nick be injured or sick? If he'd been in an accident of some sort, no one would think to tell her. How would she ever know?

No. If the accident were bad enough, she'd be sure to hear. There'd be a notice in the paper. Or Ted or Will would catch wind of it. News of that nature traveled fast in small communities.

There must be another reason. Could he have taken exception to her last letter? Surely, he could see her side. His sister and her children simply could not live with them. The cabin wasn't big enough. Besides, she wanted him to herself. Was that so much to ask?

On this point, she'd stand firm. If he wanted to keep their engagement secret for a while, so be it. If the only house he could afford for them was a remote cabin, she'd join him and gladly. But share that cabin with four additional people? No. She knew her limits. If that was the reason for his silence, well, he'd just have to stew.

"ARE YOU GOING OUT?"

Jenny stood at the hall mirror. She adjusted her hat a smidge to the left, then turned to see Grace coming down the stairs holding a book in one hand.

"Yes, I have an appointment with Ben this morning. Teddy said you wouldn't need the buggy. Has that changed?"

"No. As long as I can have it this afternoon. I promised Stella and Mrs. Jones I would visit today." Grace hesitated. "Would you like to come along?"

Grace was actually asking for her company? The thought of visiting the Joneses wasn't appealing, but maybe she should make an effort. Meet Grace halfway.

"I'd be happy to come if I get back in time. If not, I'll send Martin home with the buggy before you need it. I'm sure Ben could bring me home." She turned back to the mirror, pulling down a few of her curls, so they framed her face.

"You certainly seem to be seeing a lot of him lately."

Jenny studied Grace in the mirror. Was it her imagination, or had her sister-in-law's voice taken on an edge of acidity?

"He's working on that case for my friends, remember?"

"Oh, yes. Your *Indian* project."

Definitely acidic.

"They're not a project. They're my friends."

"No need to be touchy. A word to the wise, though? You might want to be careful how much time you spend alone with your single male friends. *I* know you've known Ben long enough you consider him your brother, but not everyone sees it that way. And in a town this small, such familiarity between two unmarried *friends* . . . well, people *will* talk."

Stella Jones, for one. After the glares that woman gave her when she found her in Ben's office, well, Jenny's only surprise was how long it had taken Grace to mention it.

She sighed and pulled on her gloves. So much for meeting halfway.

"Look. You can tell Stella I have no romantic interest in Ben. After today, I doubt we'll be spending time together. Yellow Bear's case was tried on Tuesday. Whatever the outcome, my 'project' as you call it, is over. I'm only meeting Ben to find out how it went—plain and simple. If Stella is interested in him, she's welcome to him. I won't stand in her way."

Turning, she walked out and shut the door firmly behind her. There. That sounded convincing, didn't it? Not a single tremor or warble to her voice. So why did she feel like crying? With a shake of her head, she marched down the sidewalk.

"To Mr. Bennet's office?" Martin asked as he helped her into the buggy.

"Yes. Thank you."

She leaned back against the cushions of the buggy, burrowing her hands into her muff. On a nice day, she would have walked to Ben's office, but the rain and snow of the past two days had left the roads a muddy mess. The clouds hung low and heavy over the mountains, promising more snow and mirroring the mood inside her.

In truth, the thought of Ben and Stella together rankled. Maybe if it were someone else, like Sara, for instance. Then she'd be happy for Ben. Her best friends marrying each other? That would be wonderful.

Except . . . it wouldn't.

Not really.

Oh, what was wrong with her? When had she become such a selfish person? She wasn't willing to share her home with Nick's sister. And she wasn't willing to share Ben with . . . anyone.

That's what all these near tears and the lump in her throat were about. Today she must say goodbye to Ben . . . again. She'd known it for a while now but had pushed the knowledge aside, choosing to live in the moment. But Yellow Bear's case was over. And she would marry Nick by the first of the year. Her loyalty must be to her husband, not her childhood friend. As Ben's would be to his wife someday, whoever the lady might be. She knew it would not be Nell. He'd told her their courtship ended months ago. She hadn't asked why.

A year ago, Ben was merely a sweet memory of a boy she'd known in her past. But having known the grownup Ben these past eleven months, well, the thought of a future without Ben in it seemed bleak indeed. She would miss those moments when something would strike her funny, and she'd look up to see her amusement echoed in Ben's eyes . . . she'd miss the way his eyes would crinkle when he was about to tease her about something . . . the answering spark that would come into his eyes when she suggested a new adventure . . . the way he ran his fingers through his hair when he was frustrated or concentrating on something. She would miss his sense of justice . . . his need to champion the weak and vulnerable. She would miss . . . him.

Jenny swiped at the tear that *would* well up, no matter how hard she tried to keep it back. Enough. Time to grow up. Time to do the right thing, no matter how hard it might be. Ben was not part of her future. It was time to say goodbye.

SHE KNEW THE NEWS WASN'T GOOD THE MOMENT SHE STEPPED into Ben's office. He stood looking out the window, arms folded, his hair a tousled mess. When he turned to look her way, the weariness in his face made her want to go to him, pull him into her arms and promise everything would be all right. Instead, she clenched her hands together inside her muff and waited.

He shook his head in response to her unspoken question. "I'm sorry, Jenny. I did all I could."

"Which is more than anyone else would have done. You said his chances weren't good."

He gave a bitter laugh. "Had I known how minuscule they would be, I wouldn't have taken him on."

"Yes, you would." She walked over to the chair across from his desk and sat. "Come, tell me all about it."

He studied her face a moment, then came and threw himself into the chair across from her. "You sure you want to know?"

"Yes. Tell me everything."

Ben leaned back in his chair and steepled his fingers. "Well, when I first got to Laramie, I made an appointment to see Marvin Thomas. He's a lawyer who's well known for his work on behalf of the Indians. When I told him about Yellow Bear and how I planned to defend him, he laughed. Wouldn't work, he said. I argued that just such a defense had worked in at least ten other cases. Didn't matter, he said, since none of the other cases involved Indians."

She waited for him to continue, but he didn't. He simply studied the ceiling tiles and tapped his fingers together.

"And," she prompted.

"And . . . he was right."

"That's it? That's all you're going to tell me?"

He sat up, elbows on the desk between them, eyes intense. "Jenny, I was good that day in court. The arguments were clear, the precedents were there, the reasoning sound. I had passion, I had justice on my side, and still, the jury found him guilty. *Unanimously*. Guilty. Had a white man been in Yellow Bear's shoes, that case wouldn't even have come to trial. They would have married them off and given their blessing. But Yellow Bear begged Harlow twice to be allowed to marry Bridget, and he refused. This case wasn't about justice . . . it was about power and keeping the Indian in his place."

Jenny tasted the same bitterness she heard in Ben's voice. Poor Yellow Bear. Poor Bridget. And that poor, poor baby. How would Bridget, Blind Woman, and the baby survive now that Yellow Bear was gone?

"So he'll be away for five years?"

"Actually, the judge was lenient. He was only sentenced to two."

"So maybe you did convince somebody."

Ben shrugged.

She felt his despair. Two years or five, either way, the baby was in danger. Miss Whitney said Indian babies were twice as likely to die during their first year as white babies. What chance did it have?

"We'll see that Bridget has everything she needs."

Ben nodded. "I promised Yellow Bear I'd help."

"And I will help too." Though she'd lose the bulk of her inheritance when she married Nick, she'd still have the money that came to her from her mother. Not much, but enough to help. "I'm sure Mrs. Willoughby and Sara will help as well. Between all of us, we'll make sure Yellow Bear's family doesn't starve. And when he gets out, they can marry. She'll be of age by then."

"They shouldn't have to wait." Ben pushed to his feet and began to pace. "What good can it possibly do anyone that Yellow Bear spend two years in jail?" He plowed his fingers through his hair again, causing the ends to stick up even more haphazardly. "It's times like this when I don't know why I continue in this business. It's not the way it's supposed to be. The law should benefit everyone, not just the powerful."

He looked at her with an expression so bleak, she couldn't help herself. She rose and went to him, reaching out and clasping both his hands in hers.

"*That's* why you continue in the business. Because our world needs men like you . . . men who'll stand up for the weak and powerless and fight for their rights. Your voice made a difference this week and not merely with the judge. I'm sure of it." She reached up and turned his face, so he looked straight at her. "Thank you. Thank you for fighting for men like Yellow Bear."

She lifted onto her toes, meaning to place a kiss against his cheek, but either he moved, or she did, because instead of cheek, her lips met his. At the first touch, they both stilled. Then, Ben's hand cupped her neck, and he deepened the kiss, pulling her closer, drawing her in.

Their first kiss had been exciting but way too short; their second, incredibly sweet; but this . . . this was like coming home. She leaned into him, winding her arms around his neck, threading her fingers through his hair. He tasted of coffee with a hint of peppermint. His lips devoured hers, but unlike Nick's kiss, which underwhelmed, this one left her weak and wanting more.

Nick! Oh, no.

Tearing her lips from Ben's, she pressed her fingers against them to hide their trembling and to keep them from betraying both her and Nick by returning to Ben's.

"I can't. I . . . I'm sorry."

She pulled out of his arms and turned for the door.

"Jenny. Wait!" He caught her by the wrist. "Can't we at least talk about this?"

"No. Ben. I'm sorry. What just happened was a mistake. I should never have . . . we must never . . . I'm sorry. I have to go."

She tried to pull loose, but he held tight.

"You know as well as I do that that kiss wasn't all me. You were enjoying it as much as I was. Are you sure you want to call it a mistake?"

He wasn't making this easy. She closed her eyes and drew a shaky breath. "Yes. Because . . . because . . ." she opened her eyes and raised her chin, forcing herself to look him in the eye. "There's someone else. Ben, I'm engaged to another man. You made your choice a long time ago when you chose Nell. I'm not a woman like Nell, and I never can be. And I'm promised to someone else."

For a brief moment, she saw the hurt—raw and angry—then, as if a shutter came down across his face, it vanished. He let go of her wrist and stepped back. Features hard as granite, he gave a slight bow.

"I see. Please forgive me. It won't happen again." His voice was January cold.

With a sob, she flung open the door and fled through the outer office, vaguely aware of Frye staring at her from his desk, mouth agape. She didn't care. All she wanted was to get out. All she wanted was to get home.

When she reached the street, she forced herself to slow to a walk, but when she turned the corner in front of Mrs. Allen's, a small boy barreled into her legs, nearly bowling her down.

"Whoa there." She grabbed the boy by the shoulders, steadying them both, and looked down into eyes as green as moss. She hadn't seen eyes that color for over three months, and now they stared up at her accusingly as if Nick himself were standing in front of her, knowing exactly where she'd been and what she'd done.

Glancing up the street, she saw a woman hurrying along, a young girl in tow and a toddler on her hip.

"I'm sorry," the woman said, breathless, as she drew near. "He run off before I knew he was gone. Did he hurt you?"

"No. I'm fine. A little startled is all."

"Calvin, ask the lady's pardon."

"'Scuse me," the boy mumbled. He would've taken off again if she hadn't still had a grip on his shoulder.

"Etta Mae, take your brother, will you? And watch Davey for me while I go see about our bags."

For the first time, Jenny noticed the stage parked three doors down. "You've just arrived, then?" she asked the girl as the woman turned away.

"Yes. All the way from Montana."

Suddenly the names clicked. Calvin, Etta Mae, Davey.

"Anna Marie?"

The woman turned at her call, bewilderment in her eyes. "I'm sorry. Do I know you?"

"Yes. I mean, no. Well, of course, we've never met, but Nick has told me so much about all of you, I feel as if we already know each other. I'm Jenny."

Nick's sister didn't look anything like him. A delicate blond, the woman possessed a fragile beauty that cried out for protection. No wonder Nick wished to provide for her.

"Nick. You mean Nick *Sparrowhawk*?"

Jenny nodded.

"How do you know my Nick?"

"Well, we're . . . he's . . ." Now, this was awkward. If Nick hadn't told his sister about her, what was she supposed to say? "We're . . . good friends. Didn't he mention me in his letters?"

The tiny woman drew herself to full height. "His letters?" She gave a bitter laugh. "I haven't heard from my husband since

July. In fact, I wasn't even sure he was still living in this area until you mentioned his name. So if you're his good *friend*, maybe you'd be so kind as to tell him his wife is in town?"

Had the lady slapped her, Jenny couldn't be more stunned. "I . . . he . . . your *husband?* Nick Sparrowhawk? Your *husband?*"

"Nigh on seven years, all the good it's done me. He sticks around long enough to give me another baby, then it's off again until I can track him down."

Ice settled in Jenny's core. Nick Sparrowhawk. Married.

"Yoohoo, Miss Westraven."

Oh, no. Not now. Turning, she saw Mrs. Stacia Allen waving to her from the corner, face radiating pleasure.

"I thought I saw you passing by. You must come in. I finally have that item you've been wanting."

Of all days for his letter to come. Thankfully, Anna Marie had no way of knowing what Mrs. Allen meant. And she planned to keep it that way.

"I'm sorry, Mrs. Allen. The item will have to wait. I'm terribly late for an appointment."

Gathering her last shred of dignity, Jenny lifted her skirts and practically ran down the street toward home.

Chapter Thirty-Two

Flames gyrated behind the fire's grate, their dance hypnotic. Jenny sat cross-legged on the rug in front of them, holding Nick's letters in her lap. She toyed with the blue ribbon tying them all together.

How had it come to this? All their plans . . . all their dreams . . . dashed with two simple words.

My husband.

Nick had a wife. Not a sister. A wife!

As soon as she'd reached home, she'd fled to her room, pleading a headache. Now two hours later, after an extended crying jag, she could claim the headache for a fact—along with a stuffy nose, puffy eyes, and an overall feeling of malaise.

She wanted—no *needed*—to read through those letters again, to see where she'd interpreted Nick wrong, but she couldn't summon the energy. How could he be married?

Two simple words and her dream of a home in a cozy log cabin vanished as quickly as the wisps of smoke off the fire in front of her, taking with it visions of curly-haired babies with striking green eyes.

None of it made sense. Why would Nick tell her about his *sister* and *niece* and *nephews* and beg her to allow them to live with them? Was he somehow demented? Surely he knew once the two of them met, any hope he might have of keeping any of them would end. It simply made no sense.

She pulled on the ribbon, letting the letters fall free. Maybe the answer was in here somewhere. Some hint of insanity. Some glimmer of the truth behind his deceit.

She scanned the first letter: *My dearest Miss Westraven . . . I can't stop thinking of you and of our kiss . . . dare I hope you care for me as much as I care for you?*

Those words alone were enough to make the bile rise in her throat. Why, oh why, had she kissed him? Thank goodness a kiss was all they'd shared. If Anna Marie hadn't come to town, if she'd already married Nick, she would have been ruined.

Had that been his plan all along? To trick her into giving away her virtue before the truth came out? If that were the case, why mention Anna Marie at all? She sighed and shook her head. This was all so confusing.

She forced herself to continue reading, looking for answers.

I can understand why your uncle wouldn't approve of me. If you were my niece, no one would be good enough, but we don't need his approval. If someday I'm lucky enough to call you my own, I'll be the richest man in the world. We don't need your inheritance.

Those words had once convinced her of the depth of Nick's love. Now they rang false. Of course, he could overlook her inheritance. Anything he'd gain in pretending to marry her would be temporary at best. She'd been so long accustomed to men wanting her only for her money, she found it hard to believe she had something else they might want.

She read through letter after letter, wincing at every declaration of love, but finding no answers. Then finally his last letter, the most puzzling of all, the one leading to the two weeks of silence between them.

I have almost completed the cabin and can't wait for the day I carry you over its doorstep. I long to see your beautiful face at my table every morning . . . in my bed every night. But first, I must beg a favor.

Would you share our home with Anna Marie and the children until I'm able to build another? It won't be forever—six months, a year at the most. I promised to bring them to Wyoming as soon as I could provide a home. I cannot break my promise.

There. That paragraph didn't make any sense at all. Why would he make such a request, knowing if she were to grant it, their future together was doomed as soon as Anna Marie arrived? Was the man a lunatic?

Or was Anna Marie lying?

But that made no sense either.

How had she been so blind? She, who prided herself on being able to spot a fake . . . a gold digger . . . an opportunist, had fallen for nothing but sweet talk and lies. He'd known exactly how to play her.

Worst of all was what her stupidity cost Ben.

That kiss today was special—far deeper than anything she'd shared with Nick. But more than that, their friendship, their interests, their past, their . . . well, *everything* they shared was so much deeper, so much more than anything with Nick, but she'd refused to admit it. All she and Nick truly shared were pipe dreams on paper. And today, when she'd told Ben about Nick—she'd hurt him. She'd seen it in his eyes. And she hated herself for it.

Now it was too late. No use wishing she'd met Anna Marie one day earlier . . . one hour earlier. She'd made her choice, and for Ben's sake, it was for the best. She wasn't the type of wife he needed. He deserved so much more. She drew trouble and always would. Today's fiasco was evidence of that.

She stuffed the final letter back into its envelope and tied the stack together again. What a pile of worthless, meaningless words. With a flick of her wrist, she launched them into the fire, watching as the flames first licked the edges, then flared up, bright and furious, curling the corners of the packet. Minutes later, nothing was left but a pile of ashes.

Chapter Thirty-Three

"**G**ot a moment for an old friend?"

At the sound of Ted's voice, Ben looked up from the papers on his desk, a stab of guilt piercing his conscience. He hadn't seen any Westravens in nearly two weeks. Not since he'd made a fool of himself with Jenny. He'd filled the intervening days with work, arriving early, staying late, stumbling home in the wee hours to get some sleep. Though so far, sleep had proved elusive.

"Good God, man. You're looking rough. Have you been sick? Is that why you haven't been to dinner for a while?"

"No. Just busy."

Ted studied him, his eyes so much like Jenny's Ben had to look away.

"I've had a few cases lately that are taking most of my time." Not true. He had a few cases he *allowed* to take most of his time.

"I'm sorry to hear that because I'm not here simply for a social call. There's something I'm hoping you can help me with." He pulled an envelope from his jacket pocket and laid it on the desk between them.

"A legal question?"

"A problem, more than a question, though I have some questions as well. Read that and see what you think."

Ben reached for the envelope, pulled out the several sheets of paper, and read the first few lines.

Whereas a wife is entitled, as a matter of right, not only to the support and maintenance of her husband but also to his love and affection. It follows that if any woman by the exercise of any arts or wiles, alienates . . .

He glanced over at Ted, eyebrow raised, "An alienation of affection suit?"

"Keep reading."

Anna Marie Sparrowhawk, the plaintiff, summons Jeanette Elizabeth Westraven—

"What the—?"

"Keep reading."

. . . in a plea of trespass, in which the plaintiff claims for the defendant the sum of $100,000, the ground of which complaint is as follows:

Whereas, the said plaintiff is a good, true, faithful and honest woman. . . . That she was married March 15, 1892 to F. Nicolas Sparrowhawk . . .

He skimmed through the particulars of the marriage, landing on the next paragraph.

That in July of 1900, or shortly thereafter, he became acquainted with the defendant, a single woman . . . was seen engaged in an amorous embrace with the defendant in a public alley . . .

Dash it all. Someone else witnessed that kiss.

Upon arriving in Wyoming, the plaintiff discovered a packet of letters from the defendant in her husband's possession . . .

Ben flung the papers onto the desk. "What does Jenny say to all this?"

"That's just it. I can't get her to talk. Ever since the papers were delivered to the house, she refuses to leave her room. Her maid tells me she barely eats or sleeps, just sits staring into the fire for hours on end. Frankly, I haven't seen her so distraught since our parents died."

"But surely she said something about whether the claims were true."

"She told me she and Sparrowhawk had a secret engagement. She planned to marry him as soon as he finished a cabin he was building for them. She knew about Anna Marie, but Sparrowhawk told her she was his sister."

"Should be a simple case then. She can't be charged if she didn't know he was married. She simply needs to prove she didn't know. She has letters from him, I'm assuming. They should back up her story."

"Yes. I thought about that too, but when I asked her for them, she burst into tears." Ted hooked a hand around the back of his neck and massaged it, giving Ben a sheepish look. "I'm afraid I took a tactical retreat. I don't handle tears well."

Ben could relate. The thought of Jenny crying made him want to punch someone. A certain leather-wearing, long-haired, green-eyed lying piece of scum, to be specific. He pushed to his feet, pacing to the window and back.

"So, how do you plan to handle this?"

"That's what I wanted to ask you. Grace's father thinks the suit is probably no more than a veiled attempt at blackmail. The Sparrowhawks know we won't want the scandal. He says I'll likely be hearing from their lawyer soon with an offer to settle. Tells me I should take it."

"Is that what you want to do?"

"Frankly, the thought of giving them anything sticks in my craw, but for Jenny's sake, I will. If any of this gets out, the newsmen will pounce on it like a bear on salmon. She'll be ruined."

Ben sank into his office chair with a heavy sigh. "You think it's blackmail then? Not a legitimate grievance by Mrs. Sparrowhawk?"

"Did you see the amount she's suing for? No way she'd ask for such an outrageous amount unless she knew the family she's dealing with. And to have a suit ready within days of arriving in town? Oh, she knows what she's doing. They've probably had this in the works for months."

Ben sat forward, focusing his gaze on Ted's. "And what if we could prove that? What if we could expose them for the scam artists they are? Free Jenny's name and pay them nothing? Wouldn't you want to do that?"

"Heck, yes. But the risk is too great. If we let this go to trial, Jenny's name will be paraded through the papers from here to New York. You know how ugly these cases can get. Uncle Clarence would . . ." Ted huffed a short laugh. "Lord, I don't even want to imagine what Uncle Clarence would do if he got wind of this. No. Much as it pains me, I think we have to pay."

"Promise me this, then. If they do approach you about a settlement, you'll let me represent you? I don't want you to pay a cent more than necessary. And whatever you do, don't approach them first. They've got to believe you'd be willing to take this all the way, or they're going to stick you for all you have." He looked down at the papers again. "Do you know who's representing Mrs. Sparrowhawk?"

"Phineas Pratt."

Ben snorted. "Sounds like a case he'd jump on. Here's what I suggest. Sit tight until he contacts you. In the meantime, I'll send word to his office that I'll be representing Jenny and request they share their evidence. That way, we'll know how strong a case they've built against her. My bet is they don't have a lot and are hoping the threat of the suit will be enough to get money from you."

"You'd be willing to help us then?"

"How could you even question that?"

"Oh, I don't know. Somehow I thought when you heard about this latest scrape of Jenny's, you wouldn't want to touch it with a ten-foot pole. After all, if it weren't for the way the two of you've been acting these past few months, I might have seen this coming."

"What's that supposed to mean?"

"What it means is I knew my sister was acting like a woman in love. But I thought she was in love with you. Sparrowhawk didn't enter my mind."

"How could you think she was in love with me?" Try as he might, he couldn't keep the bitter edge from his voice.

"Come on. I'm not blind. Besides, I know the reason Uncle Clarence sent her to Wyoming in the first place."

Their kiss? Great. "Look, I can explain—"

Ted held up a hand. "No. No need. I haven't been married so long I don't understand the temptation to kiss a pretty girl when the opportunity arises. Frankly, it's the reason I invited you to visit in the first place. I hoped whatever started in Newark might have a chance to develop here. And I thought it had. You should see the two of you together. You're either snipping at each other like an old married couple or acting all gooey-eyed. I figured it was only a matter of time before you came asking for my permission to marry her."

Had he been that obvious? He wanted to bury his head in embarrassment, but instead, he leaned back, crossed his arms, and glared at Ted, hoping that would shut him up. It didn't.

"Then suddenly you stopped coming around. And Jenny wouldn't come out of her room. A lover's quarrel I suspected until I saw that lawsuit. *Sparrowhawk?* Didn't even know he was in the picture. Sure, she seemed a little star-struck last September, but that was months ago."

"Wait a minute," Ted's eyes narrowed. "You knew about him, didn't you? That's why you stopped coming around. She told you about her engagement."

He gave a terse nod.

"And you still want to help her out of this mess? Why?"

"Look. You're right. I do love your sister, but Jenny doesn't love me. I guess I could be petty and use that as an excuse not to help, but I can't. If there's something I can do to help her, I'll do it. And if it brings some measure of pain to the blackguard who put her in this mess, then so much the better."

Ted stood and held out a hand for him to shake. "Jenny made a big mistake picking that man over you. If she doesn't already realize it, she will."

He returned his friend's firm grasp. "It doesn't matter now. What matters is making sure Sparrowhawk gets as little of her money as possible. Let me know when you hear from Pratt, and I'll see what I can dig up on Sparrowhawk."

~

SHADOWS. JENNY HAD COME TO LOVE THEIR COMPANY. SHE found comfort in closing the drapes, turning down the lamps, and sitting in a room lit only by firelight. The outside world simply faded away. Maybe she should stop the clocks and cover the mirrors as well. Lord knows mirrors weren't her friends these days.

Someday she'd put forth an effort. Let Molly dress her, arrange her hair. Maybe she'd even leave the room.

But not tonight.

Even tomorrow was questionable.

Why couldn't everyone leave her alone? People were so careful to let a person grieve when there was a death. Why couldn't the same rules apply to the death of a relationship? Instead, every day either Sara or Ted or Molly were at her door demanding things of her she wasn't able to give.

Two weeks ago she'd had her life mapped out, right down to her future child—a boy with curly brown hair and green eyes— named Harrold for her father. Today? Nothing. No plans. No dreams. No future.

She lay back against the pile of pillows stacked against the headboard of her bed and watched the shadows from the fire flicker against the silk canopy above her.

A soft tap at her door and Molly peered in at her. "Excuse me, miss. Your brother would like you to join him in the library."

"Tell him I have a headache."

Molly came into the room and stood for a moment, shifting her weight from one foot to another.

"Honest, Molly. My head is pounding. Tell him whatever he wants will have to wait."

"Begging your pardon, miss, but he said if you told me you wouldn't come, I was to tell you he had a telegram ready to send to your Uncle Clarence. If you don't come down, he's sending Martin with it to the telegraph office tonight."

Jenny weighed her options. Ted could be bluffing. He had no more interest in Uncle Clarence hearing about this latest mess than she did. Besides, Uncle Clarence and Aunt Matilda were in Paris right now. By the time the telegraph found them and Uncle Clarence could do anything about it, she could easily be hiding out with the Skivingtons. Not worth leaving her room tonight.

"Tell him to come up here if he wants to talk."

Molly didn't budge.

"He said if you still wouldn't come down, I was to tell you he's sending a note to Mrs. Parkhurst."

This threat had more bite. Mrs. Parkhurst had been by several times . . . had even made it as far as her door on one occasion, but each time Ted headed her off. If he allowed a breach in his protection, she was doomed. Weighing a few minutes spent with Ted in his office against a few hours spent with Mrs. Parkhurst here in her bedroom was no contest. With a heavy sigh, she pushed to her feet.

"Oh, very well. Tell him I'll be down in a minute."

"Do you want me to help you change your gown?"

"No. I'll wear what I have on." She knew Ted and Grace had probably changed for dinner, but she saw no reason to make the effort for a simple trek downstairs.

"May I help with your hair then?"

"I'll take care of it. Just tell him I'm on my way."

Molly curtsied and left the room, the stiffness of her posture a sign of her disapproval, but Jenny didn't care.

She walked over to her dressing table and studied herself in the mirror. So this was how a homewrecker looked after two weeks in seclusion. Heavens. No wonder Molly wanted to help. Any seductive wiles Anna Marie claimed she had were long gone. The dark, wine-colored wool of her gown left her looking sallow and wan. And her hair! Medusa-like spirals sprang every which way. She picked up her brush and tried to make some headway, only to give it up and pull it all back with a ribbon. There. If Ted wanted her downstairs, he'd simply have to take her as she was.

A few minutes later, she stepped into Ted's office. Unlike the rest of the house, which clearly had Grace's stamp on it, this room oozed warmth and masculinity, much like Ted himself. Her brother lounged in his large leather office chair, hands laced behind his head.

"Glad you could make it, sis."

Normally she'd have responded to the jab with a barb of her own, but to do so would take more energy than she could muster. Instead, she simply raised an eyebrow at him and sank into a chair next to Grace who sat working on a needlepoint seat cover.

"I'm assuming from the level of threats you used, you have something vital to relate?"

Ted shot a glance in the direction of the fireplace. "Actually, it was Ben who suggested you join us."

Oh, God, no. She whipped her gaze to that side of the room. Sure enough. There he stood. Or rather leaned, arms crossed, shoulder propped against the fireplace mantle, looking at her with an unreadable expression.

She didn't want to look at him, yet somehow she couldn't bring herself to look away. And then she saw it, sparking from the depths of those dark eyes. Pity. If only she were Aladdin's genie and could whisk herself away in a puff of smoke. She pushed one of her wayward curls behind her ear, knowing the effort was futile. She should have let Molly help with her hair at least.

Ted cleared his throat. "Before we meet with Mrs. Sparrowhawk's lawyer, Ben thought it might be best to hear your side of the story and give you a chance to refute the accusations she's making against you."

"Why'd you bring *him* into it?" Could she sound more childish?

"You told me to take care of it."

Yes. Like Uncle Clarence took care of things. He'd call Mr. Ainsley, money would change hands, and the ugliness would all go away.

Ben walked over from the fireplace and perched himself in front of her on the edge of Ted's desk. "Your brother would be foolish to try to take on the Sparrowhawks without legal representation."

Oh. Of course. Ben was Ted's Mr. Ainsley.

"What do you need to know?" She refused to look at him. She couldn't . . . *wouldn't* subject herself to that gaze of pity again. Instead, she kept her eyes focused on the lace trim on the cuff of her sleeve, plucking at its pattern.

"For starters. You can tell me what you knew of Mrs. Sparrowhawk. She claims you knew all about her before she ever came to town. She says you called her by name the day they first arrived as if you were expecting them."

"Well. I was. But I didn't know she was his *wife*. Nick told me he had a sister—Anna Marie. And two nephews and a niece whom he missed very much. He hoped to make enough from his last cattle drive to send for them. That's why I wasn't surprised to see them get off the stage. I thought he'd finally saved enough to pay for their move."

"Do you have anything to corroborate that? Any letters he sent you?"

"No."

"Are you sure?"

"Yes. After she told me she was his wife, I went back and looked. There was nothing in the letters specifically stating she was his sister. He always referred to them as Anna Marie and the children."

"When did he tell you she was his sister?"

"On our camping trip. He told me all about his little niece, Etta Mae, and his sister, who'd been recently widowed. He said he was taking on extra jobs to help bring them out here."

Ben nodded and looked at Ted. "We can assume then, unless Mrs. Sparrowhawk has concrete evidence to prove otherwise, her argument will be a case of 'he said, she said' with no weight either way. If this case were to come to trial, the most likely course they'd pursue would be to prove Jenny the type of woman to intentionally break up a marriage. They will also need to prove she pursued Mr. Sparrowhawk rather than the other way around." He turned back to her. "After the camping trip, who suggested you correspond through letters?"

"He did."

"And I'm assuming those letters did not come through the post since Ted tells me he never saw any."

"No. Nick told me Mrs. Stacia Allen often served as a go-between for some of the cowboys in similar circumstances. He told me to drop by her store in a couple of days, and she would have something for me."

"How many letters did he send you?"

"I don't know. Twenty?"

"You told me the two of you were engaged. I'm assuming his proposal and your acceptance came through those letters?"

She nodded, once more unwilling to look at him.

"Good. I'll need you to give me his letters then. I won't read through them or use them unless I have to but having them on hand should give us something to fight with."

"I can't."

"Jenny, this is no time to be missish," Ted said. "Ben said he wouldn't read them unless he had to."

"I know. It's not that. It's just . . . I don't have the letters."

"Why not?"

"I burned them."

"What?" for the first time since Jenny entered the office,

Grace joined the conversation. "Why would you do something so feather-brained?"

"I didn't know about the lawsuit then. All I knew was the man I thought I would marry was nothing but a liar and a fraud. I looked through his letters because I wanted proof he'd told me Anna Marie was his sister. All I found were a lot of empty promises and lies. So I burned them." Jenny bit the inside of her lip. She wasn't going to cry. Not in front of Ben. But if the questions continued in this vein, she didn't know how she could keep from it.

"We'll work around it," Ben said. "As far as they know, you still have them. If you give me the gist of what was in them, we should be able to bluff our way through. Now maybe you can shed some light on this piece of evidence for me." Ben picked up a file off the desk and shuffled through some of the papers. "Here we go." He drew out a single sheet of paper. "Apparently, they have a signed affidavit from a Winston Sanford III of New York City stating he withdrew an offer of marriage when you told him you were in love with a married man?" Ben held her gaze, one eyebrow raised.

She cleared her throat. "I didn't say that. Not specifically. Though I may have let him infer it. He . . . umm . . . he was one of the suitors Uncle Clarence brought by after . . . well, after I returned from Newark last spring."

"Oh."

Yes. Oh. How could something that felt so clever six months ago now feel so foolish?

"Oh? That's it? Oh?" Grace's voice shook with incredulity. "How could you let someone infer a thing like that?"

Ted caught her eye. "Jenny? Ben? What are we missing here?"

She looked down at her hands, twisting them in her lap.

Ben heaved a sigh. "Before sending Jenny out west, your uncle tried to marry her off. Several men proposed, but instead of simply telling them no, she told stories about herself to convince them they didn't really want to marry her. Her way of letting them down easy."

"Oh," Ted said.

The room fell silent.

"How damaging would a statement like that be?" Ted asked.

"If the case were to go to trial, Pratt would need to prove Jenny deliberately set out to destroy the Sparrowhawk's marriage. Anything they can find to tarnish her character and paint her as a homewrecker would obviously work to their advantage."

Ted shook his head. "What else do they have?"

Ben picked up his file again. "Well, they list Jenny's letters as evidence, of course."

"Nick gave the lawyer my letters? Why?"

"My guess is to build their case against you," Ted said.

"*Their* case. What do you mean? This is *Mrs.* Sparrowhawk's case, not Nick's. I understand why she wants to sue me. But why would he help her? He's as guilty here as I am."

Ben and Ted exchanged a look.

"Do you know something I don't?"

"Not really," Ted said. "But Ben and I suspect Sparrowhawk was in this from the beginning. How else would they already have an affidavit from one of your suitors in New York? Why else would he have been so careful not to mention the word 'sister' in any of his letters? Look at the amount she's suing for. Sparrowhawk knew your net worth before he ever began pursuing you. I wouldn't be surprised if they've pulled something like this before."

So he'd lied about his love, as well as everything else. Jenny could hardly swallow against the huge lump lodged in her throat. Of course, he had. When had anyone ever pursued her for anything other than her money? She blinked. Hard. She thought she'd found someone who loved her for herself, but he was just like the others after all.

"Did you read my letters?" Her voice sounded as dead and empty as she felt.

Ben cleared his throat. "Um . . . no. Just a few snippets their lawyer singled out. Like this one: ' . . . I know how you feel about Anna Marie and the children, but on this, I must stand firm. I will not share you.'"

Ted let out a curse.

"Ted! There are ladies present," Grace said.

"I'm sorry. But Jenny. You wrote that? We might as well take your entire trust fund, and mine as well, and hand it to them."

"Excuse me for not knowing the man was a liar and a fraud." Her voice thickened with the tears she was trying so hard not to shed. "I thought I was writing to the man I loved—the man I was going to marry—about his *sister*. I didn't want to share my home with his *sister*. And yes, I do understand the irony, given where I'm living, but he told me he'd built us a cabin. A *two-room* cabin. Can you imagine sharing a space that small with his sister and her three children?" She dashed a tear away from her cheek. "Even I wasn't so in love and stupid as to believe that scenario would work."

Ted pushed to his feet. "That pretty much proves it, doesn't it? He deliberately asked that of her knowing no woman alive would agree to that arrangement. He gets the answer he's looking for, sends for his wife, and wham. They spring the trap."

"Looks that way."

"So what do we do now? Is there any way we can come through this without giving them everything they want?"

"I think so. Remember, as far as they know, we still have Sparrowhawk's letters to Jenny. They won't want to go to court any more than we do. Sure, they have enough to guarantee you'll pay something because if any of these things were to become public—the affidavit, the letters—Jenny would be ruined. But I think we can negotiate. Pratt told me they'd be willing to meet and discuss a settlement as early as next Wednesday. Shall I set up a meeting?"

"Yes."

"No." The word came out much louder than Jenny intended. All eyes turned her way.

"That's not what *I* want to do. I don't want to settle. I'm not guilty. They are. I'm willing to go to court to prove it."

"Jenny." Ted squatted in front of her chair and took her hand. "I know you're angry. I am too, but fighting this is too costly. No matter the outcome, your reputation would be in shreds by the time it's over."

"I don't care."

"Well, I do." Grace laid down her needlework and glared. "You may not care about *your* reputation, but *I* care about my husband's. If you're painted in public as a homewrecker and loose woman, the ramifications will affect all of us. You live in our home. The scandal will adversely affect your brother's business interests, as well as any social standing we might have in the community. Do you care about that?"

"I'll move out. I have my monthly stipend. I can rent a room in town. You may tell your mother and the Joneses and anyone else who asks whatever you like. I'm sure when news of the trial comes out, they'll understand. But I won't stand back and let these people have what they want. If I let them take our money, if I don't fight this, then I might have the community's respect, but I won't have my own."

She stood up, eye-level with Ben, and forced herself to look at him. His expression was once again guarded, but with no sign of pity now.

"You said there was a chance the Sparrowhawks have pulled this con before. Why do you think that?"

Ben shrugged. "It's too smooth. Everything has flowed too flawlessly right down to his knowing what to ask you in his letters. My guess is this is how the two of them make a living. He comes to a town, scouts out a likely suspect, and makes his move. If he's successful, he sends for the wife. If not, he moves on."

"But he was in town a whole year before I arrived. How could he know I would come here?"

"I'm pretty sure he didn't, but he met your brother shortly after coming here and knew about you." Ben exchanged another look with Ted. "Besides, Ted believes he tried his scheme on others in town before you but failed."

Jenny whirled around to look at Ted. "Really? You have proof?"

"Nothing concrete. But maybe a place to start."

"And if we could prove it . . . could show they deliberately trapped me, then we could clear my name and not pay them a cent?"

Ted held up a hand. "Yes, but that's a pretty big 'if.' Believe me, I've thought the same things you have, Jen, but frankly, I'm not willing to pay the cost."

"The cost to you or to me? If you're holding back on account of me, don't. I told you I don't care."

"You have no idea how a scandal like this will affect the rest of your life. Besides, Grace is right. If the scandal touches you, it touches us all."

"But me most of all."

"Yes."

"If it were your reputation at stake, would you fight for it or give them what they wanted?"

"It's not the same, and you know it."

"Why not? Why does it have to be different simply because I'm a woman?"

"Because it is. In our society, an unmarried woman who loses her reputation loses everything. You'll have no hope of gaining a husband or family of your own."

"Right now, that doesn't sound like such a bad thing."

"But it will. When all this passes, and you want to return to life like it was, you'll no longer have that option—no more invitations, no more parties, nor more dinners or outings. You are consigning yourself to a life of seclusion and loneliness. Can you live with that?"

"What I can't live with is knowing I allowed them to walk away scot-free. No. That I actually *paid* them to do it. What will keep them from pulling the same scam again and again if someone doesn't stand up and fight them?" She turned back toward Ben, unable to look him in the eyes this time. She focused on his collar instead. "I know I have no right to ask this of you. You were right. I *am* 'trouble.' It seems to follow me wherever I go, and the worst part is, the people I care about most end up getting hurt. But you are the best lawyer I know. If you were to take this case, I know you'd have more chance than anyone of winning it. If you don't want to, I . . . I understand. But would you at least consider it?"

He took so long to answer she forced herself to look him in the eyes. If only she could read his thoughts. Did he despise her? She'd been such a fool. Honestly, if he refused her, it was no more than she deserved.

Finally, he answered. "You do know, with the evidence we have now, you have about as much chance of winning this case as Yellow Bear had of winning his. Less, in fact."

She nodded.

"And you're still willing to try?"

"I am."

He looked at Ted, then back at her. A small smile formed at the tips of his lips. "It wouldn't be the first time the three of us have tempted fate. What do you say, 'All for one?'"

At the mention of their favorite childhood motto, Jen couldn't help returning his smile.

"'And one for all,'" she said, Ted chiming in. For the first time in weeks, she no longer felt alone.

~

Trial moved up two weeks STOP Date set for December 21 STOP Plea for delay denied STOP

Ben slammed the telegram onto the counter. There wasn't a curse word strong enough for what he felt. Two days? How was he supposed to make it back to Lander in two days? Besides, he wasn't sure Mr. Abernathy could leave right away, and without Abernathy, they had no case.

He forked his fingers through his hair. Things were going so well. His lead in Cheyenne was a good one, but this Denver connection was even better. Mr. Abernathy was everything they needed and more. Somehow the Sparrowhawks must have gotten wind of what he was up to and had managed to move the trial date.

Well, their machinations weren't going to work. Not if he could help it. He'd have to talk Abernathy into leaving today. They'd miss the opening day of the trial, but Matthews could carry them through, and please God, he'd be there in time to mount the defense.

He scrawled a reply and handed it to the telegraph operator.

On my way STOP Use every delay tactic STOP Witness on board.

They'd get there on time. They had to. And when they did, the Sparrowhawks were going to pay.

Chapter Thirty-Four

Jenny swallowed against the dryness in her throat, fisted her hands to keep them from trembling, and followed Mr. Matthews into the courtroom. She felt the gaze of hundreds on her though she kept her own eyes trained firmly on the back of Mr. Matthew's black suit.

At the older lawyer's advice, she'd dressed in her most sober outfit—a dark blue merino wool with a high neck and long tight sleeves—and pulled her hair into a sensible bun. Well, as sensible as her curls would allow.

If only Ben were here, but the trip from Denver was a three-day journey in the best of weather. Snow had started early this morning and continued to fall. If it didn't let up, Ben could be delayed for the remainder of the trial.

Please, God, no.

A rustling on the opposite side of the court marked the entrance of Mrs. Sparrowhawk. She leaned on the arm of her lawyer, looking hardly more substantial than dandelion fluff. If Jenny didn't know better, her sympathies might have been drawn to this pale, wounded woman. She carried a lacy white handkerchief in one frail hand and used it to dab at her eyes as Mr. Pratt settled her into her seat.

Jenny fought the urge to roll her eyes and turned her attention to the bailiff who called for them all to rise for the honorable Judge Hammond.

He took his seat behind the podium with a curt nod for them all to be seated. Square-jawed and steely-eyed, the man was about the same age as Uncle Clarence and every bit as intimidating. Jenny struggled to maintain eye contact when he looked her way.

Ben told her Judge Hammond was no-nonsense but fair. She certainly hoped so. She turned to study the twelve men in the jury box.

She didn't recognize a one. Most likely, they came from ranches and farms and small towns outside of Lander. With all the press this case had received, Mr. Matthews had struggled to assemble an unbiased group of men. One thing was certain. These twelve were all more willing to look at Anna Marie than they were at her.

Not a good sign.

The only one willing to hold her gaze was an elderly man with a bushy gray beard whose thinly veiled look of contempt reminded her of Monsieur de la Roche, her mathematics instructor at Madame Delancey's.

She almost expected him to say, "Mademoiselle Westraven, if you spent half the time working your figures as you do avoiding them, you would be done by now."

She moved her attention to Mrs. Sparrowhawk's lawyer, who stood to give his opening statement. A short, wiry man with thinning hair, he reminded her of Mrs. Willoughby's bantam rooster who strutted around the hen yard with the greatest sense of importance. She fought the urge to smile.

No. No smiling. Not today. She'd heard it a million times growing up if she'd heard it once, "Ah, that one. She has the face of an angel until she smiles. But when she smiles, she's an imp through and through."

Those men on the jury were not going to see the imp. Not if

she could help it. She forced herself to gaze at her gloved hands folded demurely in her lap. If Anna Marie could play the wounded wife, she would play the angel.

With an effort, she focused on Mr. Pratt's words.

" . . . evidence will show that Miss Westraven, through wiles and seduction, deliberately and maliciously tore Mr. Sparrowhawk from the bosom of his family, robbing his wife of his company and support. You will see letters written in Miss Westraven's own hand practically begging Mr. Sparrowhawk to abandon his wife and children . . . you will hear testimony to Miss Westraven's wanton and predatory behavior . . ."

Wanton? Predatory? Really? She knew how to flirt, yes. There wasn't a girl in her social circle who didn't. A girl unwilling to flirt was destined to stand on the outskirts of any ball or assembly, and standing on the outskirts was never her forte. But Mr. Pratt didn't know her. For that matter, except for a rare few, no one here knew her. And that was a problem. Anything Mr. Pratt told them, they'd accept as truth.

She glanced at the jury box to find all twelve pairs of eyes on her. She dropped her gaze. Best not give them any more reason to consider her bold and jaded. The lawyer's words were more than enough.

Finally, Mr. Matthews rose to make his opening remarks. He had none of Mr. Pratt's dramatics, but his even-toned manner helped settle the staccato beating of her heart. She let out a long, slow breath.

" . . . in short, we will prove Miss Westraven is no seductress, but simply a victim of the lies and manipulation of a pair of slick charlatans who sought to take advantage of her youth and inexperience to gain a portion of the Westraven fortune."

Surely the jury would listen to this man's reason and not get caught up in Mr. Pratt's theatrics. Please, God. Let the truth shine through.

$\sim$

Jenny sat in the holding room adjacent to the courtroom rubbing her throbbing temples. Yesterday was harsh, but this morning was even worse.

"Would you like me to see if I can find you some headache powders?" Ted was the only one other than Mr. Matthews allowed in the room with her while the court recessed for lunch.

She shook her head. "I'll be fine."

"Mr. Matthews warned us this early part would be rough. We're hearing their slant on the story right now. But we'll get our turn. And he's doing a great job exposing the bias of their witnesses."

As much as the poor man could. The most excruciating part of the morning had been realizing how much of the evidence was fact. Mr. Pratt began by reading the *Town Topics* articles. Though Mr. Matthews was quick to point out society women often found themselves the victims of gossip, there was enough truth amidst all the innuendo to make a chink in her character.

Then there'd been Winston. Who'd have believed a man who thought as highly of himself as Winston Sanford III would take the time and expense to travel all the way to Wyoming to testify against her? He'd explained some of that away by saying he'd made the stop on his way to the west coast for a honeymoon trip, but she wasn't fooled. No one traveled a hundred miles from the nearest railroad without seeking some sort of vendetta.

Oh, she'd wounded him, no doubt. Not a heart wound, but a pride wound, which for someone like Winston was far worse. Hearing him throw her foolish words back at her in front of the entire courtroom was humiliating. Why had she felt the need to spare his feelings? Why couldn't she have simply said no?

Nor was Mr. Sanford the only easterner to make the trip to Lander. The courtroom overflowed with journalists and reporters from New York and Washington and everywhere in between. Conspicuous in their absence were Uncle Clarence and Aunt Matilda. Once the news of her trial reached the eastern papers, Uncle Clarence wired from Paris that he would not be a party to this "circus." He'd completely washed his hands of her. She should be grateful for small blessings.

But the worst testimony of the morning came from Mrs. Jones. When Will told her she'd made a powerful enemy the night of the Jones' dinner party, she hadn't believed him.

Now she did.

According to Mrs. Jones, Jenny was a wanton jade who had tried to steal the attention of every man in Lander. In her rendition, Monsieur Dumont had practically been engaged to Stella until Jenny walked in and, with her brazen wiles, stolen him away.

And the prosecution still wasn't finished presenting their case. Jenny dropped her head onto her crossed arms on the table in front of her. How she wished she could close her eyes and simply disappear.

"Rough morning?"

Her head whipped up at the sound of Ben's voice. He stood in the doorway, looking calm and solid. Pushing back her chair, she launched herself into his arms. She wanted, no *needed,* to hold him. More than she needed to breathe. A pause and then his arms came around her, pulling her close. For the first time in forever, she felt . . . safe.

What followed was embarrassing and totally out of her control. Sobs. Gut-wrenching, snot-inducing, ugly sobs.

Ted brushed past them, mumbling something about water and headache powders. Somewhere at the fringes of her consciousness, she felt a tug of concern for the state of Ben's suit jacket, but mostly she clung to him and wept.

He held on, rubbing a hand up and down her back and murmuring, "It's going to be all right, Jen. I promise. It'll be all right."

Finally, the sobs subsided and she pulled away. "I'm so sorry. I don't know what came over me."

She must look a full blown mess.

He handed her his handkerchief. Taking it, she mopped her

face and blew her nose and then had no idea what to do with it. Finally, she dropped back into her seat keeping it wadded between her hands on her lap.

"When did you get back?"

"Early this morning. We left the stage at Rongis. The stage driver decided to overnight there because of the weather, so Mr. Abernathy and I hired a couple of horses and came the rest of the way on our own. I managed to catch a couple hours sleep before coming here."

"Is Mr. Abernathy the witness from Denver?"

"Yes." Ben took a chair next to her. Placing his fingers beneath her chin, he turned her head, forcing her to look at him. "Jenny, I know this morning was difficult. It'll probably only get worse, but you have to trust me. No matter how bleak things look, tomorrow will be better. I promise. I want you to go out there with your head held high. No tears. Let them say what they want. The truth is coming. Can you do that for me?"

She swallowed and looked away. "I don't know." She wanted to be brave. She did. But the thought of facing all those hostile faces again . . .

"Come on. Where's the Jenny who rode Cousin Harlan's cow? Or bounced back after a bear attack? You can do this. You know you can."

She sought his gaze again, fighting back tears. "You'll be there?"

"Right by your side."

"Do I have time to use the wash room?"

Ben glanced at his pocket watch. "We have around ten minutes."

She firmed her lips and nodded. "Give me a few minutes to freshen up, and I'll be ready."

"That's my girl."

She'd take on a thousand enemy arrows just to see him look at her like that.

Chapter Thirty-Five

The first testimony of the afternoon was a tear-filled one from Mrs. Sparrowhawk. Jenny envied the woman's ability to shed tears without marring her beauty. When the first one fell, at least five men, including the judge, whipped out their handkerchiefs.

Ben appeared completely unaffected. He scribbled notes on his pad of paper, sometimes passing them to Mr. Matthews who would then scribble some notes of his own and pass it back. Neither man reacted to the woes of the woman on the stand, so Jenny determined to ignore her theatrics. So far Anna Marie's testimony had covered how many years she and Nick had been married and the depth of their love for each other.

She held up a basket filled with letters Nick had written her during their two years of separation and spent five weepy minutes reading through samples of the endearments he'd shared. They didn't vary much from the ones Jenny had received. Apparently he wasn't too original.

"And then the letters stopped?" Mr. Pratt asked.

"Yes."

"When was this?"

"Sometime in late July. We'd had flooding that month, and I

thought the weather might have delayed his letters. But week after week went by and nothing." She stopped to dab at her eyes. "I feared maybe there'd been an accident or something worse. Finally, I packed up the children and came to Lander, the last place I knew he'd been."

"Could you tell the jury what happened the day you arrived?"

"Well, we had no more than got off the stage, when Calvin—that's my son—takes off. I ran after him and find him talking to this fancy-dressed lady. I apologized, thinking he's bothering her, and she says, 'Anna Marie' all friendly, like we've known each other for years. 'Do I know you?' I said. 'No,' she says, 'but I feel like I know you on account of Nick telling me all about you.' Well, you can imagine that got my attention. When I asked her how she knew my husband, she got all red and took off like a scared rabbit. Then I got to talking to the proprietress of the store who was standing there and asked her if *she* knew Nick Sparrowhawk. She says, 'Of course I do. He's the sweetheart of that young lady.' I'm afraid I near fainted with shock."

"And when you confronted your husband about this, what was his response?"

"He told me I should have stayed in Montana. He was in love with her."

Here Mrs. Sparrowhawk broke down completely, burying her face in one of the handkerchiefs that had been proffered, her fragile shoulders shaking.

Mr. Pratt turned to the judge. "That's all I have, your honor."

"Will there be a cross examination?"

"Yes, your honor." Ben stood.

The judge held up a hand. "We'll allow the witness a few minutes to compose herself."

"Of course."

Anna Marie took in a long, shuddering sigh and raised her head. Dabbing at her eyes once again, she gave the judge a watery smile. "I'm fine," she said.

"Are you sure?" Judge Hammond asked.

"Yes."

"All right, Mr. Bennett. You may proceed."

Ben walked over to Anna Marie. "I understand how difficult this must be for you, Mrs. Sparrowhawk," he said, voice low and sympathetic. "I'll keep this short."

"Thank you."

"Why did your husband leave Montana?"

"He wanted to find work."

"Were there no ranches in Montana? Why move so far away from you and the children?"

"He said he wanted a fresh start. He'd trapped in the Winds when he was a boy and wanted to get back here. So he came ahead and said he would send for us when he got settled."

"Two years seems like a long time to get settled. When did your husband become a ranch manager for the Harrises?"

"Last January."

"Almost a year, then. That's a pretty stable position. Why didn't he send for you and the children then?"

Mrs. Sparrowhawk drooped, touching a hand to her forehead. "The birth of our last child left me unwell. Nick said he wanted to have a home built before he brought us here. I was waiting for him to send the money for us to come here."

"I see. Yet, without his knowledge, you managed to bring yourself and your children to Lander anyway. If you'd wanted to come to Lander earlier, you could have? With or without your husband sending the money?"

"I suppose, but I wanted to respect my husband's wishes."

"Why do you think he didn't wish for you to come earlier? I'm not a husband, but if I were, I cannot imagine wanting to be separated from my wife for almost two years."

"I told you. He wanted to have a home built."

"And to your knowledge, has he started to build that home?"

"No."

Jenny stared at the woman. No? What about the cabin Nick had written about in his letters? Was that all fantasy as well?

"So your husband has been in the Lander area for almost two years, has held a stable job for almost a year and has yet to build a home for his wife and family? In fact, he's not in any visible way, even working on it?"

Mrs. Sparrowhawk made no answer.

Ben paced a few steps away. "Back to your first day in Lander. You said Miss Westraven greeted you in a friendly manner. Did she seem to know who you were?"

"Yes. She called me by my given name, and here I didn't know her from Adam."

"But when you mentioned Nick was your husband, how did she respond?"

"She turned tail and ran."

"Did she appear upset?"

"Scared more likely."

"Why would she be afraid?"

"Because she was doing things with my husband she hadn't ought to do."

A low murmur filled the courtroom.

"Silence." The judge banged his gavel.

When the crowd quieted, Ben continued. "But why the sudden change? Didn't you say she knew your name from the beginning?"

"She did."

"But it wasn't until after you told her you were Nick's wife that her manner changed?"

"Yes."

"Thank you, Mrs. Sparrowhawk. I have no further questions."

Anna Marie returned to her seat. Mr. Pratt patted her hand, presented her with a fresh handkerchief, then stood to face the bench.

"I would like to call Miss Stella Jones to the stand."

Stella? What part did she have in any of this?

With ramrod straight posture, Stella came to the front, swore her oath and took her seat, nose and chin held high.

"Miss Jones, thank you for being here today."

The queen deigned to respond with a slight dip of her head.

"I know this will not be easy, but will you tell the court what you witnessed on the afternoon of September 8 of this year?"

Her voice rang out clear and cold. "I saw Miss Westraven and Mr. Sparrowhawk wrapped in a lewd embrace in the alley behind the livery."

A collective gasp rocked the courtroom. Dear Lord. It was Stella. That flash of blue silk. Jenny dropped her gaze to her lap, praying the jury would read her discomfort as maidenly distress and not guilt.

She peeked at Ben from beneath her lashes to gauge his reaction, but he showed no sign of surprise. He scribbled notes on his pad as if Stella's announcement was of no concern.

Stella's description of the kiss was far more lurid and scandalous than Jenny remembered. She felt exposed, as if she were in one of her childhood nightmares where she found herself standing in front of all her classmates wearing nothing but a camisole and drawers. She forced herself to keep her head up as Ben rose to cross examine.

He leaned against the railing separating the courtroom from the witness box and talked to Stella as if they were old friends. Stella didn't seem to mind. Well, of course not. Hadn't she spent the better part of the last two months haunting Ben's office?

"Tell me, Miss Jones," Ben said. "How far were you from the couple when you witnessed their kiss? Were you as close as you are to Miss Westraven now?"

"No. Further."

"As far away as from here to the door?"

She shook her head. "Closer."

Ben turned and walked up the aisle. "When I get to the right distance, tell me to stop."

She stopped him about two thirds of the way up.

"So you were twenty, maybe twenty-five yards from the couple?"

"I suppose."

"You said you recognized Mr. Sparrowhawk because of his hair. Did he have his back to you?"

"Yes."

"Where was the woman standing?"

"On the other side of him with her back against the wall of the livery."

"Hmmmm. I'm about the same size as Mr. Sparrowhawk. For sake of demonstration, let's pretend I am he. Was he standing sideways in relation to you?"

"No, I only saw his back."

Ben turned his back on Stella. "Like this?"

"Yes."

"Mrs. Blackstone, would you be willing to lend me a hand?" Ben held out a hand to a woman seated on the aisle and helped her rise, then placed her between him and the door. He looked back at Stella over his shoulder. "Now, Miss Jones, would you say Mrs. Blackstone is standing in the same position as the woman you saw with Mr. Sparrowhawk?"

"Maybe a little to the right."

He moved Mrs. Blackstone to the right. "Now?"

"Yes."

"Can you see Mrs. Blackstone's face from where you are sitting?"

"No."

"Her body?"

"No."

"What do you see?"

"Her skirt and a bit of her hat."

"Thank you, Mrs. Blackstone. You may take a seat."

Ben turned and walked back toward the witness box. "So, Miss Jones, what you're telling me is you saw neither the face nor the body of the woman Mr. Sparrowhawk was kissing."

"Not fully, but I knew it was Miss Westraven."

"You said in your earlier testimony, you did not witness the end of the kiss, so the face of the woman in question was shielded from your view the entire time. Yet, you know without doubt it was Miss Westraven?"

"Yes. I recognized the skirt she was wearing. The woman with Mr. Sparrowhawk had on a green divided riding skirt exactly like the one Miss Westraven was wearing that day. I was with her when she bought it at the mercantile."

"Is she the only woman in town to own a skirt like that?"

"No. Miss Dickinson bought one too, but the woman I saw was too short to be Sara."

"And those were the only two skirts of that color at the Lander Mercantile?"

"No. There was an entire rack of them."

"So presumably other women in Lander could also own a skirt of that style and color."

Stella was slow to answer. "I suppose so."

"Yet you say without a shadow of a doubt the woman you saw was Miss Westraven even though you never saw her face and the article of clothing you identified could well have been worn by any number of women in Lander."

"Yes, Mr. Bennett. I have no doubt the woman was Miss Westraven." Ice laced Miss Jones' words.

"Very well. Now, how well do you know Mr. Sparrowhawk?"

"Mr. Sparrowhawk? Why, not well at all."

"But you know him."

"I know *of* him. I wouldn't say I *know* him."

"And during the time you've known *of* him, did you believe him to be single or married?"

"I don't know if I've ever thought about it either way."

"Is it true he was once a ranch hand on your father's ranch?"

Miss Jones' chin came up another fraction of an inch. "I really couldn't say. Who my father hires has never been my affair."

"But you spent the summer of 1899 on your father's ranch. Surely you would have known the men who worked there."

"I have no reason to mingle with the hired help."

"No? Yet you allowed Mr. Sparrowhawk to escort you to the Founder's Day Ball that year?"

Two spots of color stained Miss Jones' cheeks. "I don't remember that. No."

"You don't remember your escort to a dance held a little over a year ago?"

"I've had many escorts to many dances. I don't remember every one of them."

"But whether you remember or not, I have witnesses who would verify Mr. Sparrowhawk *was* your escort that day. Would you have accompanied him if you knew he was a married man?"

"Of course not."

"Thank you, Miss Jones. You've been most helpful."

Most helpful, indeed. But not the least bit happy about it.

Mrs. Stacia Allen gave her testimony next, telling how she had served as postmistress for Jenny and Nick's love letters.

"Could you describe what happened on November 21 of this year?" Mr. Pratt asked.

"Well, it was late morning, and I'd just seen Miss Westraven pass by my store. I was surprised she didn't come in because she'd been in almost every day the two weeks previous to see if Mr. Sparrowhawk had sent her another letter. Up until that time, there'd been letters back and forth almost every day, but then suddenly, he stopped sending any. So when I saw Miss Westraven walking by, I ran to catch her because I finally had a letter."

"Tell me what you witnessed next."

"Well, I saw her at the corner of my building talking to a woman with three young children. I called out to her and waved the letter for her to see, and she took off like I'd threatened her with a loaded pistol."

"Was this behavior usual for her?"

"Oh no. She had always been so friendly before. I thought

maybe she'd come down sick or something. Then the lady she'd been talking to asked me if I knew Nick Sparrowhawk. I said of course I did. That he was Miss Westraven's sweetheart. Well, she turned as white as whey. 'Nick Sparrowhawk is my husband,' she says. And that's when I realized why Miss Westraven was acting so queer. She wasn't sick. She was guilty. Guilty of carrying on with another woman's husband." Mrs. Allen delivered her last sentence with the censor of a judge.

"And that last letter Mr. Sparrowhawk sent Miss Westraven, do you still have it?"

"No. When I saw the notice in the paper about the lawsuit, I felt it my bounden duty to give the letter to you as evidence."

"Mrs. Allen, I have a packet of letters here. Could you look at them and tell me if they are the same letters Miss Westraven gave you to give to Mr. Sparrowhawk?"

Mrs. Allen shuffled through the packet. "Yes. They are. I recognize the handwriting and the lavender sprig painted in the corner of the envelopes. Miss Westraven always wrote to Mr. Sparrowhawk on that paper."

Mr. Pratt addressed the bench. "Your honor, I would like to submit these letters into evidence."

Judge Hammond gave a nod.

"I have no further questions."

"Would the defense like to cross examine?" The judge asked.

Ben stood and paced in front of Mrs. Allen. "Tell me, Mrs. Allen. How did you become a go-between for Miss Westraven and Mr. Sparrowhawk?"

"Mr. Sparrowhawk asked me. He knows I have a soft spot in my heart for cowboys. Mr. Allen, God rest his soul, was a young cowboy when I met him. My father never thought he was good enough for me on account of his being a hired hand, but he won my heart anyway. And there never was a better husband, no matter his humble beginnings. So when I see other young couples whose families don't approve, I try to help them out now and again."

"Did you know Mr. Sparrowhawk was married when he asked for your help?"

"Certainly not. I would never condone such behavior."

"So when Mrs. Sparrowhawk told you he was her husband, that was a surprise to you?"

"Surprise? You could have knocked me over with a feather!"

"As a shop owner, you know most of the people here in Lander. And I'm sure there's been plenty of talk when the news of this trial came out. Did anyone you know indicate they knew Mr. Sparrowhawk was married?"

"None that I know of. Everyone was as surprised as me."

"You say you've acted as a go-between for other young couples before, is that correct?"

"Every so often, yes."

"Did you ever send letters from Mr. Sparrowhawk to any other young ladies before Miss Westraven?"

Mrs. Allen darted a look at Mr. Pratt. "Pardon?"

"Has Mr. Sparrowhawk ever requested your services as a go-between before this?"

She cleared her throat. "I don't recall."

"Are you sure? He's lived here for less than two years. Surely, you can remember if he asked you to deliver letters for him before."

Mrs. Allen did not reply.

"Must I remind you that you're under oath, Mrs. Allen?"

The woman shot him a glare. "Well, maybe there was one other time."

"Maybe?"

"Yes. But it didn't last long. Not like with Miss Westraven."

"Thank you, Mrs. Allen. I have no further questions."

Whispers rustled throughout the courtroom as Mrs. Allen took her seat. Clearing his throat, Mr. Pratt rose to his feet. "Gentlemen of the jury, I would like to share the contents of two of the letters between Miss Westraven and Mr. Sparrowhawk. From this letter dated November 4, 1900, which Mrs. Allen verified as one she sent, I quote: '*I know how you feel about Anna Marie and the children, but please understand. I cannot share you. I (selfishly, I know) want you all to myself.*' And Mr. Sparrowhawk's reply, dated November 17, 1900: '*My Darling, forgive me for not sending my answer sooner. What you ask—to give up my wife and children—is difficult, but I cannot refuse you. Life is not worth living without you. From now on, Anna Marie and the children are no longer my concern. I rend them from my life.*'"

The room erupted in talk.

Judge Hammond rapped his gavel. "Order," he called. "If members of the audience cannot keep quiet, I'll have them removed from the courtroom."

For the first time since the trial began, Jenny let her eyes travel to where Sparrowhawk sat behind the prosecution's table. Green eyes met hers, a hint of mockery in their depths. The lying, scheming scoundrel. Did he think he'd won?

Suddenly, the long delay between her final letter and his response made perfect sense. He'd never meant for her to receive it. Each word of that letter wasa lie designed to bring them to this very moment.

Had Ben not put a hand on her arm, she might have launched herself at the conniving devil. Instead, she narrowed her eyes and returned his gaze with a glare so hot she hoped it scorched him.

This wasn't over. Not by a long shot. She wasn't going down without a fight.

Chapter Thirty-Six

"Put me on the stand tomorrow. I want to testify."

Ben suppressed a smile. For the first time in weeks, the fire was back in Jenny's eyes.

"No. Absolutely not," Ted said. "I don't want you any more involved in this farce than you need be. Ben, tell her she doesn't need to testify."

Ben leaned back in his office chair, contemplating the two siblings. They never looked more alike than when they were fighting each other, blue eyes snapping, chins jutting at the same stubborn angle. Technically, Ted was right. Jenny's testimony was unnecessary. Mr. Abernathy's witness alone should be enough to turn the tide.

Yet, if they didn't put Jenny on the stand, no one would hear her side of the story. The newsmen were having a heyday with those letter excerpts Mr. Pratt had read today. Few people remained who didn't believe her to be a vile homewrecker. He understood her desire to be heard.

And why not? Once the rest of the facts were revealed, her side of the story would put a face to Sparrowhawk's treachery.

"She doesn't need to testify." Ben held up a hand to silence Jenny's protest. "*But* . . . if she's willing, it might be beneficial. It's really the only way to show her side of the story. Yes, we can win this without her. We have the evidence, but without her version of the events, the public will be left with a skewed perception of Jenny's character. If it were you, wouldn't you want the chance to set things straight?"

Ted crossed his arms and scowled. "Isn't there any way to show her true character without putting her on the stand? You know how brutal cross-examination can be. Believe me, Pratt will do everything he can to twist what she says."

"If there were another way, I'd use it. But without Sparrowhawk's letters, only Jenny can speak the truth of what was said between them. I'm confident I'll be able to get Nick to perjure himself in his testimony tomorrow. He'll have to if he doesn't want to convict himself. And when I make his lies evident, then everything else he says will be suspect. Everyone will know Jenny told the truth."

"Yes," Jenny said. "All I'm asking is that you let me tell the truth. Please?"

Ted closed his eyes and sighed. "All right. Testify."

With a squeal, Jenny threw herself into Ted's arms. He looked at Ben over her shoulder. "I hope I don't regret this."

"HOW DO I LOOK?" JENNY SMOOTHED A HAND OVER THE front of her jacket.

Beautiful. She only ever looked beautiful. But that wasn't the answer she sought.

"Perfect. Demure and sensible." He wished she hadn't scraped her hair quite so tightly into that bun, but the deep navy of her suit turned her eyes to sapphires.

"I'll do my best not to smile."

"What? Why?"

"Never mind. Anything else I need to know?"

"No. Just be yourself. Answer my questions the same way you did in my office last night, and you'll be fine."

"What about Mr. Pratt's questions?"

"Like I said last night, be honest. If he makes you angry, *be* angry. Don't hold back your emotions. In this case, they can only work in our favor. Oh, and one last thing," He walked over to her and laid his hands on her shoulders, peering down into her eyes. "I'm proud of you."

Surprise etched her features. "You are?"

"Not many women would be willing to put themselves in the public eye, let themselves be misrepresented and talked about like you have in order to see justice take place. You're doing a good thing. I don't want to give too many details, because, frankly, the emotion you wear on your face is probably our best defense, but once the court hears the evidence we have against the Sparrowhawks—well, you'll see why it's vital their scam ends here."

"Time to go." Ted called from the hallway.

Together they walked to the courtroom, taking their seats at the front. The familiar surge of energy that coursed through Ben whenever he reached this point in a trial was back. He was ready to do this. Mr. Penrose and Mr. Abernathy were holed up at the Fremont waiting their turn to testify this afternoon. He'd registered them under assumed names and instructed them to lay low overnight. Knowing Mr. Abernathy's stake in the outcome of this case, he had no doubt they had.

Mrs. Sparrowhawk and Mr. Pratt were already seated. The woman might look fragile and innocent, but he knew better. After today, she'd need a lot more than her looks to garner sympathy in this town. He'd make sure of it.

He built his case slowly, calling on Sparrowhawk's boss Mr. Harris and a cowhand who'd worked with Sparrowhawk as his first witnesses. Their sole purpose was to inform the jury and remind the audience that for almost two years, Nick Sparrowhawk had lived in their midst as a single man.

Next, he called Nick to the stand. With each blatant lie Nick told, Jenny's face grew more and more indignant. He hoped the men on the jury took note.

"And so you're telling me, Mr. Sparrowhawk, you had no intention of pursuing Miss Westraven until she began to pursue you. What did she do to encourage you?"

"You were there. On that hunting trip last fall? You saw her. Every time I'd turn around she'd be there—offering me coffee, picking me berries, asking me to help her shoot a gun. One night, she came out to talk to me in her nightgown. I may be married, but I'm not dead. You got a beautiful armful like that throwing herself at you, well, what's a red-blooded man supposed to do?"

Ben balled a fist. He'd never been so tempted to punch a witness.

"A decent man would let the girl know he was married," he ground the words out.

"Oh, I did. Didn't make a whit of difference. Made her all the more interested if you ask me."

Ben slowly unclenched his fist. He would not lose his cool.

"But why the letters, Mr. Sparrowhawk? Once you left town, you easily could have severed your relationship with Miss Westraven. If you truly wanted to stay faithful to your wife, why court her with your letters?"

"Who says I did?"

"You're denying you and Miss Westraven exchanged letters? I'd say the evidence would hardly be in your favor."

Sparrowhawk glanced over to the table where Jenny's stack of letters sat beside his lone one. "Seems kind'a one-sided to me."

"Mrs. Allen has already testified your letters were as regular as Miss Westraven's. We know you wrote to her. My question is why? What did you hope to accomplish?"

Sparrowhawk shrugged. "Nothing in particular. After the hunting trip, she dragged me into a back alley and kissed me. A man will do a lot of things for kisses like that. If she wanted letters, I'd give her letters." He winked at the audience.

This was getting them nowhere. The sooner he got this blackguard off the stand and revealed him for the flimflam artist he was, the better.

"One last question, Mr. Sparrowhawk. Mrs. Allen testified yesterday that you'd used her as a go-between. Could you explain?"

"Sure. A few months after I arrived in Lander, I'd gone into Mrs. Allen's to buy some ribbons for my daughter. Planned to mail them in my next letter home. Well, Mrs. Allen comes up to me and says she has something for me. She hands me a letter and says she'd be glad to deliver a reply to the interested party for me. But once I took the letter home and realized what it was, I wrote back to the woman in question and told her I was a married man. That was the last of it."

"There was only the one letter?"

"Yes."

"And you told the woman you were a married man?"

"Yes."

He might have known a man who made his living lying would have a smooth story to tell, but Sparrowhawk's blatant perjury surprised even him. Ben glanced at the judge. "I have no further questions, your honor."

Jenny came to the stand with fire in her eyes, pledged her oath and took her seat.

"Miss Westraven," he began. "How long have you known Mr. Sparrowhawk?

"Six months."

"How did you meet?"

"We met at Harris' Road Ranch when our stage stopped there on the way to Lander."

"And in the six months you've known Mr. Sparrowhawk, did he ever tell you he was married?"

"No."

"When did you find out he was a married man?"

"On November 21 when I met his wife."

"Before November 21, how would you have described your relationship with Mr. Sparrowhawk?"

"He was my fiancé."

"He asked you to marry him?"

"Yes."

"Would you have accepted him if you had known he was a married man?"

"Of course not."

"Even if you thought his marriage was in trouble?"

"No."

"And yet, in your letter dated before November 21, you speak of Anna Marie and the children. Could you explain how that came to be?"

"Certainly. Mr. Sparrowhawk told me Anna Marie was his sister and the children were his niece and nephews."

"When did he tell you this?"

"Shortly after we met. Sparrowhawk was our guide on a hunting trip I took with my brother and some friends. I'd been attacked by a bear, but I wasn't hurt because of the quick thinking of several of my hunting companions." He noticed she didn't mention Sparrowhawk's part. "That night I couldn't sleep. Every time I tried, I would dream of the attack and wake up in a panic. I decided to walk down by the lake to clear my head and found Sparrowhawk there. When I told him of my nightmares, he told me about his niece who had nightmares and how he calmed her. Then he told me about his sister Anna Marie, how she and her children were the only family he had and how he hoped to bring them to Wyoming someday."

"Did he ever mention Anna Marie and the children in his letters to you?"

"All the time. He told me he would soon have enough to pay for their stage fare to Rawlings and hoped they'd be able to join him before we got married. Then he asked if I would be willing to have them live with us."

"And *what* was your answer?"

"I told him no."

"Why?"

"Because Ni—Mr. Sparrowhawk said he was building a small two-room cabin. I couldn't imagine the five of us living in such cramped quarters. I told him I was willing to wait until he could build a separate cabin for his sister's family, but I did not wish to share him."

"And in your letter, dated November 4, the one read in court yesterday, you were referring to not wanting to share *living quarters*, is that correct?"

"Yes."

"If we were to read the rest of your letters," he gestured toward the stack on the table, "would they verify that?"

"If all my letters are included there, yes."

"Thank you, Miss Westraven. I have no further questions."

Mr. Pratt jumped to his feet before Ben had a chance to take his. He reminded Ben of a fox he'd once seen sneaking around his Cousin Harlan's chicken yard.

Don't let him rattle you, Jenny girl.

"Miss Westraven. You tell us this story about a cabin Mr. Sparrowhawk was supposedly building. What if I were to tell you I've read your letters in their entirety and never saw any mention of a cabin?"

Jenny raised her chin. "Then I would say you didn't have access to *all* my letters, sir."

"And the letters Mr. Sparrowhawk wrote to you? You say they would support your claim that Mr. Sparrowhawk asked to marry you, yet I don't see any here. Why is that?"

"Because I burned them."

"Excuse me? I didn't catch that."

"I burned them, Mr. Pratt."

"You *burned* them." The sneer in his voice was unmistakable.

"How convenient for you."

"Convenient for Mr. Sparrowhawk maybe, but certainly not for me."

"No? Why burn them, if you weren't trying to hide something?"

"I burned those letters the night I learned Mr. Sparrowhawk had a wife. I burned them because that's what a woman does when she finds out her fiancé is a liar and a cheat. I burned them because I never wanted to read his false promises again. It was the *natural* thing to do, but it certainly wasn't convenient. When I received notice of Mrs. Sparrowhawk's suit, you can imagine just how *in*convenient that one rash act turned out to be. But if you wish to gloat over its convenience for you and your client, Mr. Pratt, by all means. Go right ahead."

This was the Jenny he knew and loved—strong, passionate, willing to fight. Surely her fire was winning over more of the audience than just him.

"But without those letters, Miss Westraven, it's simply your word against his, isn't it?" Mr. Pratt wasn't backing down.

"Exactly." Jenny replied. "It will be interesting to see which of us is proven the liar, don't you think?"

"Oh, I have no doubts on that score. You have to admit, you have far greater motivation for lying than he has."

"Do I?" Clarence Westraven at his haughtiest would be no match for his niece right now. She glared down her dainty nose like a queen presented with a toad. "To be sure, if I lose this trial, it will cost me far more than money. I've already lost a great deal—respect, reputation, friends. But you can't make me believe Mr. Sparrowhawk has nothing to gain by lying. In fact, I can think of 100,000 reasons. That *is* the amount asked for in the suit, isn't it?"

"*Mrs.* Sparrowhawk is suing for that amount, yes, in light of all you have taken from her and her children and the emotional stress involved."

"And last I knew, a wife's property belongs to her husband,

or has that law changed?"

When Mr. Pratt did not reply, Jenny continued, "I've been heiress to a large fortune my entire life, Mr. Pratt. I know all the ways money can motivate people. Believe me, Mr. Sparrowhawk is not the first man to lie to me in hopes of gaining access to my money. He's simply the first who wasn't willing to marry me to get it."

Ben wanted to stand and applaud, but contented himself with giving Jenny's hand a squeeze under the table once she returned to her seat. He stood up to call his next witness.

He heard a gasp behind him when he called Mr. Daniel Jones. Mrs. Jones, maybe? Or Stella?

"Mr. Jones," he began. "How long have you known Nick Sparrowhawk?"

"A little under two years. I employed him as a ranch hand when he first arrived in the Lander area."

"While he was in your employ, did you believe him to be a single man?"

"Yes."

"What led you to believe this?"

"He wanted to court my daughter."

A collective gasp this time sounded from the audience.

"He asked you if he could court your daughter?"

"No. He's not man enough for that. He courted her behind my back, much the same way he courted Miss Westraven behind her brother's back."

"How did you come to find out about it?"

"My wife brought me a stack of letters she found in my daughter's room. They were letters Sparrowhawk had been writing to her without our knowing."

"A stack? Not just one? How many would you say there were?"

"Maybe ten . . . fifteen, I'm not sure."

"Did you read them?"

"I did."

"And in any of them, did Mr. Sparrowhawk tell your daughter he was a married man?"

Mr. Jones snorted. "Hardly."

"What were the nature of these letters?"

"They were love letters—filled with nonsense meant to turn my daughter's head. In the last one, he asked to meet her out behind the bunk house. As you can imagine, I staked out that bunk house until I caught the two of them together. Then I sent him packing. Told him if I ever saw him near my ranch or my daughter again, I'd shoot first and ask questions later."

"Did he ever try to contact your daughter after that?"

"He may have tried, but he didn't succeed."

"How do you know?"

"Because I took my wife and daughter to Europe for six months. Courtin's a little more difficult with an ocean in between."

Doubt crossed the faces of some of the men on the jury. Mr. Jones was a respected member of the community. Mr. Pratt chose not to cross-examine, so he moved on.

"Your honor, I would like to call Mr. William Penrose to the stand."

Neither Sparrowhawk so much as flinched as the elderly man took the stand. Maybe they'd seen so many of his like in the past ten years they didn't recognize him.

"Could you please state your name and occupation for the jury?"

"I am William Penrose, attorney-at-law, from Cheyenne, Wyoming."

"How long have you been practicing law, Mr. Penrose?"

"Thirty-five years."

"Could you please tell the jury how you and I met?"

"Our law office received a letter from you asking if any of our attorneys had been involved in an alienation of affection suit within the past ten years. I responded, and we set up a time to meet late last month."

"Could you relate to the jury what you told me in that meeting?"

"Certainly. Seven years ago, I was approached by a prominent rancher in Cheyenne asking for help in an alienation of affection suit. The suit asked for a considerable amount of money, but of greater concern to the gentleman was what the suit would do to the reputation of his daughter. He asked me to meet with the injured wife and seek a settlement before the matter became public.

"Apparently, the gentleman's daughter had been carrying on a clandestine relationship with one of their ranch hands through letters and secret meetings. One day a woman showed up at the ranch claiming to be the man's wife and, a few days later, she named the daughter in an alienation of affection suit. We had the girl's letters to help prove her side of the story and probably could have prevailed in court, but my client was adamant in not wanting the matter to become public. So we settled."

"Could you describe the couple?"

"I never met the husband, but his wife was thin and fair, and heavily pregnant at the time. Most striking were her eyes which were a deep shade of blue—almost purple. I don't believe I've ever met anyone with that particular shade before or since."

"Do you remember her name?"

"After you contacted our office, I went back through my files. Her name was Anne Spirrow."

"Does the plaintiff in today's case, Anna Marie Sparrowhawk, bear any resemblance to the woman you dealt with?"

"She does indeed. In fact, it's my opinion they are one and the same."

Mrs. Sparrowhawk did an admirable job of acting. She managed to look hurt, shocked and indignant all at the same time. Mr. Pratt did his best to undermine Mr. Penrose's credibility in his cross examination, but the seasoned lawyer held firm.

Yes, it had been seven years. Yes, he had only met with Mrs.

Spirrow on the one occasion. No, he'd never met the husband so could not speak to any resemblance between the man and Mr. Sparrowhawk. No, his clients could not testify because they'd moved from the area shortly after the incident and he'd lost contact with them. But he remembered Mrs. Spirrow well and she was sitting in the courtroom today as Mrs. Sparrowhawk. Of that he had no doubt.

Ben read speculation and doubt on the faces of the jury when they looked at Mrs. Sparrowhawk where before he'd only seen pity. Strike two. Now to bring it home.

"I would like to call my last witness, Your Honor. A Mr. Charles Abernathy."

Sparrowhawk paled and sat forward in his seat. Good. This name struck a chord.

As Mr. Abernathy walked into the room and took his seat, Sparrowhawk brought his hand up to shade his face. Adrenaline coursed through Ben's veins.

"Could you state your name and occupation?"

"I'm Charles Abernathy, owner of the Adaline silver mine of Leadville, Colorado."

"Mr. Abernathy, you and I met less than a week ago in Denver. Can you explain to the court how that meeting came to be?"

"My lawyer contacted me last week and told me he had someone he wanted me to meet. You see, he's been working on an investigation for me for the past five years, and he believed you might provide us the information we sought."

"Would you tell the jury the story you told me that day?"

"I'd be happy to." Mr. Abernathy cleared his throat and turned to the jury. "I'm a simple man. Don't know how to do much else except mine silver, but I once possessed two treasures —and I'm not talking about my mines. I came to Leadville, Colorado, back in the late 70s and was lucky enough to strike it rich. But before I did, I was even luckier to meet and marry the most beautiful and loving woman God's ever made. What she saw in me, I don't know. She was a lady—through and through—and I was nothing but a poor miner, but she married me anyway.

"She'd come to Leadville on the advice of her doctor on account of her lungs being poorly. He said the mountain air would cure her, and it did. We didn't have much. We lived in a tiny cabin on our claim about a hundred yards from our mine, but that didn't matter. We had each other. And soon, we had a baby girl—my beautiful Coraline. She took after her mother and a good thing too, because we all know I ain't much to look at."

A few in the audience chuckled, proving they were in tune to the man's story. Mr. Abernathy nodded to the room, then continued.

"Well, it weren't long after Coraline was born that I struck a main vein of silver at the mine, and we were in business. The money started pouring in as we took more and more silver out, and I built Ada and Coraline a fancy new house in Denver. Trouble was, I was never home to enjoy it. I'd get home some weekends but not all, so it took me a while to notice Ada was doing poorly again. It started with a head cold that never quite went away. Before I knew it, she'd wasted away."

Mr. Abernathy's voice wavered, and he took a moment to continue.

"The doctor said," he pressed his lips together and swallowed hard. "The doctor said my Coraline would be the next to go if we didn't get her out in the open air, so I hired a hunting guide to take us way up into the mountains. We camped out all summer long, and she grew strong and healthy again. I could tell she'd taken a shine to the young guide I'd hired, Ned Sparrow was his name, but I didn't think much of it. She was young, not yet 15, and he was almost twice her age. He'd always acted a perfect gentleman when I was around, so I had no idea what was happening between them.

"At the end of the summer, we returned to Denver and Coraline continued to be strong and happy. Then one morning a woman appeared at our door. She had a young child in her arms and one hiding behind her skirts. Coraline invited them in. She introduced herself as Mrs. Ned Sparrow and asked if we could tell her where to find her husband. Well, I was surprised, of course, because Ned never mentioned a wife and family all the time we were together, but I gave her the address he'd left me for his pay and didn't think much more of it.

"Looking back, I remember Coraline getting very quiet. She kept to her room most all day for several days. Then I received a letter telling me my sweet Coraline had been named in an alienation of affection suit by the Ned's wife.

"I was plumb bowled over. But when I showed the letter to Coraline she told me that yes, she and the young man had been secretly engaged. They'd come to an understanding during our camping trip and had been exchanging letters since. When I asked her to show me his letters, she told me she'd torn them up and placed them in the waste bin the day his wife came to our door.

"I went to my lawyer with what I knew, and he told me if we fought the suit in court the scandal of it all would ruin my daughter, so I did as he suggested. I met with the wife and settled.

"After that, I thought we could put the whole mess behind us. Chalk it up to a lesson learned and move on, but one morning Coraline didn't come down to breakfast. I went to her room to get her and," here Mr. Abernathy paused, visibly trying to control his emotions. "and . . . she was gone."

"She'd run away?"

"No, no. If only . . ." He swiped a tear from his check. "She was dead. She'd taken a bottle of her mother's laudanum. There was a letter. It said . . . it said . . ." The man stopped, pinched the bridge of his nose and took a long, deep breath before continuing. "There was going to be a baby. She couldn't bear the shame it would bring me, especially after I'd paid so much to make the scandal go away. So she took her life and the baby's too. She didn't know . . . she didn't know . . ." Mr. Abernathy was weeping openly now. Ben pressed his own handkerchief into the man's hand and swallowed against the lump in his own throat. This was the part of his job he hated—laying bare these raw emotions to the world. But if justice was to be served, they had to be brought into the light.

"Mr. Abernathy, why are you here today?" He spoke as gently as he could.

"I've been searching five years for the man who stole my daughter and grandbaby from me. I swore at my Coraline's graveside I would find him, and when I did, I'd make him pay. When you showed me the picture you had of Mr. Sparrowhawk, the one of him standing by that bear, I knew my search was over."

"Are you telling me Nick Sparrowhawk and Ned Sparrow are one and the same?"

"That's exactly what I'm saying."

"The man who ruined your daughter is here in this courtroom?"

Mr. Abernathy pointed a finger at Sparrowhawk. "Right there on the second row. Yes, I see you. Hiding behind your hand like the coward you are. You're a liar and a thief. But your thieving ways end today."

The rest of the trial was little more than formality. The jury left the room to discuss their verdict. Five minutes later they were back—a personal record for Ben.

"Gentlemen, have you reached a decision?" Judge Hammond asked.

"We have, your honor. We find in favor of the defendant."

The courtroom broke into applause. Ben wanted to let out a whoop and gather Jenny into an embrace. Instead, he turned and clapped Matthews on the back. He'd been certain the jury would find in their favor, but one thing he'd learned in his years as a lawyer. The verdict wasn't final until the jury spoke.

Somehow Jenny's hand found its way into his. He wasn't sure

if she reached out to him or he reached out to her, but now it was there, he didn't plan to let go.

When Judge Hammond rose to dismiss the court, Nick Sparrowhawk bolted from his seat and ran toward the exit. He was met in the doorway by Sheriff Allen.

"Will he go to jail?" Jenny asked.

"Absolutely. On charges of fraud and blackmail. Also, Mr. Abernathy plans to sue for the wrongful death of his daughter. He and Anna Marie won't be pulling this stunt ever again."

"Good." Her eyes sparkled with unshed tears. "That poor man . . . Mr. Abernathy . . . I had no idea . . ." With her free hand, she swiped her fingers under her eyes.

"Yes, but thanks to you, he can finally have justice." He wanted to say more, but Sara, Maddie, and Mrs. Willoughby were almost upon them. Reluctantly, he dropped Jenny's hand as the ladies pulled her into a hug. Someone clapped him on the shoulder, and he turned to shake Ted's hand.

"You did it."

"*We* did it."

"And you were right. Jenny was amazing on the stand. The other testimony would have sufficed, but hearing from her . . . Let's just say, I've never been more proud of my little sister."

Ben grinned. "She was great, wasn't she?"

"The Willoughbys have invited everyone to their house for a celebration dinner. Will you be there?"

"Wouldn't miss it, but first I need to see to Mr. Abernathy and Mr. Penrose."

"I'll come with you. I'd like to thank them both for being here."

Ben glanced at Jenny, but she was still occupied with the women who had gathered around her. No matter. He'd see her tonight. For now, it was enough to bask in the satisfaction of the moment. Victory felt good. Very, very good.

Chapter Thirty-Seven

Jenny peeked into the holding room. No Ben. Where was he? They'd barely had a chance to talk after the verdict was read. She'd been hugged and congratulated by so many people, but there was no one she wanted to celebrate with more than Ben.

His satchel sat open on the table. If she waited, surely he'd come back for it. She'd told Mrs. Willoughby and Maddie she was coming to get her cloak and reticule, which she was, but she had so hoped to see Ben. She'd wait a few minutes more.

She ran her fingers over the soft leather of his satchel. Was it really just yesterday she'd sat here in absolute despair? Then Ben arrived and everything changed.

She'd always known he was a good lawyer, but seeing him in action, knowing he was fighting on her behalf . . . . She closed her eyes, remembering the feel of his strong hand in hers when the verdict was read. She'd felt so safe, so anchored. She hadn't wanted to let go.

Could there still be a chance for them after all her foolishness with Nick? That was the real reason she'd come to seek him out. She wanted to talk to him, tell him how sorry she was . . . how foolish she'd been to ignore her feelings for him.

Oh, why didn't he come? Her gaze snagged on a letter lying open on the table, a familiar letterhead blazoned across its top. Had Mr. Goddard written to Ben?

She shouldn't snoop, but her own name jumped out at her. Leaning closer, she read:

You always were a risk-taker, but taking on Miss Westraven's case may be your biggest risk yet. The majority here think you a fool, but somehow I'm betting on you. Though I would never have advised you to take such a case myself, you will certainly make a name for yourself if you prevail.

Should that occur, I would like to offer you a full partnership with my firm. You have to admit, you're wasting your talents in that two-bit Western town. The big cities of the east are where you should be, and I can think of no better city than Newark. I wouldn't be surprised to see you named judge someday.

I would be proud to call you partner. Also, Nell has instructed me to tell you all is forgiven.

Nell. Ben had told her he and Nell were no longer courting, but he'd never told her why. Had Nell broken things off and was now regretting it? Nell *and* full partnership. Weren't those Ben's dreams?

Those dreams would never come true with her in the picture. Despite their victory, her reputation was in shreds, ruined by the publicity the trial had garnered. Mr. Goddard was right. Ben had enormous potential, but to reach it, he needed someone like Nell as a wife. Not her.

Jenny grabbed her reticule and cloak and hurried to the door. Thankfully, the hallway was still empty. She couldn't afford to see Ben now. If she did, she'd be tempted to hold onto him with everything she had. But she wouldn't do that to him. He deserved to realize his dreams.

~

BEN GLANCED AT HIS POCKET WATCH AS HE RACED UP THE steps to his boarding house. Just enough time to change before heading to the Willoughbys. He looked forward to celebrating, but he hoped to spend time alone with Jenny most of all.

"Well, well, if it ain't the conquering hero. Didn't think you'd ever show up."

The familiar mocking voice stopped Ben in his tracks. Turning, he saw his stepbrother leaning against the door jamb of Mrs. Kavenaugh's parlor.

"Bet I'm the last person you expected to see today."

Today or any day.

"Is everyone all right? Letty? Lucas?"

"All fine. And Ma too, thanks for asking." Roy sauntered into the parlor and dropped onto the couch, beckoning Ben to follow. He wore the same irritating smirk that always made Ben want to punch him.

But never again. His fighting days with Roy were over.

Ben drew a deep breath. "So, why *are* you here?"

"Couple'a reasons. First off, I'm on my way west and thought I might as well drop in and see if the brouhaha in the papers was true."

"Brouhaha?"

"You know, the trial of the century and all that. Can't pick up a paper these days without seeing your name. Quite a performance you put on today."

"It wasn't a performance. I was doing my job."

Roy shrugged. "Suit yourself. I'm not here to argue. In fact, the real reason I stopped was to thank you."

"For what?" Rearranging his face?

"For the mine. You didn't need to do that."

Oh.

"Yes, I did."

"Well, maybe you did, but if I was in your place, I doubt I'd'a done it. And, much as it pains me to admit it, you were right."

"About what?"

"It needed to be sold. Foster put me in touch with that buyer you'd lined up, and I was able to make a tidy little profit. Enough to give me the chance to make some real money mining. I'm headed to Alaska."

"*Alaska?*"

"Yup. Have you heard what's happening up there?"

"Some."

"They're finding gold in the sand, man. It's everywhere. A buddy of mine has a claim there and with my capital to put into machinery, we're bound to make a fortune. Hey, if you want, I could probably invest some of your money for ya. Bet ya'd double it in no time at all."

"No, thanks."

"What's the matter? Afraid to take a risk? That's not the way I heard it."

"What do you mean?"

"When I came into town yesterday, it took less than ten minutes to hear everyone's opinion about your chances in court today. Let's just say there weren't many who thought you were backing the winning horse."

"Miss Westraven is not a horse."

"Hit a sore spot, did I? Well, no need to go all stiff-lipped on me. I'm just saying, you took a mighty big risk there, but looks like it paid off. Not much different than mining. You should give it a try."

"No, thanks, but I wish you all the best. Unless . . . you're not taking Lucas with you, are you?"

"Naw. He's sitting all right and tight at the ranch where you put him. You were probably right there also. Seems to have settled him down a good bit. Ma's happy anyway, so I'm happy too."

"Good to know."

Roy shoved to his feet. "Well, I better be on my way. Stage leaves bright and early." He pulled a packet from his pocket and threw it at Ben.

Ben caught it midair. "What's this?"

"Don't know. Some letters Ma found when she was going through your Pa's things. She said I should give them to you."

Ben glanced at the address on the top envelope:

Mr. Lester Bennett

Lead, South Dakota

The handwriting was Grandma Janssen's. Probably letters she'd sent to Father over the years.

Roy held out a hand for him to shake. "Guess this is goodbye, then. I'll let you know how things go in Nome. If you change your mind, I'll keep my eyes open for some investment opportunities. It's the least I can do."

With that, he slapped his hat on his head and strode out the door.

Well. This was a first. Neither of them yelling or coming to blows? Given time, they might manage an amicable relationship.

As long as Roy stayed in Alaska.

Chapter Thirty-Eight

Winter camping wasn't nearly as cold as she'd expected. Though, to be fair, she and Maddie had spent the last three days in the sheep wagon huddled around the woodstove while the wind blew incessantly. But today, though crisp, the breeze was calm and the day was sunny. Jenny was happy to sit outdoors amongst the sheep and sage.

No. She wasn't cold at all. Except for her nose. And maybe her toes. Yes, if they sat outside again tomorrow, she most definitely would wear an additional pair of socks.

But even at night, when the temperatures dropped to near zero, she'd been cozy and warm inside her canvas tent provided she kept a hot water bottle near her feet and the bearskin rug thrown over her pile of blankets. Emerging from her cocoon each morning wasn't pleasant, but she'd stay all wrapped up until Rob left camp with the sheep. Then Maddie would call to her, and she'd dash to the wagon to dress by the warmth of the stove.

All in all, she was taking to this camping life like a duck to water. And Ted hadn't thought she'd last a week. Well, today marked her sixth day, and she wasn't ready to call it quits yet.

Her initial plan had been to join Maddie and Rob immediately after the trial, but Ted convinced her to stay with him and

Grace through Christmas. She was glad now she had. A blizzard hit Christmas Eve, blanketing the Sweetwater range in two feet of snow. Tent camping in the cold was one thing. Riding out a blizzard in a canvas tent was quite another.

Besides, those quiet days spent snowbound with her brother and sister-in-law went a long way toward forging a new relationship between her and Grace. Who would have guessed her letter expressing her qualms about living with Nick's supposed sister would be the key to unlock communication between them? They still weren't kindred spirits, but this Christmas marked the beginnings of a friendship.

When a warm spell hit after the first of the year, Ted arranged for the Skivington's camp tender to take her and her camping equipment out to Maddie and Rob's camp. She'd return to Lander when Jackson came to move camp again. Ted must be worried about her to allow her to camp in the middle of January. Truth be told, she was beginning to worry about herself.

Everything brought tears these days.

Maddie told her she was in mourning—not for Sparrowhawk per se, but for the death of a dream. Luckily, a good portion of that dream had been laid to rest this week with the realities of rustic living.

Cooking on a wood stove, for instance. Well, cooking in general for that matter. She hadn't realized how much she'd taken that particular skill for granted. She'd always simply showed up in the dining room at the appropriate time and been served. Out here, she'd had the opportunity to take part in the process, and it was humbling. Bless Maddie and Rob for their willingness to eat her runny eggs and blackened biscuits without a word of complaint.

Maddie had taught her much, but she was no more capable of running a household by herself than a ten-year-old child. No, she wasn't prepared to be a poor man's wife. Not that it mattered. Chances were slim she'd be anyone's wife.

That part of the dream was the hardest to let go. She'd

always assumed someday she'd meet a man who'd love her the same way her father had loved her mother . . . that someday she'd marry.

Memories of Ben surfaced—the comfort of his hand holding hers, the warmth of his arms around her, the sweet fire of his kisses. Her eyes burned. She forced her gaze upward to catch the tears before they fell. She would not cry again.

She would *not*.

Yes, she *was* mourning the death of a dream, but what Maddie didn't know, that dream had nothing to do with Nick and everything to do with Ben. But she needed to let it go. Let Ben go. She wouldn't be the reason he never achieved his own dreams. She couldn't forgive herself if she was.

What she needed was a new dream for her life—something fulfilling, worthwhile. Maybe she could be a missionary teacher like Miss Whitney. Or maybe she'd pursue a career in law. Some of her favorite memories this past year were the days she'd spent in the law office. She'd come alive searching law books, digging up cases, looking for ways to find justice for people like Mrs. Dalrymple and Lewis Yellow Bear.

Could she be looking at her situation all wrong? Maybe this disaster, like Ted's illness, had actually bought her freedom. Uncle Clarence and Aunt Matilda had squelched her dream of a career in law last spring, but what was to stop her now? Her reputation couldn't be more tarnished. And, after that very public court battle, regardless of the outcome in her favor, her uncle had written to tell her she was on her own.

She turned to Maddie, eager to share her new idea, then stopped, somehow reluctant to bring such a fragile hope into the open for fear it too would turn to dust. Oh, where was her courage? Her usual willingness to jump into new adventures? Had Sparrowhawk taken that too?

Just over the next rise the two sheepdogs began barking furiously. Rob pushed to his feet.

"I'd better check on that."

As he wove his way through the herd, one of the sheep fell in behind him.

"Do the sheep usually follow him around like that?"

Maddie laughed. "No, not all of them. Not any of them, in fact, except Fred."

"Fred?"

"Yes. We named him after Rob's little brother because he was always getting into scrapes. When he was a tiny lamb, way last summer, he fell off a cliff and landed on a ledge, breaking his leg. Rob had to climb down to get him. We splinted the leg, and it healed, but in the meantime, Rob carried him around whenever we had to move the flock any distance. Since then, Rob can't go anywhere without Fred following him."

"Like Mary's lamb?"

Maddie chuckled. "Pretty much. Rob won't admit it, but he loves that lamb about as much as Fred loves him. They remind me of the story of the lost sheep."

"What story is that?"

"Oh, you know. The one in Luke where the shepherd goes to find his lost sheep?"

Jenny shook her head. She'd learned early on the Skivingtons knew more about the Bible than anyone she knew, with the exception of Aunt Bethany maybe.

"It's the one where a shepherd has a hundred sheep, but when he loses one, he leaves the other ninety-nine and searches everywhere for the one that is lost." Maddie stopped knitting and looked out over the flock of sheep. "Before we started sheep ranching, I don't think I ever paid attention to all the sheep references in the Bible, but now we've been out here . . . well, that little lamb has taught me more about God's love than a hundred sermons."

"How so?"

"When Fred was little, he was our number one troublemaker. He climbed all over the other lambs, tormented the mother sheep, and got lost every time Rob turned his back. I can't count the number of times Rob set off looking for him. He'd find him caught in a thorn bush or stranded on the wrong side of a stream. Really, it's a wonder that lamb survived. That's when Rob started calling him Fred. Said he'd never seen any creature so prone to trouble other than his brother Fred."

Jenny felt for Fred. Hadn't she heard those same words said about her?

"But every time Fred got lost, Rob would search for him. He never gave up or said he was too much trouble. He'd leave the other sheep and go off looking until he found him. Then, one day he found him caught on that ledge with a broken leg. Once his leg healed, Fred never wandered off again. In fact, if I want to find Fred, all I have to do is look for Rob." Maddie's knitting needles flashed in and out of her yarn. "There's a verse in Isaiah that says we're all like sheep who've wandered away. We're all Freds. Sometimes it takes being broken for us to understand God's love and learn to follow."

Jenny wrapped her arms around her knees. She looked out over the grazing sheep, some in bunches, some off on their own. Rob was wending his way back to them, Fred trotting at his side.

"How do you know?"

"How do I know what?"

"How do you know God loves us that way?" She'd never thought of God as loving. When she pictured God, she thought of someone like Aunt Matilda or Uncle Clarence, only a lot bigger and more powerful, of course. Someone distant and cold. Quick to find fault.

"Because He told us He does. In the Bible. He calls himself a good shepherd—one who is willing to die for his sheep. The Bible is His love letter to us."

Jenny didn't like the sound of that. The last love letters she'd read had been full of lies and empty promises. But this was God, not Nick. And God was truth. That much she remembered from her catechism class long ago.

"If you want to know what God is like, read what he says

about himself. You'll see." Maddie looked up from her knitting. "Rob and I usually take turns reading to each other in the afternoons. If you'd like, we could read together."

"Read what together?" Rob sat down next to Maddie.

"The Bible. I was telling Jenny how Jesus calls himself the Good Shepherd."

"Ahh, yes. The Good Shepherd. Nothing like setting the bar high for those in my profession."

"Doesn't look like you're doing too badly."

Jenny followed her gaze and had to smile. Rob was stretched out again on the other side of Maddie. Fred lay beside him, resting his head on Rob's leg while Rob scratched him behind his ears. The look on Fred's face was one of utter contentment.

"Why were the dogs barking?" Maddie asked.

Rob shrugged. "By the time I got there, they'd calmed down. I left them there just in case. So, are we going to read? If not, Fred and I may take a nap."

Maddie looked to Jenny with a question in her eyes.

"I'd like to if the two of you don't mind."

"Of course not. We're always reading something out here."

"Either that or napping," Rob added.

Jenny laughed. "Does that mean you want to nap now? We could always read later."

Rob sat up. "Naw. I'm teasing, is all." He reached for his bag and pulled out a book covered in worn, black leather. "Where shall we start?"

"How about Matthew?" Maddie said.

For the next seven days, Jenny spent afternoons on the hillside with Maddie and Rob, reading through Matthew, then Mark, Luke, and John. As the story of Jesus unfolded, Jenny saw God's compassion in a way she never had before. He truly did seek out the troublemakers and outcasts. Maybe Maddie was right. Maybe she had needed to be broken before she could learn to follow.

~

Jenny stood on the boardwalk in front of Ben's law office. She shouldn't be here. She'd promised herself, she'd let him go. Yes, her two weeks with the Skivingtons had changed her in ways she hadn't imagined. She now had a feeling of worth and belonging unlike anything she'd ever known, but that didn't mean things between her and Ben had changed.

And yet, she wanted to see him. *Ached* to see him. It had been almost a month since the trial. Three-and-a-half weeks since they'd been together. Twenty-five days since she'd talked to her best friend. She had no idea how many hours that made. They must measure in the thousands. It certainly felt that way.

She'd hoped with time this pain of cutting him out of her life would lessen. Instead, each day seemed immeasurably worse. Today, she just wanted to talk to him . . . to see his slow smile . . . to drown in that dark gaze of his. Just a quick visit, that's all, and she'd be off.

She dashed up the steps to his office before she could talk herself out of it. Mr. Frye looked up as she stepped into the outer room.

"Well, well, if it ain't Miz Westraven. Haven't seen you in a while. Thought maybe you'd had your fill of lawyers and such."

"Would it be possible for me to see Mr. Bennett? Or is he busy?"

"He ain't here."

Disappointment struck hard. "When will he be back? I could wait or come back later."

"Wouldn't do you no good. He's gone."

"What do you mean?"

"Went back east. I kinda figured you knew, seeing how you haven't been around to see him. Yessiree, this office has been downright lonely now Mr. Bennett's left town. No more young ladies milling about."

Gone? Back east? Not down the road to see a client, not up

the street to the bank, but gone? Just like that? Without so much as a goodbye?

He must have taken Mr. Goddard's offer. Well, of course, he had. Wasn't that his dream? The goal he'd been working for these past five years? And it wasn't as if she'd made herself available for that goodbye. She'd avoided being alone with him at the celebration party and run off to Maddie's the first chance she had.

She took a deep breath. This was for the best. Really. Seeing him every day and knowing she couldn't have him would be far too hard. This way, they could make a clean break. Like pulling sticking plaster from a wound. Best over and done.

"Miz Westraven?"

Mr. Frye came around the desk, a worried frown on his face.

"Are you all right? Do ya need me to get you some water? You're as white as a pail of milk."

"No. No. I'm fine." Turning, she almost knocked the poor man sideways. "I'm sorry. I need to go."

She ran the two-and-a-half blocks to Ted's bank and made her way blindly into his office. He and his assistant were looking through some papers on Ted's desk. Both men looked up as she walked in.

"Hey, sis. I'm glad you came by. I want to talk to you about tomorrow. Could you hold on a few minutes, though? I'm trying to get Judson all set before Grace and I leave town."

Jenny sank into a leather armchair to the left of Ted's desk. That's right. Ted was leaving too. While she was away, he'd surprised Grace with plans for a belated wedding trip to Europe. They were leaving tomorrow on the stage.

Could her world get any bleaker?

"Why didn't you tell me?" Jenny cut into what Ted and Judson were saying.

Bewilderment shaded her brother's face. "Tell you what?"

"About Ben. Why didn't you tell me?"

336

Ted turned to his assistant. "Could you give us a minute? I'll come get you when I'm done."

Judson left the room, closing the door behind him.

Ted pulled his desk chair next to Jenny and sat. "You have to admit, there wasn't much time when you got home last night. You were so tired. And this morning, you were still in bed when I left. I figured it could wait until this afternoon."

"You *were* going to tell me?"

"Of course. I know how much Grandma Janssen means to you."

Wait. What?

"Grandma Janssen?"

"Isn't that what we're talking about?"

"No. I'm talking about Ben. He's gone."

"Yes. Back east to be with Grandma Janssen. Shortly after you went to stay with the Skivingtons, we got a telegram from Aunt Bethany. Grandma Janssen's very ill." Ted reached over and took her hand. "Jenny, there's a good chance she's not going to make it."

Jenny struggled to make sense of what Ted was saying. Ben had left because of his grandmother. Elation coursed through her only to be checked by the gravity of Ted's words. "What do you mean she isn't going to make it? She's not going to . . . she won't really . . ."

"I don't know. Aunt Bethany made it sound as if Ben might miss seeing her altogether if he didn't leave right away."

Grandma Janssen couldn't die. Last spring, she'd been as vibrant and spunky as ever. Aunt Bethany and Grandma Janssen were like two peas in a pod. Jenny couldn't imagine one without the other, and she couldn't imagine a world without both those dear ladies in it.

Poor Ben. Grandma Janssen was so much more than a grandmother to him. She was mother, father, family all rolled into one. Losing her would be a terrible blow. Losing her on top of the loss of his father . . .

"I must go to him. He shouldn't be there all alone. Not if . . . not if she . . ." She couldn't bring herself to utter the word.

Ted squeezed her hands. "I thought you might feel that way. In fact, that's what I wanted to talk to you about. Uncle Clarence is sending his private rail car to meet Grace and me in Rawlings. There's no reason you couldn't ride back with us. But it would mean leaving in the morning. Do you think you could be ready?"

"Of course I could." She pushed to her feet, then stopped. "Wait. Have you spoken to Grace about this?" This was Grace's dream trip. She didn't want to ruin it.

"Yes, and she told me to tell you, you're welcome to join us. Not to Europe, of course"—a twinkle lurked in Ted's eyes—"but we'd love to have your company on the trip to New York."

She threw her arms around his neck. "Thank you. Thank you. Have I told you lately you're the best brother ever?"

He laughed and hugged her back. "Now, much as I'd love to have you stay here and say wonderful things about me, I've got a dozen things to do before we leave, and you need to go home and pack." He opened the door for her. "And, sis?"

"Yes?"

"Could you try to keep your packing reasonable because I know for a fact Grace won't. I'm afraid between the two of you, there won't be room on the stage for any passengers."

Chapter Thirty-Nine

Grandma Janssen was dying as surely as the snow was falling outside her New Jersey home. And Ben was helpless to stop it. The last few days, he'd seen death creep ever closer, claiming his grandmother's body bit by bit.

Oh, there'd been that brief period of hope when he'd first arrived. For the first time in days, Aunt Bethany said, Grandma sat up in bed, smile huge, arms open wide for "her boy." She'd eaten a bowl of Bethany's chicken soup and called him her tonic. That hope was short-lived. Now, death sat heavy in the corner of the room as Ben watched Grandma sleep, taking note of every labored breath, wondering if it would be her last.

How could she have changed so much in a few short months?

When he'd walked into her bedroom the first day home, he almost hadn't recognized her. She'd never been a big woman. But somehow, her strength had always given her stature.

Her illness stripped that from her. She lay in her bed as frail and delicate as a newly-hatched bird. The only thing unchanged was her beautiful smile and the love that always shone for him in her pale, blue eyes. But today, those eyes were closed, and he was beginning to wonder if he'd ever look into them again.

He leaned over to brush a strand of her long, white hair from her face. He should have written more letters while he was gone. He knew how much his letters meant, and yet his correspondence had been few and far between these past eight months.

Grandma Jannsen began plucking at her bedsheets as if even their flimsy weight were too much for her fragile body. He reached out and took her hand between his own. The skin was a deep, mottled purple and felt paper-thin beneath his fingers. This hand had once clothed him, fed him, stroked his hair each night before he fell asleep. This woman had once been his whole world. Now she was slipping away. He kissed her fingers and set her hand gently down across her stomach.

Standing, he paced beside her bed.

He hated this. Hated the way death was taking his family, one member at a time. If only there was a way to fight back. But death was powerful. Too strong for him.

The words of a poem he'd once recited in school chased across his mind, reminding him of hope.

Death, be not proud, though some have called thee
Mighty and dreadful . . .
One short sleep past, we wake eternally
And death shall be no more; Death, thou shalt die.

"Lester?" Grandma's reedy voice cut into his thoughts.

He turned to see her watching him, her blue eyes lucid for the first time in days.

"I'm here, Grandma."

"Stop your pacing and sit. I need to talk to you."

"Yes, ma'am." Even in the throes of death, she had the ability to command.

Sitting, he took her hand again.

"Dear, Les. Such a good boy. Your father will be so proud."

How many times had she said those words to him growing up? How many times had he wished they were true?

"There's something I need to give you." Her words were slow and slurred. "In my wardrobe. A blue bandbox."

When he didn't move, she grew agitated. "Get it, son. Now."

He went over and opened the doors of her wardrobe. Up on the top shelf were several bandboxes of varying shapes and colors. He took down one in a pale blue print—the only blue he saw—and carried it over to the bed.

With a palsied hand, Grandma tried to lift the lid. Seeing her struggle, he reached over and did it for her. The inside was filled to the brim with letters.

"These are for you."

He picked one up and glanced at the return address. South Dakota. These must be the counterparts to the ones Roy had given him. But there were so many. Hundreds of them.

"I'm sorry, Lester." The words were little more than a whisper. He had to bend to hear what she was saying. "I should have given them to you earlier. I always thought we'd have more time. All of us. More time."

He reached over and squeezed her hand. Remembering the words of the poem, he said, "We will, Grandma. We do. We have eternity."

But her eyes were already shut. He wasn't even sure she heard him.

BEN TOSSED ON THE NARROW MATTRESS OF HIS CHILDHOOD bed. Why had he come in here? He couldn't sleep. But Aunt Bethany had been adamant.

"You need your sleep, Ben. You haven't slept more than an hour or two since you got here. You'll be no use to your grandmother if you take sick. Go along, now. I'll wake you if there's any change."

So here he lay . . . chasing sleep that wouldn't come. With a groan, he sat up and turned the lever on the lamp beside his bed. Its flickering glow cast shadows across the room. His gaze snagged on Grandma's hatbox sitting on his old desk.

So many letters. He remembered his childhood excitement every time a letter came from Father. He couldn't wait for Grandma to read them. He'd make her read them over and over. But in his memory there'd never been this many of them.

He walked over and opened the box. Picking up the one on top, he glanced at the postmark. January of last year.

Wait. Last year?

Looking closer, he saw the letter was addressed to him. And it was unopened. Why hadn't Grandma given it to him? He'd still been in Newark then. Flipping through the next twenty envelopes, he saw they were all the same. All addressed to him. All unopened.

Curious now, he turned to his satchel and pulled out the stack of envelopes Roy had given him. He'd brought them along, intending to give them to Grandma. No point in that now. Undoing the twine around the packet, he thumbed through the envelopes. Most of them were in Grandma Janssen's handwriting, but about a third of the way through, he came across one he recognized as his own boyish cursive. He opened the envelope and scanned the contents:

Papa,

How are you? Grandma says I growed 2 inches in the last six months and she can't keep me in clothes. I think maybe I'm tall enough now to be a big help in your mine. School will be out in one month. Please send for me.

Your son,

Lester

How many of those letters had he sent over the years? Probably one a month from the time he could write. If Father had granted his requests sooner, would the outcome have been the same? He shrugged. No way of knowing now. He folded the letter to put it back in the envelope and noticed something written on the back. Grandma Janssen had enclosed a postscript.

Lester (it read),

You ask if little Les is ready to come to you yet. I know he wants to come, but I fear it would not be wise. Though he is growing, and yes, all of eight years old now, he is still quite small for his age. I fear he's inherited his mother's frail health. Dr. Douglas advises against sending him to so isolated a location. Of course, we welcome a visit from you whenever you can make it.

Cordelia

Ben read through the message twice. What was this? Frail? He'd rarely been sick. In fact, the only time he remembered Dr. Douglas visiting on his behalf was that summer he broke his leg.

Puzzled, Ben opened a few of the earlier letters and scanned through them.

Little Les is much too young for such a rough environment . . . Have you considered Les's schooling? He's an exceptionally bright boy. . . Les has been poorly all winter.

Seems as if every time his father asked for him to come, Grandma made some excuse as to why he shouldn't. All this time, he'd thought Grandma Janssen was on his side when in reality, she'd worked against him, going so far as to manipulate the truth to get her way.

He shook his head, hoping to clear it. Why? She knew how badly he'd wanted to live with his father. But deep down, he knew the answer. He was all she had.

As a kid, he'd never considered what would happen to Grandma Janssen when he went to live with his father. Would they have made return visits to see her? Most likely not. His father's visits east were rare enough as it was.

He flipped through the stack of letters to see if any more were in his handwriting. He no longer felt right reading more of Grandma's, as if he were going behind her back, snooping into things he was never supposed to know.

He flipped past another in her handwriting, then froze. This one was addressed to him, and across the front in bold ink someone had printed the words, RETURN TO SENDER. Any guilt he'd felt evaporated with those three words. He pulled out his penknife and slit the envelope.

The letter was dated October of 1887, shortly after his disastrous trip to South Dakota.

Dear Les,

I hope you're doing well and are happy to be back in Newark. All is well here, but I miss you. I know you felt you never fit in here, and maybe that's my fault. If I'd insisted you come live with me sooner, maybe things would have been better. Grandma Janssen tells me you're angry about my wife and family. That you didn't know I'd remarried. I wish I had known that while you were here. We could have talked—man-to-man. Cleared things up.

But he hadn't wanted his father to know. Hadn't wanted to admit how hurt he felt—how stupid, for not knowing.

I want you to know my love for Roy, Letty, and Lucas in no way diminishes the love I have for you. You are my first-born son, whom I love more than life itself. I'm so proud to be your father. My only regret is I couldn't be the father you needed when you were a baby. That I couldn't be there to watch you grow into the fine young man you've become.

Cordelia tells me you don't want to receive letters from me. I can't promise you that, but I'll try not to write so often unless you tell me otherwise. I hope after you read this letter, you'll give me another chance.

Love,

Papa

Ben pinched the bridge of his nose, forcing back the tears. If only he'd read those words as a twelve-year-old. How different his life would have been. Had he truly said he didn't want his father's letters? Maybe in a fit of pique, but surely Grandma Janssen knew he wasn't serious.

He sifted through the letters in the hatbox, opening them this time and scanning the contents. True to his word, his father had continued to write. When Ben made the football team . . . graduated high school with honors . . . made captain of his college football team . . . passed the bar exam—a letter for each milestone and many others in between. Everything Ben worked so hard to obtain—the praise, the affirmation, the love—was there. Had been all along.

Burying his head in his hands, Ben wept, mourning for the first time since his father's death all that was lost.

Chapter Forty

She was too late.

Jenny sat in her uncle's closed carriage on a side lane in Mt. Pleasant Cemetery. She'd asked Wilson, her uncle's chauffeur, to pull over the moment she realized the graveyard service had already started.

Too late.

Those two words had been the story of her day.

She'd arrived at Aunt Bethany's to be informed her aunt had already left for the church to attend Grandma Janssen's funeral. She'd arrived at the church to find everyone had already left for the graveside. Now she'd arrived at the cemetery to find everyone gathered around the grave, heads bowed in prayer.

Too late.

Surely, that was the saddest phrase in the English language. Grandma Janssen was gone. Jenny had missed the chance to see her one last time, to hold her hand, to tell her how much she loved her.

Too late.

The heads of the people gathered around the grave came up, signaling the end of the prayer. As the crowd dispersed, some gathering in small clusters, others hurrying toward the row of parked carriages, Jenny caught her first glimpse of Ben seated beside Aunt Bethany, head still bowed. She drank in the sight of him. As she watched, he stood and helped Aunt Bethany to her feet. Together, they walked to the head of the grave and dropped in the single rose they each held in their hands.

If only she'd been a few minutes earlier. If only the traffic had been less congested, or Ted and Grace's ship had left at an earlier hour. She could be with him now, holding his hand, finding comfort in their shared sorrow.

Well, what's done was done. She'd go to him now. She reached for the door handle, then stopped short. Mr. Goddard and Nell were standing by Ben now. The lawyer reached to shake Ben's hand. His daughter latched onto Ben's other arm as if she belonged there.

Maybe she did.

Somehow in the mad race to reach Newark, Jenny'd forgotten all about Mr. Goddard's letter. The fact Ben had come to Newark for his grandmother did not negate the fact he'd been offered a job. Full partnership. That was Ben's dream. And from the looks of things, he and the Goddards had picked up right where they left off.

Ben bent his head toward Nell's, listening intently to whatever she was saying. She looked elegant and poised, the perfect lady. She was everything Ben needed. Everything Jenny was not.

Jenny tapped on the roof of the carriage. "Take me back, Wilson."

"You're not getting out, Miss?"

"No. It's too late."

Chapter Forty-One

Ben pulled another handful of law books off the shelf and set them in the packing box. He hadn't needed to pack up tonight. Mr. Goddard told him he could take as long as he wanted. But the alternative, a lonely evening at Grandma Janssen's, held no appeal.

What a grueling day. Not the best for making life decisions, as Mr. Goddard pointed out. But why postpone the inevitable? Newark held nothing for him anymore. Even full partnership lost its allure. The city felt too crowded, the air too dirty. No. His heart . . . his home was in the West. It was time to step up. To be the man his father expected him to be. He would head back to Lead, take up the family interests in person rather than from afar and finally be the big brother Lukas and Letty needed.

The fact he was still hoping that home would include Jenny probably made him out to be a fool. He hadn't heard a word from her since the trial. She hadn't even sent a note of condolence, though he knew Aunt Bethany had sent a telegram the night Grandma died. But hope was slow to die.

He'd go back to Lander. He'd see her one last time before returning to South Dakota. Maybe if he heard her refusal straight from her lips, he could finally let her go.

The door behind him opened and shut with a click. From the corner of his eye, he could see the hem of a woman's dress. He sighed.

"Nell. I'd rather not get into this tonight." He turned his head toward her and stopped short.

Jenny.

Had the fact she'd been on his mind all day somehow conjured her up? He blinked, but she didn't go away. In fact, she looked remarkably unlike any vision he'd ever imagined. She looked . . . solid. Real.

And here.

"I'm sorry. I know you weren't expecting visitors. But I was too late this morning for the funeral, and Aunt Bethany said if I never take any risks then how will I know, so I came because, well, I needed to see you and I'm so sorry about Grandma Janssen and . . ." Her voice trailed off into a sob.

He didn't know what she was babbling about, but the fact she was here, HERE, not thousands of miles away, turned the flicker of hope he'd all but snuffed out into a roaring flame.

He opened his arms, and she ran into them. The bleakness in his soul fell away. All he wanted was to hold her . . . to breathe in her essence . . . to bask in the sheer rightness of it all. How long they stood there, him holding her, her holding him, he didn't know. A minute . . . five . . . a lifetime? But all too soon, she pulled away.

He took a few steps back and sat on the edge of his desk, knowing if he didn't put some space between them, he'd reach out for her again. He crossed his arms. She was talking, all flushed and bothered, but all he could focus on were her lips looking soft and warm. He knew exactly how they'd taste.

"Ben?"

"Hmmm?"

"Are you listening to me?"

"Of course," he lied. "I still can't believe you're here. How did you get here? When?"

"Last night with Grace and Ted. I came to Aunt Bethany's as soon as their ship sailed. I had so hoped to be in time, but from what Aunt Bethany said, we were still on the train when your grandmother died."

"I'm glad you came. Do you plan to stay?"

She gave a little laugh and shrugged. "I was so focused on getting here, I never gave any thought to what I'd do . . . after. I suppose I'll stay with Aunt Bethany for a while. She's going to be so lost without your grandmother. After that? I don't know."

He was willing to offer some ideas but wanted to tread slowly. Her break-up with Sparrowhawk was still new. Maybe he'd stay for a while too. He needed to settle Grandma Janssen's affairs before he left anyway.

Jenny's gaze roamed the room. "It seems strange to be here . . . in this office . . . after all that's happened. I always did love this room." She stepped toward his desk and laid a hand across her heart in a gesture of mock horror. "Why, Ben Bennet, are you actually organizing your law books?"

"Hardly. Unless you call packing them up, organizing."

"Packing? But why? Don't tell me Mr. Goddard rescinded his offer of full partner."

"How'd you know about that?"

She flushed. "Oh. Well. I saw his letter on the table after the trial. I didn't mean to read it . . . it was just . . . there and all." She gave a smile that didn't quite reach her eyes. "I should have said something. Congratulations."

"I didn't take the job."

"What? But Ben, it's what you've been dreaming of for years."

He couldn't help himself. He reached out and took her left hand and pulled her toward him until she was standing less than a foot away, eyes level to his.

"Funny thing about dreams, Jenny." He kept her hand captured in his own. "Sometimes you chase one so long, by the time you get there, you're no longer the person who originally dreamed it. All my life, I've had but one dream. Oh, it took a lot of different forms, but basically, it was the same. I dreamed someday I'd have my father's approval—that he'd want me as his son. I'd say to myself, if only I can finish top in my class . . . or make captain of the football team . . . or graduate law school . . . or pass the bar exam . . . then, he'll notice. Then he'll want me. But you know what I've learned these past few days?" She shook her head, tears glistening in the corners of those beautiful blue eyes. "I never needed to do any of those things. I didn't need to earn his love. I already had it, just because . . ." He clenched his jaw and swallowed hard against the tightness in his throat. "Just because I was his son."

Jenny reached out with her free hand and cupped his cheek. He closed his eyes. Did she have any idea how good that felt? Reaching up, he covered her hand with his own, then turned his head and pressed a kiss into her palm.

Maybe it was her touch. Maybe it was something he thought he was reading in her eyes, but he no longer wanted to take things slow.

"Don't get me wrong. I still have dreams. They've changed a little, is all. Now, I dream of going back to South Dakota and making things right with my family. Not running away anymore when things get tough between us. I dream of making my home in the West, where things are new, the air is clean, and you can see for miles if you want to. I dream of practicing law, not to make a name for myself or impress my father, but to bring justice where there is none, to help people like Yellow Bear who have no voice. I dream of coming home to a ranch house tucked in amongst the trees alongside a gently-flowing river and finding . . ." He paused, afraid of her reaction, then pushed ahead. "And finding you."

Her eyes widened, but he saw none of the reluctance he'd expected. "I love you, Jenny. Do you think someday . . . maybe . . . you could love me too?"

"Oh, Ben," she said, cupping his face with both hands now. "I love you now. I do. More than you can imagine, but . . ." He winced against the word. "I'm not what you need. You deserve someone like Nell or Stella. Someone who'll always do the right thing. Someone whose name hasn't been broadcast in every newspaper between here and California. Someone who's not always getting into trouble. Someone—"

He couldn't hold back. Leaning forward, he silenced her lips with his own. She hesitated a second, then slid her arms around his neck. That was all the encouragement he needed. He deepened the kiss, breaking after a minute or two to kiss her eyelids, then the soft flesh by her ear and along her jawline before returning to feast on her lips.

"I don't deserve this, Ben," she murmured against him. "I don't."

He pulled away, forcing her to look at him. "Neither do I. Didn't you hear what I said? We can't earn love. It's a gift."

"But you also said I was too much trouble.'Stay away from Jenny, and all will be well?' Remember?"

"No. I don't remember, but it doesn't seem to be something you'll ever forget. I was drunk out of my mind that night, Jenny. And angry . . . and jealous . . . and in a bucketload of pain. Don't hold what I said under those conditions against me."

"Sometimes those conditions bring out the truth." Her words were barely a whisper.

"And sometimes they simply reveal how big a fool someone can be. I was so jealous of Sparrowhawk. I did my best to protect you from that bear, but in the end Sparrowhawk saved the day. And there you were looking all limp-eyed at him, calling him your hero. All I had for my efforts was a shredded shoulder and a mauled ear."

She reached up and traced the edge of his scarred ear, sending a tremor through his entire body. "I came into your tent that morning to tell you how grateful I was. I couldn't believe you'd sacrifice yourself for me, but then you were so nasty. I believed your words rather than your actions. *I* was the fool.

You've shown me true love over and over again, but all I could hear were Nick's empty promises. Can you forgive me?"

In answer, he kissed her again, reveling in the silky softness of her lips, drowning in the feel of her in his arms. Finally, he broke away.

"So that's a yes? You'll marry me?"

She tipped her head, dimples flashing. "Why, Mr. Bennett. I don't believe you've asked."

"I said I wanted you in my home and that I loved you. Marriage was implied."

"I'm sorry, sir, but I've learned from experience not to put stock in implications. I need to hear the words."

"Very well." He kissed her right dimple. "Miss Jeanette Elizabeth Westraven"—he kissed her left one. "Would you do me the honor"—he kissed the tip of her nose—"of becoming my wife?"

"I'd be delighted, Mr. Bennett, but it's only fair to warn you, I can be a bit of trouble. And I have dreams of my own, you know. What would you say if I told you I wanted to be a lawyer?"

He grinned. "I'd say you'd make one heck of a lawyer. And as for trouble? Turns out, you're just the trouble I need."

Acknowledgments

With a debut novel, it's hard to know where to start with the gratitude. So many have had a part in this journey.

First and foremost, I want to thank my Father God for instilling in my DNA a love for story and a desire to create. He is my daily inspiration.

To my husband Kurt, my biggest cheerleader and fan—I could never have done any of this without your constant support and, at times, definite prodding. I'm so blessed to be walking this journey of life with you.

To my sister Marjorie who has probably read this book more times than anyone, thank you for using your incredible copy-editing skills on my behalf.

To my editor, Kristin Avila—this story is infinitely stronger thanks to your suggestions and insight.

To Evelyn LaBelle of Carpe Librum Book Design—you brought Jenny to life with your beautiful cover.

To my writing community of friends and teachers: ACFW, My Book Therapy, the IN group, my MBT Huddle ladies—you have all had an incredible influence on this book through your willingness to teach, brainstorm, encourage, and pray for me and my writing.

To Rachelle Gardner for believing in this story. Your vote of confidence and invaluable advice over the past four years have gone a long way toward making this book a reality.

To my kids, Jared and Megan, and all my extended family who have supported my writing over the years, and to all my friends who continue to ask, "how's that book coming?"—thanks for keeping me on track.

A special thanks to my mom and father-in-law who were huge champions of my writing. They never lived to see one of my books in print, but in my heart, I know they know and are cheering from heaven.

Finally, to all of you who have read this book, thank you. I hope you enjoyed it!

About the Author

A south-Texas transplant to the good life of Nebraska, Kathy Geary Anderson has a passion for story and all things historical. Over the years, she has been an English teacher, a newsletter and ad writer, and a stay-at-home mom. When she's not reading or writing novels, she can be found cheering (far too loudly) for her favorite football team, traveling the country with her husband, or spending time with her adult children. *The Trouble with Jenny* is her debut novel. For more information on upcoming releases, visit www.kathygearyanderson.com.

www.ingramcontent.com/pod-product-compliance
Lightning Source LLC
Chambersburg PA
CBHW031609100726
47898CB00006B/1717